"MADAM, MUST I ALWAYS RESCUE YOU? IT APPEARS THAT YOU ARE YOUR OWN WORST ENEMY."

Adam's deep voice sent a tingle through her entire body. It terrified her to admit it, but she was happy to see him.

"It appears so, Your Grace," Jewel managed to squeak out.

"Did it ever occur to you that you could have broken your fool neck?" His forefinger flicked at the curl she'd tried unsuccessfully to tuck behind her ear. His voice was low, his warm breath brushing her cheek. "This is what we have servants for. To help you when you need assistance. I do believe we had this conversation the first time we met."

His gaze met hers, his charcoal-colored eyes boring into her, melting her insides. She contemplated whether all their meetings were going to be so turbulent.

Adam speculated if it would be safe to set Jewel upon her own two feet. Now that his initial shock had subsided, anger reared in his veins. What if he hadn't been here? No, he didn't want to think of that. He shook his head. "What in bloody hell were you doing up there?" he demanded.

She pointed to the mistletoe, which happened to be directly over his head, and the minx in her took over. She reached up on her tiptoes and placed a kiss on his cheek. "Welcome home," she said softly.

Adam glanced up at the mistletoe, then back at her. His anger seemed to vanish like a puff of smoke. He arched a black brow. A sly grin appeared on his lips. "My dear, I think we can do better than that."

BOOK YOUR PLACE ON OUR WEBSITE AND MAKE THE READING CONNECTION!

We've created a customized website just for our very special readers, where you can get the inside scoop on everything that's going on with Zebra, Pinnacle and Kensington books.

When you come online, you'll have the exciting opportunity to:

- View covers of upcoming books
- Read sample chapters
- Learn about our future publishing schedule (listed by publication month *and author*)
- Find out when your favorite authors will be visiting a city near you
- Search for and order backlist books from our online catalog
- Check out author bios and background information
- Send e-mail to your favorite authors
- Meet the Kensington staff online
- Join us in weekly chats with authors, readers and other guests
- Get writing guidelines
- AND MUCH MORE!

**Visit our website at
http://www.zebrabooks.com**

THE DUKE'S LADY

Brenda K. Jernigan

Zebra Books
Kensington Publishing Corp.
http://www.zebrabooks.com

ZEBRA BOOKS are published by

Kensington Publishing Corp.
850 Third Avenue
New York, NY 10022

First Printing: May, 1999
10 9 8 7 6 5 4 3 2 1

Printed in the United States of America

This book is dedicated to the memory of Bonnie Dittman, who died much too young of breast cancer. A portion of the proceeds of this book will be donated to HOSPICE, so they can help those who can't help themselves.

First, I would like to thank God for giving me the ability to tell a story. And to my husband Scott and my son Scott Alex for all their words of encouragement and support.

And to my critique partners past and present—thank you for sticking with me through the years. Jerri Johnson, Trease Gibson, Lori Biesemeier, Starla Criser, Kathy Williams, Cindy Procter-King, Ruth Morrison. And a very special thanks to Bonnie Gardner and the Harnett County Library—I couldn't do it without you.

Prologue

Death would be better than this.

The cold, blue water called to her.

Escape . . .

Escape now!

Down, down, down, into the cold Atlantic Ocean she sank. The saltwater burned her back, making the pain twice as bad as it had been before.

Tired . . . so tired. How easy it would be to give up to the cold murky darkness. Somewhere in the foggy recesses of her mind, she heard Jean's voice. "Never give up, *petite*, always be a fighter." Moving arms laden with lead, she struggled, fighting her way up toward the light. It was so far away . . . too far away. Her lungs felt as if they would burst before she could get air. Just as her head reached the surface, a blackness engulfed her, and Jewel knew no more pain . . .

One

Some called him the Devil. . . .

Some called him worse.

Adam Trent smiled slightly as he drew his steed to a halt and stared at the sight before him. He had many reasons for his cold indifference, but none that he cared to share.

The foggy mist had broken from around the massive gray rooftop as the last clouds cleared and the sun beamed down, taking away the castle's cold, grim appearance. Briercliff stood high on the granite cliffs, overlooking the sea below. It was as if all his Cornish ancestors sat watching him . . . waiting . . . wondering. . . .

Adam shook his head and drew his gaze away from his ancestral home. Unbuttoning his white linen shirt, he slipped the garment off and laid it across his saddle. He could almost picture his late grandfather scowling down at him, reminding him of his status in life. But his bred-in-the-bone independence took over, and as usual, the Duke of St. Ives ignored the vision and did as he pleased.

The powerful, black stallion shifted beneath Adam's thighs; he leaned low over Star and gave the beast its head. The wind whipped at Adam's black hair, and the saltwater that sprayed high from beneath the horse's pounding hooves felt cool on his bare chest. This morning he wanted to taste the brine on his lips and feel the sun bake into his already bronzed skin—the two things he'd missed most since returning to England. He glanced out to sea, and something on the horizon caught his attention. Reining in his horse, he stared, muscles tightening at the sight of the brig.

He missed commanding his own vessel. When his grandfather died over a year ago, Adam had had little choice but to return to England and take over Briercliff. He wasn't sure he liked being a duke, but he'd learned to live with his British birth. However, America still held his heart. Watching the ship's billowing sails, he wondered if this had been the burning vessel he'd seen late yesterday. Evidently not, because she moved at a fast clip.

Star pranced underneath him. Even the stallion sensed his restlessness. It wouldn't be long before he had his affairs in order, so he could return home. Of course, he had one more thing that could hold him here.

"Adam, ol' chap. Adam!"

Adam turned and saw his good friend, Jonathan Hird, waving to him as he nudged his horse down onto the beach.

"If you hadn't noticed, ol' boy, the season has changed," Jonathan remarked as he rode up alongside Adam.

"Has turned a mite cold. But it feels damn good this morning." Adam slipped on his white linen shirt, leaving it unbuttoned. "When did you arrive from London?"

"Just before that hellish storm last night. I thought perhaps Briercliff had slipped into the sea. However, I find little damage. I suppose you've been making bargains with the Devil again?" Jonathan asked with a sly twinkle in his eyes.

"Me?" Adam's brow arched. "Make bargains with the Devil? You've been listening to the gossip-mongers again. I will admit, however, *he* has been known to make a deal or two with me." He couldn't help but smile. "Damn, Jonathan, it's been too long. But I know you better than to say you missed the country life. Therefore, I'll assume the clubs and gambling must have taken their toll, and you're looking for rest and recuperation. So what brings you to Cornwall?"

"Never could fool you," Jonathan admitted. "Thought I'd better give the ladies a break from my charm and wit. Besides," he added with an insouciant shrug, "without you there, it was much too easy. I need a little competition every now and then."

Suddenly, Jonathan turned serious, an action completely against his nature. "Actually, I've brought a missive from Hawk." Jonathan reached into his coat and pulled out the note. "I had a hell of a time convincing the messenger I could be trusted."

Jonathan handed Adam the letter. Adam immediately recognized the seal and wasted little time breaking the wax and reading the message.

"Bad news?"

"Not yet." Adam frowned. "But something's afoot. Hawk thinks a meeting of importance will take place soon, but has no idea when. I'm to do a little investigating in London." Adam looked up. "I appreciate your promptness, Jon. I know you don't want to be involved, so I'll try to keep you out of our war."

Dismounting, they let their horses roam free. "There are times, Adam, when I think you're damn crazy." Jonathan shook his head with disbelief.

They walked over and sat down on a group of ash-gray rocks that lined the Cornwall coast. Both men stared out at the foamy whitecaps in the choppy, dark blue sea.

Jonathan sensed an aloofness about Adam, and wondered if he'd ever know him completely. It struck Jonathan how well matched Briercliff was for Adam . . . distant, and forbidding. But Jonathan liked his friend no matter what his mood. They were alike, yet so different. Even with his own height at six feet, Adam still towered over him by at least three inches. Where Jonathan had sandy brown hair, Adam's raven black hair and slate-colored eyes gave him a rakish air, or so Jonathan had heard many a young woman comment.

He had learned from their long friendship to always watch Adam's eyes. They were the Devil's eyes and could be as dark as midnight when he was angry, turning from light gray to pitch black.

"I heard you were in a bit of a tiff this morning. Is anything wrong?" Jonathan plunged straight into the problem.

"Wrong? I take it you've spoken to Giles?"

"Your butler is informative." Jonathan grinned.

A sigh escaped Adam's lips. "The estate runs efficiently; I have no money problems. What could possibly be wrong?" Cynicism marred his features as he glanced out to sea and quietly said, "It's time I returned home."

"This is your home!" Jonathan threw up his hands. "I'd hoped you'd remain at Briercliff this time."

"In an odd way I like the castle, but this place can run itself just as it has for the last eighty years without me. I've a few minor details to attend to before my affairs will be in order. I only need to find the right solicitor; then I can return to Four Oaks. That's where I belong, and I've been away from the plantation much too long. Elizabeth assures me everything is fine, but spring will be coming soon, and with it, new crops will have to be planted. I don't want the burden on her shoulders." The war with Great Britain had been going on a little over a year, and so far had not affected New Orleans. Adam wondered how much longer that fact would hold true.

"It's been ages since I've seen your twin. How is the fair Elizabeth?"

"As sassy as ever. She's changed so much you probably wouldn't recognize her." Adam grew quiet as he turned to his friend. "Lately, Jon, I've had the strangest feeling I can't seem to shake." He raked a hand through his hair. He felt dead inside—as if a part of him were missing. Restlessly, he sought *something,* yet he didn't know precisely what.

"Ol' boy, I think you've been in Cornwall much too long." Jonathan's mirth showed. "There are no women on this god-forsaken coast. You're simply bored."

Adam's eyes snapped up. He thought of the countless female faces with names he couldn't even remember, and his laugh came out harsh. He stopped a moment, feeling that restlessness once again, and rubbed the back of his neck. "Maybe there *is* someone special out there. But I doubt it. Thus far, I've found only tiresome females who are scheming for the wealthiest titled gentlemen. Have I made my point?"

"Quite nicely, I might add. Obviously, I've hit one of those touchy spots of yours," Jonathan observed none too subtly.

A sharp whinny drew Adam's attention. He jerked his head in Star's direction. The muscular stallion pawed the air and pranced around in a circle, snorting. What in the bloody hell had him so agitated? Adam slid off the rock and took off running. "Come on, Jon. Something has that beast worked up."

"Easy, boy," Adam said, soothing the high-strung stallion. Adam grabbed the bridle and tried to calm the horse by stroking its neck. "Back up so we can see what you've found."

He stared at the damp beach. "My God . . ."

Quickly kneeling down, Adam placed his hand on the clammy body sprawled face-down in the sand. "Bloody hell!"

"Is he alive?" Jonathan asked right beside him.

Adam pulled the slimy seaweed away from the listless form. The weed had done its job by holding the lad firmly to a piece of burnt wood. His ragged, bloodstained shirt was in tatters. Long white lash marks were visible through the shredded material.

Placing two fingers on the youth's wrist, Adam checked for a pulse. "He's still breathing, but only just." Shifting his weight to the other knee, Adam frowned. "He's a tough one to have survived a severe beating and the ocean, too. Let's get him off the beach."

Jonathan went to round up the horses while Adam, still on his knees, reached to turn the youth over. The lad had a slight build and medium-length chopped black hair. Whoever had cut his locks must have been in a hurry, Adam thought, observing the uneven cut, but at the moment that was the least of his worries. Would the boy last through the night? Very gently, Adam rolled him over.

"Damnation!" Adam jerked his hand back as if he'd been burned. A pair of creamy white breasts peeked through the torn shirt. *This was no boy!*

Having returned with the horses, Jonathan peered over Adam's shoulder and said, "By Jove, it's a woman."

Dumbfounded, Adam could only stare at the once-delicate face that hinted at past beauty. Even in her god-awful condition, there was something about her that gripped his attention. At the moment she appeared ethereal, and he had to blink several times to shake away the feeling that he was dreaming. He clamped his lips tight as strange, unfamiliar emotions stirred deep within his gut.

Adam moved in a trance-like state, forgetting his friend's presence for the moment. His fingertips brushed the girl's cheek and found her hot with fever. Her lips were cracked and swollen, but he could well imagine their normally full, soft touch. My God, the damage that had been done! A crescent of beautiful, black-fringed lashes only heightened his desire to see her eyes. The urge to shake her and make her come to life overpowered him, and he couldn't drag his gaze from this waif of a girl who stubbornly clung to life by a gossamer thread.

Then another woman's face flashed through his mind, and a sudden pain twisted his heart as he remembered another time eerily like the present.

Adam had only been nine when he'd found her lying in the surf much like this. He recalled the helpless feeling of a young child desperate to save her. With only the muscles of a boy, he'd not been strong enough to carry her to safety. He had screamed and cried until he grew hoarse, but no one had come. In the end, he could only hold his mother and tell her how much he loved her. Something had died within him that day.

Adam pulled off his shirt and wrapped it around the girl. She weighed no more than a feather, he thought while he held her in his arms. This time he had the strength of a man and needed no one. By God, it wouldn't happen again!

"Here, let me hold her while you mount," Jonathan said.

Adam glanced at his friend, having forgotten he was there. But he was loath to relinquish her.

"For God's sake, Adam. I'll give her back. You can't possibly mount the horse with her in your arms."

Adam knew Jonathan was right as he handed the child-woman to his friend while he himself mounted his horse. When he took her back, a soft moan escaped her lips, and tore through him like a burning knife. She lay lifeless, cradled in his arms. He carefully brushed a wet lock from her cheek, wishing he could ease her pain. He felt a strong urge to lightly brush his lips across her forehead, and tell her everything would be all right. But instead, he murmured, "I won't let you die, my sweet. . . . On that you have my promise."

Glancing up, he noticed Jonathan already in the saddle, smiling that lopsided grin of his. Adam gathered the reins. "Let's make haste, and wipe that damned smile off your face!"

As they made their way up the rocky path, Adam prayed it wouldn't be too late to save her. Abruptly he ceased, realizing he hadn't prayed for anything in a long time. He shook off the confused feelings and concentrated on maneuvering the horse through the rocks.

Reaching the top of the cliff, he urged Star into a gallop, covering the distance to Briercliff in record time.

Jonathan stabled the horses while Adam climbed the castle's steep stone steps at a run. He pounded on the double oak doors. With the girl held securely in his arms, he swept past an openmouthed butler as soon as the doors swung open.

"Annie! Annie!" He heard the impatience in his voice. Damn it, where was she?

A plump little Scot scurried into the hallway. "Why ye be makin' such a ruckus? Just look at ye soakin'—oh, my lord, what have ye here?" Annie's eyes traveled to the bundle held in his arms. "What a wee thin' ye be carryin'." She placed her hand on the girl's forehead. "Why, she's burnin' up with fever, Your Grace! Who is the wee lass and where did ye find her?"

"I'll explain later," Adam said curtly. He took the stairs two at a time while Annie scurried to keep up with him.

"Which room?" he shouted over his shoulder.

"The yellow one."

As they entered the designated bedroom, Annie rushed over to the high four-poster bed and pulled out a small wooden footstool. Stepping up, she threw back the covers. "Wait!" Annie halted him as he started to lay the girl down. "Don't be puttin' her down yet. Poor thing's soakin' wet." Annie frowned. "And I might be addin', so are ye. I'll fetch some towels to dry ye both."

Hurrying to the adjoining dressing rooms, Annie brought back a handful of soft towels and began drying the girl off the best she could while Adam held her. "These clothes will have to be disposed of."

"I quite agree." Adam reached for the first button of the girl's blouse.

Annie smacked his hand. "Ye'll no be stayin' in here. 'Tis no place for a mon." She raised her brow and placed both hands on her hips, reminding him she was more like a grandmother than a housekeeper.

"For Christ's sake, I've glimpsed her body already." He

felt uneasy about leaving. What if she died? Yet he knew
Annie was very capable.

Adam stared hard at Annie. Finally he sighed, knowing
how stubborn she could be. "All right, Annie. I'll change
my clothes and be in my study should you need me." Bending down, he laid the girl on the bed, feeling a strange re-
luctance to leave her in someone else's hands—even Annie's.

After Adam left, Annie cut the remains of what had been
a shirt with a pair of shears, pulling the scraps of material
from the long, angry welts. This seemed easier and far less
painful for the wee one.

When she removed what was left of the lass's chemise,
something fell from the clothing and landed on her foot. She
bent down and picked up a folded oilcloth that resembled a
belt. Unwrapping the thick material, she found a faded brown
parchment with ragged edges, indicating it had been torn in
half. Carefully, she opened the paper and stared at the scrag-
gly lines of a drawing. A big black X had been marked in
the left hand corner.

Unable to make any sense of the document, she refolded
the paper and had started to lay it on the table when she
saw a bold script on the back side. "What's this? 'Tis writin'
I be seein'," Annie mumbled as she walked over to the window for a better look in the sunlight. The words were in
French, but she could make out a name . . . Jewel.

"Jewel, 'tis a good name," Annie whispered. She liked the
sound, and it surely applied to this wee one. When she was
well again, she'd be a beauty to behold—a treasure plucked
from the sea.

Adam reached his study to find Jonathan pouring two
brandies. "I thought you could use this right about now, ol'
boy." He held the glass up and motioned to him.

"Perhaps you'd better make mine a double," Adam said.
"But first, I need to send for the physician." Adam rang a

bell, then bent over his desk and quickly penned a note. When Giles appeared, Adam gave orders to dispatch it by messenger at once.

Taking the stiff drink, he sank down in one of the wing-back chairs that flanked the fireplace and shut his eyes. He could still see the girl's features. Her face hadn't been blistered, so evidently she'd been in the water overnight and spared the cruel sun. Could she have been on the burning ship he'd spotted late yesterday? The piece of burnt wood he'd found her clinging to supported that theory, but what could one so small and frail have done to cause such abuse? Shifting, he stretched his legs out in front of him, crossing them at the ankles. He opened his eyes and stared at the flames. The girl stirred up feelings he'd thought were long dead.

Adam let the brandy and the fire's warmth take the cold from his bones. It was only September, but already a chill lingered in the air, especially in this cold, damp castle. And he thought of his warm airy plantation home, thinking it would be a welcome sight when he finally returned.

"Adam, who do you suppose she is?" Jonathan asked the question that was on both their minds.

"I wish I knew. Maybe when she awakens we'll have some answers."

"If she awakens," Jonathan softly replied.

Two

Adam threw another log onto the grate and watched the sparks shoot high before falling harmlessly along the stone hearth. The room had grown quiet, except for the crack and hiss of the fire. With the fresh wood, the flame once again grew bright.

For the dozenth time, he glanced at the mantel clock, then at Jonathan dozing in a chair. When would Dr. Perkins come down with his report? He had been upstairs for over an hour. Just how long could it take to examine one small female?

A sharp rap on the door drew Adam's attention and woke Jonathan.

"Enter!" Adam called out.

Dr. Perkins set his bag on the small marble tabletop by the door. "Your Grace, I've just finished my examination."

"Good. We're most anxious to hear your report." Adam placed his drink on the liquor cabinet and picked up the crystal decanter. "May I offer you a brandy?"

"No, thank you." The doctor held up his hand. "I've another patient to see this afternoon. Perchance another time."

Adam leaned against the liquor cabinet and crossed his arms. "How is she?"

"You have a dreadfully sick lady on your hands." Dr. Perkins's gray brows drew together. "Can you tell me anything about her?"

"Very little, I'm afraid. We found her on the beach this morning. I had hoped you could tell us more as a physician."

"I can't give you specific details. But I'd say she's about sixteen or seventeen and appears to have been in good health before this occurred." Dr. Perkins sighed. "It's such a shame to see one so young who's obviously suffered at the hands of a madman."

"I couldn't help but notice that myself." Adam rubbed his chin. He hid his surprise that the young woman was older than she appeared. Bracing himself for the inevitable, he asked, "What chance do you give her for lasting the night?"

"I honestly don't know. I've applied my special ointment made of berries and roots, which heals from within, and I hope it will leave few scars when she's recuperated. But that is the minor problem. The thing that concerns me most is her high fever. I don't know if she's strong enough to physically fight, or has the fortitude to live. I'm afraid the next two days will be very critical."

Dr. Perkins shook his head as his tired eyes met Adam's. "Her condition is extremely grave. I've instructed Annie to administer a spoonful of laudanum every four hours." He shrugged. "There's little else I can do."

Adam frowned and looked at Jonathan, who merely shook his head. Helplessness surged within Adam. Not knowing what else to say, he gulped the remainder of his brandy, thinking the scorching liquid would help. It didn't. He escorted the doctor to the entrance hall, his thoughts on the young woman fighting for her life upstairs. He barely heard Perkins's parting remarks.

"I'll check on her tomorrow. If anything should go wrong tonight, don't hesitate to summon me. Good day, Your Grace."

Adam fought the urge to rush upstairs, and instead returned to his study.

Jonathan sat with his feet propped casually upon the hearth, indulging in a third brandy. His gaze met Adam's as he entered the room. "It looks as if you'll be having a guest for a while. What will you do with her?"

"Do?" Adam paused and stared at his friend, then let out a weary sigh as he sat down. "Hell," he said, raking a hand through his hair. He had obligations in America and would be leaving soon. He shut his eyes and pictured her again in the sand. His chest tightened. He'd seen men die, but the thought of the lady upstairs not surviving bothered him more than he cared to admit. Christ! Was he getting soft to be so affected by the plight of one probable stowaway?

Again he glanced at Jonathan, remembering his earlier question. "I'm going to help the girl recover, then send her on her way. That is, after I have a few answers." Adam said the last more to himself than to his friend.

Adam stood, stretching his long legs. He reached over and slapped Jonathan on the back. "Come on, Jon, I need to check on some of my tenants." Adam felt the need to keep busy and take his mind off the girl. "They might need some help after last night's storm. How about riding out with me?"

The day passed with one long repair job after another while Adam and Jonathan helped the farmers who had the most damage. As they neared Briercliff, Adam glanced at his friend, feeling a little guilty. In his effort to keep busy and keep the demons in his mind at bay, he'd pushed a little too hard and he could see the results in the way Jonathan slumped in the saddle. Adam wanted to smile, but instead asked, "Can you stay for dinner?"

"Every bone in my body aches." Jonathan rubbed the back of his neck. "I remember now why I chose to give up such physical exertion. Too much liquor," he confessed. "Thanks for the invitation, but I have a bit of clerical work I've been putting off. It seems to have stacked up since I've been in London. I'll see you in a couple of days. By the way . . ." He turned in his saddle. "Next month I'm having a few friends up from London for a dinner party. Going to give them a taste of the country life. I'd like you to come. But I

should warn you, Colette will be there." Jonathan frowned.
"You might say she invited herself, hoping she'd get to see
you.

Adam grimaced with disgust. "Will that woman never give
up? Colette thinks I'll be her next husband. But she's not
the wife I'd choose, providing I wanted one." Adam paused,
then gave his friend a long look. He knew Jonathan had
never cared for the lady's shallow personality.

"I must admit, she has eyes only for you." Jonathan chuckled, and being the devilish fellow he was, couldn't resist adding, "Be careful. I've heard she usually gets what she wants."

"Laugh, damn you," Adam replied. "Lady Colette will
find she can't have everything she wants—especially if she
wants me." He nudged his horse forward, bringing an end
to the topic.

Stopping at the entrance of Briercliff, he turned to his
friend, "Thanks for your help today, Jon." Suddenly, Adam
could no longer control his impatience to be home. It was
only natural to be anxious to see how his little sea urchin
was doing. As master of Briercliff he was responsible for
her.

Jonathan left, and Adam turned his mount down the long
drive and urged his steed into a gallop. When he reached
the stables, he dismounted and tossed the reins to a groom,
then strode toward main house. He entered through the oak
doors and wasted little time climbing the stairs. He ignored
his growling stomach and weary body.

Annie smiled as he strolled into the room. "Good evenin',
Your Grace. Have ye had yer dinner?"

"No, Annie, I'm going to bathe and change clothes first.
I just stopped to see how our guest is faring." Adam's gaze
drifted to the sleeping girl who appeared so small and helpless lying in the large bed. Her labored breathing echoed in
the room as if she fought for each breath, and her coloring
was still not good. Adam couldn't seem to control the sudden
tightness in his chest. "How is she?"

"There's no change." Annie shook her head. "I've managed to get a wee bit o' chicken broth down her and o' course the medicine. But I do fear her fever will shoot up tonight. It usually does."

Adam noticed the fatigue lines around Annie's eyes. Her brown hair streaked with gray always reminded him of how precious the little woman was to him. He never doubted that he and his sister, Elizabeth, had caused a few of the gray streaks when they had been small. If the truth were known, he'd probably caused several more over the last year. "After I eat dinner, I'll relieve you for the night," he said.

"Dinna be botherin' yerself!" she protested. "I can take care o' the lass myself. Besides, she'll be needin' her medicine."

"I assure you, I'm quite capable of administering a spoonful of syrup."

"But sir!"

"No arguments! I'll be back after dinner," he said firmly as he shut the door.

Precisely at eight o'clock, Adam returned as promised.

Annie explained the exact dosage of laudanum that the patient was to receive, then lectured him about keeping cool compresses on her forehead. Turning to leave, she added, "Take good care o' Jewel and call should ye be needin' me."

"Jewel?" Adam turned to Annie. "Why did you call her by that name?"

"Oh, beggin' yer pardon, Your Grace. I be forgettin' to tell ye." Annie fumbled in her pocket. "I be havin' it here somewhere," she muttered.

It had been a long day, and Annie's vagueness wore Adam's temper thin. "What are you talking about?"

" 'Twas just this very mornin' when I undressed the wee lass—I dinna ken what it is." She finally pulled a piece of folded paper from her pocket. "What do ye make o' it?"

Carefully, so as not to cause further damage, Adam unfolded the faded brown parchment. He scanned the paper, taking in the very detailed drawings. The French words had faded in places, but Adam could make out the words for "Bay of"—unfortunately the other word was not legible. The paper had been torn exactly in half, and one was no good without the other. Studying the map, he thought something looked vaguely familiar, but couldn't quite put his finger on it. "I don't see any reference to a name, Annie."

"Look on the back, sir."

Adam turned the map over and saw the inscription. In French it read: "TO MY BELOVED JEWEL, MAY THE TREASURES OF THE WORLD BE YOURS." The name scrawled on the bottom was JEAN.

"What do ye make o' the parchment?" Annie asked.

Adam read it again. So her name was Jewel. But Jewel what? And who was Jean and what right did he have to refer to her as his beloved? Adam scowled, not liking any of the possibilities that ran through his mind. Could she be nothing more than a common doxy? No. He refused to believe the worst just yet. Perhaps Jean was her brother or maybe her father, Adam reasoned. Somehow that thought sat better with him.

Why in the world would she have a map? Evidently it was valuable, and possibly the reason she'd been beaten. He tucked the folded paper into his pocket for safekeeping. All but forgotten, Annie stood with her hands on her hips, tapping her foot and awaiting a reply.

Adam turned his attention back to her. "I beg your pardon?"

"I do say, mon, where has yer mind been? I've been talkin' for the last few minutes. Come to think o' it, ye've not acted like yerself since ye found the lass."

Adam, not wanting to comment on his thoughts, gruffly swore. "Annie, damn it, what did you say?"

"I asked, what ye be thinkin' about the drawin'?" Annie replied in a rather offended tone.

"It's possibly a treasure map; however, this half is no good without the other." His gaze strayed to the bed, wondering if the girl was as innocent as she looked. "She could have stolen it. Remember, we don't know anything about her. I guess we'll have to wait for all our answers until she's recovered." He rubbed the back of his neck. He really didn't need a discussion just now. "Good night," he said, dismissing Annie.

After she left, Adam once again turned his gaze upon Jewel's small and delicate features. Short black hair framed her oval face, and soot-black eyelashes rested on her flushed cheeks. Reaching over, Adam felt her forehead. It still burned with fever.

He moved to the washstand, where he poured fresh water into a porcelain bowl, then carried the bowl back to the bed. He sat down on the edge of the bed, closely watching the rise and fall of her chest. Balancing the bowl on his legs, he tenderly brushed the hair back from her face. He dipped a cloth and squeezed out the excess water, then placed the damp compress on her forehead. When the cloth grew warm he followed the procedure again, but this time he wiped down Jewel's arms and bare chest, trying everything to bring her body heat down. How strange it felt to take care of someone again. Adam remembered taking care of Elizabeth when they were younger. Even though they were twins, he had always seemed years older. But she hadn't been as cooperative as this patient. She'd usually fussed about staying in bed. Of course, Elizabeth had never been as sick as the lady before him. Again he applied the soothing water, and held the moist rag to her parched lips to relieve the dryness.

The hours passed slowly. After a while, Adam stood and rolled his head on his shoulders to alleviate the tension and pain in his neck. Picking up the basin, he moved back to the washstand. That was when he heard a moan so soft he thought perhaps he'd only imagined it. He jerked around.

Easing down onto the bed, he took her hand in his and rubbed his thumb over her soft palm. "I'm here, Jewel. Just rest and get well," he whispered.

Compassion stirred deep in his soul. But compassion was all he could ever feel for this mysterious woman who had drifted into his life, he told himself, despite the strong attraction that swept his body.

Suddenly, Jewel's eyelids flew open. She reached up and grabbed Adam's shirt. She stared directly at him. "P—Please don't let me die." The soft plea slipped from quivering lips. Adam grabbed her arms so she wouldn't fall. Slowly, he lowered her back to the bed, then leaned closer so he could hear her softly spoken words. She had a very slight French accent, but not a normal accent—it was somehow different.

"I—I'm so cold. C-can't get warm." Her head thrashed from side to side. "Don't let them hurt me. Don't leave me— please," she begged, grasping his hand.

The words, though choppy and brief, affected Adam deeply. He became lost in the brown velvet softness of her feverish eyes, and found he had been holding his breath. He let it out slowly, thinking how small she looked in the midst of the pillows that surrounded her.

Before he could move or say anything, Jewel's eyes closed and once again she slipped back into the deep sleep she'd been in before. She still clutched his hand. Her lips quivered from fever-induced chills.

Adam loosened her fingers from his hand, then quickly retrieved two quilts from the chair, tucking them around her. He waited. The quilts didn't help. Nothing seemed to help. Her shivering increased. Swiftly, he removed his boots and shirt, and thought for one brief second about removing his breeches, but decided against it. He wanted to keep thinking of this young lady as a child that needed protection—nothing more. Otherwise, it would be far too easy for one thing to

lead to another. He also didn't want Annie to have an attack
of the vapors when she found him in bed with Jewel the
next morning.

He slid under the covers, pulling the blankets over them,
being careful of Jewel's raw back as he placed her next to
his long frame. Her skin felt dry and hot to the touch.

Gliding one arm under her head, he draped the other over
her waist, the radiating heat from Jewel's body quickly en-
gulfing them both in sweat. Still, he held her close, offering
her his body's warmth and comfort. Somehow he had to stop
her chills. It seemed like hours before he felt her relax and
the trembling ceased.

Exhaustion finally claimed Adam, and he relaxed. Not
since he'd been a boy had he experienced such a peaceful
contentment. Again he remembered his mother's death, but
this time the outcome would be different, he vowed. The
woman cradled in his arms would live because he'd saved
her life.

Jewel turned over and faced him, snuggling her head on
his shoulder. A strange protective sensation washed over
Adam. He wondered just what he was getting himself into.

If he wasn't careful he could have deep emotions for this
slip of a girl. But that was impossible; he knew nothing about
her. He rubbed his calloused hand over her soft arm. The
skin felt cool and damp. The fever had broken. And Annie
had thought him incapable of caring for Jewel. "I guess I've
shown her," he murmured before drifting off into a long-
awaited sleep. Tomorrow, he had a long ride into London.

The early morning sunlight filtered in through the white
batiste curtains, bathing the room in soft yellow. Adam
opened his eyes to find Jewel snuggled next to him, her arm
draped across the black hair of his chest. Careful not to dis-
turb her, he slipped out of bed and retrieved his shirt from
the chair.

He heard her soft mumbling, and walked over to the bed. "What did you say?" he asked.

"Hold me," she said sleepily.

Adam chuckled. "I'd like to, luv, but I've other pressing matters this morning." He realized she didn't know what she was saying, but he hoped she would awaken today so they could really talk. Perhaps then he could extract her from his mind.

She slept like an angel. But what if she wasn't one? His brow wrinkled with the unpleasant thought as he buttoned his shirt.

God, he needed some answers!

Three

Images filled her dark world.

First, a flash of blue—beautiful, tranquil—then flashes of white as two ships bobbed like tiny corks in the middle of a stormy sapphire sea. Billowing canvas sails flapped in the wind, catching her attention just before someone yelled, "Come about!"

Suddenly, a loud explosion jarred her, followed by shouts of panic from all directions. The sails came tumbling down, and she saw blood . . . lots of blood.

Jewel tossed and turned in her fever-induced sleep, trying to cry for help, but the sound wouldn't come.

Somewhere a man screamed in agony. Blood oozed between his fingers as he turned and glared at her. She gasped at the sight. His cheek had been ripped open from his mouth to his ear.

The grotesque face was too close for comfort as he reached out and grabbed her wrist, sending the small, bloody knife she held skittering across the deck. Jewel tried to swing out, but someone held her arms. She couldn't move.

She couldn't breathe.

She was going to die.

When she looked again, her attacker had disappeared, and Jewel slipped back into the timeless void she'd been in before.

Peaceful sleep . . . no pain. Such a blissful state. She wanted to stay here forever.

She felt something cool on her forehead, and her eyelids fluttered open and she found herself staring into the Devil's black eyes. Her bottom lip quivered as she pleaded, "Please, don't hurt me."

The words had barely been uttered before she drifted back into a foggy state of sleep. She felt the comfort and warmth of the Devil, and vaguely heard his softly spoken words, which left her with a feeling of contentment.

Strong arms cradled her close, yet she sensed those same arms were capable of crushing the very life from her body. But for now they offered her comfort.

Jewel rose from the depths of her sleep and blinked, letting her eyes adjust to the light.

She lay upon her stomach encompassed in fluffy, white comforters strewn across her. She wasn't quite sure she wanted to crawl out of her warm cocoon, but she sensed that she must. Raising her head, she recoiled at the soreness that seemed to cover every inch of her body. "Oh!" The moan escaped her.

Pushing herself up onto her knees, despite protesting muscles, she managed to stay in a crouched position until the blackness that threatened to once again engulf her faded away. She must have been very sick to feel so awful, she thought as she slowly turned and sat up so she could take in her surroundings.

Pale yellow walls trimmed in white gave a bright and cheerful appearance to the room . . . to this *unfamiliar* room. She sat upon a four-poster bed made feminine by a yellow-and-white canopy. Rubbing her hand across the smooth comforter, she had the strongest feeling that she didn't belong there.

The lacy curtains fluttering by the open window caught her attention. Where? . . . How? . . . What? Frustration seized her.

Where was she? Nothing looked familiar. Nothing! She was dead. She just knew it.

Slumping in defeat, she leaned back against the headboard, but immediately gasped and bolted upright. Sharp, burning pain shot through her body, letting her know she was very much alive.

She winced at the throbbing in her head and back, and reached up to massage her temples. What in the world had happened? How had she gotten here? *Think, Jewel. Think.* She remembered a ship, but what ship? And why was her memory so vague? Lost in her confusion, she barely heard the creak of the door.

"Ye done an' woke up, lass." A stout little woman entered the room with a tray in her hands. " 'Tis aboot time."

Startled, Jewel tried to scream, but her lips were so parched that only a squeak slipped out as she warily watched the older woman's slow and unhurried movements—a woman she didn't know.

" 'Tis good to be seein' those wee eyes open." The lady tilted her head to the side and smiled. "Why, ye have the darkest brown eyes I've ever seen. They're simply beautiful, lass. I knew they would be." The chattering woman winked at her cheerfully.

Setting the tray down on the bedside table, she bent over and squeezed Jewel's arms in an affectionate gesture. "There will be no frownin'. It'll be causin' lots of wrinkles on that bonny face. Take it from one who knows."

Jewel tried to laugh at the bouncing little lady with the gray hair, which only made her head hurt worse. She cleared her throat and managed to whisper, "Water."

Immediately, a glass was brought to her lips. After a few cooling sips Jewel apologized. "I'm sorry I frowned at you. It's just that I've been sitting here trying to remember what happened." She tried to ignore the quiver of her stomach and her ice-cold hands. "Do I know you?" Even her own scratchy voice didn't sound familiar.

"Nay, lass."

"I see," Jewel said, even though she really didn't see at all. "If I don't know you, then how did I get here?"

"Adam found ye on the beach."

"Adam? Beach?" Jewel's confusion grew. "I'm sorry, I don't understand."

"Ye don't remember a thin', lass?"

Jewel shook her head, despair wrinkling her brow. "I don't know where I am, and I can't for the life of me remember anything but my name."

"And that bein'?"

"My name is Jewel. . . ." She paused a moment. "I—I can't even remember my surname." Exasperation infused her nervous voice and tears burned her eyes.

Stepping up on the stool, the nice lady sat on the bed and patted her hand. "Now, lass, don't be a worryin'. The doctor said this could happen. 'Tis quite common with an accident, but yer memory will be returnin'," the woman assured her, brushing her hair off her forehead. "And probably when ye least be expectin' it."

The motherly gesture caused a lump in Jewel's throat. "Where am I?"

"First, let me introduce myself. My name is Annie Pritchard, and I've worked for His Grace since he was a wee bairn."

"Who?" Jewel raised a brow in question.

"His Grace, Adam Trent, Duke of St. Ives. Ye be stayin' at his castle, Briercliff, in Cornwall. 'Tis Adam's country estate, and lucky for ye he be hatin' the city and 'twas in residence, or ye might never have been found."

Jewel realized she was in England, and the fact didn't surprise her. She also had a feeling that England spelled trouble for her. Perhaps her memory would come back little by little, but until she knew who these strangers were, she'd best keep anything she remembered to herself.

"Well, I'm thankful to His Grace, and I'm sorry I've caused so much trouble for both of you."

"Dinna fret yerself lass. For a while we didn't think ye'd survive. The important thin' now is to get ye well. Are ye hungry?"

Jewel nodded, smiling once again at Annie's kindness. She seemed a caring person with her mothering ways, perhaps someone who could be trusted. But trusted for what?

Jewel's stomach rumbled in anticipation as she smelled the food brought in earlier. Annie slid from the bed and picked up the tray, placing it across Jewel's lap. Jewel reached and pinched off a bit of bread, then spread the remainder of the slice with thick, creamy butter and jam, savoring every mouthful. "This strawberry jam is very good."

"I took the chance ye'd be awake this mornin'. Eat slow, lass," Annie cautioned. "The wild strawberries I found in the glen last spring. Maybe when yer able, I can show ye where they are. 'Tis a beautiful place."

Jewel wiped her mouth with the linen napkin and laid it on the tray. "I didn't know I was so hungry. It must have been days since I've last eaten."

Tired of sitting without support, Jewel tried to prop a couple of pillows behind her; however, stiffness prevented even this simple task. Annie fluffed the bolsters and helped ease Jewel back, but the minute her shoulder touched the pillows, she let out a blood-curdling yelp.

"Damnation! My back hurts! What happened to it?" Looking down, Jewel noticed for the first time the bandages wrapped around her midsection. "What are all these bindings for?" She looked up to see Annie gasp. "What's wrong?"

"Ye language, lass. 'Tis not considered very lady-like to be swearin'," Annie cautioned, then added, "Ye really canna remember a thin'?"

"No." Jewel tried to recall anything. "I remember a ship, but nothing more."

Annie spent the next half hour explaining how Adam and

Jonathan had found her on the beach. She also told Jewel that Dr. Perkins had made a special ointment, hoping to prevent the scarring of her back.

"You said beaten." Jewel mumbled the words. "I wonder what I could have done to deserve such harsh treatment."

"I don't know." Annie shook her head. "Mayhap you fell afoul of somebody truly wicked. But it does a body no good to brood," Annie said firmly as she removed the tray. "Let's be takin' one day at a time, and before ye know it yer memory will return. I'm sure ye canna have done anythin' wrong."

Jewel's eyelids felt heavy. "I fear I'm still very tired."

"I've probably tarried too long, but 'tis good to have someone young here again. Everyone has grown much too serious over the years. Rest now, lass. Rest be the best medicine. I'll look in on ye later."

Adam wasn't a man to be kept waiting. But waiting was just what he had been doing until yesterday when word had arrived that the *Merry Weather* had finally docked in London.

Mid-afternoon, he set out for the rendezvous point. The usual meeting place had been changed to a tavern called The Black Lady. Adam strode down several cobblestone streets, heading in the direction of the docks. Now the tavern lay just ahead.

Pausing, he read the crooked sign over the door. It hung by a single bolt and appeared ready to fall at any given moment. The sign swayed and squealed as he pushed open the black wooden door. Luckily, the sign held.

Ale and sweat infested the stale air as he peered through the smoke lingering above the scattered tables. Adam carefully moved between the patrons. Spying a vacant table in the corner, he headed in that direction. The wall would provide good protection for his back, and he had an excellent

view of the door. His gaze traveled over the riffraff and vaga-
bonds who called this place home.

Swinging the chair around, he adjusted his faded brown
jacket and sat down. At the moment, Adam didn't resemble
the Duke of St. Ives. His face sported a three-day growth of
stubble, but he had to look like the occupants of the pub if
he didn't want to draw attention to himself.

"Ale, luv?" The black-haired wench placed a mug on the
table. Adam tossed her a coin and watched as she made her
way to another table. Her black hair reminded him of Jewel,
and he wondered if she had regained consciousness. He
hoped that when he returned home, she'd be able to answer
his many questions.

Adam rubbed the coarse stubble on his chin. He still
couldn't fathom the beating she'd received; however, he did
know she possessed a haunting beauty that intrigued him and
kept her in his thoughts more than he liked to admit.

The door swung open, and Adam saw his contact enter.
Cameron looked around the room before moving into the
dim light. Adam raised his hand and immediately gained his
friend's attention.

"Mate." Cameron nodded as he took his seat. "How have
you been faring?"

Adam smiled at the code they used. If he didn't answer
correctly, Cameron would know something was wrong.

"By the seat of me pants, lad, by the seat of me pants."
Adam chuckled.

Leisurely, they drank ale and talked in their darkened corner.
Cameron passed him the packet unnoticed under the table.

"How's Jackson?" Adam asked.

"He's up to his ass in Creeks."

"Really?" Adam smiled. He could almost picture Hawk
astride a horse with a gun in each hand ready to do battle.
"Sounds like he's enjoying himself as usual. He's always
liked a good fight."

They continued their discussion while drinking a second

mug of ale. As they stood to leave, Adam slipped the papers into his coat. They had started for the door when a big, burly hand reached out and grabbed Adam's left arm.

"Whatcha hurry, mate?" the intoxicated bloke mumbled.

Adam didn't say a word as he shook off the man. His menacing stance should have been a warning for the offender. But it wasn't.

"I'll just be relievin' ya of that packet, mate. The way you're clutching the thing, I'd say it were worth somethin'."

Adam noticed the room had grown quiet in anticipation. "Then again you could be mistaken," Adam said as he turned to leave.

"He's got a knife!" Cameron shouted.

Adam swung around, raising his left arm to deflect the blow and at the same time throwing a right jab to the sailor's midsection. His opponent fell backwards and hit the floor with a loud thud. Feeling the man was out cold, Adam once again started to leave.

He was almost to the door when the hairs on the back of his neck warned him something wasn't right. He spun around, drew his gun, and fired just as his adversary pulled out a pistol. Adam's bullet nicked his assailant's hand, and the man dropped his gun to the floor.

Walking over to the man, who lay sprawled on the floor, Adam searched the sailor's face to see if he recognized him. The sailor looked scared, and Adam decided the man wasn't a British spy. His only fault was that he was drunk.

Adam and Cameron parted outside the tavern. Even though killing wasn't second nature to Adam, he had come to accept it as a part of the secret life he'd chosen. This time, it had been avoided.

Now it was time to take care of his other problem. He was heading to Briercliff.

* * *

Dr. Perkins entered the room, followed by Annie. "It's good to see your eyes open, young lady."

"Thank you."

"Lie very still. I'm going to remove the bandages from your back." Carefully, he detached each dressing until Jewel's skin was exposed. He then took warm water and sponged off the thick white medicine.

Pushing down gently on the thin streaks, he asked, "Does this cause you pain?"

"A little." She jerked. "But I can tell I'm not as sore as I was a week ago. Sometimes my back feels tight, and I do experience tenderness if I move suddenly." Jewel felt a little more soreness than she admitted, but she longed to get out of this bed.

"That's to be expected. The tightness comes from the healing process. I have an idea that you're experiencing a little more pain than you let on, my dear."

"Look, Annie, do you see this?" The doctor pointed to the once-bloody cuts on her back. "The welts have turned pink and are no longer angry and red. I say, they've closed up nicely, and that's a very good sign. Once again, my miracle salve has done its job."

"If I'd not be seein' with me own eyes the before and after, I'd never be believin' it was possible!" Annie exclaimed.

"What is it?" Anxiety twisted Jewel's insides as she turned her head to see them. How awful could her back look?

"My dear, you will be very fortunate. You'll have scars, but I believe your scarring will be minor. You might have red marks now, but given time, they should fade."

Jewel pulled up her gown, then turned to face the doctor. "Dr. Perkins, how will I ever repay you?" She glanced down at her hands before looking back at the doctor. "I'm afraid I'm short of funds, but I'll gladly work off my fee." She felt herself blush.

The doctor took her hand in his and gazed into her eyes.

"You don't owe me a thing. His Grace has taken care of everything. He'll be pleased that you will be up and about upon his return. Perhaps you should stay in bed just a few more days." Dr. Perkins smiled. "Just give it time, my dear."

Jewel waited a good hour after everybody had left the room before deciding to test her legs. There was no way she was going to stay confined any longer. Throwing back the covers, she quickly came to an upright position—too quickly. The room began to spin, and she grabbed the edge of the mattress to steady herself. She had to wait for the dizziness to subside; then slowly she opened her eyes and tried to focus on the rug far below. This had to be the tallest bed she'd ever seen—her feet dangled well above the floor.

Gathering up her courage, she shoved away from the mattress and landed on wobbly legs that gave way the minute she hit the floor. She landed on her derriere with a thud.

"Ouch," she mumbled, rubbing her backside.

Then she spotted a stool just under the bed. "I could have used you before I fell." Pulling the stool out, she used it to brace herself as she tried to stand. Her legs felt like limp straw, but they held. It was amazing how weak her body had become, but she was determined not to give in to that feebleness.

She placed one foot in front of the other until she reached the window. Perspiration covered her brow and her chest heaved with her efforts, but she had achieved her small goal.

The breeze felt cool on her damp skin. What she had thought was a window was actually French doors that led out onto a balcony overlooking a yellowish-green meadow. A small creek ran in front of white stables that were surrounded by whitewashed fences. Adam Trent must have had many horses to fill a building so large.

Jewel longed to be outside, but knew she would have to wait until she felt stronger. Even this short walk had left her legs feeble and unstable. Turning back to look at the room, she marveled at the wealth of the man who'd saved her. Lavish Queen Anne furnishings accented the feminine decor. The Oriental carpets had deep greens and golds with just a touch of black.

This room probably belonged to the lady in Lord Trent's life, Jewel mused. She remembered Annie saying he wasn't married, but since the first day, she hadn't said anything else about him.

Jewel wondered about the man who'd saved her. Evidently, he wanted nothing to do with her because she'd yet to see him. If that was the case, then Jewel decided she'd treat him with the same indifference. She hadn't asked to be here. *He'd* brought her to his home. She would get well, thank the duke for saving her, and then go out of his life. But where was she going to go? She couldn't go home. She didn't even know where home was.

A gnawing fear of the unknown seeped through her body. Her eyes started to moisten, and her stomach twisted with apprehension at not knowing what the future would bring. What if he threw her out?

"What ye be doin' out of bed?" Annie scolded from the door. "Are ye forgettin' what the doctor done and told ye? Here, let me help ye!" She hurried over and took Jewel by the arm, guiding her back to the bed. "You're doin' well for the first time up, but I wouldn't be overdoin' it," Annie said more gently.

"Annie, what is the duke like?"

"Like no other mon I've ever known," she answered with quiet authority. At Jewel's look of surprise, she added, "Of course, I'm a wee bit prejudiced. He's fierce like a lion on the outside, but if you can break past his hard shell ye'll see a kind mon." Annie smiled as she straightened the bed linens. "Ye'll meet him soon and can judge for yerself."

After that description, Jewel wasn't sure how much she

looked forward to the prospect. "What if he doesn't like me?"

Annie cocked her head to one side and gave Jewel an appraising look. "He'll be likin' ye, lass. I've no doubts on that matter."

Jewel wasn't so sure. Why should he like a perfect stranger? He probably wouldn't like her at all. Exhausted from just those few minutes, she appreciated Annie's assistance more than she knew as Annie helped her into bed.

"Tomorrow we'll be gettin' ye up and dressed. I'll show ye the house, but I want ye to promise ye'll let me know the minute ye tire."

"But Annie, I have no clothes! I have nothing."

"Don't be a-frettin', child. Remember the wrinkles," she teased. "I'll find ye something to wear. That ye can be sure of." Annie fluffed the pillows as Jewel climbed up on the bed, then pulled the covers over her. "Rest now. Tomorrow will be here before ye know it."

Jewel's temples throbbed as she snuggled gratefully under the white comforter. She knew she wouldn't try to get out of bed again, but tomorrow would be different. She couldn't wait to get back to her old self again—whoever that was, and she also found her apprehension growing at the thought of meeting this mysterious man who sounded both formidable and kind and whose house she was living in. She sighed, and her heavy eyelids drifted down, but her mind wouldn't rest as she pondered all the unanswered questions.

She had to find her knife.

Jewel's eyelids flew open.

A knife? Why in the world had she thought of a knife?

Maybe something evil *did* lurk in her past. Or maybe *she* was the evil person. . . .

Lord, she hoped not!

Four

Jewel awoke bright and early to a slight nip in the air. Today she was going to leave this room and see just how big Briercliff was. Stretching her arms overhead, she felt a tightness in her back that soon gave way to a nagging itch. Another good sign her back was healing.

She slid out of bed and found her legs were not as weak as the day before. Grabbing a lacy shawl, she made her way to the French doors. The glass doors swung open and moist, salty sea air poured in. The stone of the balcony floor chilled her feet. Pulling her shawl closer to ward off the brisk air, she glanced to her left and saw the white misty fog beginning to separate, leaving in its wake a view of the sea. Behind the wispy curtain of mist, the sea roared as it flung itself against the rocky shore.

Wrapped in her solitude, Jewel shut her eyes and found she felt very much at home with the sea. But that tranquility was soon erased as she envisioned two ships: one the victor, the other the prey. The remains of a broken ship surrounded by smoke, blood, and death half-crystalized before her eyes. Memories.

"No!" An agonized whisper slipped passed her lips and she covered her ears, trying to block out the screams of death. Her eyes flew open. She gripped the railing so hard her knuckles had turned white. She didn't want her memory back if it was anything like what she'd just envisioned.

"And a good morning to ye, missy. How would ye be

feelin' this morning?" Annie asked cheerfully as she walked into the room.

Jewel took several deep breaths. By the time she'd turned away from the railing, she'd managed to regain her composure. Her gaze lit on the clothes Annie had thrown across her arm. "Good morning, Annie. I feel much better," Jewel lied. "I see you've found something for me to wear?"

"Now, 'twould seem all the women round here are a wee bit larger than ye." Annie held up a pair of trousers and a shirt with a shame-faced look. "However, the cook, Marie, suggested that I be tryin' some of her son's clothes on ye— that is, if ye don't mind?"

"Mind? Of course not. I'd wear anything to get out of this room." Jewel found herself getting caught up in the kind lady's merriment. She absolutely didn't want any more flashes of gruesome memories.

"Speaking of clothes . . . what happened to the ones I had when I came here?"

"They were no better than rags, lass, so we burned 'em." Speaking matter-of-factly, Annie laid the garments on the end of the bed. "Adam would not like findin' ye in men's garb, him bein' of the gentry, but he's not due back till tomorrow, so we thought 'twould be all right."

"Thank you, Annie. I don't see why His Grace would care. Besides what he doesn't know won't hurt him or us." So that was why Jewel hadn't met His Lordship. She had thought he was purposely avoiding her. What kind of man would take the time to save her, then leave before he found out if she would live?

"Now, for a bath." Annie pulled the bell cord, signaling the servants to bring the water up from the kitchen. Fifteen minutes later, the hip-tub was filled, and Jewel lay back in the steamy water, enjoying the scent. She was thankful the water didn't burn her still-tender back.

"This soap smells wonderful."

" 'Tis the fragrance of lavender, and 'tis Elizabeth's favorite, too."

So Elizabeth was the lady in the duke's life. Jewel wanted to know more about this person, but since Annie didn't say anything else, Jewel hesitated to ask. Of course, it was none of her business. However, it explained the female decor of this room. Perhaps His Lordship had gone after Elizabeth. *That* could be his most urgent business.

And where did Jewel fit in once they returned? She wondered about that as she lathered her arms. Would she be sent to the servants' quarters or sent away? And how the hell was she going to get home? She slid under the water to rinse off the soap, then emerged thinking of the unknown. Scared, she pushed her worries aside and patiently sat while Annie washed her hair. Jewel reached up, and for the first time she realized her hair was short.

"You know, Annie, I don't even know what I look like," Jewel admitted.

"We'll be fixin' that shortly. To be sure, a few weeks ago ye wouldn't have wanted to see yerself, but yer bruises have faded now, so I think it'll be all right." Annie helped her from the tub, providing a soft sheet for drying off.

After dressing in the clothes provided, Jewel walked over to look at herself in the mirror. She didn't recognize the person staring back. Placing her hands on her cheeks, she sighed. This definitely wasn't the face she remembered. Again her memory was jarred as she recalled her carefree days on an island daydreaming over the fashionable magazines that her tutor, Mr. Lovall, had provided, hoping that one day she might be as beautiful as the grand ladies. But look at her! She had a boy's figure and the one thing that had been pretty was now gone—gone was the silky, black hair that had hung to her waist, and there was no memory of the face that stared back at her.

"What happened to my hair?" Reaching up in dismay, she fingered the strands that just touched her shoulders. Then she remembered a man . . . no, a captain lacing his fingers through her long black hair as he jerked her to her knees and savagely hacked off her long hair, throwing it at her feet. When Jewel opened her eyes, two tears had run down her cheeks. She didn't know who she had been before today, but she knew some terrible things had happened to her. The question was, what part did she play in all these scenes?

"I didna mean to upset ye, lass. Yer hair will grow back." Annie squeezed Jewel's arms.

"It—it's not that. It—it's just that for a moment I could see a man cutting off my hair."

"Did ye recognize him?"

"No." Jewel shook her head.

" 'Tis a good sign. Yer memory will be returnin' 'fore long and ye'll have all yer questions answered to be sure."

Jewel couldn't stop staring at the stranger's . . . no, *her* reflection. Just who was the woman who stared back? She pinched her cheeks to bring out a soft pink color. Shrugging her shoulders, she decided there was not much she could do about her appearance until she was completely well.

She felt a vague familiarity about the clothing she had on. She didn't feel the least bit strange in pants, but she didn't comment as they headed slowly down the stairs. According to Annie, ladies would never dream of wearing such garments.

Looking at portraits of the Trent ancestors that hung along the walls, she noticed they all had cold and unhappy countenances. She could truthfully say she was glad she didn't have to meet any of these men. The present duke would probably be bad enough.

First, they entered the sitting room, where the rich cherrywood paneling smelled of beeswax and a large white Persian rug sprawled across the oak floor. Jewel stepped on the thick carpet, skirting the family crest boldly dominating the very center of the rug.

Sapphire blue surrounded the outside edge of the crest,

and in the center a bold knight dressed in armor sat astride
a mighty black stallion. The mantle draped above the helm
was blood red. Under the knight was sprawled the Latin for
the motto *one so bold*.

Velvet drapes of the same sapphire blue hue covered the
windows. Everything in the room proclaimed the wealth of
the Trent family.

"It's beautiful," Jewel finally said.

"I think so, too," Annie admitted. "This carpet took over
two years for the weavers to finish. I daresay there's not
another like it."

Just how wealthy was this man? He must have paid a small
fortune for a rug of this quality, Jewel thought.

"Lass, I've some things to be doin' in the kitchen," Annie
explained. "Ye can stay in here if ye like or ye can come
with me."

"I'd like to see the cooking area, if you don't mind. I
promise not to get in the way."

The place reminded Jewel of a beehive with so many people coming and going. The aroma of freshly baked bread
scented the air as a big, gray-clad woman stood in the center
of the room, swinging a leg of lamb as if it were a mere
chicken bone. Jewel decided quickly that the cook wasn't a
woman to be crossed. Jewel glanced around the kitchen and
noticed an abundance of everything. It appeared they were
preparing enough food to feed an army.

"Are we having company?" she asked the cook.

"Not company, but His Grace." The cook picked up a pot
full of hot broth and a big spoon and moved to the fireplace.
"A messenger just arrived with a note from His Lordship.
He sent word he'll be here tonight for dinner, so there are
many things to be done." When she finished basting the lamb
with broth, she looked at Jewel. "His Grace insists his staff
eat as well as he does; that's the reason you see so much

food," the cook explained as she carried the roast over to the fireplace.

"Annie, let me help here. I feel strong enough." Jewel smiled hesitantly. She felt useless just sitting and watching others work.

"Nay. Besides, ye have just gotten out of bed."

Jewel straightened her shoulders and prepared herself for an argument. She knew she'd have her hands full convincing Annie. "I promise I'll tell you if I get tired. There must be something easy I can do," she suggested hopefully. "All of you have done so much for me, it's the least I can do."

"Adam would have my head and ye would hear the roar of the lion himself." Annie shook her white-capped crown. "Now, be a good lass and go on back to the sittin' room. I'll check on ye later."

"Go to the sitting room? And do what?" Jewel mumbled. "No, I don't think I will." She wandered down the hall past the stairs to what she thought would be the study. Her curiosity about the duke had to be satisfied.

The sharp odor of cherry tobacco pricked Jewel's nose as she opened the door. How masculine the room appeared. A sense of power and strength emanated from the dark, massive furniture. She wondered what His Lordship was like. "Probably old and ugly," she murmured to herself.

Bookshelves lined the wall behind the desk, reaching from floor to ceiling. Hundreds of leather-bound tomes on every conceivable subject filled the space. Pulling down a text, she carefully opened it to the first page and scanned it swiftly. She could read, so she must have had some kind of education.

Putting the volume back in its place, she began cleaning with the feather duster she'd found. Jewel stretched up high, but the pain in her back reminded her all too quickly that she wasn't fully recovered.

A pair of blue leather wing-back chairs soon glistened from her efforts. Next she tackled the mantel, carefully picking up each vase. When she'd replaced the last one, she glanced up and noticed a large portrait hanging above the mantel. She had to back up to get a better look. An older, distinguished man stared down at her. His finely chiseled face had strong aristocratic features. However, his strange coal-black eyes dominated his attributes, and compelled her attention as his black piercing pupils seemed to stare right through her so much so she found it impossible to glance away. How silly, Jewel thought. The painter must have been in a hurry because no one had eyes the color of midnight.

Casting off the eerie feeling, she turned back to the task at hand, moving over to the large, mahogany desk. Its rich colors matched the bookcase perfectly. She picked up a paper lying on the top, trying to get some feel for the man. The sheet she held was a ledger from a farm that was probably on his estate. Putting it back, she shook her head as she looked at the messy desktop. It was hard to decide where to start. Her knees buckled, and she could tell her legs felt just a little wobbly. She'd just finish this last thing, and then she'd find a chair where she could rest.

Stacking all the documents to one side, she began to dust. In her haste, she bumped the largest stack of papers, and watched as they scattered in disarray over the floor. "Damn," Jewel swore as she got down on her knees to retrieve the papers. Annie's words came back to her and Jewel bit her lip in consternation. Hadn't Annie warned her how particular His Grace was? That was all Jewel needed . . . to anger a man she had yet to meet.

She rose with her arms full of papers and glanced at the painting. If he looked anything like this painting, he stayed in a bad mood. Perhaps he wouldn't notice the documents were out of order if she just spread them across the desk.

Engrossed in her task, she didn't hear the door open.

Five

Adam's eyes narrowed as he watched a young lad going through his papers. A muscle twitched in his cheek. By God, no one entered his study unless invited! Pulling out the gun he kept tucked in his belt, he eased across the room with a quietness that years of training had taught him.

Catching the lad off guard, Adam wrapped his arm around the boy's neck and jammed a revolver into his back. He felt a smug satisfaction when the boy yelped.

"What are you looking for, son?" Adam growled in a low, menacing voice. "I assure you that everything in this room belongs to me, and you better damn well have a good excuse for being here. I strongly suggest that you slowly turn around."

Adam felt the boy stiffen, and it took a moment before the lad spoke. "You're hurting my back! For an old man, you sure have a mean grip. Remove that damn gun, and I'll do as you request."

"As I request! Bloody Hell!" Adam's shouts vibrated the windows. "You've some nerve, son." Not waiting for the boy to move on his own, Adam grabbed him by the shoulders and spun him around.

The angry words Adam was about to hurl at the boy caught in his throat as a pair of angry brown eyes looked up at him. Eyes that he'd seen only briefly before. Eyes that now held him spellbound.

Jewel? No, it couldn't be. Surely she was still in bed, he

reminded himself. Wasn't that why he had ridden so hard from London? Was it possible? Could this be the same person?

"Jewel?"

A young woman stared up at him, her anger having vanished, and he could see she was as shocked as he. "Yes," she replied softly. "A-are you His Grace?"

Adam nodded slowly. His gaze rested upon the feather duster she held in her hand and his temper flared once again, but this time for a different reason. Did she think she had to earn her keep? She couldn't possibly be well and should be in bed regaining her strength . . . not playing downstairs maid. He had a staff quite capable of cleaning.

"What are you doing in here?" he snapped.

Jewel gasped at his abrupt tone. Of course she was snooping, but she couldn't tell him that. He had taken her by surprise, for she'd never seen a man who . . . who was so much a man. The man before her stood . . . tall . . . powerful. He took her breath away.

So *he* was the magnificent lord of the manor, the one she half-dreaded, half-anticipated seeing, and he was making it plain he didn't approve of her. Jewel couldn't fathom why he was so upset. Evidently, he had a very low opinion of her if he thought she would stoop to thievery.

"I'm sorry I've been so much trouble to you and Annie. I thought to make up for it by dusting that thing"—she pointed behind her—"you call a desk. For your information, I was not prying." She looked to heaven and asked for forgiveness. "I've no reason to," she stated as she gazed straight into his dark eyes. What had happened to the softness she'd seen there only moments ago? His eyes had now turned to pitch black. Just like the portrait over the mantel. The one she'd assumed was his portrait.

"Is that your father?" She nodded at the picture above the fireplace. She could see the simple question threw Adam completely off guard, and again his expression changed.

"My grandfather," he answered abruptly. "Who has nothing to do with this conversation." His eyes traveled over her, taking in every inch of her appearance. "No wonder I thought you to be a lad—look at the way you're dressed, in a blousy cotton shirt and black breeches. Men's garb, to be precise!" He threw her an irritated scowl.

"Perhaps not." She shrugged. "But I saw the painting earlier and wondered. You do look a lot like him, you know," she finished lamely.

Jewel stared into his dark, brooding eyes and took note of his strong chin. She remembered all of Annie's warnings as they tumbled through her mind. "The roar of the lion himself. He hates havin' anyone in his study. He'll be havin' me head." Then, completely without warning, Jewel swayed, all the excitement having drained her strength. Luckily, a pair of strong arms caught her just before she hit the floor, and carried her over to the settee and sat her down.

"You shouldn't be out of bed so soon. I'll have Annie's hide for this," Adam growled.

"No, don't!" Jewel laid a hand on his forearm, feeling his tense muscles beneath her fingertips. "It's all my fault," she admitted. "The doctor said I could get up, and I persuaded Annie to let me come downstairs. I—I've just overdone it a little. I'll be fine, really." A strange shiver of delight hammered through her. She found his presence a little overwhelming.

The chestnut riding jacket the duke wore fit snug across his broad shoulders, and his handsome face was deeply tanned. He radiated an aura of power that intrigued and drew her. Even though she sensed Adam could be very dangerous.

But for now he touched her almost tenderly. Concern softened the harshness in his eyes, and she wondered if she'd really get to know him before she left.

"Who are you?" His words broke into her thoughts, making her jump.

She wished she could answer that question. She wasn't

sure what he would do when he found out she didn't know. Would he turn her over to the authorities?

"I do not know," she finally said softly.

Surprised, Adam raised one black eyebrow. "What do you mean . . . you don't know?"

"I cannot remember anything but my first name." She paused. "The doctor said in time my memory will be restored. I'm sorry I've been so much trouble."

Adam realized he was staring at her slightly parted lips, wondering how they would taste. Then he remembered his previous nights in London where Jewel had plagued his dreams. She wasn't like the sophisticated ladies with whom he usually kept company. She looked more like a child than a woman. She was so small. Yet he could see signs of a radiant beauty—once she regained some of the weight she'd lost—and he itched to reach out and touch her short hair.

Knowing where his thoughts would lead, he turned his attention back to Jewel's outlandish tale. "You've not been any trouble. I just wish the devil I knew where you came from and what brought you to my doorstep, but I guess that will have to wait. Let's get one thing straight from the start. You do not earn your keep by working in my house. You're to be a guest in my home until we can find out where you belong. I trust I've made myself perfectly clear on that point."

The tone of his voice hinted he wasn't accustomed to repeating himself or having his instructions questioned. Perhaps she should humor him and be a little obedient. But some inner tingling told her that obedience wasn't a part of her personality.

A mischievous light stirred deep within her, and she gave him a small smile. "Yes, I understand. But you must also understand, I need something to do, unless you would like me to die from boredom."

Adam smiled, and she held her breath. His chiseled jaw relaxed and his eyes sparkled, taking away his stern expression. Why did she sense smiling was something he rarely did?

"I guess I should go back to my room," she said. "I promised Annie I wouldn't overdo." Jewel stood to leave, but instead of making a graceful exit, her foot slipped on the rug, and she fell right back into Adam's lap. *Uncle Jean had told her she would outgrow her clumsiness one day . . . she was still waiting.* Her eyes widened as the snippet of memory flashed through her mind. Was this something? Perhaps a beginning to who she really was.

"Well, now." Adam chuckled. "If you wanted me to carry you, you had only to ask." He looked down at her, his lips mere inches from hers.

Jewel's cheeks grew warm from Adam's bold stare. Had anyone ever looked at her the way he did? Could he tell how fast her heart hammered or how many butterflies fluttered in her stomach? His arms felt like steel around her, and a strong tide of emotions flowed through her. She was surprised when he hadn't removed his arm from around her.

"I—I think I can walk." But as she took a step, her knees trembled so badly from the duke's closeness that she had to clutch his sleeve.

It was the only invitation Adam needed. He swept Jewel up into his arms and carried her to her bedroom before reluctantly setting her back on her feet. The desire to kiss her became overpowering. What a natural temptress, he thought. And again he questioned his reaction to her. Normally, he could distance himself, but this one—confused and bewitched were feelings he didn't care for.

"You'll not have to wear men's clothing again," he said in a firm voice.

"But these clothes are fine," Jewel argued, sweeping her hands over her attire. "We couldn't find anything else that I could wear, and Annie told me you had burned my clothing."

"If you'll let me finish," Adam said patiently. "I bought

a few things for you while I was in London. I hope they fit."

"But . . ." Jewel started to protest further. Then she noticed the boxes stacked in the corner of her room. There were at least thirty. He had bought her all that? "How did you know my size? You really shouldn't have . . . I don't even know you . . . why did you buy so many?" Overwhelmed by surprise, she was astonished that he'd been thinking of her while he'd been gone.

He looked suddenly as if he considered a very grave matter. "So far I've found you to be clumsy, you have a temper, and you talk excessively when excited. We'll have to work on that problem before you drive me daft." He smiled this time.

"A deep breath will be required to answer all your questions, my dear. First, I told the dressmaker you were about the size of my sister, maybe a little shorter. Since the seamstress has sewn for my sister before, she already had her measurements. Second, I thought it better that you be clothed." His lips curved into a smile as he thought, *Better for me.* "Third, you're right. I don't know you, but we are getting ready to correct that. I'll have Annie bring dinner up here tonight, and we'll dine together. Now, does that answer all your questions?"

She gave him a slight nod. "Thank you, but you shouldn't have spent so much." Yet she found it pleased her that he had been so thoughtful.

"Don't worry about money, my dear. I think I can afford a few gowns. Besides, my sister can always wear them if you cannot. Now, if you'll excuse me." He turned and started for the door. "I'd like to wash up before we dine. The trip from London was very dusty. I'll send Annie up in a minute."

Jewel frowned. His sister could wear them? And she'd thought he had been thinking of *her* when he'd bought the clothes. He was only being practical. She sighed, pushing aside her disappointment. What did it matter what he thought? Except, she admitted, he wasn't the old gentleman she had first imagined. Quite the contrary. He was very good-looking, and probably half the women in London were in love with him. She'd best make sure she didn't fall under his spell.

Jewel hadn't realized how tired she'd been. A bath was just what she needed. Waiting patiently for the servants to fill the tub, she found herself looking forward to dinner tonight and excited at the prospect of learning more about the mysterious man she'd just met.

After she bathed, Annie spread a clean sheet on the bed and instructed her to lie down so she could attend her. Taking a few drops of sweet-smelling almond oil, Annie massaged the streaks that ran lengthwise down Jewel's back, to ease the tightness.

"What would ye like to be wearin' tonight? Adam has bought ye some beautiful things." Annie wiped her hands on a towel.

Jewel rolled over, pulling the sheet around her. "I haven't had a chance to look at anything yet," she confessed. "Pick something soft. I'm still a little tender."

Annie sifted through the many boxes until she found a soft dress and held it up for Jewel's approval. The white silk gown had tiny roses on the neckline and appeared to have a loose fit with gathers under the bust. Tiny pink ribbons flowed down the back.

" 'Tis perfect!" Annie smiled.

Jewel touched the silky material and thought it would feel cool on her skin, so she nodded her approval. Annie helped her slide the gown over her head, and Jewel found the garment to be a flawless fit, just as His Grace had said.

She swirled around for Annie to see, marveling at the way the material caressed her skin. "What do you think?"

"Ye be lookin' pretty, lass. Ye won't even be needin' lip color, like most women do. When yer hair grows out ye'll look just like a princess."

"My hair *is* ugly, isn't it?" Jewel reached up and touched the short hair that fell just below her ears, then glanced back to the mirror with a frown. "What can I do with it?"

"Why, to be sure, we can do somethin'." Annie brushed Jewel's black hair until it shone. She applied water on the gleaming tresses, feathering them around Jewel's face to give her a bewitching look. "Do ye like that?" Annie asked.

"It's a big improvement." Jewel could see Annie was pleased with her creation, and Jewel had to admit her hair did look better. She felt like a *real* lady. Hearing the knob of the door rattle, she turned to stare.

Unannounced, the door swung open.

Six

Jewel's breath caught in her throat.

Casually leaning against the door frame, the duke filled the entrance with his broad shoulders and rugged handsomeness. A pulse throbbed in his neck where dark skin contrasted against cream-colored linen. She found it impossible to tear her gaze from him.

As he pushed away from the door, she couldn't help noticing how his breeches clung to his muscular thighs. His manner was one of supreme confidence, yet there was something about him that was untamed and savage. Somehow Jewel knew she'd never met anyone like him before.

He moved toward her. His gaze traveled over every inch of her body. She felt shy and unsure of herself, and she prayed her nervousness would go away before dinner was served.

"Are you ready to dine, Jewel?"

His textured, masculine voice sent shivers down her spine. "Yes. I find I've quite an appetite tonight."

"Excellent." Adam nodded to Annie, acknowledging her presence. "Can we have dinner served now?"

"Yes, Your Grace."

He offered his arm. When Jewel placed her hand on his sleeve, her fingers trembled. After he escorted her to the small, round table that had been set up earlier in her bedroom, he placed a soft pillow behind her back so she would be comfortable. What a contradiction His Lordship could be.

One minute he was hard and disapproving, and the next he was concerned with her comfort. Some deep intuition told her there was more to this man than he let people see.

Adam poured a glass of his finest wine, and watched as the rich, burgundy liquid touched her lips. He still couldn't believe she'd survived. He felt as if he'd breathed life back into her body, willing her to live. No matter who she was or what she had done, Jewel would have his protection until she recovered her memory. She took another sip. "How do you like the wine?" he asked.

She nodded her approval. "It's very good and has a rich flavor. I like wine, but I've always preferred rum." She gasped. "Wait . . . I remembered. Your Grace, I remembered! I like a drink called rum."

"That is a good sign, and a mighty strong drink for a lady. Maybe it will not take long for your memory to return." Propping his arm on the table, he leaned forward. "Interesting you should mention rum. It's hard to get here in England. However, I have tasted this drink in Louisiana and purchased a bottle in the Jamaican Islands," he said thoughtfully. "Our cook, Marie, makes a very tasty bun. I enjoy using rum."

Adam stared at his visitor as he sampled his own glass of port. Could it be possible that Jewel wasn't from England? And if not England, then where? He noted that her face was still thin from her recent fever, but he intended to restore her good health with plenty of food.

Their conversation stopped briefly when the servants filed into the room laden with silver serving platters, steaming with rich aromas. They lifted the lids to reveal rare roast beef nestled in a bed of small boiled potatoes.

Jewel felt wonderful after the delicious feast and three glasses of wine. Having enjoyed the meal so much, she now realized that she'd finished eating and had talked very little. Adam must think her rude. Then again, why should she care what he thought? But she found she did care. Taking another sip of wine, she looked from beneath her lashes to find

Adam watching her. His dark brows were drawn together, and his eyes were full of questions she couldn't answer. Again, she found herself wondering why he would bother with her.

"You've quite an appetite, young lady. Most women I've known pick at their food and don't do the cook justice."

Jewel laughed huskily. "I guess I do have a good appetite. I'm sure it isn't very lady-like, but you have a superb cook, and the meal was simply wonderful!"

"I'm glad you enjoyed the roast." Adam smiled. "Your accent sounds French. Do you perhaps speak the language?"

Jewel shrugged her shoulders. "I don't know."

"Vous avez les plus beaux yeux brune, Mademoiselle."

Jewel felt the heat of her blush. She had understood every word. He had told her she had beautiful brown eyes. *"Merci, Monsieur. Je parle francais."*

"Well, now there's another clue in figuring out who you are. We'll have your memory back in no time. Until then, remember you're to be my guest." Adam wasn't sure he was doing the right thing, but for some strange reason he couldn't send her away, at least not yet. And he had no earthly idea why he felt as he did other than that he liked her.

"Thank you." Touched by his thoughtfulness, she reached across the table and laid her small hand on his. She was a perfect stranger to him, yet he wasn't throwing her out.

The mere touch of his warm skin under her fingertips produced a tingling she was unprepared for. Gasping, she withdrew her hand and tried to cover her uneasiness. "T-tell me something about your family," she stammered.

Adam's eyes met hers, and he knew she'd felt the same exhilaration. It would be easy to lose himself in the depths of her brown eyes. They reflected her innermost thoughts and could prove useful as a mirror into her soul. Realizing she felt the same was of little comfort. He had no time for a woman. He also needed something stronger than wine, and reached for the brandy decanter, pouring a liberal portion into the glass. He wasn't accustomed to talking about himself, but telling her a little couldn't hurt.

"I don't know where to begin," he admitted. "I was raised here in Cornwall, but left when I was eighteen. You know how young men like to sow their oats." He chuckled, for he'd definitely done just that. "I've sailed all over the world and found the place I loved most was America. I've a twin sister who lives just outside New Orleans, Louisiana."

He relaxed as he continued to speak of his American home. "My plantation, Four Oaks, is surrounded by moss-covered trees and four very large oak trees. It's a comfortable place, and most certainly doesn't have the formality of England."

"But you're English! Does not your loyalty lie with England?"

"I'm only half English. My mother was an American."

"This isn't your home?" Jewel asked. "After all, you are a duke."

"In a way, yes. I am the Duke of St. Ives by birth, but this was my grandfather's and my father's home. I'm here now because of my grandfather's death and to get the estate running smoothly. Then I'll hire someone to oversee Briercliff before returning to Four Oaks."

An odd flutter of panic stirred in her stomach at the thought of his leaving. She'd never felt so thoroughly confused. "You'll be going home before long? Will you book passage on a ship?"

"You've a strange habit of asking double questions, sweetheart." He winked at her in a teasing mood. "I have my own ship. As a matter of fact, I have three—this one is called *Wind Jammer*. She's a clipper, and I daresay there's not another quicker."

Jewel saw an excitement enter his eyes as he spoke of his vessel. It was easy for her to picture him standing at the helm, the wind blowing his hair, and for a fleeting moment another face flashed before her, but it was so brief she couldn't catch the image. Thank God this image wasn't as scary as the other images.

Adam watched as she stared at him, but he could tell her mind was far away. Perhaps she was remembering some little something, and he wondered what her life had been like before she landed on his shore. She was full of life, and wasn't in the least bit shy around him. He liked that. Maybe no one had taught her to play the aloof seductive role that most women played.

"Where's the *Wind Jammer* now?" she asked. "May I see her one day? She sounds beautiful, Your Grace."

Adam started laughing. She'd just done the same thing—asked two questions at once. "Please, call me Adam."

"Thank you, Adam."

He liked the way she shyly said his name, her accent adding a different sound with its mixture of French and English. If he could only put his finger on where he'd heard it before. "She's in the colonies right now, transporting spices and other goods from the West Indies to America. I left my first mate, Derek, in charge. And in answer to your first question—when I'm ready to return home, I'll send for Derek to pick me up. You can see the ship at that time."

"Then you'll be leaving soon?"

"I'm not sure. As I said, I still have some business matters to clear up here first. And I need to find out just who you are and where you belong." Adam noticed the look of apprehension that crossed her face, and wondered what had caused it.

"I see," she said softly.

Noting the disappointment in her voice, Adam came around the table to help her out of the chair. His hand slid down her arm. He felt her tremble at the mere brush of his fingers. He knew he was too close—her breathing became shallow.

Slowly, she looked up into his eyes. "You're handsome,"

she murmured, swaying toward him. "I didn't mean to say that. Annie said that ladies should be demure."

Adam grinned, thinking the wine had loosened her tongue as he reached out to steady her. A pink blush covered her face. Of course, he'd been guilty of keeping her glass full all night. If she could read his thoughts right now, she'd be smart and run out of the room to safety. God, she was beautiful, and he'd love to find out if her skin felt like satin all over. How he ached to touch her wine-sweetened lips. But Adam thrust aside the thought as soon as it formed. She still seemed an innocent child, much like his sister, he told himself. He'd not take advantage of her.

Finally, she looked down at her feet and murmured, "I'm sorry."

"Don't apologize, my lady." He put his finger under her chin and tilted her face up so he could see her eyes. He looked deep into their depths and found a burning passion, making him forget all earlier thoughts of her being a child. He groaned. Again the urge to kiss her grew like a fire within him. Jerking himself back to reality, Adam realized that he couldn't kiss her as he wanted to. This attraction to her was insane. It made no sense at all. Gently, he brushed his lips against her forehead. "Good night, my lady."

The shutting of the door brought Jewel's attention back. Adam was gone, and she didn't know if she was happy or sad. If only he were old and ugly or had a scar or two, then resisting him would be easier. But he was simply beautiful.

"Good night, Adam," she whispered to the closed door.

Breakfast consisted of blueberry muffins and jam. There were also generous portions of ham and bacon. Jewel was afraid she'd feel awkward after the previous night, but Adam acted as if nothing had happened. She wasn't sure how men and women were supposed to act. Perhaps he kissed every woman he knew.

They enjoyed a pleasant conversation much as they had the previous night.

After breakfast, Adam bade her good day and went to his study to work, leaving her to entertain herself. Jewel soon learned this was his usual custom, so she began to visit the kitchen staff, knowing he would disapprove if he found out, but needing someone to talk to. She soon learned all the servants' names, and would laugh while she helped them with their small tasks.

The days soon settled into a routine. She saw very little of Adam during the day, but at night he always appeared for dinner and provided her with stimulating conversation about Briercliff. They were developing an easy relationship, and a few times she felt that Adam was reluctant to bid her good night. However, he never kissed her on the forehead again, much to her regret. But when she expressed a desire to go outside, he did promise to take her riding very soon. She was beginning to feel like a member of the family, and it seemed she had known Adam longer than a month.

The next three weeks, she spent her time reading; however, she soon became bored and looked for other ways to occupy herself.

Finally, one morning she saw Adam ride off on his black stallion. Now, she decided, was the perfect time to cure her restlessness. Every time she had mentioned going outside, Adam had told her she wasn't well enough. There were times when he treated her much like a child, and she wondered if that was the way he really saw her.

She had a terrible longing to be outdoors, and now was her opportunity. She quickly dressed and hurried from her room.

Once outside, Jewel wandered across the back lawns of Briercliff. She stopped and stared up at the grayish stone contrasted against a bright blue sky. The structure might not be the largest in England, but it was certainly impressive.

Annie had told her a little about the castle. It was, of

course, large, with thirty-four rooms. There were two three-bedroom cottages, two fish ponds, and an active church on the grounds. Jewel found the leaded windows that stretched across the back of the house to be beautiful. The ballroom was easily identified by the many floor-to-ceiling windows and several French doors.

She turned away from the castle and walked down the stone steps, noticing the back lawns were in layers, each level leading to another. After reaching the second section, she found Annie working in the flower beds.

"What are you doing?" Jewel asked.

The little lady was startled, but quickly recovered and looked around at her. "Workin' in my flower garden, lass. 'Tis nice tae see ye outside."

"It's wonderful to be here. I'd have come out sooner, but His Grace kept insisting I wasn't well enough." She sighed. "I've been shut up much too long. This time I didn't bother to ask," she confessed. "What are those things you're planting?"

Annie held up a tiny round ball with a point on one end. "They're called bulbs. I plant them in the fall and by spring we'll be havin' bright rainbow colors. I'm also plantin' daffodils and crocuses. 'Tis said when ye see the first crocus peek out of the ground, spring can't be far behind." She stood up, stretching her back muscles. "Would ye like to be helpin' me?"

"May I?"

Jewel glanced down at her pretty dress of heather blue with the faintest thin white stripe running through the material. She really should go and change, but the October sun felt much too good on her skin, and she didn't want to miss one ray. Shoving aside the guilt about soiling her new gown, she was soon down on her knees, digging in the soil.

"My mother liked flowers," Jewel admitted right out of the blue.

"Ye remember her, lass?"

"I—I can almost picture her in a flower garden, but it must have been a long time ago," she said sadly, "because I can't remember her face."

"The important thing is ye remembered."

"I guess you're right," Jewel admitted as she scooped out two more small holes.

Annie laughed, and Jewel turned to see what had amused her. "What's so funny?" she asked, puzzled to find Annie watching her.

"Lass, one thin' we now be knowin'! Ye've never planted bulbs in yer life." She pointed at the row Jewel had just finished. "Ye've just inserted that whole line of tulips upside down. Points must be pointin' straight up—not down." Annie laughed, stopping to wipe the tears from her eyes. "Lass, ye don't know how much ye have brightened up this household."

"Well, they fit better with the point down." Jewel chuckled, then pushed the hair from her face, smudging her cheek in the process. Her hair was extremely unmanageable, causing her to brush it often from her face.

Annie showed her the correct way to plant the bulbs; then, for the rest of the late summer afternoon, they worked in the garden. The day grew warm, and Jewel ended up streaking her once-lovely dress in many places as she wiped the dirt from her hands from time to time.

"And a good afternoon, ladies. Is Adam about?" a male voice inquired from behind them.

Both turned to see who had spoken; however, the sun's glare blinded Jewel and she couldn't make out the intruder. Shading her eyes, she stared at the gentleman who had interrupted their tranquility.

"Jonathan!" Annie stood and hugged his neck. "Ye've stayed away much too long."

"It's good to see you, too." He smiled at her. "I had to go back to London unexpectedly and have just returned," he explained. "Adam wasn't in his study. I thought he might be out here."

"Nay, he rode out early this mornin', but we be expectin' him back for dinner. Do stay and eat with him," Annie said.

"Since you've twisted my arm, I'd be delighted." Jonathan turned his attention to Jewel. "Perhaps you should properly introduce us, Annie." He grinned at her with a breathtaking smile. "I presume this has to be the girl from the beach."

" 'Tis Miss Jewel."

Jonathan brought Jewel's hand to his lips and gently placed a kiss there. "It's a pleasure to meet you. I'm glad to see you've recovered nicely, for you look nothing like the frail waif we found that morning. The last time I saw you, you were a very sick young lady. I now see why Adam has been keeping you under close wraps."

"You found me?" Jewel asked, puzzled.

"Well, yes, I mean no . . . I mean yes and no." Jonathan chuckled.

"I'm not sure you've said anything." She laughed good-naturedly.

Jonathan's face had taken on a shade of pink. "It's been a long time since a woman has gotten me tongue-tied," Jonathan confessed. "I was with Adam when we found you on the coastline. I must say, if I had known you looked like this, I'd have taken you home myself."

Warmth spread across her face. She had the feeling Jonathan could be quite a charmer. Perhaps it was the twinkle in his eyes that spoke of a devil-may-care attitude. But before she could respond, Adam rode up on his magnificent black stallion.

Immediately, she sensed his gaze upon her and wondered why he was frowning. Could it be because she had disobeyed him and was outside without his permission? There were times when he treated her like his own personal property.

"Hello, Jonathan, have you been waiting long?" Adam asked.

"No, I've just arrived. I was explaining to Jewel how we had met. I'm surprised you didn't tell her about your best friend." Jonathan chuckled.

Adam dismounted, walked over to Jonathan, and gave him a none-too-gentle slap on the back. "Well, seeing that you are my best friend and a scoundrel to boot, one could understand the slight oversight. Wouldn't you agree?"

"Ah, praise from the king." Jonathan grinned broadly. "What's wrong? Afraid I'd steal her?"

Adam ignored the comment. Instead, he focused his attention on Jewel, and didn't bother to hide the irritation in his voice. "Mademoiselle, I believe I bought you a nice wardrobe. It would seem there is something amiss with that garment."

She looked down and saw the soil marks on her gown, but she really didn't see a problem. The garment could be washed, and surely a little dirt never hurt anyone. She was not a child to be ordered about. She was a woman! Couldn't he see that? And what was wrong with the way she was dressed? Hadn't Annie told her she'd had on breeches when she was found?

"I've been planting flowers," Jewel said. "Do you expect to keep me locked behind Briercliff walls, never to see the sun again?"

She saw his brow raise slightly. A sure sign, she'd learned, that she'd vexed him. He was getting ready to speak, but Jonathan spoke first, saving her from Adam's tongue-lashing.

"I think you look charming. And Adam must agree some fresh air would do you a world of good. However, most ladies don't care for the sun."

Her anger surfaced. "Evidently, I'm not most ladies," she snapped. She'd tried her damnedest to please Adam lately. Well, she was through trying. "Jonathan, I look forward to your company tonight. If you both will excuse me, I need to change into something more *suitable* to His Lordship."

Jonathan covered his mouth to smother his laugh. "I see

you have your hands full, Your Grace, and somehow the thought pleases me."

After she left, Adam looked at his friend, an eyebrow arched in question. "Dinner?"

"Your invitation is a trifle tardy. I believe Annie invited me earlier. You don't mind, do you, ol' boy?"

"Of course not." Adam scowled, a small twitch starting in his jaw.

"I'll be damned." Jonathan grinned. "I never thought I'd see the day. You are jealous, ol' boy!"

Once they were in Adam's study, Jonathan accepted a drink from Adam, who warned him, "Don't get any ideas about Jewel. She's a sweet child."

"Child!" Jonathan nearly choked on his brandy. "Adam, you've been in the country too long. She is a woman if I've ever seen one, from those velvety brown eyes and that creamy skin—" Jonathan stopped in mid-sentence. "But don't worry, I'll try to suppress my charms."

"See that you do," Adam growled, sitting down in his favorite chair and casually propping his feet up on his desk.

"You wouldn't be trying to keep *our* little lady all to yourself, would you?" Jonathan gave Adam one of his lopsided grins.

"Of course not," Adam retorted. Then, in a calmer tone, as if regretting his outburst: "I just don't want to see her hurt. Jewel cannot remember anything about herself except her name."

"You're joking! So you don't know any more than you did the day we found her?"

"Well, I've learned a few things, but not much. She speaks French, and she enjoys rum." Adam gave him a rueful smile. "She's certainly not a debutante from Almacks. As you saw earlier, she thought nothing of being half-clothed. Yet there is a certain naivety about her." He sighed. "I can't figure her out. We found what looks like a treasure map with her first name written on it. But the diagram is only part of a larger map."

Jonathan sat up, intrigued. "What did she have to say about it?"

Adam shrugged. "Nothing."

"Nothing?"

"No, I haven't shown it to her yet. The doctor suggested I wait until she's completely recovered physically." He reached in his desk drawer and pulled out the parchment, then tossed it across the desk. "What do you think?"

Jonathan studied the map. "It's hard to tell with only half a chart, but this looks like the Gulf of Mexico to me. I'd wager your friend—you know, the pirate—could possibly shed some light on this map."

"You mean Lafitte, that scoundrel! If this drawing is worth anything, he'd sell his soul for it. The man lacks scruples, but no better friend could I find. You do have a good point, though. If Jewel doesn't recognize this place, I'll take it with me when I return home."

"Speaking of the United States, I have another message from General Andrew Jackson." Jonathan handed a letter to Adam.

Tearing the envelope, Adam quickly read the note, then frowned. "Things are getting worse at home. I need to do a little investigating in London to see what I can pick up. I also think it's time to send for the *Wind Jammer.*"

"So soon? Are you going to take Jewel with you?"

"No, I think it's better that she stays here," he answered in a low voice. "At least until we find out more about her. Her life could possibly be in danger."

"You're probably right," Jonathan agreed. "If you're ever caught, you'll be hung for treason."

"In my eyes it's not treason." Adam's look hardened. "I think the United States should be allowed to govern themselves. After all, I'm part American."

"I know, and I agree with you. One day perhaps I'll go

and see this country you love." Jonathan realized he probably could be hung for that treasonous statement, but he knew Adam wouldn't be loyal to this new nation without just cause. "By the way, while you're in London, I'll be glad to keep an eye on Jewel." Again he saw the muscle in Adam's jaw start to twitch.

"Thank you." Adam let out a long, controlled breath. "But remember, the lady is mine."

"So, you do care!"

"Let's put it this way. I found her. She belongs to me!" he stated in no uncertain terms.

Jonathan couldn't help laughing. "You talk as if Jewel is a piece of goods to be bought and sold, and the person who had possession was her owner. I think you're in for a rude awakening, ol' chap."

Before Adam could issue a stinging reply, the study door opened and the subject they had been discussing entered the room. Jewel was a vision of femininity. Her simple dress was made of white percale that fitted at the top and gathered with soft pleats at the waist. The bottom of her skirt had a muslin flounce trim. She wore a pink embroidered Spencer jacket with puffed shoulders and long velvet sleeves that fitted over the bodice and accented her tiny waistline, and her hair had been tied back with a soft pink ribbon of lace.

The two men both stood as she walked over to them, but Jonathan moved first, claiming her hand. He placed it in the crook of his arm. "Let me escort you into the dining room. I must say you look lovely tonight, my dear."

"Thank you," Jewel murmured.

Jonathan glanced over his shoulder. "Are you coming, Adam?" Jonathan was well pleased with the black look he received.

Jewel noticed extra candles had been placed on the dining room table. Soft light bathed the room, and in the middle of the table was a beautiful centerpiece of orange and yellow cut flowers. She took her seat across from Jonathan, and Adam sat at the head of the table.

The quail was delicious, but most of all she enjoyed Jonathan's carefree company. He was such an imp, making her laugh often. Even Adam seemed to finally relax as he told her about the mischief he and Jonathan had gotten into when they were younger.

Jewel kept wiping the tears off her cheeks. She didn't know when she had laughed so much.

Seeing her eyes glisten with laughter, Adam once again found himself wondering about the lady. He knew Jonathan was trying his damnedest to be charming, and it irritated him. But despite that, Adam was surprised the evening proved so enjoyable. He now found he'd hate leaving her, but he knew he must.

"Jewel," Adam said, gaining her attention, "I'll be departing for London in a couple of days."

"Why?" Her brow furrowed but her eyes never left his.

"Why?" He couldn't believe she had asked why . . . instead of just accepting his statement. He certainly couldn't tell her the truth, and he wasn't accustomed to explaining *why* he was doing things; however, there she sat, waiting for his answer.

"I've decided to let Jonathan oversee Briercliff when I return to America, so I need to see my lawyer to sign the necessary legal papers. Perhaps if I'm lucky, I also will hear something about you while I'm there. Enough time has elapsed. Someone should be asking questions." Of course there was another reason, the most important of all, but she'd have to accept the excuse he'd just given. "Jonathan has agreed to keep an eye on you while I'm gone so if you need anything, he'll be near."

"I will look forward to your company, Jonathan." Jewel presented him with the most dazzling smile. Then turning to Adam, she said, "Have you decided when you'll be sailing?"

Adam clenched his teeth at the way she smiled at

Jonathan. Why didn't she look at *him* that way? Since that night when she'd blurted out that he was handsome, she'd treated him as an older brother—an aging duke. She could at least look a little sad, he thought. Instead, she seemed happy at the prospect of seeing more of Jonathan. Damn woman! It was a good thing he didn't care a fig for her . . . as it was, she was driving him crazy enough.

"I'll be sailing the first of the year," Adam stated bluntly. His previously good mood having disappeared, he found he didn't want to discuss his leaving any further. "Good night, Jewel." Standing abruptly, he looked at Jonathan. "Shall we have our brandy in the study?"

Well, she might not have a memory, but she certainly knew when she'd been insulted! Jewel raised an eyebrow, having picked up the damn habit from him. She wouldn't give Adam the satisfaction of seeing how his words stung her. Slowly, she placed her napkin on the table, then rose from her chair.

She turned to Jonathan, addressing him deliberately. "You have made dinner very pleasant tonight. I hope to see you again soon." Turning, she walked out of the dining room with her head held high, but before she got completely through the door, she looked over her right shoulder. "Good night, Your Grace."

Adam smiled grimly. He'd noticed the high color that stained her cheekbones and knew he'd made her angry, but at the moment he required some distance from her. He also needed to speak with Jonathan in private, he realized with a weary sigh. Tomorrow, he would make amends. He'd promised to take Jewel riding, and that was just what they would do.

Yes, tomorrow would be *their* day.

Seven

The next morning, seeing the door to Jewel's room ajar, Adam gently pushed it open and leaned against the doorway while he watched with amusement as she jerked the silver-handled brush through her ebony tresses. Her hair crackled and shone, and Adam wondered if she longed to use that brush on him.

He knew she saw him in the mirror, and he wanted to laugh at her rigid back as she attempted to ignore him. It didn't seem to bother her one bit that she was dressed in a rose-colored robe. There didn't seem to be a modest bone in her body, and he wondered about that. Just what kind of upbringing had she had? In every other way she appeared a lady.

Evidently, she was still a little upset over his rude dismissal of her the night before.

"Don't you ever knock?" Jewel snapped, eying him from the mirror.

"Not in my home, I don't," he drawled, a slight smile upon his face.

Her reflection glared at him. "If you're trying to point out that this is your home—I'm well aware of that fact."

From the way he looked, her rudeness hadn't fazed him. His casual manner irritated her. "Still angry about last night?" he asked casually.

"What makes you think I'm upset?"

"Well, for some strange reason your hair seems to be taking a lot of abuse. I wouldn't be surprised if it all fell out, the way you're brushing it." He chuckled.

She slammed the brush down and turned to face him. "Is there something I can do for you?"

His eyes twinkled devilishly. "Sweetheart, there's a lot you could do for me. However, I'm going to do something for you."

"Oh." Jewel looked skeptical. His easy humor caught her off guard.

"How would you like to go for the ride I promised? I thought we could take a picnic lunch."

She jumped up, forgetting her earlier irritation. All she could think about was getting beyond those castle walls and out into the fresh air. "Do you mean it?" Seeing Adam nod, she ran over, threw her arms around his neck, and placed a light kiss on his cheek. "Thank you! I'll be dressed in a moment." In her excitement, she hadn't thought twice about her small display of affection, or the fact that her arms were still wrapped around his neck.

At his sharp intake of breath, she suddenly realized the position she was in. Before she could retreat, his arms went around her waist, and she felt his breath hot against her forehead and his hard muscular body beneath her fingers. She tried to pull away, but his grip tightened.

With only a robe between them, Adam liked the feel of Jewel's firm young body pressed next to his. He reached out and stroked the curve of her throat with his knuckle, thinking perhaps they should have their picnic here in the bedroom. What a delicious thought!

She wasn't good at hiding her emotions, and somehow he knew he'd always be able to look into her liquid brown eyes and see the truth. At the moment, he could see doubt, but there was a passion that burned deep, a yearning he'd seen other women pretend to feel. God help him, he wanted to taste the fire and lose his soul in this woman's charms.

Bending his head, he gently brushed her lips. His voice

sounded raspy as he struggled for control. "Sweetheart, I think you should get dressed . . . unless you can think of something else we could do?"

Remembering that Jewel wasn't one of his paramours, he released her. But the move was so sudden that she stepped back on her gown and lost her balance. Quickly, he reached to steady her. She really was clumsy, he thought, but adorable.

Jewel trembled. She had no idea what to say. Adam's lazy smile made her breath catch, and she felt that she was falling under his spell. And the worst thing was that she couldn't seem to stop herself from feeling this way. Being only a temporary part of his life, she could never be anything more to him. Hadn't he already told her he was leaving and, memory or no memory, she'd be on her own? The feelings she had for him were nothing more than gratitude. After all, he had saved her life, so it was natural to find her rescuer attractive. Wasn't it?

The gleam she saw in his gray eyes scared her because she didn't quite understand it. "I—if I am to ride, I'll need something to wear other than a gown. Should I wear the breeches I had on earlier or did you buy me something?"

"I did." Adam grinned. "It's deep purple. Would you like me to help you find it?"

"N-no," she stammered, pushing him out of the room. "I'll find it myself. I'm sure it's not proper for you to be here, especially when I'm not dressed."

He turned around, catching her hand in his. He lifted her fingers and placed a brief kiss. "I think it's the most proper time."

Jewel's thoughts were on Adam as she finished dressing. He could be so charming, and for one brief moment when he had held her, she had wanted something more. Even though she wasn't sure exactly what she wanted from him. He confused her.

Her spirits were high. Finally, she would see this strange land she found herself in. She looked into the mirror and liked what she saw. The deep purple velvet made her skin look creamy and smooth, and it also brought out tiny flecks of purple in her eyes. The white muslin petticoats hung just below the hem of her skirt, giving it the appearance of lace trim, which also matched the lacy front of her blouse, and a snug-fitting jacket accented her small waist.

Annie pulled Jewel's hair up to one side, pinning a hat of purple and white ostrich feathers there. The ends of the feathers came down and barely touched her high cheekbones. Of course, she didn't need rouge since Adam usually kept her cheeks tinted pink.

Worried she'd taken too long, she flew down the stairs, practically knocking Adam down.

"Slow down, sweetheart. You're going to be the death of one of us yet. Here, let me look at you." Adam stood back, giving his approval. "You look lovely, but then I knew you would when I picked out that color."

She had a moment to look at Adam's attire. His riding jacket was made of the same rich material as hers. Most men wouldn't dare wear purple, but then she was finding out that Adam Trent wasn't like most men. Yet upstairs, she'd really been aware of his manly ways. She felt her body grow warm as she continued to take in Adam's clothing. His white shirt opened at the neck, revealing golden skin. The brocaded waistcoat matched his black riding pants, and his Hessian boots glistened from hours of polishing. Just one look at him spoke of his noble background.

Once outside, they found the horses had been brought around front. Marie gave them a blanket and a basket packed with food. Jewel draped the blanket over her arm and held the wicker basket while Adam placed everything on Star.

Walking over to her mount, she marveled at how tall the animal appeared.

"Jewel, I don't think you've ridden before," Adam informed her.

"What makes you say that?"

"You're on the wrong side of the horse, my dear. You mount from the left."

"Oh," Jewel mumbled, embarrassed at making a fool of herself once again. She moved around to the other side. "Adam, this horse is too high. I think I need a smaller one."

Adam chuckled, and the groom's head snapped up in amazement. Apparently, laughter from Adam was not a common occurrence. The groom smiled to himself, then shook his head.

"I think this afternoon is going to be an interesting experience for both of us." Adam helped her up before mounting himself.

"Don't be afraid or the horse will sense it," he instructed, showing her how to hold the reins properly.

"I'm not afraid," Jewel said confidently.

Adam was pleased at how fast she learned to handle her mount. Her ostrich feathers had slid a little further down her face, but it made her look delightful. Accustomed to being around women who had to have every little hair in place, Adam found Jewel a refreshing change.

The crisp beautiful morning made Jewel appreciate her jacket. Autumn colors flecked the countryside as they rode away from Briercliff. She turned and looked back over her shoulder. The castle appeared to watch over the valley and the sea, a fortress high on the cliffs of Cornwall.

"Briercliff is beautiful," Jewel commented, turning back to him.

They rode along steep cliffs that fell to a sea littered with fang-toothed rocks and shallow reefs. Adam smiled as Jewel peeked over the edge. He explained that the many coves were havens for smugglers. They could hide themselves and their loot in every nook and cranny without fear of discovery.

The unending presence of the sea breathed ceaselessly over their shoulders. One slip and they would tumble to their death. "I sure hope this horse knows what he's doing, because I most certainly don't."

Adam chuckled, but ignored the sharp cliffs as he focused his attention instead on the sway of Jewel's hips and the confident way she sat on her horse. She was afraid—he knew from the way she tightly gripped the reins—yet she refused to give into it. She was proving to be a Pandora's box, filled with exciting facets to her mysterious personality.

"You're doing extremely well handling your mare," he commented.

She smiled at his praise. If he only could see the handful of mane she had gripped in her hand, he might change his mind.

Soon they were through the narrow passageway and she was able to breathe a sigh of relief. They continued on to the small village of St. Ives, which Adam had said was his favorite. It charmed her with its harbors, thatched-covered cottages, and small lanes. Making a right turn, they followed a path to the docks where a fisherman unloaded his catch of the morning.

"Good morning, Your Grace," the bushy-faced fisherman called out to him.

"And a good morning to you, too, Cyril. How did you fare this morning?"

"Not bad, Yer Lordship. Fishing was good today—even netted a conger eel." The proud fisherman's face beamed before he reached into his basket and pulled out the unusual catch.

The slimy snake writhed in the air. Jewel gasped. She dropped her reins, causing the mare to sidestep. Adam reacted quickly, soothing the horse with soft words. He reached over, patted the mare's neck, and retrieved the leather straps.

After a moment he handed them back to Jewel, holding her hand a little longer than necessary.

She hated snakes—that much she could remember—but when she looked again, it wasn't a snake the man held. The warmth of Adam's hand calmed her trembling. Somehow, he seemed to give her strength.

"Sorry, miss, if I startled you," Cyril said, stuffing the creature into a basket.

"T-that's all right. What is that ugly thing?"

"That was a conger eel, and they're not good for anything, but can give a most painful bite. So always be careful should you encounter one."

Jewel smiled down at the fisherman. "I'll remember that, Cyril, and let's pray I never see one of those slimy things again."

His laughter shook the bright red curls on his head. "If you'd stay for dinner, I've caught some mighty big lobsters we can steam, and I do believe that's His Grace's favorite meal."

"Sounds wonderful, Cyril, but we'll have to decline this time," Adam told him. "I'm taking Lady Jewel to the copper mines, and we still have a good ride in front of us. However, you can send a few lobsters to Briercliff . . . perhaps for supper."

"Very good, Yer Lordship. You'll have them tonight."

After bidding good day, they rode up into the country. Jewel was surprised at how well Adam got along with the commoners. He knew all their names and stopped to ask each about their families, and if there was anything he could do for them. She could see how much his people cared for him. Sneaking a glance at Adam, she couldn't help the smile that touched her lips. He presented a hard exterior, but deep down he seemed a good man, one she could easily fall in love with, even though she knew that could never be possible.

Several hours later, they reached the tin and copper mines. Jewel became eager to stretch her legs. She listened to Adam as he instructed her not to leave the horses while he talked to the foreman of the mining operation. "I promise it won't take long," he said.

She felt certain she'd never seen a place such as this. The land was different. Stark sentinels of stone guarded the entrance to the shaft where dirty, sweaty men poured out of the mine for a noontime break. One man in particular seemed to stare at her with a lurid grin upon his face. She shuddered at the way his gaze roamed over her body.

Turning away from him, she spotted an odd-shaped building with steam belching from the chimney.

Adam had told her not to move, but the building wasn't *that* far away. Her curiosity got the better of her. She would come right back, Jewel promised herself as she wandered over.

When she drew closer, she noticed a young man with sandy brown hair standing in the door. He seemed like a harmless lad as he addressed her. "Good day, miss. Might I help you?"

"Hello," Jewel greeted him. "I hate to bother you, but I was curious about His Grace's mines. Just what do you do here?"

"This here's the smelting building." The young man laughed at her puzzled expression and went on. "I see I've need to explain further. First we finely grind the ore that is brought up from the mine. Then it's mixed with a liquid, and the metallic minerals float while the gangue sinks. That way the metals can be melted down, and we're left with a fine copper product."

Jewel nodded. "Are the mines deep?"

"Some are. There's one shaft that goes down several hundred feet 'neath the sea. Ye can actually hear the water rolling overhead."

"Really! It sounds terribly dangerous. What keeps it from caving in?"

"Our shafts are from rock instead 'f dirt like some mines.

We've never had a cave-in," he told her. "Would you care to see, m'lady?"

"No, thank you." Jewel held up her hand. "I'll take your word for it, but I appreciate your taking the time to tell me about your work, and I'm sorry I took you away from your meal."

"Don't mention it." He tipped his hat. " 'Tisn't 'ften we get to see a pretty lady round here." He picked up his sandwich and started to eat.

Jewel decided to pick some purple heather she had seen earlier. It was located near a large boulder, but was in the opposite direction from where she should be. If she hurried, Adam would never know she had wandered off.

Bending down, she snipped the lovely flowers, thinking to make a small bouquet for their picnic. She turned to leave, but the leering man she'd seen earlier loomed directly in front of her, blocking her way.

"Well, well, missy, have ye come down 'ere just to brighten up me day?" He grinned, revealing gapped teeth.

Jewel's breath caught in her throat. She didn't like the way he was ogling her, and he had some nerve obstructing her way. Squaring her shoulders, she decided she'd just walk past him. "I don't know what you mean, sir," she snapped. "Kindly get out of my way." She took a step to move around him.

He reached out so quickly, she couldn't avoid the lecherous fingers that clamped around her arm. He jerked her next to his sweaty body, then dragged her further behind the big boulder. "Ain't it a fact ye came behind this here rock just so I could get a feel of yer tits? I seen the way ye flirted at me earlier."

She struggled as his grubby hands began groping under her jacket, pinching her breast painfully while he fumbled with her buttons. "Please," she pleaded.

"I'll please ye, honey—just give me a moment." He nuzzled her neck, sliding her jacket to the ground.

His sweaty smell made her sick. She beat her fists on his chest, momentarily startling him. He yanked her arm behind her back, causing her to scream out in pain.

"So ye like it rough, do ye?" He slapped her, knocking her head sideways as he tried to keep her quiet. "Scream again and ye'll regret it."

Jewel didn't realize she was screaming until the blow brought back another time—she'd screamed then, too. An evil man in a blue uniform stood talking to his first mate. Her fingers clutched the hilt of her knife, but she must have made a noise because the captain swung around as her weapon came down, catching the fleshy part of his cheek. He grabbed at the ripped flesh, causing blood to ooze between his fingers. Like an injured animal, he roared before capturing her wrist. He threw her across the deck, knocking the breath from her lungs.

Angrily, the captain swiped the blood from his cheek, revealing a jagged slash that ran from his ear to the edge of his mouth. Bending down, he clutched the small weapon before he straightened back to his full height. "Damn you!" he swore as he wrapped his fingers in her long, black hair, yanking her to her knees. "I could have gone easy on you, my dear little miss, but now you'll taste the cat-o'-nine-tails." With the bloody steel blade he savagely hacked off her hair, throwing the remains at her feet.

Someone was shaking her. Her memories quickly faded, replaced with the danger at hand. She glared at the miner, no longer afraid, then spat in his face. He cursed a colorful string of oaths, but loosened his grip as he wiped his face. Quickly, she pulled her knee up, catching him in the groin. Immediately, he released her as he grabbed his crotch.

"Damn bitch, ye'll pay for this," he croaked out.

Seizing the opportunity, she turned and ran from behind the boulder, but stopped short as she slammed hard into Adam's chest.

He looked at her rearranged clothing, and she saw an uncontrollable rage surge through him. Taking her by the shoulders, he held her from him to view the rest of the damage. His gaze stopped on her cheek, where she was sure a purplish mark lingered.

"Did he hurt you?"

A muscle twitched angrily in his cheek as his eyes turned to pitch, reminding Jewel of death. She shivered beneath his fingers. His voice was threaded with anger, and she could sense his barely restrained violence.

"N-no," she whispered in a struggling voice.

"Where is he?"

With trembling fingers, she pointed to the rock, and watched as Adam started around the boulder. The miner was staggering, but looked up when Adam approached him. The miner took a step backward, but stopped while he tried to size Adam up. Evidently he decided that Adam was a fancy bloke, and more than likely wasn't even armed. The miner didn't care for fancy blokes. The smirk on his face said as much when he spoke up. "Come on, Yer Lordship, if you want a piece o' me."

Adam didn't get a chance to reply as the man charged him, hoping to put a head in his gut to knock him down, but Adam easily stepped aside. When the miner came at him a second time, Adam reached out and grabbed him by the throat.

"My lord, I meant no harm. Just having a bit of fun," the miner struggled to choke out as he gasped for air.

Jewel could see Adam was killing the man with his bare hands. She grabbed Adam's sleeve and tugged to get his attention. "Adam, please! I'm fine," she pleaded. "He has learned his lesson. Just let him go." Adam didn't seem to hear her.

But Adam had heard her. Didn't she know she could have been raped or even killed, all for what this man called "a bit of fun"? She was damn lucky he'd heard her scream and arrived in time.

He stared down at the man held in his grip. "No one crosses me and lives to tell about it! You'd best remember that for your future health." Reluctantly, Adam let the man loose. "Get out of here. You no longer work here!"

The foreman ran up and stood beside Jewel before he moved over to Adam. "Your Grace, I'm so sorry this happened."

Still angry, Adam turned, stopping the foreman dead in his tracks. "Michael, if ever I bring this lady with me again and one of your men steps out of line . . . you'll pay for it!" His lethal voice sent chills up Jewel's arms.

Speechless, Michael nodded.

Jewel found she couldn't move. She now had seen another side to Adam . . . the fatal side . . . the side she hoped never to see again. And she'd glimpsed another side of herself, too. She'd stabbed a man, and she really didn't feel any remorse. Just what kind of person was she? Her body started quivering. Something evil lurked in her past, and she felt as if it were waiting to reach out and snatch her back within its grasp. She took a gulp of air, wishing the tidbits of memory would mesh together . . . would tell her something. She needed answers, not more questions.

Adam joined her. He shoved her trembling hands out of the way and fastened her jacket.

"Are you sure you're all right?" Once again his voice was calm.

She nodded, then looked up into his face. Was that really concern she saw in his eyes? She couldn't be sure, but at least she could hope. Tenderly, he brushed the dirt from her cheek, and she wondered what he was thinking.

"Why, Adam?" Jewel asked. He'd almost killed the man with his bare hands. She liked to think he rarely restored to violence. She had to know.

"Because he touched you," Adam said simply. "Isn't that enough?"

Eight

Taking Jewel's arm, Adam escorted her back to the horses, where he helped her mount, then mounted himself. Michael ran over, evidently not wishing to anger His Grace any further. "Good day, Your Grace. I'll have the copper ready by the time you've requested."

"Good." Adam nodded. He tightened the reins and nudged Star into a trot, heading away from the mines. His hands trembled with barely leashed anger, but he looked straight ahead, trying to clear his mind. Despite the fact that the miner had caused trouble before, killing three other miners, the thought of almost taking the man's life turned Adam's stomach. But the worst thing was that he'd lost control of his emotions, and a man who did that could soon find himself dead. Adam's jaw tightened. It wouldn't happen again.

Jewel glanced at Adam from time to time, wondering what was running through his mind. Perhaps it would be better to leave him with his thoughts. She now knew why he was admired—and feared. He wasn't a dandy, and he could most definitely back up any threats he made. She respected him, and hoped his anger would never be directed at her.

After what seemed like an hour, she couldn't bear the silence any longer, so she asked, "Why will you be needing copper?"

"I'll be taking it back to America, for my ships. We line the bottoms with copper to prevent rotting and to make the ships faster.

Unfortunately, the conversation ended there. Jewel could think of no way to get Adam out of his pensive mood, so they became lost in their own thoughts and rode another hour in silence.

The country again changed from the ash-gray rocks of the mines into the golden colors of late fall. Glad to be away from the mines, Jewel rode beside Adam until she grew weary from the constant jostling in her saddle. "Will we stop for lunch soon?" she asked with a hopeful glance.

He indicated a spot up ahead. "See that group of trees? I believe it's the perfect place. We'll stop there."

The once-beautiful blue sky began to darken as thunder clouds edged their way across the horizon. Jewel hoped the rain would hold off until they returned home; she didn't want anything else to spoil their day.

But she couldn't help the groan that escaped her lips when she dismounted. The rough handling at the copper mines had taken its toll.

Jewel spread a blanket out beneath a large English oak tree while Adam retrieved the basket of food that had been prepared for their lunch. He proudly produced two wine-glasses that had been carefully packed in a linen cloth. Soon they feasted on cheese, biscuits, and roasted chicken, topped off with white wine.

While they ate, he eased back against the tree trunk, crossing his booted feet as he kept Jewel entertained with stories of his sea journeys, describing the beautiful ports he'd visited.

She listened eagerly, glad that his earlier angry mood had dissipated. His vivid descriptions of white sandy beaches and crystal blue seas were easy for her to imagine when she closed her eyes. She wondered why everything about the sea held such a strong fascination for her.

Adam stood and pulled her up with him. "Come with me."

Together they walked across the field to a thicket of thorny bushes. She thought it impossible to go farther, until Adam pointed to a well-hidden path behind a little wooden gate.

"Where are we going?"

"I want you to see something." He refused to elaborate as he tugged on her hand.

They walked down a well-trodden path until they came to a clearing and a beautiful spring. Bending down, Adam scooped up a handful of water and drank, then offered her some of the liquid cupped in the palm of his hands. She had to hold his hands to bring them to her lips, but the intimacy of the act surprised her, and she drew away as soon as she'd taken a sip of the sweet, cool water.

"Thank you," Jewel said as she wiped a droplet of water from her chin. Looking over at Adam, she noticed his intense expression. "It's beautiful here, and the water tastes fresh and clean." She grasped at anything to lessen the funny feeling stealing over her. "I can see why you like coming here. How did you find this place?"

"This is the Madron Well." He waved his hand over the water before he stooped to pick up a smooth pebble at the water's edge. "I used to come here when I was small," he said more or less to himself before skipping the rock across the water. "Would you like to hear the legend?"

Jewel nodded, wondering what kind of story could go with what appeared to be an ordinary spring.

Adam moved near her and draped his arm around her. This time she didn't pull away, but laid her head on his shoulder, prepared to listen.

"Many years ago there was a poor crippled lad by the name of John Trelilie. All his life he had been forced to walk upon his hands. In 1650 he had a dream. He was told in the dream to wash himself in the Madron Well. At first he didn't think anything about his vision, but he had this same dream again three times. The third time, it's said, he knew he had to find this well. At that time, it was not an easy task to get here, for the ground was covered by thorns and thistles. John had to crawl. By the time he reached the well, he was cut and torn, so he crawled into the water to wash himself, just as the dream had instructed. When he climbed out, he no longer had to crawl, for he could walk upon his feet."

"What a beautiful story." Tears gathered in Jewel's eyes.

Adam turned her around. "Ever since that day, this has been known as the healing well." Her tears told him she felt things deeply. Perhaps too deeply. She was so delicate-looking that he couldn't help feeling he had to protect her. He liked touching her and holding her. Too much, by far. He wanted to kiss her mouth, but something stopped him. Instead, he placed a kiss on the end of her nose.

"My story wasn't that bad?" he quipped.

She smiled and they walked hand and hand.

Returning to their picnic, Jewel poured Adam the last of the wine, then cleaned up the leftover food and neatly packed everything into the basket.

Adam sat back and leaned against the large, brown tree, watching her as she worked. She couldn't imagine how badly she'd scared him at the mine. Without thinking or talking himself out of it, he reached up and pulled Jewel over to him, letting her back rest against his knee so she would face him as he spoke.

"Jewel, I'm sorry you had to witness that scene at the mine." He paused, surprised at himself for apologizing. He didn't make amends to women, especially ones that had disobeyed him. But somehow this young lady was different. The very thought of her being afraid of him was something he didn't want. He needed to make her understand.

"The next time I tell you to stay somewhere, I mean for you to do just that!" He saw her eyes widen, and he softened his voice before he continued. "You could have been killed." He brushed a stray hair from her neck. When he saw the faint bruise, his jaw tightened. The miner should have died.

"I'll listen the next time," she promised. "I just hate that the whole thing happened."

"Tell me something." Absentmindedly, Adam rubbed his fingers across the back off her neck. "How did you get away from him? He was quite a bit bigger than you."

"I hit him."

"My sweet, you're not that strong."

"I am when it comes to hitting in the right places." She blushed, but he saw the grin she tried to hide.

Adam chuckled. "I'd wager you didn't learn that at finishing school."

"Probably not," she murmured, acutely aware of the gentle stroking of Adam's fingers producing a pleasurable sensation throughout her body. She lifted her eyes to his, only to be captured by the softness that lurked in their depths. Had she ever been kissed before? Had she ever felt these strange longings now surging though her?

His arms tightened around her, pulling her closer while his gaze held her spellbound. She wondered if she should draw back, but much like a child looking into a secret treasure chest, her curiosity pushed her on.

What would it be like? Her anticipation grew. She was getting ready to find out because his lips were drawing near. His breath was but a whisper upon her face. The first tender brush of his warm lips made her heart catch in her throat, and her eyelids closed. She was lost in a dreamy world she never knew existed.

What Adam intended to be a chaste kiss was rapidly crumbling beneath him as he tasted the sweetness she offered him. Her soft, beguiling mouth became the only invitation he needed as he gave in to his longings and deepened his wine-drenched kiss. She responded by wrapping her arms around his neck and pressing her body to his.

God, she felt good! He should release her. He hadn't planned this. What could one small kiss hurt? Clutching Jewel to him, he gently parted her lips with his tongue, ex-

ploring her velvety softness. The once-tender kiss became a
tantalizing excitement that unsettled Adam as he teetered on
the brink of ripping off her clothes and easing the desires
that ran rampant through his body. The very taste of her was
like no other before. He had always been in control . . .
until now.

Shy at first, Jewel became an apt student as Adam's touch
released a burning passion in her. She couldn't hold anything
back, nor did she want to. She was curious if she was doing
this correctly. Had she done this before . . . with someone
else? Surely, she could remember such a jolting sensation.
Trembling, she responded to his kiss, exploring his mouth
the same way he had hers.

The brazen move surprised Adam. He lifted his mouth and
struggled to restrain himself even though his blood pounded
through his veins. Never had he felt such strong desire. He
brushed his fingertips across her warm cheeks, and found
himself memorizing every facet of her delicate features. He
saw passionate eyes burning with desire just before her eyelids fluttered shut, and he claimed her mouth again. The taste
and fragrance of her drove him crazy. She was an angel.

No, Jewel was a devil.

But he didn't care. His lips moved along her neck, and
his self-control slipped another notch as he unlatched the buttons of her jacket with dexterous fingers. He slid his hand
beneath her blouse. Capturing a full, ripe breast, he rubbed
his thumb back and forth across her nipple, and felt it harden
with desire.

A bolt of lighting struck a tree across the meadow with
a loud explosion, jerking Adam back to his senses. A groan
of frustration tore from his lips. He pulled away. "I fear it's
going to rain," he murmured.

"Yes, rain."

Adam smiled at her. She didn't seem aware of the thunder
as it rumbled across the sky, issuing a warning of what was
to come. And he felt rather pleased with himself, but he

knew they would have to leave—even if he didn't want to. He looked past Jewel's wild eyes, noticing her puffy lips. Could she be as innocent as she seemed?

Struggling to control his ragged breathing, he whispered, "As much as I hate to, we need to be going. My sweet, you must be a goddess—a goddess from the sea sent to tempt me. And sweetheart, you have, so beware."

He watched as she lowered her eyes shyly and began buttoning her blouse. At least she didn't act as if this was something she'd done before, and that eased his mind. But he had no desire for her to feel guilty, and he was pretty sure that was how she felt. He could read it in her eyes.

He brushed her hands aside and helped with the last button. Placing a finger under her chin, he tilted it up so he could see her eyes before he spoke. "This was my fault, Jewel. I'll try to control myself in the future."

The breeze had turned to a gusty wind laced with moisture as they rode hard towards Briercliff, trying to escape the threatening downpour but to no avail. The rain finally caught up with them. By the time they reached the castle their clothes were soaked through.

Annie met them in the foyer with towels, attempting to dry their bodies the best she could. "I'm not sure this riding habit will ever be the same."

Glancing over at Jewel, Adam let out a howl of laughter. The ostrich feathers had somehow become plastered to her face, and the cute little hat hung by a single pin. She looked like a drowned rat. Perhaps an adorable rat, but drowned just the same.

With her hands resting on her hips, she cut him a sideways glance. "What's so damn amusing? I'm tired, sore, and soaked to the bone. And you think it's funny!"

"Didn't they teach you in finishing school that ladies don't swear?" Adam chuckled as he noticed the glare in her eyes.

Jonathan walked out of Adam's study and into the foyer. "You'd better watch out, ol' boy. They say a woman is worse than a tiger when she has her hands on her hips."

Humor made Adam's eyes water as he bowed graciously. "My pardon, madam," Adam said, "but you do appear like a drowned rat, and the ostrich feathers were simply my undoing."

Jewel reached for her apparently forgotten hat, then turned to look at her image in the hall mirror. Seeing the sight, she laughed, too, and she jerked the limp thing from her head. "Your pardon is accepted, sir, but before cackling about my appearance you should be taking a look at yourself."

This time Jonathan was the one guffawing. "The lady gives as good as she gets. Yes, sir, nothing like a spirited woman. I do believe she got the better of you on that one, ol' boy."

"Oh, be quiet," Adam growled.

While Adam relaxed in a tub of steamy water, Jonathan sat on a nearby stool. "I take it you two are getting along better," he said.

Adam knew he referred to Jewel. He smiled, remembering their afternoon. "I guess you could say so."

Jonathan folded his arms across his chest, and seemed to be studying him for a moment before he asked, "Is there something you'd like to tell me, ol' boy? Especially since I detect a gleam in your eyes. Just what did you do today?"

Adam took his time lathering himself with soap before answering his friend. "Oh, nothing much. We went to the mines and I ordered copper for my ships. With the English blockade of the colonies, materials are hard to come by."

"And that was it?"

Adam grimaced, remembering the scene with the miner. He wasn't going to answer Jonathan's questions like a bloody schoolboy, so he changed the subject. "I'm surprised to see you this soon."

"I received a juicy tidbit from London that I think you just might be interested in. It seems there's a party tomorrow night at the Earl of Ludlow's town house. My source seems to think you can pick up some interesting information there."

"I see." Adam rubbed his chin. "The last message from Hawk indicated an important meeting would be taking place soon. Perhaps this is the one." Adam paused for a moment, knowing what he must do. "Looks as if I will be leaving at dawn."

Adam and Jonathan waited in the dining room. When the door opened, Adam's breath caught in his throat at the lovely vision of femininity entering the room. Jewel's shoulders were not creamy white, but a golden hue, and his gaze lingered there much too long as he noted the way the neckline of her dress caressed her shoulders. The stunning gown had numerous silver and metallic threads woven into the elaborate fabric. As she turned around, the light caught each thread, giving her the appearance of being wrapped in diamonds. She wore her hair pulled back, where she had fastened it with silver netting.

The shimmering material enhanced the sparkle in Jewel's eyes, and tonight they were almost as black as Adam knew his own to be. At this moment, he wasn't sure he wanted Jewel to remember her past. But he was quick to remind himself that he'd be leaving soon and she would be out of his life. He must remember that.

Jewel had to take a second look at the two gentlemen in her life. They were dressed just alike in black breeches and white linen shirts that opened halfway down their chests. She noticed the frown on Adam's face, and wondered what had caused the creases in his brow.

"Please excuse our casual attire, my sweet," Adam said,

sweeping his hand toward the table. "We've decided to do a bit of fencing after dinner. We didn't think you'd mind our lack of etiquette tonight."

She moved around the table to her place. "No, of course not, providing you let me watch."

Jonathan held a chair out for her. "We'll welcome an audience, but who will you cheer to victory, milady?"

Jewel gave him a wicked smile. "There are some secrets one should never tell."

Their banter was interrupted as the servants entered the room with silver trays. The delicious lobster Cyril had sent was served with melted butter. They also had fresh fish and small potatoes. Jonathan's manner made him easy to talk to, and he seemed like a good friend already, even though she had only known him a short time. She told him about their day, leaving out the episode at the mine and, of course, the picnic.

After dinner, Jewel went to freshen up, leaving the men to their brandy. Upon returning, she found them gone, but the clanging sound of metal caught her attention. She followed the noise down a long hallway toward the back of the house. She'd not ventured into this part of the house before. She passed many rooms until she reached a set of double glass doors.

Cautiously, she opened the doors and looked into what she assumed had to be the grand ballroom. The room was enormous. Three crystal chandeliers hung high above the floor, and the walls were not walls at all, but a series of windows and mirrors, making the room seem wide and spacious.

Slipping into the ballroom unnoticed, she watched in fascination as Adam and Jonathan parried back and forth. Adam's agility was amazing. His swift speed reminded her of a bird of prey toying with his victim.

Something told Jewel she'd seen this done before. She was sure of it. She glimpsed a flash of another match, but instead of Jonathan and Adam, a man and woman fenced and laughed as they played their game. As quickly as the vision came, it vanished, leaving Jewel to wonder if *she'd* been the lady she'd envisioned.

The scraping of steel blades brought her attention back to the two men. It was plain to see that Adam was the far superior swordsman and was only toying with Jonathan. But how would she know that? Where had her knowledge of fencing come from?

"Jewel, I didn't realize you'd come in," Adam said, only slightly winded as he spoke.

"You're very good," Jewel complimented him.

"Thank you." He nodded. "Perchance you know something about fencing?"

Was he mocking her? She wasn't sure, but the next words out of her mouth seemed to surprise them both. "Yes, I believe I do. Would you care to fence with me?"

Laughter burst forth from Adam and echoed in the empty ballroom. It did nothing but make Jewel determined to show him she was as capable as she had boasted. She only hoped she was the woman in her vision—she might be mistaken. But she'd like to take the duke's arrogance down a notch.

Getting his laughter under control, Adam managed, "Are you absolutely daft, my sweet? I do *not* fence with women. Hell, you probably can't even hold a sword, much less swing one."

"Wait a minute, Adam," Jonathan came to the lady's defense. "I think she's serious. Would you care to fence with me?"

"Thank you, Jonathan." She smiled her gratitude at his vote of confidence. "Let me change into some trousers. I'll be right back." She turned to leave. "At least you're not a pompous ass," she declared over her shoulder.

She heard the faint echo of Adam's swearing in the ballroom as she raced up the stairs.

"You permit her to wear trousers, ol' boy?" Jonathan asked, continuing his teasing once Jewel was gone.

"Most certainly not," Adam snapped, then began to pace the floor. "She can't possibly know how to fence. And she could get hurt!" He ran his hands through his hair, giving his friend a puzzled look. "Did you say trousers? I told her to burn them."

"Cool your feathers, ol' friend." Jonathan enjoyed the way a wisp of a girl could get Adam perturbed. "I'm not out for blood. The swords will be tipped, and she can wear your mask. She'll probably tire very soon, and that will be the end of it." Jonathan moved over to a nearby table and took a sip of cool water. "What can it hurt?"

Returning to the ballroom, Jewel announced, "I'm ready." Jonathan poked Adam in the side, "No pants, eh?"

Adam noticed her breeches immediately. His gaze couldn't help being drawn to the tight fit. Damn it, hadn't he told her to get rid of those things? Didn't she know how enticing she was in breeches, especially ones that seemed to hang on her every curve? "I thought I told you to throw that garment away."

"I believe you did." Jewel slipped on Adam's mask, and in so doing utterly ignored his statement, but not before she glanced at him from beneath her lashes and found him scowling.

She met Jonathan in the center of the room. They crossed swords, and she felt the palms of her hand begin to sweat. Could she do this? Or would she make a complete fool of herself?

"En garde." Jonathan saluted.

She touched his sword in salute, and suddenly she relaxed. This felt natural—a real part of her. They started to move, and Jewel found herself swift and agile, not showing any of her usual clumsiness.

Jonathan calmly parried her thrusts, but he realized fast that she was a skillful swordsman not to be taken lightly.

He could tell she watched him intently, judging each of his movements before he made them. He lunged at her, but she stepped aside with amazing speed.

In an unexpected move, she sent his sword flying across the room in one quick movement that took him completely by surprise. He stumbled and fell backwards.

She pointed the tip of the sword to his heart and gave a throaty laugh. "Surrender or die!"

Jonathan felt a little stupid lying on the floor, especially since a woman had put him there. Adam would never let him live this down. "I'll surrender to you any day, milady, for you already have my heart." He clapped his hand over his chest, and they both burst into laughter like two over-grown boys.

"By George! You're good," Jonathan complimented her.

"I think I've done this before," Jewel quipped in a playful mood. In fact, she had surprised herself. She wondered where in the world she'd learned to handle a sword with such ease. She was sure that fencing wasn't considered lady-like. So far nothing she'd done was especially lady-like.

Adam had been watching in utter disbelief. Jewel was good, damn good. Here was still another twist to the sea goddess he'd pulled from the sea. So feminine, so petite, yet she could fence better than most men. When would he find the key to unlock her mysterious past?

"I believe you've indeed done this before. I'd say you've had a bloody good teacher," he snapped, his temper barely simmering. "Would you care to tell us who?"

A tear hovered in the corner of her eye. Adam's words stung, for he knew she couldn't remember anything. And what she did remember wasn't very pleasant. He'd been so different this afternoon. Why did his personality seem to change so quickly? Well, she was tired of keeping track of his moods.

She straightened her back as she removed the mask and dropped it on the floor. The teardrop slipped quietly down her cheek. Damn him! She was glad he was going to London! She definitely wouldn't miss him one bit!

She longed to tell him so, but at the moment, she couldn't find her voice. Before she embarrassed herself further, she turned and ran from the room.

Adam watched her hasty retreat, feeling like a complete jackass. Why hadn't he just complimented her on her fencing instead of tearing into her? He couldn't explain his actions, nor anything else he'd done since she'd come into his life. He didn't want to hear Jonathan's criticism either.

Adam's steady gaze lingered on his friend. "Good night, Jon. I'll be leaving at daybreak." Abruptly, he walked to the door. "I'd appreciate your looking in on Jewel."

Jonathan stood in the empty ballroom, shaking his head.

Jewel changed into her nightgown the minute she got to her room. She hated him! He was mean!

Blowing out the light, she lay in the darkness, crying into her pillow. She truly had no one here, and loneliness threatened to smother her. She swallowed and took a deep breath. Hearing the door open, she figured Annie was coming in to check on her. But Jewel didn't want to see anyone, so she didn't look her way.

The bed sagged. "Jewel?" Adam whispered.

She stiffened, but refused to turn. "Go away."

His hand touched her shoulder. She wiped the tears away with the palm of her hand and sat up. "What do you want—to make fun of me again?"

She heard Adam sigh. Then he reached out and pulled her into his arms before she could protest. Unable to hold back any longer, she sobbed like a child.

"I'm sorry, my sweet," he said. "I don't know what comes over me, especially where you're concerned. You truly are an excellent swordsman, but God knows, where you learned fencing is beyond me." He rocked her back and forth, holding her tightly within his arms.

She finally stopped crying, and sniffed. "Do you really think so?" she murmured into his shirt.

"Indeed I do."

"I wish I could remember who I am."

"I know you do." After a lengthy pause, he said, "Jewel, I'll be leaving at daybreak."

She leaned back and looked at him. The moonlight coming in through the windows provided only a darkened image of his face. "I thought we had another day," she said. She'd forgotten she didn't want to see him anymore.

"My plans have changed." He didn't bother to elaborate. "I want you to look at something while I'm gone."

"What?"

Letting go of her, he reached over and lit the wick of an oil lamp. "When we found you"—he reached inside his coat and pulled out a folded piece of paper—"this map fell from your clothing. I've been waiting until you were well before I gave it back to you. Here, look at it."

She took the tattered map and carefully unfolded the parchment. It appeared very old. The minute she looked at it she realized it was only half a diagram, but still she recognized nothing.

Adam turned the map over so she could read the inscription. He tensed, waiting for her to say something. "Do you recognize this diagram?"

"No . . . not exactly. It's a map, but I don't remember where or why I'd have it." She sighed. "This is so frustrating."

"Take some time, sweetheart. I'll leave the diagram with you. Maybe other things will come back." Adam paused a moment, then said, "Jewel."

"Yes."

"Do you remember this Jean?"

"Jean," she repeated aloud, uttering the syllable slowly in

French. "The name is familiar and I have a good feeling inside when I say it. I don't remember exactly who he is, but . . ." Her voice grew quiet. "I do remember he's someone I love."

A coldness settled around Adam's heart. She couldn't possibly love this man. Noticing how lost she appeared, he pulled her back into his arms, clutching her tightly. Was she in love with another man?

"Please stay with me tonight," she whispered. "I don't want to be alone."

Adam groaned inwardly. Did she know what she asked of him?

But he knew tonight he'd behave. He would be content just to hold her, for she was just a lost soul, and he knew how cruel the world could be. Adam found he didn't want to be alone either.

Turning the wick down, he laid her head on his chest. He ran his fingers through her hair until he heard her soft, even breathing. How small and fragile she felt in his arms. He ached to kiss her and make her forget about the other man. And make him forget that he knew nothing of the lovely woman he held in his arms. But he settled on her trust. Deep down he felt she'd trusted him with her life and she wasn't wrong . . . he'd kill any man that tried to hurt her.

Nine

The overcast October sky made the morning dampness seem just that much cooler as Adam rode away from Briercliff.

He inhaled deeply, filling his lungs with cool, crisp air as he tried to shake the cobwebs from his brain. Sleep had eluded him last night as he'd held Jewel in his arms. So many confusing thoughts raged a war in his head, and still he lacked answers for the myriad emotions the lady evoked in him. He felt an attraction to her—perhaps that was an understatement. It was more like lust. Hadn't he already proven that at the picnic?

But love her—no. He didn't believe in love. The few couples he knew that professed love when they married soon found others to occupy their time. No, it was lust, plain and simple. Damn, he needed a woman! He'd been too long without one. He would have to take care of that problem in London.

Three hours into his journey, Adam's sleepless night began to take its toll. His mood blackened, his shoulders ached, and still, thoughts of Jewel nagged at him.

He paused for some tea at the next tavern. Hurriedly he swallowed the brown brew, and burned his tongue in his haste. "Bloody hell," he swore, causing the man sitting next to him to jump when Adam stood to leave. He tossed a few coins on the table and stalked from the tavern. His mood had little improved.

Frigid air slapped his face the moment he opened the tavern door. The wind whipped his greatcoat around his legs as he tramped to his horse; at least the tea had helped take the chill away.

The misty morning had cleared, leaving in its wake a biting wind. Adam jerked the collar up on his coat, trying to get extra warmth. He would not stop again until he reached London.

And he would not think about the lady he'd left behind. No, that was something he would not do.

At four in the afternoon, Adam arrived at his town house. Giles had been sent ahead the day before, for which Adam was grateful. All he could think of was a hot bath and bed. His feet felt like lead as he climbed the stone steps of Trent House. The four-story town house held an elegant charm, and right now looked damn inviting.

"Good evening, sir," Giles greeted him at the front door, taking his coat.

"Giles, I'm going to bed. Be sure to wake me in two hours. I'll be attending a party tonight. Have Byron prepare my clothes," Adam said gruffly.

"So you're going to Ludlow's affair tonight." A feminine voice called from the parlor. "I thought maybe we could go together."

Adam glared at the butler. Didn't he know better than to let Colette in the door?

Giles shrugged his shoulders helplessly, then mumbled under his breath, "Sorry, my Lord, but the lady was insistent."

Adam knew that fact all too well—impossible was more like it. "What are you doing here, Colette?" he asked.

"Now, Adam, is that any way to greet me after all this time?" She sauntered over and draped her arms around his neck, greeting him with a kiss and choosing to ignore his coolness. "I've missed you."

Adam groaned silently as she pressed her body into his.

Feeling himself tighten, he removed Colette's arms from around his neck and waited until she backed up a step. She hadn't changed a bit. Her tempting lips beckoned him, and for a brief second he thought about bedding her and ridding himself of this damn yearning. But staring down at her, he thought only of getting Colette out of his house.

"I repeat, what are you doing here?" He tried to keep a leash on his temper.

"My, aren't we in a pleasant mood," she commented, running a finger down his chin.

"I'm tired, Colette." He sighed while flexing his neck with his hand. "I just want to go to bed."

She closed the distance between them again and ran her fingers up the back of his neck. "That does sound like fun, darling," Colette murmured, suggestively rubbing her breasts across his chest.

Adam felt himself harden as she smiled up at him, and he could see the victory in her eyes. Adam grabbed her by the arms. When she thought he would kiss her, he instead began shoving her towards the door.

"Good-bye, Colette," he snapped.

"But Adam!" She tried to resist his efforts to push her to the door. "I thought we could go to the party together. I've already broken my other engagements because of you."

Adam didn't feel like having this conversation. He was too bloody tired. He looked at her. Maybe she could prove useful. Sighing, he gave in. "I'll pick you up at eight."

Smiling candidly like the mouse who'd gotten the cheese, Colette stood on tiptoe and kissed him again. However, this time it was a long, drawn-out kiss, and just for a brief second he was responding, but again he pulled away with a firm movement. "See you tonight, darling." She smiled and sauntered out of the house.

Adam slammed the door and headed for his inviting bed. This time he slept like the dead. All too soon Giles shook him rudely awake. Adam still felt tired, but at least his head was clear of cobwebs, he thought as he slid his arms into a stylish royal blue coat that his valet held for him. He checked the watch tucked in his fob pocket. It was time.

He wished he hadn't promised to take Colette to the dance, but he had, so now he'd have to live with the decision. He reminded himself that his plan to gather information would work out better if he arrived with someone.

Adam picked Colette up precisely at eight, and for once she was ready on time. She was dressed in a pale green gown with pink ribbons threaded through her hair, and she wore long white gloves. There was no question, she was a stunning woman.

Adam was silent as they rode to the earl's house. Colette snuggled next to him, trying to engage him in conversation, which only irritated him. What had seemed vivaciousness before was now merely annoying chatter.

They arrived with several other couples, and the Earl of Ludlow and his wife greeted them at the door. Once inside the main ballroom, Adam scanned the crowd. His gazed fixed on a group of men gathered by the rear doors. They were precisely the gentlemen he needed to talk with, but first he'd have to rid himself of Colette. He glanced down in annoyance, hoping it would prove to be an easy task.

"Let's dance, Adam, it's been such a long time," she purred as clutched his arm.

He nodded once, then led Colette to the dance floor, where he purposely engaged her in light conversation, trying to avoid the subject of their relationship. But it didn't work.

"Adam, dear, when are you ever going to admit that you love me?" she whined.

Adam gritted his teeth. He found he hadn't missed her one bit.

"You know I'd make a good wife, and I possibly would consent to have at least one child."

"But Colette, you're mistaken," Adam said in a rather bored tone. "I simply don't love you."

"That's a lie!" She stiffened in his arms. "I refuse to believe you don't love me. Haven't you been my constant companion this past year? That is, until you escaped to that dreadful Briercliff. What you see in that isolated location is beyond me," she said, exasperated. "After all we've shared, you simply must feel something for me," she persisted. "Besides, I come from a good family, and you'll need someone to carry on your name."

Adam didn't like these stupid games, and especially tonight he hadn't the stomach for them. "Colette, if I were you I'd let the subject drop."

"It's that other woman!" she spat, and Adam tightened his hand around her waist. She smiled sweetly up at him since she'd gotten a response.

"What woman, Colette?"

"The one you found on the beach," she said smugly.

"How did you hear about that?" he snapped out, staring at her from beneath hooded eyelids. "I asked you a question," he repeated, his patience wearing thin.

"I saw Jonathan at the club about a month ago. I wanted to know when you were coming to London. He said not to expect you anytime soon. Seems you'd found some chit on the beach, and you were taking care of her. Adam, how could you bring some commoner into your house!"

The music ended. Adam firmly and none too gently took Colette by the arm, and escorted her over to a corner where they couldn't be overheard.

"Adam, please, you're hurting my arm!"

"What I do in my home, madam, is none of your affair!" Adam snapped. He spun her around to face him, blocking her from probing eyes. "How many people have you told about my house guest?"

"Only a few." Colette pouted. "Adam, you know I don't gossip, but people have been waiting for us to announce our engagement. I had to say something. So I told them you had rescued a young woman and you felt responsible for her until she was well enough to leave."

She put her arm through his. "Bringing me here tonight was so sweet, darling," she added.

"Don't change the subject. I escorted you here tonight as a friend, and I will see you safely home. But I've never had any intention of marrying you." With his lips grim in vexation, Adam ran his hand through his hair. "I told you before, Colette, it's over. Accept it. And I'd rather you not contribute gossip about Jewel."

"Jewel?"

"The girl I found on the beach is young, and I'm trying to find out something about her," Adam explained because he didn't want Colette doing anything vicious—which she was quite capable of. "She's helpless. Do you understand?"

"I see," Colette replied. Automatically, she assumed Jewel must be a mere child since Adam had pointed out her youth. Smiling, Colette chided herself for being so silly as to be jealous of a youngster. Maybe she could help Adam. That way it would get the girl out of his life faster.

"You know, Adam, you might try talking to Captain Lee. He asked me what I knew about the girl at a gathering a fortnight ago."

"Why did he want to know?" Adam asked.

"I'm not sure." Colette snapped open her fan and began waving it in front of her face. "He seemed interested, as if he knew something."

"Is he here tonight?"

"No. At least, I don't think so." Colette stared at him above her fan, trying to judge what he was thinking, but as usual his eyes were dark and unreadable. "Adam, please, will you be sweet and get me some refreshments? I'm simply perished after that dance."

"I'll get a glass of punch, but after that you're on your own. I have some gentlemen I need to speak with."

"Oh, Adam, you're not going to leave me all by myself?" She pursed her lips in a well-practiced pout.

"I'm afraid so," Adam stated. "I'm sure you'll find another gentleman to help occupy your time." After getting Colette her punch, Adam excused himself to cut his way through the crowd to the other side of the room.

Colette watched him go. Her eyes narrowed. There simply must be a way to get him back.

The small group was already deep in a political discussion when Adam joined them. Looking around at the distinguished gentlemen, he spotted the United States ambassadors to Great Britain: Pinkney, King, and Monroe. They were three honest men trying to find a way to settle the disputes between America and Great Britain. Adam wanted to laugh because they definitely had their hands full.

The British Navy was famous for press-gangs, which Americans hated. Many a man had been hit on the head and found himself on a British ship when he awoke. Adam himself had lost some of his crew that way. The brutal discipline, the rotten food, and backbreaking work were sometimes hard to survive. And a troublemaker could taste the cat-o'-nine-tails. If that didn't work, there was hanging.

Adam knew the ambassadors had been struggling in London to appease both sides. Great Britain had much more important matters on her mind, and didn't believe that her former colonies could be forced into a fight, since they had nothing to fight with. Arrogant bastards, Adam thought.

"Tell me, Monroe, do you think you'll have your treaty ready for the meeting next week at Whitehall?" Ludlow asked. He was a stout fellow in his early fifties, and considered to be a moderate.

"We've worked hard, my lord, to bring peace between our countries," Monroe stated firmly. "However, whether the

United States will sign a treaty without mention of impressment will be doubtful."

Captain Percy shook his head. "Why the colonists think they can grant citizenship to any rabble is beyond my understanding. One can no more change one's nationality than he can the color of his skin."

Pinkney spoke up for the Americans. "That may be true, but as you know, the United States is a nation made up of all nationalities in the first place, so it can sympathize with people wishing freedom from the countries from which they hail."

Ambassador Pinkney turned toward Adam. "Your Grace, it has been a while since we've seen you. Come join our conversation and be of assistance. You've been to the United States. Is it as bad as these gentlemen seem to think?" He swept his hand toward the group.

Oh, how he'd love to tell them what he really thought, but he'd have to choose his words carefully if he were to gather any information. These men believed him to be true to England and her cause. Adam thought a moment before he spoke. "The United States is made up of hardworking people, I agree. But on the other hand, they should not be ungrateful to their mother country." Adam looked at the earl. "After all, England has helped them through some difficult times."

"Hear! Hear!" the British gentlemen cheered.

Pinkney's face reddened. "Well, of course we're grateful, but we don't like the blockade of our ports, and we're quite willing to do something about it."

"Really?" Adam said, playing his part the best he could. "Do you have anything to fight with?"

"We have a small navy," Monroe answered, "and it's growing. It has already challenged the British blockade on the Eastern Coast."

Adam saw his expression change when Monroe realized he'd sounded boastful. He hurried to add, "Gentlemen, let me point out the others and I are here to end the war between our countries."

Adam watched as the assembly of men nodded their heads in agreement.

The three Americans, evidently feeling they had overstayed their welcome, bid an early good night.

After their departure, the rest of the group moved out to the terrace so they could smoke and enjoy the fresh night air.

Adam cupped his hand and lit a cheroot. Assuming a bored expression, he asked, "Tell me, Captain Percy, how do you think the war is *really* going for our country?" He knew Captain Percy was one of England's top commanders, and could provide him with valuable information.

"England has a navy superior by far to those young upstarts," Percy boasted. "Still, we have discovered the Americans are quite a stubborn lot! Pigheaded I believe is the word." He chuckled. "We've been working on a plan that just may give us the power we need to tame them."

"Such as?" Adam drawled.

"I'm really not at liberty to discuss such matters," Percy said bluntly.

Ludlow cleared his throat. "Captain Percy, do you not realize you are speaking to a duke?"

Percy flushed with embarrassment. "I beg your pardon, Your Grace, but surely you can understand such military secrecy."

Adam nodded, politely accepting Percy's apology, though he really felt like choking the man. "One never knows *who* the enemy could be," Adam admitted, wondering how he was he going to get the details. He didn't have long to ponder the question because Ludlow spoke next.

"You might like to know, Captain, that His Grace has lived in New Orleans for several years and knows quite a bit about the territory."

A spark of interest appeared in Percy's eyes at that tidbit.

"Certainly, that is good news. We could put to use such valuable knowledge, but I think you'll admit a party is not the proper place to discuss these matters."

"I quite agree, Captain. Perhaps I could meet you at a later date." Adam wondered why that particular territory was important. So far, New Orleans had escaped the war on the East Coast, but now it sounded as though his American home might be drawn into the battle.

"Two days from now we're having a meeting at my town house,"Percy said. "We would be most grateful if you would attend."

"I'll look forward to, perhaps, being of some service to you and my country," Adam said. Of course, he didn't say which country.

"Gentlemen, gentlemen." Ludlow held up his hand. "Enough business for tonight." He glanced at Adam. "Tell me about the young woman you've found. I've only heard bits and pieces, and we all know how things can be exaggerated." His eyebrows shot up as he asked, "Did you really find her half-dead and washed up on the beach?"

The hairs on the back of Adam's neck stood on end. He now found himself the center of attention, the one thing he didn't need. Evidently, Colette had done a good job of spreading the rumor. Now that the subject had been brought up, perhaps someone here might know Jewel's identity.

Adam cleared his throat. "As chance would have, I did find a young woman near death. I think she must have been washed overboard the night of the terrible storm. It really was a miracle she survived at all."

"Who is she?" asked the earl.

"That, gentlemen, I wish I could say. She seems to have developed a temporary loss of memory."

"Do you suppose she was a bonded slave?"

"No!" Adam said, a bit louder than he had intended. "Or at least, I don't think so. Her first name is Jewel—that much we do know. So far she has been unable to tell me much about herself. Have you gentlemen heard of anyone that could be missing? She's petite with black hair and brown eyes."

Captain Percy spoke first. "I did hear Captain Lee comment when he heard that you'd found someone. It seems he lost a girl overboard on his ship. Perhaps you can speak with him. It could be a lead."

"Yes, Captain, it does seem so. Where can I find this Lee?"

"He's sailing on a small mission for me, but will be in port the end of November or the beginning of December."

Adam nodded. "Good, I shall see him then." The conversation drifted on to lesser matters. Adam didn't know Captain Lee personally, but had met him on a couple of other occasions. He'd seen him enough to quickly form an opinion. He thought Lee to be a sneaky bastard. Yet Adam would put his feelings aside just in case Lee did know something about Jewel.

Colette walked over to the group. "Adam, darling, it's time for dinner, and I know you must be starving after your long journey from Cornwall."

Adam frowned at the interruption. But he realized he had accompanied Colette tonight, and he probably couldn't gather any more information, so he held out his arm and escorted her into the dining room. The rest of the evening was spent listening to her chatter.

What a shallow woman thinking only of herself, Adam thought as he sat back and listened to her endless talk of parties and teas. Again, he wondered why he had ever been attracted to her.

Later that night Adam sat in his library, staring into the fire. The cool night brought a chill to the room. He grabbed another log and threw it in the hearth. Sparks rose, then spiraled up the chimney. He warmed his hands a few moments before returning to his chair, where he picked up a lead-crystal glass. He took a swallow of brandy, feeling the warmth spread its magic. The tension in his shoulders began to ease as he watched the fire's hypnotizing vibrant red and orange colors. A black-haired beauty danced among the flames, her face soft and radiant. Liquid brown eyes spoke of their trust, and soft lips beckoned him. "Damn," Adam swore. He swallowed the fiery liquid in one gulp, immediately regretting his action as tears sprang to his eyes.

He rose to pour another stiff drink, berating himself for acting like a young pup in heat. It had only been this morning when he'd seen Jewel, and here he sat daydreaming of her. This time he took a slower sip of brandy before turning back to the fire. He'd be damned if he would let the girl get under his skin.

Yes, he wanted her, and the quickening in his loins told him just how much—but he'd overcome it. After all, he was thirty-five, not a young chap of eighteen who couldn't control his emotions or his life. Come January, he would leave, and he wouldn't see Jewel again.

So it was best he forget her now!

Forcing his thoughts to business matters, he let his mind wonder over the tidbits of information he'd heard. He most certainly was pleased with what he had learned tonight. He looked forward to his meeting with Percy; however, the information about Captain Lee was a different matter. Could Jewel have been on his ship? And worse, could Jean be a seaman aboard Lee's ship?

Adam stood, picked up his glass, and moved over to his desk. A shifty-eyed devil, Lee was not someone Adam would turn his back on. Opening the desk drawer, Adam retrieved a sheet of white paper and laid it in front of him, then reached for his quill and dipped it in the India ink. He scribbled a note asking Lee to meet him upon Lee's return. He powdered the ink before folding the slip of paper and sliding it into an envelope. Holding his seal, he dripped wax on the letter and placed his royal mark on the envelope.

This encounter could prove to be very interesting.

Ten

When Adam arrived at Captain Percy's, he found a group of men sitting around a massive table. An unfolded map was the center of everyone's attention.

"Gentlemen." Adam nodded his greeting before moving over to take his seat.

Captain Percy waited a moment, then continued on with the meeting, pointing to the chart. "I believe you will all recognize this as a diagram of New Orleans and the Gulf of Mexico. We have decided that it would be most beneficial for England to take control of New Orleans. Thereby, we would gain access to the Mississippi River."

Adam shook his head. "The land is treacherous territory, and will be rough sailing. If you are not aware, New Orleans is surrounded by bayous, small streams, and swamps. Men have entered there never to be seen again. The area is a maze that few can navigate," he pointed out. "How do you hope to overcome this?" Adam hoped to discourage Percy, though what he said was true. Only fools would venture into those swamps.

"Precisely what I thought when I first heard this plan," Captain Percy said, nodding in agreement with Adam. "As you know, there is a cluster of islands about sixty miles off the coast of Louisiana that are controlled by a group of outlaws. We have heard they would sell their own mother if the price was right."

"So you plan to offer them money?"

"That's correct, Your Grace. A good sum of money, too. I'll send Captain Lockyer and Lieutenant Williams to make Lafitte an offer."

"And what will that offer be, Captain? That is, if you are at liberty to say," Adam asked.

"By all means, Your Grace. After all, we are all loyal British subjects. My men will offer Lafitte forty thousand dollars, land, and a British citizenship."

Adam rubbed his chin. "Your plan sounds good, Captain. I've never known a pirate yet who could refuse money." He managed a brief smile. He had his doubts about the money, but Jean Lafitte would laugh outright at the offer of British citizenship. Lafitte wasn't an ordinary smuggler. He was a gentleman's pirate with his own set of morals. Adam really didn't think his friend would take the offer, but Adam wouldn't take the chance. "When will you carry out this scheme, Captain?"

"Our plans are not complete. There are still some arrangements to be made. We're training new troops, and of course that will take time. I hope to send two ships, *The Brig* and *Sophie,* to Barataria in about eleven months. At the moment, we are planning for a departure date of September 3, 1814."

Good, Adam thought. He would have time to sail home and warn General Jackson. He also wanted to talk to Lafitte. It had been a long time since Adam had seen his friend. And they needed to talk.

The rest of the meeting proceeded smoothly. Percy shook Adam's hand warmly as he left the house and stepped out into a foggy London night. Adam signaled for his carriage to go on ahead. Shoving his hands in his pockets, he preferred to walk along the Thames and do some thinking.

Mentally, he ticked off a list of supplies he'd need for his ship and then composed a letter to Jackson. As he climbed the steps of his town house, the excitement of returning home surged through him. Gripping the brass doorknob, he opened the great mahogany door, and the scent of a house seldom

occupied rushed out to meet him. It would be grand to see
Four Oaks and his sister again, but he had to admit there
were a few things here he'd miss—such as Annie, Jonathan,
and . . . Jewel. He could shut his eyes and almost feel Jewel
within in his arms and smell the scent of . . . of her hair.
What was he going to do with his little sea treasure?

Jewel ran her hand over the indentation in the pillow where
Adam's head had lain. Closing her eyes, she caught his scent
on the covers, and secretly wished he would be next to her
when she looked again. It didn't work. The bed was as empty
as before.

She was still alone.

Adam had been so tender the night before. Of course, before that he'd been cold and unfeeling. He seemed to keep
her on the brink of insanity. She was truly perplexed by what
the man thought of her. At times, it seemed nothing more
than pity, and she didn't want his pity. She wanted him to
see her as a woman, and a small part of her wanted him to
care. She would miss Adam while he was gone. Tears started
to form, and threatened to spill over her bottom lids. Slowly,
she wiped them away. Crying wouldn't help; she must learn
to stand on her own two feet. Adam would be sailing for
America before long, and then she would be without him
forever.

And still the question of what she'd do haunted her. She
couldn't stay at Briercliff forever. She must have had some
kind of life before she arrived here. But from the glimpses
she'd remembered so far, she wasn't too sure she wanted any
part of the other life.

"Good mornin', lass. 'Tis a mite chilly this mornin'." Annie appeared bright and cheerful, as she did every morning.
"Good Lord, the fire is cold. I'll be stirrin' it up before ye
catch yer death of cold." While Annie added kindling to the
fire, a maid brought in some hot cocoa and warm rum buns.

"Mmm, the chocolate sure helps this morning," Jewel said as she held the cup between her hands to warm them. "I'm a bit colder than I thought."

"Don't be mentionin' it, lass. Adam said tae be takin' special care of ye."

Jewel glanced up with widened eyes. "He did?"

"Of course he did." Annie opened the curtains, then walked over to Jewel's side, lowering her voice so no one could hear. "I think he likes ye, lass, more than even he'd like tae admit." Annie had a knowing look as she winked at Jewel.

"Did he say so?"

"Nay, didn't have tae. I raised the lad, and can see it in his eyes." Annie smiled. "I've seen the way his gaze follows you round the room. And I've been seein' Adam round other women before, but never have I seen him look at them the way he looks at ye."

"You're imagining things. He's just being kind." Jewel knew what Annie said wasn't true, but she had managed to brighten her spirits anyway.

"We'll just be seein', lass, if ol' Annie ain't right. Now, what would ye like to do today?"

"I'd like to stay busy, and since Adam isn't here to fuss and order me about, I'd like to do some cooking."

"There no be a need. We've a cook."

"I know," Jewel admitted, "but for some strange reason, I've a desire to work, and it's something I feel familiar with."

Jewel helped Annie around the house, or as much as Annie would let her. But eventually Jewel grew bored, and decided to spend the afternoon in the kitchen. At first, Marie was reluctant to let anyone in her kitchen, but when Jewel expressed a desire to learn how to make rum buns from the very best cook, the ice melted from around Marie's heart.

Jewel found she knew quite a bit about cooking, and she ended up teaching Marie a few new tricks with spices and seasonings.

When Jewel told the cook her desire to make rum buns one morning for Adam, she could see she had risen another notch in Marie's estimation.

Jewel moved from one task to another, giving herself little time to sit and ponder her future—she also didn't have time to think of Adam. Sometimes at night it was all she could do to climb the stairs and fall into bed. Keeping up this hectic pace, she found the time went by quickly, and before long a month had passed. And still no word from him.

In the three months she'd been at Briercliff, her hair had grown, and now hung just below her shoulders. Jewel gazed at her reflection in the mirror while she ran a silver brush through her tresses. She'd gained weight, she noticed, touching her cheeks with her fingers. But something was still missing, and she couldn't quite figure out what. Hearing a knock at the door, Jewel turned.

"Jonathan has come tae take ye ridin', lass," Annie announced. "He's waitin' downstairs."

Jewel quickly dressed in a black and white riding habit. Jonathan had promised to spend the day with her. She found herself looking forward to seeing him again because she'd missed the way he made her laugh, and she hoped he might have some news of Adam. Just maybe Jonathan could tell her a little more about the duke.

Glancing out the window, she could see the low, gray clouds indicating another damp and cold day. Didn't the sun ever shine in this godforsaken country? But even the weather wouldn't dampen her spirits today. She truly enjoyed the cool, crisp mornings, even though she felt the chill more than everyone else. Annie had suggested Jewel might have come from a warm climate and wasn't used to the cold like the people in Cornwall.

Jonathan choked on his tea when she entered the drawing room. And it took him a minute to recover.

Jewel's cheeks flushed with embarrassment. He stared as if he'd never seen her before. "Is anything wrong?" she asked. "Perhaps I'm not dressed correctly, but you said we could go riding." She glanced down at her outfit.

He chuckled. "No, my dear, nothing is wrong. I was just admiring your beauty, and it simply took my breath away."

"You've the tongue of a silver fox, Jonathan Hird. I'll have to be most careful," she bantered back. "But thank you for the compliment."

"Here, I've brought you something I think you might want." Jonathan handed her a sealed note.

Recognizing the seal of the duke of St. Ives's, she carefully broke the wax open, holding her breath. Adam had written to her! How often she had wondered if he ever thought of her.

Dear Jewel,

Business has taken longer than I expected. I hope to be home the week of Christmas. We are invited to Jonathan's for a Christmas Eve party.

I hope things are well for you—and Jewel, I do miss you.

Adam

Looking up at Jonathan, she smiled. "Adam said you're having a Christmas party and I'm invited."

"That's correct. And I'm sure you will be the belle of the ball."

"Will there be many people there?" Jewel asked excitedly.

"I do say, London turns out for one of my gatherings," Jonathan boasted.

"I haven't been around strangers. I'm a little frightened," she admitted. "Won't they ask questions? Wonder who I am?"

"Oh, they'll wonder." Jonathan chuckled. "Don't worry, my dear, Adam and I will both be by your side at all times.

The only thing you have to worry about is the gown you're going to wear."

"A dress! I don't have a party gown, Jonathan. What will I wear?"

"I'm sure Annie will find something. Now, let's go for that ride." He took Jewel by the elbow. "Worrying about a dress is such a silly waste of time."

Rays of sunlight broke through low clouds gilding the ocean's surface with golden light as the waves rolled to shore and flung themselves onto the dark sand. Salty air tickled her nose, enticing Jewel to breathe deeply.

She had hoped to stir some memories, but nothing here looked familiar or brought back anything. Would she ever learn her true identity?

Jonathan climbed up on a large gray rock, pulling her up beside him.

"How long have you known Adam?" Jewel blurted out.

Jonathan grinned. "We grew up together."

"Then you knew his parents," Jewel pressed on, not looking at Jonathan as she spoke. "Did they ever allow Adam to have fun?" She heard Jonathan chuckle, and she blushed at her boldness. "It's just that he seems so intense all the time."

"I suppose he does. But you have to know Adam's childhood."

"Will you tell me about it?"

Jonathan propped his elbow up on his knee, his gaze directed to the sea. "I can't see that it'll hurt anything. Let me see, where do I start?" He rubbed his chin as he thought. "Adam's mother died when he was but nine. He found her on this very beach." Jonathan paused, then turned and looked at her. "Much like he found you. After that, Adam was no longer a carefree child of nine. He grew serious and learned to hide his emotions from everyone. I think that experience changed him completely. I suppose you'd say he's success-fully built a wall around himself that few can penetrate."

"What about his father?" Jewel asked, feeling sad for the child Jonathan had just described.

"I think Adam's father loved him, but the man had a hard time showing it. Instead he constantly groomed his son for the duties he expected him to assume one day. Unfortunately, that all happened sooner than expected." Jonathan looked at her abruptly. "Tragedy struck again when Adam was fifteen. His father was killed in a hunting accident."

Jewel held her breath, spellbound at the tale, her heart again going out to the young boy not yet a man. No wonder Adam seemed so distant and remote. Jonathan continued speaking, his tone conveying his own compassion.

"Adam, with the help of his grandfather, took over Brier-cliff. At eighteen, he grew restless and left the estate in his grandfather's hands. He eventually built a shipping business and made his home in America, but he had to come back to England when his grandfather died." Jonathan smiled. "I think you know the rest."

"Thank you," Jewel murmured as she stared out across the sea, thinking of what she had learned. It sounded as if Adam had lived a very lonely life as a child. She could picture him as a boy with dark hair cut in a bob, trying to please the man he looked up to. And somehow she had the feeling Adam's father had never complimented him. Instead, it was probably constant complaints. No wonder he'd grown into a hard man with a shell as thick as armor. An ache in her chest was a small reminder that Adam was becoming a part of her life. She couldn't imagine never seeing him again.

The roar of the waves and the rhythmic pounding of the surf seemed to hypnotize her into a peaceful contentment. To think she had come from somewhere out there. She was sure she had lived around the water before, because of the tranquil feeling it gave her. Perhaps she had come from someplace on the map Adam had given her. Tonight she

would study the drawing with the hope of recognizing something. Anything. She clenched her fists against the warm
rock. She had to find out where she belonged.

Jonathan watched her with an odd expression on his face.
She pulled her knees up and rested her chin on them, wrap-
ping her arms around her legs much like a child. Suddenly,
Jonathan voiced his thoughts. "Jewel, how old are you?"

"Eighteen, and I'll be nineteen on July first," Jewel answered spontaneously, then stared at Jonathan round-eyed,
seeing her own surprise mirrored in his eyes. "I remember!"
She gasped and reached for Jonathan's arm. "Can you believe
it?"

"Yes, I can." He smiled back at her, clasping her hand.
"We told you your memory would return. It just seems you
never know when a chunk will fall into place."

"I know, and I don't understand why." She frowned. "I'm
healthy now. I should remember everything."

"You will, my dear." He squeezed her hand. "But let's not
spoil today. I want to show you where I live. I've something
special I want you to see. I think you'll like my surprise."

"What is it?" Jewel asked excitedly as Jonathan helped
her off the rock.

"You'll just have to wait. Come, I'll race you to the
horses."

When they arrived at Foxmore, Jewel wondered about the
name and said, "Jonathan, how did you come by the name
of your estate?"

Amusement flickered in his gaze. "I'm an avid foxhunter
and I raise hounds. Therefore, the name came from fox,
which is my passion when in the country, and because I love
to do *more*. I put the two names together. Fox—more."

Jewel giggled at his explanation of the name. What a carefree rake he was. There wasn't a serious bone in his body.
From the size of his house, Jewel could tell he wasn't a

pauper by any means. Foxmore was not as large as Adam's home, but impressive nonetheless.

They had a light lunch of pork pie and warm gingerbread, and Jewel felt content. "Tell me, Jonathan, why have you never married?"

He grinned. "Because I could never find anyone I thought very interesting. That is, until you came along."

"Be serious!" She laughed at his flirtation.

"I am, my dear. If you ever get tired of Adam, you're welcome at my home anytime." A dimple appeared in his cheek; then his gaze grew serious. "Have you thought about what you'll do when Adam returns to America?"

She shook her head as a dejected look crept into her eyes. "No, I haven't. I just pray my memory is restored by then. I pray that I've a home somewhere. It's frightening not belonging."

Her unhappy expression twisted Jonathan's heart. He wanted to take her in his arms and offer her comfort. However, she belonged to Adam. So he decided to distract her mind with something else.

"Come, let me show you my humble abode." Jonathan guided her on a tour of his home before going to the stables.

Magnificent horses lined the stalls on both sides of the barn. Jonathan pointed out one horse that was sired by Adam's horse, Star, and sure enough the colt had the same star on his forehead. Jewel could shut her eyes and picture Adam on his prancing stallion, frowning at her with that peculiar stare of his.

They moved on to the kennels located in the back part of the stables. Jewel spied little white and black beagles darting about in play. They moved past the dogs to an empty stall.

"This is what I wanted you to see." Jonathan grinned.

Peeking into the stall, Jewel saw a mother dog with very long ears and her offspring. In all, there were five puppies wobbling on shaky legs around their mother. "They're adorable! Can I hold one?"

"Sure, I don't think Daisy will mind. Their eyes just opened a couple of weeks ago, and they're learning to walk. As you can see, they're not too good at it yet."

Moving over to Daisy, who had large soulful eyes, Jewel bent down and patted her head.

Jewel plopped down on the straw. That was the only invitation the puppies needed. Soon they began crawling on and off her lap. "What kind of puppies did you say they are?"

"Basset hounds. They hail from France and are well known for their ability to hunt small game. They have well-developed noses, and their ears actually help them to smell better. I hear their keen sense of smell is second only to a bloodhound."

Jewel held up one of the puppies. She could tell he was scared from the way his front paws wrapped around her fingers, hanging on for dear life. There were times when she felt just like the puppies. "That's okay, fellow. I won't hurt you," she cooed, trying to soothe the puppy. "He's so pretty, and has the longest ears. Look, Jonathan, most of their ears drag on the ground!" She laughed. "Do you use these dogs for hunting?"

"Yes, but not if I'm in a hurry. Believe me, bassets are not known for their speed." He chuckled. "Mostly, Daisy is just a pet." Jonathan rubbed her head. The dog rolled over onto her side and closed her eyes. The rest of the afternoon Jewel and Jonathan spent playing with the puppies and chuckling over their clumsiness.

When it came time to go home, they walked leisurely to their horses. Jewel stopped, then turned to Jonathan. Reaching up on tiptoe, she placed a kiss on his cheek. "Thank you for a most wonderful afternoon." She thought of Jonathan as a friend, or perhaps a big brother, and she truly enjoyed his company. Linking her arm through his, she said, "I hope we'll always be friends."

"You can count on it, madam. I'll always be near should

you need me," he replied casually. *Friends?* He would like to be more than that. If Adam let this woman slip through his fingers, Jonathan hoped they would become more than just acquaintances. But for now just friends was fine.

That evening back at Briercliff, Jewel surprised Jonathan with some dishes she'd prepared for dinner. For dessert, they had an outstanding strawberry cake that melted in his mouth.

"This is wonderful! Surely, I've died and gone to heaven. I can't believe it," Jonathan said, lavishing on the praise.

"Believe what?"

"Beauty and a great cook all rolled up in one little vixen." He winked at her. "I can't believe you can cook."

"Sir, you think to turn my head with your flattery," she bantered back.

After dinner she persuaded Jonathan to fence with her. She found her skills were even greater than she had first thought. But the time finally came for Jonathan to return to his home.

Jewel bid Jonathan good-bye, then elicited a promise he would soon return. Sighing, she climbed the stairs, and as usual her thoughts returned to Adam. When was he coming home? Jewel wanted to see him. She enjoyed Jonathan's company, but it wasn't the same. There was something about Adam that made her stomach flutter, and just the touch of his hand produced such comfort . . . and something more. But she couldn't put her finger on what that *something* was. Time seemed to drag by when she was alone.

She withdrew the map from the bedside drawer, and spread it out on the bed in front of her. With no identifying markings on the land, it was hard to tell the location, but it definitely appeared to be a small island. Several caverns were scattered about, and one cave lay at the end of a narrow gully. She traced the gully with her finger, feeling the parchment beneath her fingertips. Tiring, she lay back on the pillows, trying to remember. Not bothering to turn out the oil lamp, she gradually shut her eyes and soon drifted asleep.

Dreams of soft, fluffy clouds surrounded Jewel. Slowly they parted as a vision of rubies, emeralds, gold, and diamonds floated before her.

Holding a diamond up to the light, she watched fascinated by the patterns it made on the wall. "Look, Jean, I've made a rainbow." The small girl giggled.

A man looked over at her with love showing in his eyes. "Cherie, with the wealth we have here you can buy all the rainbows your heart desires. But petite, you must remember; this is our secret treasure, and no one must know about it but you and me."

"What are you going to do, Uncle Jean?"

"We're going to make a blood pact, you and I, just like pirates do. Would you like that?"

"Yes, Jean." She nodded her head, making her black curls dance upon her shoulders. "But how?"

"You'll have to be a brave girl," he cautioned her.

"I will." Jewel's eyes sparkled with excitement and admiration for the man who sat across from her.

He pulled out his knife; the blade glistened in the faint light. It was so big. Jewel's eyes grew wide as he lowered the blade and made a small clean cut on his index finger.

Jean looked up and saw a stern expression on his features. "Give me your hand, Jewel." She thrust her small palm out, determined to be brave. She trusted her uncle. He'd never hurt her. Her bottom lip quivered as he made the same identical cut on her finger.

"I'm very proud of you, petite. You're my little pirate." Holding both their hands side by side, he said, "Do you, Jewel, promise to keep secret what we've done here today and to tell no one of our treasure?"

"Yes, Uncle Jean."

*"Good." He pressed their fingers together and mixed their
blood. Then they each left fingerprints on opposite corners
of the chart.*

*Jean tore the map in half, handing one part to Jewel.
"Keep it safe, petite. And if something should ever happen
to me, remember you have wealth beyond your wildest
dreams."*

*The small child threw her arms around him. "I love you,
Uncle Jean. I'll always love you."*

Jewel gasped and sat straight up in bed. She wiped the
tears from her wet cheeks. Looking down at the map, she
searched the left-hand corner for a small brown stain. Then
she knew—she was the child in her dream.

This Jean was her uncle, but she still had no memory of
his face, and she still had no last name. But if she could
remember where she came from, Jewel knew she'd have
someplace safe to return to.

She had lived with pirates. Did that mean she was a bad
person? What would Adam say? She chewed her bottom lip.

No, she decided, she wouldn't tell him anything, not until
she had her full memory back.

The rest of the night she tossed and turned in a fitful
sleep.

And in London another person was having the same
trouble sleeping because a black-haired beauty plagued
Adam's dreams.

Eleven

Barataria Bay, just off the coast of Louisiana

Jean Lafitte knew he was handsome and a smooth talker with a keen sense for business, which made him wealthier than most men and gave him control of all Barataria. He liked to claim he was merely a privateer, not a pirate.

But at the moment, business wasn't on his mind. He paced the floor, his boot heels thumping against the worn floorboards, while his brother, Pierre, sat with his boots propped on the desk, watching Jean walk off some of his frustration.

Pierre finally sighed. *"Mon dieu,* wearing a hole in the floor will do us no good, nor will it solve our problem."

Jean grabbed a bottle of rum and slumped into a hardbacked chair. He proceeded to pour a stiff drink into one of two lead-crystal glasses before speaking. "Amazing, is it not? Months have slipped by and still no word. I feel damn useless just sitting here waiting."

Without warning, the thick oak door opened and a deckhand poked his head inside. From the lad's heavy breathing, it was apparent he'd been running, and it took some moments for him to catch his breath. "Beggin' your pardon, Cap'n, but the topsails have been spotted on the *Lin Fa*. She'll be at the dock in 'bout fifteen minutes."

"Obliged." Jean nodded. "We'll be there."

After the door shut, Jean refilled Pierre's glass with a generous shot of rum. "I pray to God Jewel's on board. You know I never wanted her on a damn ship . . . it's much too dangerous!" Jean squinted one eye accusingly at Pierre.

Pierre threw his hands helplessly. "I know, Jean. I know. You've now told me at least a thousand times!" Pierre raised his voice to match his brother's. "Hell, I'm worried, too. You know as well as I do she was raised around pirates. The sea is in her blood."

"Privateers," Jean corrected him.

Pierre paused and lifted his glass. *"Oui,* I understand how you feel—I love her, too. You can blame me if you have to blame someone, but think about it; we always came home with the most wonderful stories when we'd been at sea. Of course, we left out all the bad parts, so to Jewel they sounded like an adventure."

"I'm sorry, Pierre." Jean's voice broke slightly as he re-filled his own glass. He took a swig, then stared at the glass, thinking back to the raven-haired child who had solemnly joined with him in a bloodpact.

Jean ran a hand through his hair and blinked his suddenly moist eyes several times. "I guess I've been taking every-thing out on you, Pierre. It's just that I promised our sister before she died that I'd bring her daughter up as a lady."

"We did, Jean." Pierre leaned back in the chair with folded hands behind his head. "After we caught that English mer-chant ship, that is. It was full of schoolbooks and one very proper schoolteacher, Mr. Wilson Lovall."

"Oui, I remember." Jean's face creased into a smile. "Can I not see him now with his feathers all ruffled, telling us he would teach no one?"

"He soon changed his mind! That is, with a little friendly persuasion." Pierre laughed, slapping the side of his leg.

"Then he met Jewel and was hopelessly lost. She can charm anyone." Jean thought again about the eight-year-old pixie that had stolen his heart. She had always been full of life and eager to learn, mastering French and Spanish by the age of eleven. She'd even picked up a touch of a British accent from her tutor. Now that she had grown up, he'd had to remind some of his crew that she was not to be bothered. The few times they'd had visitors at Barataria, he'd been careful to keep her hidden away from prying eyes. If he wanted her introduced into society—and he did—it was better no one knew of her background. She'd never be accepted into the proper circles if it was discovered she'd lived with a band of cutthroats.

Jean had to admit she had real beauty, with her long black hair hanging in ringlets down to her waist, and those soulful, deep brown eyes.

Pierre broke into Jean's contemplations. "I should not have taught her to sail, but she begged so often." He waved his hands helplessly in the air. "And she was damn good! Why, she could maneuver the boat in and out of the bay as well as any of our sailors."

"If you think that was bad"—Jean leaned forward, propping his elbows on his knees—"I taught her to fence. She told me she might need to defend herself one day, and if she knew how, then I'd have someone to practice with. Can you believe that? As if I didn't get practice enough already."

Surprise registered in Pierre's face as he lowered his chair. "You taught her to fence?"

"And there were a few times she damn near got the best of me."

Pierre put down his glass and stared moodily out the window. "I miss her, too. This house just isn't the same." He slid his chair from the table. "Let's go down to the dock and see if she's come home."

Jean stood up. "Come on. Maybe we can have one of her famous dinners tonight."

The *Lin Fa,* the ship Jean had sent in search of Jewel, glided out of the morning sun and sailed smoothly into Barataria Bay, her sails down, her masts naked. Once again the frigate had navigated the narrow straits between Grand Terre and Grand Isle, the two islands that protected Lafitte's haven and home. Some sixty miles from New Orleans, it was the perfect haven for *his* band of smugglers and pirates. And Jean was damned proud.

His warehouses overflowed with merchandise worth a king's ransom—not to mention his astounding control over his gang of cutthroats, which made them respect his leadership. And he knew they would give their lives for him.

A small dingy had been launched from the *Lin Fa,* and now rowed slowly to shore. But, to his shock and dismay, not a dark head bobbed among the passengers.

All too soon, the boat pulled alongside the pier and the blood drained out of Jean's face.

Jewel's bodyguard, Ben, lay slumped over in a heap—unconscious. His head was wrapped with bloody bandages. Jewel had called Ben her gentle giant, but he reminded Jean more of a big husky bear. At seven feet, Ben towered above every man on the island, and when he was angry, one swipe of his meaty arms was enough to lay any man low. Seeing him now, in this condition, meant something terrible had happened aboard Jewel's ship, the *Morning Star.*

The men struggled as they lifted and laid the 350-pound man down as gently as they could. His chalk-white color reminded Jean of death. He glanced at the men. "Where did you find him?"

A sailor known as Drake shuffled his feet. Jean grew irritable at his silence. "Well, mate, have you lost your blasted tongue?"

"We found him floatin' on a box. Near dead he was." Drake bobbed his head as he talked swiftly, bouncing from one foot to the other.

"And Jewel?"

"Nobody, Jean, 'xcept Ben. Nary a trace of the *Mornin' Star.*"

Drake took a step back, twisting his cap in his hands.

"He's been unconscious most of the time, Cap'n, but he did come to when we brought him aboard." Drake stopped abruptly and drew in a deep breath. Only then did Jean realize that the sailor saw the fury that twisted in his gut and was evidently reflected in his eyes.

He grabbed the bloke by the front of his shirt. "Damn it, Drake! Spit it out—what did he say?"

"T-take it easy, Cap'n. H-he said they'd been tricked by the bloody English. Said the bastards burned everything. That's all I know, Jean—honest."

"Jean, let him down!" Pierre shouted as he walked up the pier and laid a hand on his brother's shoulder.

"Sorry, mate." Jean sighed. "I just need to know what happened." Slowly, he let go of the material clutched in his hands and returned the sailor to his feet. He turned to where Ben lay and, seeing the severity of his wounds, shouted, "Take him to the main house and fetch Doc."

Jean stood by the railing of his veranda and peered through a glass at the calm ocean, which undulated with a high tide. He scanned the horizon, leaning against a whitewashed column, one of sixteen that surrounded his home. With a sigh, he lowered the spyglass. No ship approached. He turned and went back into his beautiful Southern-style home, which was located in the center of the island.

He moved into the large airy bedroom through doors that opened out onto the veranda. Ben lay in the bed surrounded by pillows and looking very much out of place amid the fine furnishings. His usually tanned face was drained of color. He'd protected Jewel since she had turned thirteen. Seeing him now, Jean wondered if this meant the worst.

"How are you feeling?" he asked as he pulled a chair up beside the bed but remained standing.

Ben opened his eyes, looking sheepish in his weakened

state. "I'm sorry, Boss. I've let you down, and I wouldn't blame you none if you slit my throat."

Jean patted his arm. "Start from the beginning, and tell me what happened." Jean sat, grateful that Ben seemed better. Weak from loss of blood, Ben had been severely dehydrated, his skin pale, his breathing shallow, and for a time Jean had thought they would lose him. Several weeks had passed before Ben had been well enough to speak, but now he'd finally come around.

"It was a trick." Ben paused long enough to prop the pillows behind him. "The British ship sat heavy in the water with little firepower for protection. It looked to be an easy mark; however, when we got closer, secret panels in the ship swung open and the hidden eighteen-pounders soon left us helpless. When they pulled beside us, we were prepared to fight, but the belly of that ship was filled with soldiers." Ben paused to sip some water; then with much irony in his tone he continued. "We were no match for them."

"Why were you there?"

"I tried to talk her out of it, Jean. But she was determined after receiving your note."

Jean frowned. "What note?"

"I never read it, but she thought something had happened to you—and she mentioned something about a treasure."

Jean said nothing for a moment. This was the second time he'd heard the word "treasure." "Did they take any prisoners?"

"Aye, one."

"Who?"

"Jewel."

Jean's throat tightened. "Why?" he whispered.

Ben shook his head. "I don't rightly know, but the captain of the British ship seemed to know her. I heard him say that now he'd get his gold. I thought he meant our ship, but he gave orders to burn the *Morning Star.*" Ben took another sip of water. "Of course, they thought I was dead, but I fooled them, sliding overboard just before she blew."

"Did anyone else escape?"

"No, Cap'n."

Jean rubbed his chin as he thought. "You said the Englishman mentioned treasure. Were you carrying any on the ship?"

Ben shook his head. "No, Jean, none."

Damn. Jean's face paled. He tensed. Someone knew about the treasure. But how? "If the captain knew about Jewel, someone from within our ranks has betrayed us. Do you remember the English bloke's name?"

Again Ben shook his head. "Maybe it will come back to me later." He slumped back on his pillows, dejected. "I'm sorry, Cap'n."

"The fault is not yours, my friend." Jean reached over and squeezed Ben's shoulder. "When you're on your feet again, you can help us find her."

"Aye," Ben agreed. "I'll always remember the bastard's face. Mean he was. He'll pay when I get my hands on him."

"*Oui*, Ben." Jean stood, then nodded slowly. "The bastard will pay dearly! That I promise you."

Twelve

"His Grace has excellent taste." The jeweler smiled and leaned forward over the mahogany and glass counter. "Yes, excellent. Would you care to see the fine choker?"

Adam nodded, then glanced down at the necklace of fire opals and diamonds snuggled in a nest of blue velvet. Each opal, set in rich gold, picked up the fire from the other stones. It was magnificent indeed, Adam thought as he imagined the rare stones against Jewel's throat, pulsing with her heartbeat.

"This choker, Yer Lordship, has perfectly matched opals and diamonds." The jeweler dangled the piece from well-manicured hands. "The sparkle would make yer lady's neck appear to be on fire. I've more expensive rubies and diamonds, but by far, this piece is the finest."

"How much?"

"Five thousand pounds." The jeweler beamed.

Adam raised an eyebrow. He'd only come into the shop to pick up his repaired timepiece. "Harry, I've known you a long time. I believe you can do better, my friend."

Harry laughed. "For you, Yer Grace, I'll gladly sell this one-of-a-kind gift for a mere"—he rubbed his chin—"four thousand. I do say, you will set yer lady's heart aflutter with such an expensive gift."

Adam smiled. "I'm sure the lady will love the necklace. She has twice the fire as these opals." He placed the velvet box in his coat pocket. "Merry Christmas, Harry."

"And Merry Christmas to you."

* * *

Back in his town house, Adam buckled his bag, wondering what had possessed him to spend so much. It had to be that the holiday season had seeped into his bones. He laid two silver-wrapped boxes upon his satchel, making sure he wouldn't forget them when he returned to Briercliff. They contained Jewel's ball gown for Jonathan's party and a silver fox cape that had also cost him an ungodly sum. Good thing she wasn't a permanent part of his life, or he'd go broke.

"Is everything ready, sir?" Giles said as he entered the bedroom.

"I believe so. I'm sending you ahead with the trunks and if at all possible, I'll leave for Briercliff tomorrow."

Adam led a procession of servants downstairs, and after the bags were placed in the coach, he glanced up at the sky. "I don't like the looks of those clouds. The weather has grown colder since yesterday. Perhaps we'll have snow for Christmas." He couldn't remember when last he had looked so forward to a holiday.

"I hope it doesn't snow before we get home, sir," Giles grumbled as he climbed inside the satin-lined coach. "Snow has a way of making the roads impassable."

"Don't be a cantankerous old goat, Giles." Adam shut the coach's door. "I'll see you at Briercliff." The team of four leaped forward with a flick of the reins, and the coach bearing the Trent crest careened around a street corner and out of sight.

Pulling up the collar of his greatcoat, Adam walked to the docks. When he reached the river, he stopped and looked around before moving to the wharf. The Thames was busy today, he thought as he watched the sailors working on the docks, unloading the ships. A barrel rolled down a plank, and Adam turned in that direction. A weathered-looking waterman caught the cask and rolled it over to the deep underground caverns where London stored casks of wine, and also Adam's favorite—brandy.

Watermen of all shapes and sizes labored together, but one man in particular caught Adam's attention. Dressed in a threadbare dark jacket and trousers, the man leaned against a post, rolling a cigar. A scarf was looped warmly around his neck and a battered old cap perched on his head. Just as he put the cigar in his mouth, Adam offered him a light.

"Thanks, gov'nor," the man said without looking up.

"Can you tell me where I might find Captain Lee's ship?" Adam asked.

"Aye, I can tell you, mate. But why you'd want to know is beyond me." He looked up at Adam, taking in the cut of his clothes. His expression changed. "Begging your pardon, Yer Lordship. I can take you there if you'd like."

Adam laughed. "I've the same opinion of the captain. Unfortunately, I do have business to discuss with him. What's your name, mate?"

"Norman, sir," he said, his color slightly heightened. "You won't go telling him that I put a mark on his character now, will you?"

"Mum's the word."

"I heard tell he flogged a woman for some minor offense. No telling what he'd do to a man." Norman looked at him, one eyebrow slightly higher than the other as he added, "He's a mean one."

Adam's stance immediately grew rigid as he remembered the ugly welts along Jewel's back. He fought to maintain an expressionless face. "That's interesting. What did she do?"

"Don't rightly know. You know how rumors get started. Heard it was his doxy—some said it was a pirate, and another said it was a child." Norman shrugged. "No matter. Don't trust him none."

"I appreciate the information and the warning, Norman. It's been a pleasure to meet you." Adam extended his hand and waited for the shocked sailor to take it. "I would be most humbly grateful if you would lead the way to Lee's ship."

Adam followed the limping man down the wharf. He could feel his blood pounding in his ears at the tidbit of information he'd just heard. It could just be a coincidence, so he'd put it away for now.

They passed several ships before they came upon Captain Lee's. "Obliged," Adam said, handing Norman a gold coin. "Buy yourself a new hat for winter."

"Thank you, Yer Lordship, and good day to you, sir." Norman smiled as he walked away. "Hell, I can buy a whole wardrobe with what the fancy bloke has given me," he said to himself. "Yep, looks like it's going to be a good Christmas after all."

Captain Lee leaned back in his chair and slowly rolled a hot cup of tea between his palms as he thought of the impending meeting. Maybe, by a stroke of luck, Lord Trent had found Lafitte's niece. Absentmindedly, he rubbed his index finger across the scar on his face and sneered. How he'd love to get his hands on the little bitch who'd given him this ugly reminder, but how was he going to accomplish that task? Evidently, Adam Trent didn't know who she was, or maybe she just wasn't talking. Lee wasn't quite sure how he was going to answer His Grace's questions. He was well aware of Trent's dangerous reputation, and didn't want to cross him. He'd just have to see what happened.

Adam boarded the ship, and a deckhand led him to the captain's cabin. Rapping on the door, Adam heard a deep voice call for him to enter.

The man behind the desk stood as Adam entered the room. "Your Grace." Lee nodded his head.

"Captain, I'm glad you took the time to see me," Adam said coldly before sitting down in front of the desk.

He stared at the gentleman who sat across from him. Lee was of medium height and just a bit on the heavy side. His dirty blond hair fell over dull, bloodshot eyes—probably from a previous night of boozing, Adam thought. He also noted that Lee's looks had changed. A scar now ran the full length of his face, marring his features. Adam watched as the captain absently rubbed his finger over the still-red scar. Obviously, he hadn't had the mark long.

"It appears you've been in a bit of a scrape since the last time I saw you," Adam commented.

"I had the misfortune to tangle with a pirate's knife. But I assure you the one that did this"—he fingered his wound—"was in worse shape than I by the time I'd finished with him." Abruptly, he changed the subject. "Why did you wish to see me, Your Grace?"

"I pulled a young woman from the sea who had apparently been washed overboard. I understand you've been asking questions about her. I thought perchance you might know her identity." Adam saw a momentary glint of something in Lee's eyes before his previous guarded expression reappeared.

"Why haven't you asked her yourself?"

"You see, that's quite impossible, Captain. She has temporarily lost her memory."

"I see." What a stroke of luck, Lee thought. The girl has no memory. If in fact she was the pirate's niece, he couldn't wait to get his hands on the little baggage, and this time he wouldn't lose her.

"Well, Captain?" Adam snapped. "I've not waited all this time just to sit here. Can you help?"

"I don't know if I can be of any assistance." Lee's mind began to churn. He had to think fast. And he'd better make it good. "I had my niece on board ship when a terrible storm hit, washing her overboard. However, I don't see how she could have survived the choppy sea."

Adam rubbed his chin. "And when was this?"

"I don't exactly remember, but it was sometime toward the end of September. My dear sister has been beside herself with grief."

"Can you provide a description of your niece?"

"She was very pretty, a small girl with brown eyes and black hair."

Adam wasn't sure he liked the way this was turning out. "Well, that does fit the description of the lady I've found."

"Praise the Lord if it is! When can I get her?" Lee's eyes gleamed with anticipation. At last something was going his way. He looked into Trent's eyes and started to fidget. The man had an evil stare.

"If this is your niece, tell me why she was beaten so badly," Adam demanded.

"Surely you don't think *I* did it!" The captain feigned an innocent expression. "The girl has always been headstrong. It's really a long story, and I don't want to bore you," Lee said.

"I've plenty of time, sir," Adam said dryly.

"I see." Lee knew he had to come up with something and it had better sound good. "She ran away and got in a bit of trouble. The way she had been beaten, I'd say she was caught pilfering. She's such a bad child. That's the very reason I was bringing her home to my poor sister. And I appreciate all you have done, Your Grace. I'll be glad to take her off your hands now."

The man was lying through his teeth. Adam felt it deep in his gut.

"She's been no trouble, which leaves me to wonder if in fact we speak of the same woman." Adam rubbed his chin in thought. "I'll tell you what I will do." He withdrew a slip of paper from his jacket. "There will be a party held at Foxmore on Christmas Eve. I'll write an invitation so that you may attend." Adam scribbled the necessary information before sealing the note with his ring, which bore the Trent crest.

Handing Lee the note, Adam said, "If she recognizes you and wants to go with you, Jewel will be free to do so. Otherwise, she will remain under my protection."

"She's my niece!" Lee protested. "You can't keep her from me!"

Adam stood, slowly coming to his full height. He slammed his hands down on the desk and leaned forward. "Captain, I can do anything I damn well please!"

Captain Lee's face flushed red as he swallowed hard beneath the force of Adam's glare. Adam wondered if Lee would challenge him, but he stayed mute.

Adam turned to leave. "I will see you on Christmas Eve." He looked back and raised a brow when he heard no response.

"I'll be there," muttered Captain Lee.

After the door had shut, Lee sat down behind his desk, trying to devise a plan. He would get to Jewel even if he had to kidnap her. It might mean disposing of His High-and-Mighty Lordship, but it could be done with enough men.

He gritted his teeth, deep in thought. Slowly, his lips curled into a smile as a plan formed in his mind. He would sail his ship, *The Rose,* to Cornwall and lay anchor at Land's End. Then he would go to the party. If the duke didn't agree that Jewel could leave with him, he would make plans to pay them a visit on Christmas Day.

One way or another, the girl would be departing with *him.*

Anxious to get out of the city, Adam decided to leave that afternoon. Even though it was late, he knew he could ride at least halfway, spend the night at an inn, and be home the next day.

As he rode, Adam's thoughts troubled him. He wasn't quite sure how he felt about his meeting with Lee. A clue to Jewel's identity should have made him happy, but he found it hard to believe that she could be related to that riffraff.

Besides, many things didn't add up. If Captain Lee knew she had been badly beaten, then why was Jewel out of her cabin, and especially in a storm?

No! The man was definitely lying.

But why? Did he hope to marry her or perhaps gain wealth?

Adam remembered the map. Wealth! That had to be the answer.

Well, no matter what the reason, Adam decided he wouldn't mention his meeting to Jewel. He would wait to see if she recognized Lee.

Adam frowned and pulled his coat tighter. He should have taken his coach, and then he wouldn't be out in this biting cold wind.

But what if she *did* recognize Lee? Adam's thoughts hammered back at him. He'd have no choice but to let her go.

He was hard pressed to put his feelings into words at this moment. Would he miss her when she was gone?

Yes, he admitted, he'd definitely miss her.

Giles entered the sitting room, startling Jewel. "His Grace said to convey that he'd arrive tomorrow."

Jewel's stomach fluttered with excitement. Maybe Adam would come home early and be here tonight.

Giles turned to leave, and he didn't notice the puppy until it was too late. He tripped over the dog and landed sprawled across the floor. The pup yelped and scampered out of the way.

Jewel and Annie each took an arm and dragged Giles to his feet while Duke barked, thinking this was all a big game.

"Who let that bloody beast in the house?" Giles lost his composure. "Get that mutt out!"

Jewel, having grown out of her shyness, replied, "I'll do no such thing. The puppy's name is Duke, not mutt," she added. The shocked expression on the servant's face made her want to laugh.

Giles glared back. Jewel could see he didn't care for the way she'd spoken to him. He evidently held no illusions that she was a grand lady or good enough for Adam. And that hurt her pride just a little.

"Well, His Grace won't like it," he said.

"I'll worry about Adam when he gets home."

Giles turned and stomped off, and Jewel picked up her puppy and stroked his head. In turn, he pulled on a lock of her hair with his teeth. "You'll have to be careful to stay away from the old codger, little one."

Annie burst into a fit of laughter. " 'Tis one of the best Christmas presents ye could have given ol' Annie. The bloke has been tryin' tae boss everyone around, especially when Adam's away." She winked at Jewel. "I guess he just found one he couldn't."

Jewel placed Duke back on the floor with a stern warning to stay put. He was so adorable with a brown nose and a black mask around his face. His long brown ears dragged the ground, causing him to trip quite frequently. He'd been a Christmas present from Jonathan, and she had decided to name him Duke. Jonathan had teased her for her choice of names.

The hour grew late while Jewel sat in the drawing room alone watching the fire. She felt tired and a little disappointed that Adam hadn't made it home today. He was so strong in her thoughts lately that she jumped when the door opened. She turned in anticipation, but it was only Annie.

"I thought ye would like a wee bit of warm milk before ye went tae bed." Her gaze went to the puppy curled up at Jewel's feet. " 'Tis a sleepy pup who's had a hard day."

"I think we all have." Jewel sighed. "Christmas will be here before long."

"Why don't ye go tae bed, lass," Annie said when Jewel had finished her milk. " 'Tis sure I be bettin' Adam has spent the night elsewhere, and will be here tomorrow. Ye dunna want tae meet him with puffy bags under those pretty eyes. Besides, we've some decoratin' tae be done."

Jewel smiled. "Okay, I'm going to bed. But Annie, something has been bothering me."

"And that bein', lass?"

"I don't have a present to give Adam for Christmas."

"He won't be expectin' one. This is the second Christmas he's been home and I fear the last." Annie looked sad. "Besides, what can ye give a mon that has everythin'? Adam always gives us presents, but I think his rewards are seein' how happy he makes us. There is one thin' ye could do."

"What?" Jewel eased to the chair's edge and listened.

"For Christmas, ye could make him a few rum buns. He dearly loves them, and 'tis been a while since he has had any."

"That's a great idea! Thanks, Annie." Jewel went over and kissed her on the forehead. She was beginning to love this kindhearted woman more every day. "See you in the morning."

After a good night's sleep, Jewel awoke refreshed and excited. Today she would get to see Adam.

She took special care with her wardrobe, picking out a green day dress that reminded her of Christmas. The dark forest-green material had long, tapered sleeves, and the bodice came to a point at the waistline, accenting her waist. The skirt was bell-shaped and had a very wide hem. Jewel tied red and green ribbons in her hair, letting them flow down her back.

She felt a tug on the hem of her dress, and looked down at an anxious puppy. "Okay, fellow, let's go and see what we can get into today."

Together they went down the stairs. The puppy was on the very last step when he stepped on his ear, sending him tumbling. Jewel snickered. "You're as clumsy as I am, Duke.

We make a good pair." He followed her to the kitchen, where she opened the back door and let him outside. Moving back into the kitchen, she took a seat on a wooden bench with Annie and Marie to eat breakfast, which had become a custom with her since Adam had left.

"What smells so good, Marie?" Jewel asked, propping her chin in her hand.

"I'm fixing a roast and potatoes for His Grace's return." Marie clanked the lid down on a pot and wiped her forehead with the back of her hand.

"If I have to smell that heavenly aroma all day, I'll be starving by dinner," Jewel admitted.

"If that be the case, we'll just have tae keep ye busy," Annie said. "Let's start decoratin' the staircase with greenery."

Around noon they had finished the stairs. Their hands were sore from wiring the garland they had strung across the banisters. Annie had gone off to another part of the house to finish what she called a kissing bush, while Jewel prepared the finishing touch. She tied a big, red velvet bow to the banister and arranged the tails of the ribbons, making sure they hung just right before turning to see what else could be done.

Spotting a few green sprigs of mistletoe, Jewel decided to hang them from the chandelier in the foyer with a little of the greenery they had left from the banister.

She moved a ladder from where one of the servants had been using it, and positioned it under the chandelier. Hiking up her skirt, she carefully climbed the ladder until she stood on the next-to-the-top step. She reached up, but was still unable to touch the chandelier. Putting the twine in her mouth and the mistletoe in her pocket, she placed first one foot and then the other on the very top of the ladder.

There, now she could reach the cut crystals.

Being cautious to keep her balance, Jewel reached in her

pocket and withdrew the mistletoe and evergreen. Taking the twine out of her mouth, she tied the greenery to the center of the light and smiled at her handiwork. She had almost finished when Duke began to bark somewhere behind her.

"Be quiet, Duke. I'll be down in a moment."

But the pesky animal kept on. Jewel twisted to look over her shoulder at the yapping puppy. The ladder started to wobble. She gasped. And the next thing she knew her left foot slipped and she lost her precarious footing.

Cold hard marble loomed beneath her as she fell through the air to her impending doom.

Thirteen

The urge to return to Briercliff nagged at Adam like a thorn in his side. By the time he reached the inn, he stopped for merely an hour to eat and rest his horse, then continued on his journey. He couldn't remember when the need to return home had driven him so hard. He also knew if he spent the night, the snow would be deep by morning, prolonging his journey.

He rode all night. Fortunately, the snow fell lightly until daybreak. By the time Adam finally saw the stables of Briercliff, the flakes were falling heavily. His ears felt more like ice chunks than human flesh, he thought, his gaze all the while on Briercliff. He'd been gone much longer than he'd planned, and he wondered what changes he would see in Jewel. Would she still be the naive woman he remembered, or would she have regained her memory and become a complete stranger to him?

Stopping in front of the barn door, he handed the reins to the groom with instructions to walk Star before feeding him. Then he ducked into the barn to pick up Jewel's Christmas presents, which he had instructed Giles to leave in the tack room.

With the silver boxes tucked under his arm, he started for the main house, a slight smile touching his lips as he thought of the look on Jewel's face when she opened her gifts. Even though tiredness bit him to the bone, he suddenly felt much younger as a burst of energy filled his being at the image of Jewel. Stepping up on the porch, he noticed large evergreen wreaths tied with bright red bows adorning his front doors. Apparently someone had been busy. He brushed the snow from his coat and stomped his boots before turning the brass knob and pushing the door open.

One very frisky puppy met Adam, barking and wiggling all over with the excitement of meeting someone new. Adam bent down and scooped up the pup, scratching him behind the ears. "And where, pray tell, did you come from, little one?" He chuckled as the dog licked his chin. "I bet Jonathan had a hand in this." Just as Adam set the puppy back on floor, he heard a gasp and looked around the corner in time to see Jewel lose her footing on a high ladder.

"What the devil—" His heart caught in his throat. For an instant he couldn't move. She would break her neck if she hit the floor! He threw down the boxes. With lightning speed, he closed the distance between them and caught Jewel in midair.

Jewel's mind whirled at her close escape from injury. She'd thought she'd heard Adam's voice. Now, crushed next to his chest, she breathed in his manly fragrance as she clung to him, trying to catch her breath. But was she breathless because of her fall or because of him? She wasn't sure.

Her eyes widened as she looked up at Adam's disapproving stare. This wasn't how she had planned to greet him upon his return. She'd pictured walking down the staircase, her hand resting on the balustrade, wearing a wine-colored dress she'd been saving for the occasion . . . or at least some kind of lady-like approach. But as usual, she'd failed to be what the books she'd read referred to as demure. She brushed the hair away from her face. Apparently, she'd never fit into that appropriate feminine mold.

"Madam, must I always rescue you? It appears that you are your own worst enemy." Adam's deep voice sent a tingle through her entire body. It terrified her to admit it, but she was happy to see him.

"It appears so, Your Grace," Jewel managed to squeak out.

"Did it ever occur to you that you could have broken your fool neck?" His forefinger flicked at the curl she'd tried unsuccessfully to tuck behind her ear. His voice was low, his warm breath brushing her cheek. "That is what we have servants for. To help you when you need assistance. I do believe we had this conversation the first time we met."

His gaze met hers, his charcoal-colored eyes boring into her, melting her insides. She contemplated whether all their meetings were going to be so turbulent. Maybe she had done a foolish thing, but she wasn't going to let it upset her, especially now with Adam's homecoming. He held her as if she weighed no more than a feather, and she wondered why we hadn't put her down—not that she wanted him to.

Adam speculated if it would be safe to set Jewel upon her own two feet. Hell, she'd probably trip. Finally, he eased her down. Now that his initial shock had subsided, anger reared in his veins. What if he hadn't been here? No, he didn't want to think of that. He shook his head. "What in bloody hell were you doing up there?" he demanded.

She pointed to the mistletoe, which happened to be directly over his head, and the minx in her took over. She reached up on her tiptoes and placed a kiss on his cheek. "Welcome home," she said softly.

Adam glanced up at the mistletoe, then back at her. His anger seemed to vanish like a puff of smoke. He arched a black brow. A sly grin appeared on his lips. "My dear, I think we can do better than that."

He reached out a strong, brown hand and pulled her to him. His forefinger moved along her jaw until it came to rest just below her chin. He tilted her face up and slid his free hand behind her back. Her heart fluttered with anticipation.

His lips brushed hers tenderly, and she swayed towards him, closing her eyes. Adam's mouth changed from tender to demanding, and from somewhere deep inside Jewel could feel a sweet, hot passion take over. A desire for something more overcame her as she pressed her body next to his. To be in his arms again had been well worth the wait.

Adam explored the softness of her mouth. He tried to rid himself of all those lonely nights he'd dreamed of her just like this—those long nights when sleep had eluded him.

He moaned. She should be slapping his face, not falling into his arms. Hadn't he promised himself this wouldn't happen again, only to find the minute he laid eyes on her—damn! He broke off the kiss, realizing this could go further than he wanted. Lifting his lips, he noticed hers were moist and already swollen from his onslaught. He smiled, knowing he'd been the cause. His gaze penetrated her eyes, and he saw confusion deep in their depths. There was a sparkle there, too. Adam wondered if that was for him.

"Tell me, my sweet," Adam murmured in her ear. "Did you miss me?"

Jewel nestled her head on Adam's chest, trying to catch her breath and enjoying the way he held her close, as if he cherished her. As if she were special. She had missed him, but that was something he must never know.

"No, not a bit!" She tried to sound lighthearted.

"What!" Adam pushed her away so he could see her face, and caught her mischievous grin.

She pouted prettily. "Maybe just a little."

"Well, if you didn't miss me, maybe I should leave and take your Christmas presents with me." He turned, starting for the door.

"Don't you dare take a step out that door." Jewel laughed and grabbed his arm.

"So you did miss me?" He raised his eyebrow in question, and with a gleam in his eye, awaited her response.

She hated to give him the satisfaction, but seeing that he was in such a good mood and determined to press the point for whatever reason . . . "Yes," she said, "I missed you."

"A lot?"

"Well . . ." Jewel smiled. "Yes, very much."

"Good!" Adam seemed satisfied now, and his smile told her as much.

Someone cleared their throat, and they both jumped. "Welcome home and Merry Christmas," Annie greeted Adam as she entered the front hall. "Did ye ride all night?"

"I'm afraid I did just that." Adam walked over and gave Annie a bear hug, lifting her completely off the floor, making her cheeks as red as the ribbon on the banister. "You've been busy decorating," he noted.

"That we have. Thankful I be that Jewel's been here tae help. I dare say I couldn't have done it without her."

"I could see how she's been helping when I entered the door," he said dryly, casting a look of disapproval at Jewel.

She playfully stuck her tongue out, causing him to smile. None of this exchange, however, was seen by Annie—he hoped.

"We've just about finished." Annie tilted her head to the side, surveying the hall critically. "Except for a few things."

"And that being?"

"A yule log. And a bit more greenery."

"I think I can provide the log," Adam said. "We'll go get one this afternoon." He retrieved the packages he'd left by the door. "Madam, I believe you will have need of a ball gown," he said, handing Jewel the two silver-wrapped boxes.

She gasped with surprise. He had brought her a new dress! She and Annie had labored diligently, trying to make one of her gowns more presentable for the ball, but now there would be no need.

"Thank you." Jewel looked puzzled as she took the second box from him. "But why two boxes?"

"One is a warm cape you'll be needing for winter. And the other is your gown, which should be tried on to make sure there is no need for alterations."

"I don't know how I can ever repay you, Adam." He had given her so much, and she had given him nothing.

"I don't expect payment," he said flatly, presuming no

more would be said. He frowned at her constant attempts to repay him. They were gifts. Couldn't she understand that? Then again, maybe she was really trying to say she didn't want to be indebted to him at all. Then again, maybe he was just tired. "Now run along and try on your dress, and Jewel . . ."

She had already started up the stairs, but turned when he called. "Dress warmly," he said. "We'll take the sleigh to fetch the greenery. And one more thing."

"What's that?"

Adam picked up the long-eared puppy. "I can see by this little fellow that Jonathan's been here. He evidently couldn't wait to give you your Christmas present. What is the pup's name?"

"I named him Duke." Jewel saw Adam's smile as she finished climbing the stairs.

In her room, Jewel placed the packages on the bed. She tugged at the ribbons, and they easily slipped from the first package. Removing the lid, she grew quiet. Lying in the white tissue paper was the richest material she had ever seen, much nicer than the other gowns she'd been given. She rubbed her fingers across the blue velvet, marveling at the different shades it turned as she pressed the fine fabric. She glanced around when Annie entered the room. "What do you think?" Jewel asked.

Annie slipped the dress out of the box and shook out the wrinkles. "This is no ordinary gown, lass. Ye'll look like an angel in this."

After agreeing the dress was perfect, Jewel undressed and handed the gown back to Annie so she could hang it up in the wardrobe.

Jewel tore off the other box lid and unfolded the white tissue paper. Silver fox tails met her gaze There was a hint of blue mingled throughout the silver tails. She slipped her hand inside and felt a soft white satin lining. On the inside of the left lapel was the crest of the Duke of St. Ives. Running her fingers over the crest, she noticed not the smallest detail had been left out. Jewel tried the cape on, and was surprised to find it was a little heavy. Annie explained that the weight came from the animal skins.

" 'Tis lovely." Annie reached to rub her hand across the pelts. "I've never been knowin' Adam tae give anythin' this expensive tae Colette," Annie mumbled to herself, but was quick to hide her comment with a smile. "Ye'll not be havin' tae worry about anyone lookin' down their nose at ye. Ye'll be dressed tae the hilt."

Jewel nodded in agreement, speechless at the rich gifts she'd just received. Yet she was puzzled by a name she'd never heard. "Who is Colette?"

" 'Tis no one of importance, lass."

Jewel wondered what Annie wasn't telling her, but she knew Adam would be waiting downstairs, so she let the subject rest for the moment. Pulling on her riding boots, she was ready.

"Adam said ye were tae dress warmly. Take yer new wrap."

"But this is much too nice, Annie."

"Nonsense, lass, 'tis fur. Ye can't hurt it. Haven't ye looked outside today? It's snowin'."

"Snowing?" Jewel ran the word through her limited memory. "I saw it this morning. I don't see how I could forget anything so beautiful."

Annie chuckled at Jewel's puzzled look. "Surely ye've seen snow before?" Opening the French doors, Annie led her out onto the balcony.

The ground and trees were completely covered in white. Jewel stared in wonderment. But before she could say anything, Annie grabbed her arm, pulling her back inside.

"Ye're definitely not from England, lass." She shook her

head. "See why ye need yer cape? And take yer hat. I dinna want ye catching cold."

"Annie, you treat me like a baby," Jewel protested.

"Well, somebody has tae," Annie mumbled, pushing her out into the hallway. "Some people in this house just can't see what they have."

Down in the foyer, Jewel hung up her cape, then went to the dining room to have lunch with Adam. They kept the conversation light as they enjoyed steamy vegetable soup and finger sandwiches. Jewel told him about her trip to Foxmore. Adam never mentioned her memory, something she was glad of. There were too many dark secrets she needed to figure out.

After lunch, Jewel donned her coat and tucked her black hair under the silver fox hat. Holding tight to Adam's hand, she stepped carefully down the ice-covered steps.

A sleek black sleigh pulled by two white stallions waited for them. The thick cushions were of red velvet, and the Trent crest stood boldly on the side of the vehicle.

Adam helped her into the sleigh, then walked around to the other side and climbed into the driver's seat. He threw a fur lap rug over them, and reached for the reins. Despite the cold exterior, he seemed intent on presenting a tender side that touched her heart.

"Are you ready to go?"

"You're going to drive?" Jewel couldn't hide the surprise in her voice. She had supposed a duke would do none of the work.

"You doubt my abilities, madam?"

"No. I thought you might need some help."

Adam smiled, looking into her eyes. "I have help." He snapped the reins and off they went.

The silver fur fluttered around Jewel's face as she watched the changing scenery. Snow clung to the tree branches, making them bend over from their burden. She was amazed at how snow could change the appearance of everything, making it look so much cleaner.

She was also acutely aware of Adam's thigh pressed next to hers. She didn't need the hot brick at her feet to keep her warm. Taking a deep breath, she tried to still the butterflies in her stomach. There was something about Adam that always made her nervous, and she wasn't sure what. He effortlessly ran his vast estates. He was confident. And she seemed neither effortless nor confident.

The sleigh soon left the road, heading for a distant grove of trees. So absorbed was she in the beauty that surrounded her that Jewel hadn't said a word since leaving Briercliff.

"There, madam," Adam said, pointing to the trees, "is where we'll find our greenery."

Soon they were walking through the winter landscape. Jewel held the greenery Adam cut, all the while admiring his powerful shoulders that the greatcoat couldn't disguise. The odd tingling she experienced every time she came near him was beginning to be a nuisance.

Adam clipped two more bows of spruce and turned back to his helper. He chuckled because he could only see her face above the bundles of green branches. "Let's take those back to—"

A shot rang out. He sprung toward Jewel, taking them both to the ground.

"W-what was that?"

"Shh."

Every muscle in Adam's body coiled, waiting to spring into action. A pair of horses sounded in the distance. He jumped to his feet, then ran toward the sound. But by the time he drew his pistol to fire, there was no one in sight. Whoever it had been was long gone.

He went back to Jewel and helped her up. "Are you all right?"

"I-I think so." She brushed the snow from her cape with her gloved hands. "Were they shooting at us?"

"I'd like to think they were poachers. But that was too close for comfort." He took her elbow, and they turned toward the sleigh. "I'm going to get you back home."

"What about the greenery?"

"I'll send someone back to get it. My main concern, for now, is your safety."

After dinner they gathered in the drawing room in front of a blazing fire. Annie and Jewel busied themselves making Christmas decorations from eggshells while a very frisky puppy played at their feet. Adam couldn't help but laugh over the puppy's clumsiness.

Watching Jewel while he sipped his brandy, he noted she seemed to fit well into his family. He thought of how different she looked now from when he'd first found her. He also realized his obsession about her past wasn't as strong as it used to be. But the girl herself still puzzled him. He tried to dismiss her, only to find she crept back into his thoughts. He was sure once he found out who she was the obsession would end. Life would be as it had been: fulfilling his duties at Briercliff before returning to Four Oaks. And then what? Somehow there seemed to be an empty void he hadn't realized before.

The servants entering the room caught his attention. Even Giles had lost some of his sour disposition tonight as he lent a hand with the festive activities. He joked with Marie, who had brought in the eggnog and scones.

The eggnog was delicious, especially when laced with brandy, and the mood was festive as they sang Christmas carols around the piano.

Later, Adam brought out an armful of presents, and Jewel helped place them on a table decorated with greenery. She noticed how much younger he appeared tonight. All the hard lines had vanished from his face, and he didn't look quite so intimidating. His eyes twinkled, and she wondered if under that hard exterior there lay a gentleness he tried to keep hidden from others.

The spirit of Christmas filled each heart that night when they went to bed.

The next morning, Jewel slipped out of bed before the rest of the household. She dressed in a dark blue gown with a white lace overdress, then hurried down to the kitchen, taking care not to make a sound. When she found the kitchen empty, she breathed a sigh of relief.

She had explained to Marie what she wanted to do, and Marie had told her the best time so that Jewel wouldn't run into the regular household staff.

Now, to make Adam's present. She probably should wait for Christmas morning, but they would be tired after Jonathan's party, so she thought now would be a better time. Trying to remember everything Marie had taught her, Jewel mixed up the batter in a big brown mixing bowl, remembering to add a generous helping of rum.

While the buns baked, she brewed fresh tea and filled a pitcher with cream. The heavenly smell of the rum enticed her senses as she spread the thick white icing on the warm buns. Arranging the goodies on a silver tray with the tea, she covered them with a cloth to keep them warm, then left the kitchen.

Taking a deep breath, Jewel climbed the stairs to Adam's room. She was sure it wasn't considered proper for her to be in a man's room, but no one was around to see, so what did it matter?

It was a small miracle, but she made it up the stairs without spilling any of her goodies. Thank God! For once, she wasn't her usual, clumsy self.

Jewel opened the door and eased into the room, taking care not to wake Adam until everything was ready. She placed the tray on a table beside the bed.

Adam appeared so peaceful. She couldn't help staring at him. His tousled hair made him very appealing. Smiling, she leaned over him and touched his arm.

Adam had a sixth sense when it came to danger. Having been in precarious situations too many times, he never slept deeply. Years of training had taught him to keep up his guard.

Now he sensed that someone was in his room, and felt a presence near his bed. There were too many people who wanted him dead—especially if they'd found out about his spying activities. Easing his hand under his pillow, Adam's fingers touched the cold metal of his pistol.

As a hand touched his shoulder, he moved with lightning speed. He grabbed the arm, and with a powerful jerk he threw his assailant onto the bed and quickly placed the barrel of the gun next to the intruder's head.

Jewel! Fear lanced him at the thought of how he could have hurt her.

He calmed his breathing as he stared down at the woman now lying under him. Blinking his eyelids several times to clear the sleep, he once again focused on the intruder. The picture that met his eyes was somehow unbelievable. Either he was having a very vivid dream or Jewel was in bed with him. Impossible! For the wild-eyed tigress that met his piercing gaze told him he was wide awake.

He removed the gun from Jewel's head, keeping her trapped beneath him. Taking a deep breath, he said, "Good morning, sweetheart. May I ask what you're doing in my bed?"

"I wasn't *in* your bed until you threw me here," she snapped indignantly. The palms of her hands pushed against his chest, and she realized with a sudden shock that the man wasn't clothed. She really hadn't thought about how improper this whole thing would look to him, but when his arms tightened around her, she knew this wasn't a situation any lady should find herself in.

"Let me rephrase my question." His gaze shifted toward the crack in the curtains, then back to her. "Is there a particular reason why you're in my room at this ungodly hour?" But he had no intention of letting her answer. She could tell his thoughts were anything but friendly. His heavy-lidded gaze lowered to her lips just before he said, "I can think of many things we could do." His husky voice became a purr as he nuzzled her neck. "Mmm, you smell wonderful."

His lips took her breath away, and she had the strongest desire to melt against him. Her head spun. This was wrong. She knew some distance had to be put between them. She felt much too comfortable in his bed and in his arms.

Catching him off guard, Jewel shoved hard on his chest and scooted off the bed before he could grab her. This wasn't going at all as she had planned!

Adam laughed tauntingly. "I could come after you."

"You wouldn't dare."

He started to throw back the covers, and Jewel could see he planned to get out of bed. Did the man have no shame?

"Wa—wait a minute. You're not dressed. Oh, Adam, you're going to ruin everything." She shoved him back down before he could get out of bed.

"What do you mean *ruin everything?*"

Jewel brushed the wrinkles out of her gown. "I have a surprise for you. That wonderful smell is not me, but your breakfast."

"My what!" His brow shot up.

"Your breakfast." Jewel pulled the blankets up to his chin. "Now if you'll get yourself situated, I'll serve your breakfast in bed."

"I don't believe this. I've never had breakfast in bed." His astonishment rang clear as he smiled at her.

Jewel handed him a plate and pulled the cloth off the buns,

letting the savory rum aroma fill the air. "This is my present to you. Merry Christmas."

"Rum buns!" His eyes rolled toward the ceiling, then back to the tasty treat. "How did you know they're my favorite?"

Jewel handed him a piping hot cup of tea laced with rich cream. "Let's just say someone told me."

She watched as Adam sampled her cooking, pleasure rolling through her when she received his nod of approval.

"I refuse to eat by myself," he said. "Please join me."

Jewel fetched herself a pastry and a cup of tea, then looked around for a place to sit. Adam patted the bed beside him. She really didn't trust him after a moment ago, or maybe she didn't trust herself because she liked his kisses too much. But considering that his hands were busy with the sticky buns, she took a chance. "I wish I could give you a better Christmas present."

"Sweetheart"—he placed his forefinger under her chin, turning her face to his—"you couldn't have given me anything I wanted more. Then again . . ." His eyes gleamed.

"Adam!" So much for him being occupied with food.

"I was just teasing. I promise I'll be on my best behavior. He sipped his tea, then said, "Tell me, Jewel, have you had a chance to look at the map?"

"Yes, I have." She tensed, wondering how much she should tell him. "Bits and pieces did come back to me." She toyed with the edge of her sleeve. She couldn't tell him about the pirates for fear he would hate her association with such people. He might also turn her over to the authorities. And she still wasn't sure exactly how she had ended up at Briercliff. Had she lived with her uncle? Somehow, that notion seemed farfetched.

"I remember that I am eighteen, and that my birthday is July first. I also remember who Jean is." She waited to gauge his reaction.

Adam tensed. "Who is he?"

"My uncle."

Adam let out the breath he'd been holding. "Uncle? It's a start, Jewel. What's his last name?"

"I don't remember that, but he's the one who gave me the map. The other night I had a dream, and in my dream I was a child. I can't tell you any more, but that's when I received the map. She did remember her childhood promise of secrecy.

"Do you know where the islands are located?"

"No."

"Jewel, does the name Henry Lee mean anything to you?"

She thought for a moment. "No. Should it?"

"I'm not sure. We'll talk more of it later." Adam decided he didn't want to stir up that problem at the moment. If Lee was her uncle, Adam would have to let her leave. The question was, could he do that? Or did he want to?

"Breakfast was delicious," he said. "Don't tell Marie, but I think your rum buns are the best." He winked at her, then added, "Would you like to go with me to St. Ives today?"

"To see Cyril?"

"Yes, among others. My grandfather has always taken the villagers baskets of food for Christmas. Since he's no longer here, the duty falls into my hands. But first, I've some things to take care of in my study. We'll leave around eleven o'clock."

Jewel nodded.

"Now, unless you would like to stay and help me dress, I'd suggest you run along."

"I'll take the hint." She slid off the bed. "I'm leaving." She gathered up all the dishes on her tray and walked to the door.

"Jewel?"

"Yes?" She looked at Adam, thinking how much she really would like to stay. She was drawn to him, and she knew that couldn't be good. They seemed to be from two different worlds. And she'd probably never fit into his, no matter how much she wanted to. Something in his eyes made her realize that he would kiss her again if she moved closer. But the distance between his bed and the door might as well be a mile, because she didn't know exactly how to act. Or how he really felt about her.

"Thank you for my present," he said. "It means a great deal to me."

Fourteen

Adam worked in his study all morning, dealing with the matters that had been neglected during his absence. At mid-morning he was deep in the tedious clerical work when he heard a knock on the door.

Adam barked gruffly, "Enter."

Annie walked up to his desk, but remained silent.

"What is it, Annie?"

"Beggin' yer pardon, sir. There be a gentleman here tae see ye."

Adam's first thought was Captain Lee. "Who is it?"

"He wouldn't rightly give me his name. He did tell me tae say that ye'll be glad tae see him."

Adam shoved the chair back abruptly. "We'll see about that."

Adam went to the sitting room where the visitor had been sent. A man of medium build stood in front of the fireplace, warming his hands. He wore a sailor's coat of navy blue wool with his collar turned up so that Adam couldn't see his hair. Maybe it was Captain Lee, Adam thought again. If so, the man definitely had some nerve.

"You wished to see me?" Adam stated bluntly.

The visitor jumped, then slowly turned. "You wouldn't have gone and gotten all uppity on me now, would you, son?"

Adam relaxed as a broad smile swept across his face. He immediately recognized the gentleman in front of him, and walked over to embrace him. "Derek, you old codger. You made damn good time, but then only you could have the ocean do as you command. I hadn't expected you this soon. Did you encounter any problems on the trip?"

"No, son, not a bit. We had smooth sailing all the way." Derek took a moment to look him over. "I must tell you straight off, you look well indeed. Something here has surely agreed with you. And to think, all this time I've been feeling sorry for you, stuck in this godforsaken land."

"Things haven't been so bad, but you'd best believe I'll be glad to return to Four Oaks," Adam admitted.

Derek looked around. "I'm well impressed with your wealth, Your Lordship." He gave him a mock bow.

"Oh, shut up and sit down." Adam poured his friend some scotch, which had long been Derek's drink. "I've known you well enough, old friend, to realize my title doesn't impress you one bit. If it had, I wouldn't have had such a hard time persuading you to let me on board your ship those many years ago."

Seeing Derek sitting across from him, Adam noticed he hadn't changed much in the last year, except for a little more gray at his temples. He was a good-looking man with a gentle nature.

Adam thought back to the first time he laid eyes on Derek. The man had been standing at the wheel of the ship with the sea breeze blowing his russet-brown hair. Adam had been a young man set upon seeing the world; however, he hadn't had any sailing experience. He could remember that day as if it were yesterday. Derek had stared down at the then-young Adam. "What makes you think I should take the time to teach a dandy like you how to sail, son?"

Adam had informed him that he wasn't a dandy, and if Derek would like to see his skills, he'd be most happy to demonstrate them.

Derek had seemed to like Adam's spunk, and for some reason unknown to both, he had taken him on board his ship.

In many ways Derek had been a father to Adam, and had taken him under his wing and taught him everything he needed to know about the sea. Derek was a man of great wisdom who Adam respected above all people.

"Tell me what has been happening at home," Adam said. "Have you seen Elizabeth?"

Derek Winters looked at Adam before he spoke. "I couldn't be prouder of you if you were my own flesh and blood. I remember the first time I saw the arrogant young lad you were." He chuckled. "You were brought down a measure on your first sea trip, as I recall. I can still see you hanging over the side of the ship, retching your guts." His cheeks turned red with laughter.

"Elizabeth sends you her best and wants you to hurry home," he continued. "She said to tell you please don't marry Colette. She doesn't want her for a sister-in-law; said you could find somebody much more suitable in New Orleans."

Adam smiled, thinking of Elizabeth. "Well, my sister has always spoken her mind. I wonder where she got the idea I was going to marry Colette. I have a feeling Annie is in this somewhere."

"Who?" Derek inquired.

"Annie. You met her when you arrived."

"Aye, I met her. I must say she's all spit and fire. Wasn't too sure she was going to let you know I was here." Derek smiled. "You know, she's a right nice-looking woman. Is she married?"

"No, as a matter of fact, she isn't, but I'm not sure you could handle her. You might see gray in Annie's hair, but she *is* a spitfire. Both men laughed together, and began catching up on old times.

Annie and Jewel had been busy all morning filling baskets with fruit and baked goods for the people of St. Ives when Annie mentioned Adam's visitor.

"Who do you suppose it was?" Jewel asked.

"I dinna know. 'Tis a fact I've not seen him before. Dressed strangely, too. He was a fine-lookin' mon, but I dinna think he comes from round here."

"Well, it must be someone Adam knows, because he's still visiting," Jewel said as she tied her final ribbon. "There, that's the last basket. I'll go tell Adam they're ready, and while I'm in there I will see who your mysterious visitor is."

Seeing the drawing room door open, she paused to look at the stranger before she entered. The man seemed different from Jonathan and Adam just by the clothes he wore, but he was good-looking, just as Annie had said. His bronzed and weathered skin resembled Adam's, but the fine lines around his eyes told her he liked to laugh, whereas Adam controlled his emotions.

The stranger glanced up when she entered. Upon seeing her, he stood. "This is Colette?" Derek asked.

Adam swung around. "She's a far cry from Colette," he answered, taking Jewel's arm and escorting her to the seat beside Derek. "Derek, I'd like you to meet Jewel."

Derek bowed. "Nice to meet you, ma'am."

"The pleasure is mine. Are you Adam's first mate?"

"Aye. I see he's mentioned me."

"Yes, he has." Jewel stared at him a moment before taking her seat. She saw in his eyes the same thing she saw in Annie's—trust.

"I now know why Adam looks so well," Derek hastened to comment. "With a lovely young lady such as yourself beside me, I'd stay in England longer, too."

"Such flattery, sir, but I assure you I'm not the reason." Jewel smiled before asking Adam, "Who is Colette?"

"A lady some people think I am going to marry."

The woman he was going to marry.

Jewel started to say something, but clamped her mouth shut while she watched him. His attention drifted back to Derek, and he spoke to him. She heard little of what they said, her mind lingering on Adam's statement to her. When Adam had come home, he hadn't acted like someone who would be getting married soon, but then they had been busy decorating, and she hadn't given him a chance. He had kissed her, but not until she had pointed to the mistletoe. Had he been waiting for the right time to tell her?

She was glad now she hadn't given her heart away. She would bloody well be protecting it from him in the future! She had thought he might care for her just a little, but what was merely friendship to him, *she* had mistaken for more.

"Jewel, are the baskets finished?" Adam's question brought her back into the conversation.

"Hmm?" She lifted her gaze to stare into his searching eyes, realizing belatedly that he'd spoken to her.

"Have you and Annie finished with the baskets for St. Ives?"

"Yes." She blushed. "That is what I came to tell you. Will we still take them to St. Ives today?" She stood, prepared to leave, needing to put some distance between them.

"Of course. We'll take Annie and Derek to help us." Adam paused. "Once, you told me you'd like to see my ship. Derek has docked her in the harbor there, so I'll be able to take you aboard." Adam walked with her out into the hallway. "By the way, I have some things to discuss with Derek, so I'll spend the night on board the *Wind Jammer*. But"—his smile broadened—"I'll be home in time for the party."

Jewel didn't bother to comment. At the moment she didn't care about the party. She felt numb inside. He would leave her. Even though she'd known all along his intention was to go back to Four Oaks, she still wasn't prepared. She just nodded and said, "I'll have the carriage packed with the baskets. We'll be ready shortly."

After she left, Derek said, "I need to satisfy my curiosity, son. I've never in all my travels seen a creature so lovely. Who is she, and where did you find her? And why is she staying with you?"

"Down, boy." Adam's eyes took on a faraway look. "Yes." He rubbed his chin before saying, "She is beautiful, isn't she? Would you believe I found her washed up on the beach?" He smiled at Derek's surprise, then went on to explain just how he had come across Jewel.

"That's some story, lad. Will you be taking her home with us?" Derek asked.

"No."

"Then, my friend, you're damned crazy, if you don't mind me telling you."

"That's what I like about you, Derek. You never mince words." Adam smiled.

The conversation in the carriage was light and jovial on the way to St. Ives. Jewel noticed that Derek and Annie were getting along extremely well. Now that she thought of it, Derek reminded her a lot of Annie, who was smiling at some remark he'd just made. She appeared bubbly and much younger than Jewel had seen her lately. Adam joined in the conversation, too, but to Jewel he seemed quieter than usual. Probably thinking of that woman, she thought as her chest tightened. These feelings were new to her, but she couldn't possibly be jealous of someone she'd never met.

Around noon they arrived in the festive little village, and the coachman slowed the horses. Greenery decorated each house, and boxwood wreaths tied with scarlet bows adorned the doors. Children's laughter filled the air as they played in the streets and built snowmen. The joyous sound helped to brighten Jewel's spirits.

The sleigh stopped, and the coachman hurried to open the door. Annie and Derek climbed out first. Adam helped Jewel down from the carriage, holding her a little longer than necessary. His mouth hovered inches above her own, and he was only inches from her lips. She held her breath with anticipation. Just when she thought he would kiss her, he turned and grabbed a couple of baskets. Damn man! Why did he affect her so? Loving him would be much too easy.

Adam turned to the others. "I suggest we split up in pairs to distribute the baskets," he said. Jewel started toward Annie, but Adam, seeing her intent, quickly grabbed her elbow and took her with him. "The first place we're going to stop is Cyril's house. Do you remember him?"

"Of course I do. He was the man with the eel," she replied casually.

"Cyril's wife just had a baby, and I thought you might like to see them."

"That will be nice, but Adam, these people don't know me. Will they mind my intrusion?"

As they climbed the steps, it struck Adam just how different Jewel was from any of the women he'd known. In the carriage she'd seemed remote, and he could feel her withdrawing. She actually cared about everyone she met, and she wanted very much to be accepted, whereas he'd never cared what anyone thought.

They reached Cyril's front door before Adam answered her. He looked down into her inquiring eyes, thinking how pretty she was. He certainly would like to kiss her now, but he had promised to behave, and from now on he would do just that. Since Derek had arrived with the *Wind Jammer,* Adam's departure was eminent. He couldn't get attached to her for any reason. Yet his next words contradicted his thoughts, as they always seemed to when he was with her.

"No, they won't mind. The villagers know you're a guest in my house. You belong to me." He shrugged his shoulders. "That makes you accepted."

"I do not *belong* to you! I am not chattel, Adam," Jewel uttered.

He arched a brow, taken aback by her vehemence. She

most certainly *did* belong to him. After all, he'd found her and nursed her back to health. He had a good mind to show her just how much she was his! Her inner spirit was something he hadn't captured, and though there was something vulnerable about her, he sensed a strength she kept well hidden. He gazed into the eyes of an angel. She reminded him of a fresh flower he desperately wanted to hold, yet he had to be careful not to crush the bloom. "Have you any idea?" he murmured.

But before he could put his thoughts into action, Cyril answered the door.

"Yer Grace, 'tis good to see ya, and I am glad ya brought Lady Jewel," Cyril said, greeting them. "Please come in out of the snow."

"Merry Christmas," Jewel said, handing the basket of goodies to Cyril.

Cyril's wife, Mary, appeared from the back of the house with the newborn infant in her arms. "It's a pleasure to see you," she called, smiling her welcome.

As they stood talking, one of the younger children rushed through the door. "James has been hurt! Come quick!"

Mary shoved the baby toward Jewel, then ran out the door to see what had happened to her other child. Cyril and Adam followed her.

Jewel slipped off her coat and placed the babe on her shoulder. He nuzzled her neck, completely content to let a stranger hold him.

She walked over to the window and looked out on the scene below. It appeared James had cut his leg in a sledding accident. Jewel was surprised at how Adam took charge, ripping the child's pants leg and examining the cut. She supposed he had taken care of such things when he was aboard ship.

The baby started to fret. She rubbed her hand up and down his back, talking in a soothing voice. Glancing back out the window, she saw and felt Adam's hot gaze. Even from this distance, she could see the darkness of his eyes.

Moving away from his view, Jewel went back, sat down in a rocking chair, and began humming a lullaby to the child she cradled in her arms. The warmth of the baby's hand as he gripped her finger made her wonder if she herself would someday be a mother. Somehow the thought appealed to her. She smiled to herself.

A noise caused her to look up. Adam stood watching her from the doorway. "What's the matter?" she asked, wondering at his frown.

Adam entered the child's bedroom, and his gaze rested on the bewitching creature before him. Jewel seemed completely at ease with a child in her arms, and for just a moment, he wondered what she'd look like if that were *his* child. He shook the crazy notion completely out of his head. Why did his thoughts constantly venture in this direction when he was around her? There was something about her that he had never found before. And he was willing to lose it all—to lose Jewel? He shook the thought aside angrily.

"Are you ready to go?" His voice sounded strange to his ears as he struggled with his emotions.

"Yes," she said uncertainly.

Hell. He knew she was confused. But so was he.

After handing out all the baskets, the four of them climbed into the sleigh, and Adam instructed the driver to carry them down to the dock.

Even before they got to the wharf, Jewel could see the topsails of the *Wind Jammer*. She drew in her breath as the sleigh pulled up to the dock. "It's beautiful," she whispered.

Adam was pleased she showed an interest in his ship. Of course, she probably didn't know much about ships, he thought.

"Thank you, madam. You are looking at the fastest clipper ship to be found," Adam said proudly. "She is two hundred sixty feet long, forty-five feet abeam, and has a depth of twenty-nine feet. Notice the long and lovely lines, and the enormous expanse of sails lacking in most ships."

"Your sails are different. Most are white, but some of yours are blue."

"You're very observant. They are actually azure blue. When we're at sea, the white and blue sails make us blend into the horizon. It's a good way to escape the enemy when the need occurs. To other ships, we look like a floating cloud."

Staring at the *Wind Jammer,* Jewel knew she had been on such a craft. She shut her eyes and saw herself walking across a ship's deck. There were many men around her, but their vague faces meant nothing to her. She stepped up behind a big wheel—

"Are you feeling ill?" She felt Adam nudge her.

Her eyes flew open. "No, just thinking." She smiled. "I'm impressed, but do you not have any guns?" Was the man mad to sail the sea without protection?

"Yes, sweetheart, we are very well protected. The cannons are hidden. Come, let me show you my ship."

Jewel enjoyed the tour of the vessel. Each click of her heels upon the wood deck brought back another memory. The fact that she could sail, for instance. All the parts were starting to fit together, except for a missing piece—one she couldn't quite put her finger on.

Adam's detailed explanations amused her. I'll bet he'd be surprised if I told him I could sail this boat right out of the harbor, she mused. But then she'd have to admit the truth. She had learned all that from a pirate, and Adam probably would hate her. Jewel kept her thoughts to herself, wondering what she was going to do.

The seamen glanced at each other as she passed, and they took great pains to be cordial. Adam spoke to them with authority, and they jumped to do his bidding. Jewel could tell from the look in their eyes that Adam had their loyalty and devotion.

It was late in the afternoon when Adam and Derek walked the ladies back to the sleigh. Adam instructed the driver to stop for nothing on the way home.

He took Jewel's hand in his, but before he helped her up, he bent down and whispered, "I'll be home tomorrow night, and I expect you to be radiant for the ball." He kissed her cheek.

Jewel's gaze lingered on Adam, noticing the way the setting sun flickered across his coal black hair. She wanted to say something, anything, but couldn't find the words. Lifting her hand, she gently touched the side of his face, then turned and climbed into the carriage.

Fifteen

At long last, Christmas Eve had arrived. Tonight was Jonathan's party. Jewel found herself looking forward to the gala, although her nerves jumped at the thought of being around so many strangers.

She leaned her head against the cool windowpane. Annie had told her the weather had been strange this year, and today was a perfect example. The air had warmed enough to melt the snow. Only traces remained, and that, too, would soon vanish.

Jewel had tried to keep busy, hoping it would make the day pass faster. Behind her water splashed into the tub as the maids emptied the last buckets of hot water. Taking a kerchief out of her pocket, Jewel wiped the steam from the windowpane and peered out at the stormy sky. The dark clouds moving in looked ominous, threatening to let loose their raindrops at any moment. Her brow drew together in a frown. She could remember another such storm, but when and where? Then, too, she'd felt impending doom grow near. Her nagging memory just wouldn't cooperate. Well, maybe this bad weather would hold off until after the party.

"Has His Grace returned home?" she asked the smallest maid.

"Yes, ma'am."

Jewel stepped into the tub, wondering why Adam hadn't stopped in to see her. After yesterday, she didn't know what to think. Adam had a way of keeping her teetering on the edge. He'd been so different since he'd returned from London. He'd acted as if he'd miss her. Yet he still planned to sail. And very soon, she imagined, since Derek had already arrived. Uncertain of what she'd do, Jewel found relief as everyone fussed over her as she bathed, taking her mind off her uneasiness.

Finally, after her bath, she took a seat in front of her mirror. Annie brushed her hair until the raven highlights glistened. They decided, instead of curls all over her head, they would pull her hair up on one side. The result was breathtaking. A mass of ebony curls cascaded down the right side of her face and over her shoulder, coming to rest on the upper part of her breast. Among the curls, Annie pinned white baby's breath and ribbons of peacock blue.

Jewel placed a hint of color on her cheeks and just a touch on her lips. Long, sooty lashes framed her warm brown eyes, and for a final touch, she accented her bottom lashes with a touch of black kohl.

Annie held the dress so Jewel could step into it, then fastened the hooks in the back. Worn off the shoulders, the gown dipped in a vee in front and was trimmed with blue peacock feathers. Each little feather moved against her alabaster skin as if the dress were a part of her, seductively teasing her breasts. Although she'd been assured it was modest compared to most, Jewel thought the neckline seemed daringly low.

She adjusted the sleeves and rubbed her hand over the soft, sapphire blue velvet, noting the richness of the material. The skirt pulled up from the bottom, revealing on both sides a white satin underskirt, which had tiny seed pearls and sequins of white and silver sewn very carefully in the folds.

She watched the way the light caught each little sequin as she swayed back and forth in front of the mirror. Then she smiled. Adam had done well with his choice of dresses.

"Ye look like a delicate porcelain doll, lass," Annie commented.

Jewel did feel like a fairy princess with her cheeks warmed by a blush and eyes sparkling with excitement. She swallowed the lump in her throat. "I-I hope I'll say all the right things tonight." She bit her bottom lip, wishing the knots in her stomach would settle down. What if someone recognized her? Would she never see Adam again?

"Adam will be havin' tae keep an eye on ye fer sure."

Jewel wasn't too sure about that. He couldn't care too much if he was leaving.

" 'Tis time tae be goin'." Annie nudged her gently. "I see ye biting yer lip. Ye nervous, lass?"

Jewel nodded.

"Excuse me a minute, lass." With a pat on her arm, Annie left her standing there. When she returned, she handed a glass of deep amber liquid to Jewel. "Drink this, lass. It will help with yer butterflies."

"What is it?"

"Brandy. Believe me, ye'll be relaxed after ye have some."

Jewel swallowed, then crinkled her nose at the strong taste. Taking a deep breath, she tipped the glass and threw her head back, swallowing the rest of the brandy in one gulp as instructed. Bouts of coughing ensued, followed by teary eyes. Annie was right, Jewel thought as the warmth spread through her body, and she had to admit she did feed a little better.

With her head held high, she descended the staircase.

Adam steeled himself to give away nothing. By God, Jewel looked like an angel. And dressed in his colors. Unwelcoming desire pulsed through him. Whatever had possessed him to have the gown made with *his* royal colors?

"Your beauty will not be surpassed tonight, madam." Adam bowed gallantly before her. "And I'm happy to say I'll be your escort."

She smiled, her dark eyes sparkling with anticipation. "Arise, my humble servant." She tapped him on the shoulder as a queen would. "You, sir, will set many a lady's heart aflutter tonight."

"Ah, but will I touch your heart, madam?"

"Let's just say the night is young, sir." Her laughter floated around him when she walked over to retrieve her cape, but he followed and took it out of her hands, draping it across the banister.

"Oh, we're not going?" she said with a puzzled look.

"Not yet." Such beauty had to be adorned, he thought. He hoped she'd always have the sparkle for life he saw in her eyes. Reaching into his pocket, he withdrew a long silver box. "Merry Christmas," he said softly, handing Jewel the package he'd bought without so much as a second thought.

"Adam, you've given me so much." She glanced up at him with a glorious blush brushing her cheeks. "I've given you little in return," she said, fingering the box nervously. "You really shouldn't have."

"You're right, of course I should have waited until tomorrow morning, but I wanted you to wear this tonight." And, for some odd reason, he wanted her to look her very best tonight. He'd probably carry the vision of her with him a long time after he left.

She handed the package back to him abruptly. "You need to give this to your fiancée."

"My what?" Adam practically yelled. "What the hell are you talking about? I paid a tidy sum for this gift to have it shoved back in my hands so unceremoniously."

She looked at him accusingly. "I heard you tell Derek that you are going to marry a lady by the name of Colette."

Adam smiled, taking Jewel's chin in his hand. "My dear, you need to pay better attention, or perhaps you don't hear well." He placed the gift back in her hands. "Colette has nothing to do with this."

Should Jewel believe him? She realized he really hadn't come out and denied anything. But most of all, she had too much pride to ask anything more about Colette, and Jewel didn't want anything to spoil this night. With trembling fingers, she carefully tore the silver paper off a long velvet box. She opened the lid and gasped. Nestled on a satin bed lay ten fiery opals surrounded by diamonds. Running her fingers over the necklace, she couldn't believe Adam would give her something so beautiful and obviously costly. Especially since—

"It's gorgeous," she whispered.

Adam lifted the choker from the box and fastened it around her neck, his fingers brushing her nape. Then he turned her around to face him. She felt his gaze roam over each little stone, and she swallowed as he stared at the one large opal resting in the hollow of her throat. Why couldn't she act as if she cared naught for the man? It was something about his boyish charm and devastating smile. She almost felt the need to make Adam happy.

A rustling behind her drew his attention and he lifted his eyes. "What do you think, Annie?" Holding Jewel by the shoulders, he turned her around again.

Annie's eyes grew wide. " 'Tis beautiful. Ye've outdone yerself. The lass's neck appears tae be on fire."

"I quite agree," Adam said, coming to stand beside Annie.

Jewel tried to control the shimmering tears in her eyes. Adam was magnificent in evening attire. She did, however, keep the thought to herself this time. He was dressed in a black waistcoat studded with pearls, the perfect complement to his black overcoat. The only white Adam wore was his white linen shirt and cravat, which was tucked in the front with a mother-of-pearl pin. Yes, she mused, she'd be the envy of every woman there. He was most definitely a man in every sense of the word. Maybe he did care for her just a little. She didn't know why she was teary-eyed—perhaps it was the brandy that caused her eyes to burn and her throat to constrict.

She was happy that Adam was here, yet sad he would be leaving. How could he give her expensive gifts, then walk out of her life? Perhaps he couldn't. She'd have to cling to that thought. And she had to get control of herself. Adam had never made her any promises, so she didn't know exactly what she expected. Tonight she'd grasp what she could, and face tomorrow when it came.

"You don't like your gift, sweetheart?" Adam frowned. Jewel quickly nodded. But she didn't trust herself to speak.

Annie came to the rescue, pointing to the mistletoe. "Have ye noticed where ye both are standin'?"

"Splendid idea." Not wasting another minute, he pulled Jewel into his arms, planting a light kiss on her soft lips.

He lifted his mouth and stared at her upturned face. A bemused smile hovered on his lips. "Madam, is that my brandy I'm tasting?"

"I believe it is." Jewel laughed softly, feeling very light-headed and truly wonderful. "Really rotten stuff, too."

Adam arched a brow, then glanced at Annie. "I suppose you had something to do with this."

"Well . . ." Annie hesitated. "I didna do it on purpose. Ye see, Jewel was just a wee bit nervous, and I be thinkin' it would help cure her butterflies . . . and it has, too. As ye can see, she's very relaxed."

"You might say she is completely relaxed. And if she passes out before we get to the party, I'll have your hide, Annie."

"There's no time to get yourself in a dither, Adam," Jewel said, then giggled as she tried to usher him out the door.

As their coach drew near Foxmore, a glow could be seen in the distance. Several footmen awaited to assist them from the carriage as it pulled up to the front entrance. Emerging from the vehicle first, Adam waved away the footman who was there to help Jewel.

Soft music filled the air with an enchanting melody, surrounding them as they climbed the white marble steps. Once they entered the foyer, a maid immediately appeared to take Jewel's wrap.

"What a lovely cape," the maid commented. She turned and took Adam's greatcoat. "You have excellent taste, sir." Jewel saw the way the woman batted her eyelashes in a flirtatious gesture. Evidently she was another of his conquests.

Adam looked amused, but didn't bother to answer. Instead he moved to where Jewel stood and took her by the elbow, then proceeded to the receiving line.

"It's good to see you, ol' chap. I see you made it home safely." Jonathan's enthusiasm showed as he shook Adam's hand.

"As you can see, I'm back in one piece. And I might say I did have a successful trip. I'd like to thank you for looking after Jewel."

"The pleasure was all mine. We've become good friends." Jonathan winked playfully at her. "Tell me, Adam, did you meet Duke?"

"How could I not see one clumsy, little, flop-eared hound? But then, you knew I couldn't miss him."

Jonathan laughed. "I'm just about finished here. Let's get together later. I'd like to hear about your excursion." He then turned his attention to Jewel. "My dear, you look simply ravishing. Be sure and save me at least one dance, possibly more."

"I will," Jewel replied just before Adam led her into the main ballroom.

The lavishly decorated ballroom was filled with beautiful ball gowns in every imaginable color. There are just too many people! Jewel thought as she clutched Adam's arm a little tighter. Not having a true identity was frightening among so many strangers.

As if sensing her sudden apprehension, Adam patted her hand as he led her to a small group of people and began introductions. Jewel listened, finding it difficult to contribute to the conversation. She felt as if every eye was on her, and several times she did look around only to meet someone's quickly averted gaze.

Little did Jewel know everyone was staring at her. The women chattered among themselves, green with envy, wondering who this lovely creature with the Duke of St. Ives could be. They spoke of her beauty, and especially her clothing.

"There is not another dress in the room that can even come close to its richness," one lady commented. "Have you noticed, the dress is the duke's colors? What do you suppose that means?"

Colette happened to be in one of the groups when she overheard that particular comment. "It doesn't signify a thing. As you all know, Adam will be asking for my hand in the very near future."

"Not if he's around that young woman very much," commented a stiff matron with graying hair.

Another young woman joined in the conversation, "I envy you, Colette, if you do marry Lord Trent. He's so handsome." The young woman giggled as she stood dreamy-eyed. "Just look at him tonight. He's dashing, and by far the best-looking man here."

"You're right, of course, I'm a very lucky lady. And if you will all excuse me, I think I shall go over and join him now." Colette swept away from the group.

She stopped by the refreshments table, having grown extremely warm. Slowly, she sipped the cool champagne, remembering Adam's last words to her. He had led her to believe that this woman she saw before her was a mere child. The girl was young, but she was in every sense a woman. Colette frowned. She had seen the way every man's head had turned when the woman entered the room. She would have to inform the young chit just what kind of relationship she and Adam had.

* * *

The evening grew long for Adam as he kept his eyes on Jewel while appearing to pay no attention to her. At least she was by his side now. He glanced around the room for Captain Lee. Relief washed over Adam when he didn't spot him. Good. Lee wasn't coming. Now maybe he could relax just a bit.

But just when he did, a young dandy by the name of Charles Simmons from London approached them. Adam had noticed the young man's gaze on Jewel from the moment she'd entered the ballroom.

"Your Grace, it's good to see you," Charles said. "I must beg for an introduction to your lovely niece."

Charles couldn't seem to take his eyes off Jewel, which Adam found a little irritating. Charles waited for the introduction. Not hearing anything, he glanced at Adam. "Maybe this wasn't such a good idea," Charles added nervously.

Adam let out a disgusted sigh, trying very hard not to lose his temper and give this young buck the set-down he deserved. "The lady is not my niece," he bit out.

"I beg your pardon, Your Grace, but Colette told me this was your niece and you wouldn't mind my dancing with her."

"Really?" He drew his brows together in an angry frown, not at all surprised by Charles's explanation. "May I introduce you to Lady Jewel."

"It's a pleasure to greet someone with such beauty." Charles bowed graciously.

"Thank you," Jewel murmured, casting a glance at the crowd looking for Colette. Jewel's stomach tightened at the mention of the woman's name.

"Jewel, would you like some refreshments?" Adam asked.

"That would be lovely."

Charles, seeing this as an opportunity, asked, "Would you care to dance in the meantime?" With a look at Adam's stern face, he added quickly, "If His Grace does not mind."

Jewel was tired of these men talking about her as if she weren't here. She could speak for herself. "Why should he mind?" She laughed. "I'm the one that will be dancing." She reached out and took Charles's hand, leaving both men a little speechless.

Adam couldn't believe her boldness. The last thing he needed was to be left standing gawking at the couple dancing. He was glad she was having a good time, but she didn't have to dance with every man in the room. Turning, he made his way to the refreshment table.

From a less visible corner, Adam concentrated on the two young people as they moved around the room. It was hard taking his eyes off Jewel. It also appeared Charles was having the same problem. His eyes lingered once too often on her decolletage, Adam noted as he slugged down his third brandy. He'd break Charles's damn neck if he dared touch her!

Adam felt an arm slip through his. He looked down, and found Colette clinging to him.

"Adam, darling, you look most dashing. I had hoped to see you tonight."

"Hello, Colette," Adam answered.

"You should have joined us for the fox hunt this morning." Collette paused until he gave her his attention. "You'll never believe what happened," she went on, relating an earlier mishap, which finally made him chuckle.

Jewel had grown warm and she was glad when the music ended and Charles moved her across the floor. She noticed a woman standing very close to Adam. She wore a vivid green satin gown with a plunging bodice that made her ample figure stand out. *So, this must be Colette.* Jewel had to admit the woman was very pretty, and Adam appeared to be enjoying himself.

As they stopped in front of Adam, he handed her a glass of wine. "I believe you will like this better than my brandy." He winked.

Jewel smiled, noticing that Colette still clung to his arm with a very intimate gleam in her eyes.

"Adam, darling," the woman crooned, "aren't you going to introduce me to your little friend?"

"Yes, indeed. Jewel, I would like you to meet a friend of mine. This is Lady Colette."

"It's good to meet you." Jewel nodded to the woman in front of her, noting that Colette was about three inches taller than she. Jewel returned the woman's look, refusing to flinch at the hatred she saw there.

Colette's smile was cold and empty as she stared back. Jewel had the distinct impression that the woman thought she was worthless and not good enough to be in this crowd.

"It's nice you could get out and come to the party tonight," Colette told Jewel with a sneer. "And it was especially sweet of Adam to buy such a lovely dress so you would be properly attired." She paused before adding the final stab. Venom poured from her mouth as she attacked her victim. "I understand he found you in rags."

Before Adam could say anything, Jewel answered Colette directly. "I quite agree, it was thoughtful of Adam to purchase a grown for me, and this necklace he gave me for Christmas, needless to say . . . leaves me speechless." Her hand brushed the stones as she spoke. "It's a shame, Colette, you didn't have someone to help you pick out your dress." Jewel batted her eyes sweetly, looking very innocent.

Adam laughed out loud, drawing quite a few stares. Just about the time Colette was ready to lunge for Jewel, he stepped between them, expertly taking Jewel by the hand, escorting her to the dance floor. "I think we should waltz, my dear."

Adam couldn't take his gaze off Jewel as they whirled around the room to a soft melody. Just what kind of little spitfire did he have here? "My, don't we have a sharp tongue?"

Jewel held his stare, then laughed. "She asked for the set-down." Jewel's cheeks turned a deep pink.

"I believe she did," he replied after a second's consideration.

He pulled her closer, holding her tightly as they glided across the floor. So absorbed were they by the music that neither realized that anyone else was in the room. It was just the two of them alone.

People murmured about what a lovely couple they made, and that they seemed to waltz together as if they had been doing it all their lives. That is, all the people but one.

Colette seethed in the corner, planning how she was going to get even. Glancing at the doorway, she was surprised to see Captain Lee standing alone. She'd known Lee for a couple of years, but they usually didn't attend the same parties. She motioned for him to come over. "What are you doing here, Henry?"

"I've come to get my niece." Lee said as he eyed the room until he spotted Jewel dancing with Adam. She did look different dressed in her finery, Lee thought. Not only could Jewel supply the map he needed, but maybe he also could have a little fun on the long voyage to America. After all, the bitch did owe him something for the scar. He rubbed his index finger slowly along the red mark. But enough of that kind of thinking. He'd have to be gentle if he was going to persuade Jewel he was her long-lost uncle.

He watched Colette's eyes widen as she said, "Your what?"

"The young lady dancing with Trent is my niece."

"You can't be serious."

"Oh, but I'm quite serious," Lee said.

"Then you'll be taking her with you?"

"I hope to as long as His High-and-Mighty Lordship doesn't stand in my way," Lee sneered.

"If it will be of some help," Colette purred, "I'll try to keep Adam busy later."

"Aye, that would be a big help."

The music ended, to Adam's disappointment. He'd enjoyed having Jewel in his arms. They walked off the dance floor, and immediately Adam spotted Captain Lee. There was no avoiding him, Adam thought. They might as well get this over with. Placing his hand in the small of Jewel's back, he guided her over to where Lee stood.

"I see you made it, Captain."

"Aye, I did."

"Jewel, I would like you to meet Captain Henry Lee."

She extended her hand, which Lee took, placing a kiss there that lasted much too long. Her skin crawled. She resisted the urge to jerk free of his grasp. His cold lips caused her to shiver all over. What a strange reaction, she thought. But as she looked upon his face, she noticed a scar that ran from his ear to his mouth. She thought he had the coldest eyes she had ever seen, and for some unknown reason she didn't like the man in the least.

"Jewel," Adam said softly. "Captain Lee tells me you're his niece. Do you recognize him?"

"Niece!" That was impossible. She couldn't possibly be related to this man. Could she? "He isn't the man in my dream," Jewel whispered to Adam.

Captain Lee spoke up. "Darling, you're bound to know me. I practically raised you from a little girl. Don't you recall being on my ship? You were washed overboard. Surely you must remember."

Jewel did recall a ship and being thrown in the water, but she couldn't possibly be related to this man. Yet every hair on her body stood up at the sound of his voice.

"N-no, I don't remember."

Colette intruded. "Adam, you promised me a dance. Besides, it will give these two a chance to talk."

Adam looked hesitantly at Jewel, and she didn't know exactly what to say. Maybe if she talked to this man longer some sort of memory would return. She had to find out who she was before Adam left. So far, Lee didn't tie in to any of her flashes of memory. "Yes, go ahead. I would like to talk to the captain," Jewel finally said.

Lee tried everything to convince her they were related. She sipped her wine and listened to his prattle. Wouldn't she know if she were related to this man? Surely she would have some intuition. Instead, all her instincts told her to beware. He was dangerous.

And then her gaze lingered on the ugly scar that marred Lee's once-perfect features. And for a moment she saw a flash of blood seeping from the scar. She blinked. There was no blood. But somehow she knew this man fit into her memory. She had to get away from him.

"How is the belle of the ball?" Jonathan seemed to come out of nowhere to rescue her. "I do hope you're enjoying yourself?" he inquired.

"Jonathan . . ." She paused and took a deep breath. "Do you know Captain Lee?"

"No, I don't believe I've had the pleasure," Jonathan replied.

Lee nodded. "It's good to make your acquaintance." He shook Jonathan's hand. "I'm Jewel's uncle."

"What!" Jonathan exclaimed.

Jewel grabbed Jonathan's hand. "I believe this is your dance, Jonathan," she said, pulling him onto the dance floor with the stunned expression still on his face.

After they started dancing, Jonathan recovered from his initial shock. "Is that man daft? You can't be related to him."

"That was my exact thought. But I don't understand why he would make up such a story."

"I don't know, either. What does Adam say?"

"I haven't had a chance to talk to him since I've spoken with the captain. He's dancing with Colette."

"Well, luv, if he is dancing with her, I would wager she jerked him onto the dance floor. Jonathan laughed.

Jewel laughed, too, but she couldn't help wondering if

maybe Adam wanted to be rid of her. He had tried so hard to find out who she was and where she belonged. What if he believed this Captain Lee and sent her away with him?

"Jonathan." She hesitated, taking a deep breath. "You once said if I needed someplace to stay, I could stay with you. Did you mean that?"

"Yes, I did." His blue eyes glistened with sincerity. "Has Adam done something to you?" Jonathan asked immediately, his arms tightening around her.

"Not yet." She paused before continuing. "Jonathan, I'll not go with that captain if Adam sends me."

"I think you're cutting Adam a little short," Jonathan chided her. "I'll find him after this dance and see what this is all about."

Adam couldn't be that crazy, Jonathan thought. But if he were, Jewel would belong to *him*. And he would take care of her.

He'd make sure of it.

Sixteen

Adam was lounging against a pillar surveying the crowd when he spotted Jonathan walking purposefully toward him.

"Let's go to my study. We need to talk!" Jonathan insisted.

"Where's Jewel?" Adam asked. "Have you seen her?"

"I just finished dancing with Jewel. She said she was going upstairs to the retiring room. She should be fine there."

When they reached Jonathan's study, Jonathan swung around. "Who is this Captain Lee?" he blurted out. "I couldn't believe my ears when he told me he was Jewel's uncle. And she's pretty upset, too, I might add."

"Did she say anything?"

"Jewel doesn't believe she is related to Captain Lee in any way. However, she seems to think you might send her away with him." Jonathan gave him a long, penetrating look. "She is wrong—isn't she?"

"What the hell do you think?" Adam's temper exploded as he threw his empty glass into the fireplace, shattering it into a thousand pieces. It was bad enough he was worried, but Jonathan's unexpected question had pushed him too far.

"I don't know what to think!" Jonathan snapped as he leaned against his desk and folded his arms.

"The lady, and I do mean the one with black hair"—Adam paused, emphasizing each word—"will be going nowhere unless it's with me."

"You love her, then?"

"What the hell has that got to do with anything?" Adam

ran a hand through his hair. He barely held his temper in check. He moved to the cabinet, where he picked up a crystal decanter and poured a shot of Madeira into two glasses. Turning, he handed Jonathan a goblet. "I don't know why we're arguing when we need to think clearly. I don't trust Lee. What if he tries to take Jewel when one of us isn't near her?"

"You're right. But what could he possibly want with her?"

"You're forgetting the map." Adam explained his suspicions to Jonathan, then filled him in on everything he knew.

"What are we going to do?"

"Do?" Adam let his gaze drop to his drink. "I'm going to send her home. I hate to do it, but she'll be safer there."

"And then what? Do you think he will come after her?"

"I don't know. It depends on how much he wants the map. I wish I could tell where the diagram leads. Maybe it would tell me why he wants it so badly."

Jonathan pushed away from his desk. "We'd better get back out there."

"I agree." Adam set his glass on the desk and followed Jonathan. "I'll find Jewel."

The upstairs chamber was a good place to relax and get away from the crowd. Jewel rubbed the back of her neck, easing the tension. Her head swam. *If they don't give me some food soon, I'll be drunk.* Several ladies had been in to freshen up, but now the room was empty, and she knew she needed to get back to the ballroom, but her feet refused to cooperate.

The door swung open, and in swept Colette. "Oh, it's you, darling. Imagine me finding you hiding here. Well, now we'll have a chance to get to know each other better, won't we?" she said sweetly, seating herself on the upholstered bench by Jewel.

"I don't know that we have anything to say to one another," Jewel replied, wondering what this woman was up to.

"Well, my dear, Adam's told me quite a bit about you."

"Really." Jewel tried not to let any of her emotions show.

"Yes, he's told me everything." Colette stood, then started to pace back and forth. Suddenly, she stopped and stared straight at Jewel. "I told Adam I didn't mind you staying with us after we're married."

"He isn't going to marry you!" Jewel snapped.

Colette gave her a look of surprise. "Oh, but you are wrong, dear! Where do you think he spent his nights while in London?" Colette's slow, satisfied smile made chills run over Jewel's body. "He didn't want to break the news until after I'd met you. You see, Adam needed my approval."

"You're lying!" Jewel said with much more conviction than she felt.

"Well, we'll just see who he spends the night with to-night," Colette said, rearranging her shawl around her shoulders. She swung around, her head held high; then, with a final glance at Jewel, she left the room evidently feeling victorious.

Stunned, Jewel couldn't move. Hadn't Adam denied his intentions earlier when she'd asked him? The woman was just making it up. But what if she wasn't? An icy fear encircled her.

Jewel returned to the ballroom, hardly knowing in which direction she walked. She definitely didn't want to see Captain Lee. Soft music filled the room as couples danced. Jewel stayed close to the wall until she could escape out to the terrace. Standing in the corner by the rail, Jewel looked out over the gardens. The cold air felt good on her flushed face. Her jangled nerves had made her fidgety. She would just stand here and calm down before seeking Adam. The winds gave advance warning of the approaching storm, but the breeze felt good as it tugged at the loose strands of hair. Hearing the doors on the far end of the terrace open, she saw a couple walk out. The lighting was much too dim for her to make out their faces, and she was thankful they couldn't see her standing in the shadows as they walked down the steps on the far end.

After scanning the ballroom and not finding Jewel, Adam decided to look outside. He had made up his mind. He'd send her back to Briercliff to keep her safe from Lee's clutches. Adam knew he'd made the right decision. He needed to figure out just what the captain's intentions were. He'd join her later after he was sure Lee wouldn't be a threat.

Adam moved out one of the six doors that led to the terrace, then went down the steps to stand at the bottom. Could Jewel possibly have walked out into the gardens?

He heard a movement and peered into the shadows. A woman walked up the path. As she drew closer, Adam noticed it was Colette and she was headed straight for him. There was no telling what she had been doing, he thought.

When she reached him, she stopped in front of him and draped her arms around his neck. The next instant she pressed her body suggestively into his. He was too tired for this. However, his body took over from his sluggish thoughts. Damn! He'd drunk too much liquor. He could feel himself hardening against Colette's curves, but it was Jewel's face that flashed in his mind. The overpowering scent of sweet gardenias brought him to his senses. My God, what was he doing? He pried Colette's arms from around his neck as if she were a serpent.

"Adam, darling, it has always been so good between us," Colette cooed.

Jewel's head snapped around at the sound of Adam's voice, but she couldn't see him from where she stood. Moving in the direction of his voice, she stopped dead in her tracks. Below her, two people were entwined in a lovers' embrace. Thinking it was the couple that had come out earlier, she started to turn away. Then someone opened a door and the light caught in Adam's black hair.

She couldn't stop the gasp that escaped her lips. Swallowing convulsively, she felt sick to her stomach as a river of conflicting emotions ran through her. Gulping a breath of air, she bit her lip to keep from crying. Her beautiful evening had just come to an end.

What a fool she had been!

Jewel picked up her skirt and swung around. If that was how he felt, she would go back to the party and have the time of her life.

Adam sensed Jewel even before he heard her gasp. "Damn," he swore as he shoved Colette away from him, practically knocking her down. Taking the steps two at a time, he caught Jewel before she entered the ballroom, and spun her around to face him. "It's not what you think."

Jewel held her head high, fixing him with a cold stare. "It's not necessary for you to explain. Please let go of my arm. I intend to dance."

"I think not," Adam said.

"I beg your pardon!"

"You're going home."

"I am not!" she snapped, her voice growing louder with her anger.

"Yes, you are, even if I have to throw you over my shoulder," Adam growled. "And keep your voice down."

"Go to Hell!"

"Sweetheart, I'm sure I will someday, but not before I take care of you." Adam took a deep breath, trying to cool down his rising temper. "I can't explain now, but you must go home."

She didn't bother to respond, but her eyes shot daggers at him just before he slid his arm around her waist, holding her tight in case she decided to protest further. He then escorted her through the ballroom to the front door, ignoring her mulish silence while he helped her collect her wrap.

Once they were outside, Adam motioned for his carriage. They walked down the steps. "Things aren't as they appear. I'll explain everything later."

Jewel stopped in front of the carriage and glared at him. "I don't want to hear it! Colette is waiting for you. Try not to disappoint her." Turning, Jewel stepped up into the carriage, disappearing into its darkened interior. At the groom's hesitant look, Adam gave a reluctant nod. The servant immediately slammed the carriage door.

Adam watched as the coach pulled away. She was wrong, of course. He should have made her listen to him. But there wasn't time. The important thing was to have her away from Captain Lee. There would be time for explanations later.

Adam went back into the ballroom, nodding to Jonathan that he had accomplished his task. Once again Colette appeared at his side. By now, he was very tired of her. He bent down to Colette, his voice low and menacing. "Colette, you seem to have a hard time understanding. What we had was nice while it lasted, but it's over. You need to find someone who can give you the attention you need. However, I'm not that gentleman."

Red angry blotches stained Colette's cheeks. "Well, I never!" She clamped her mouth shut and stomped off across the room.

Adam purposely waited until after the supper before speaking with Captain Lee, giving Jewel plenty of time to reach home.

Captain Lee found Adam first. "I'll be glad to take Jewel home with me tonight. Where is she?"

"She doesn't believe you're her uncle." Adam's voice brimmed with contempt. "She'll not be leaving with you tonight."

"Your Grace, I presume you are familiar with the law." Lee returned Adam's stare; then Lee's lips curled back in a snarl. "I can prove she is my niece, and you can't stop her from going with me."

"When you can prove the fact, we'll talk. Good night, Captain," Adam stated flatly, then left.

"It appears I'll be paying the lofty duke a visit on Christmas Day," Lee remarked to himself.

Adam couldn't wait to leave the party. His conversation with Captain Lee weighed heavily on his mind. Unfortunately, Lee had been correct. If he could prove Jewel was his niece, Adam would have no rights to her.

The coach's lamplights flickered as the carriage bumped along through the night. The strength of the wind buffeted the coach from time to time. Jewel clung to the straps to keep from being tossed to the floor. Peeking out the window, she tried to see anything that might tell her how close they were to Briercliff. For a moment, she had a good mind to tell the driver to stop so she could get out, but then what? Out here in the middle of nowhere, she had no place to go. Besides, somehow she had to be aboard Adam's ship when it left. If what Colette said was true, Adam might be planning on staying here. But one way or the other Jewel would get aboard that ship.

The storm clouds had covered the moon, allowing little light to shine. The poor driver up on the box was having to fight the wind, but Jewel felt confident in his ability to get her home safely; after all, he was employed by Adam.

Jewel had drunk too much tonight. That was what had made her blurt out those sentiments to Colette and then to Adam. Her face felt hot just remembering. How had she allowed herself to care about him when he was nothing but a womanizing scoundrel?

Her head felt woozy. Other than that she was numb, and right now that was a good feeling.

What was she going to do after tonight? Her head hurt

thinking about it, so she took the coward's way out and put it from her mind until later.

It was probably just her mood, but the carriage ride seemed eternal. They hit a bump, and she felt her stomach churn again. Much more of this and she would be sick. The buggy swayed to the left; then she felt the sharp turn into the driveway of Briercliff. Finally, they were home.

"We're here, miss." The driver opened the door, and Jewel tumbled out thankful she hadn't embarrassed herself. A gust of wind caught in her dress, knocking her off balance, but easing her queasiness. The driver steadied her, and chose to walk with her the rest of the way.

"It looks like we're in for a *flaw*," he commented.

"What's a *flaw?*" Jewel questioned.

"Oh, it's much worse than a storm, my lady. Some can be quite furious. That's what we call a violent storm in these parts," he explained. "But don't worry, miss, you'll be quite safe at Briercliff. I've never seen as much as a shingle damaged round here."

"Good night and thank you," she said with a grateful smile for his help. Giles opened the door.

"Is His Grace with you, my lady?"

"No, Giles." Jewel handed him her cloak. "You can probably go to bed. I believe His Grace had other plans for tonight."

When Giles left her, Jewel was thankful to be alone. The clicking of her heels on the slate floor was the only thing that broke the silence. She dearly loved Annie, but she really didn't want to see anyone tonight.

Jewel closed the door to her room and leaned against it. A fire burned in the hearth, giving off warmth and a soft glow. A lady's maid helped her unlatch the hooks on her dress; then Jewel removed her clothing and carefully hung up the gown. She dismissed the maid and slipped into a white silk nightdress, tying the tiny pink ribbons on the shoulders and letting the streamers hang loosely down her arms. She caught sight of herself in the glass and her mouth twisted. She'd thought the gown with its pink and white baby roses at the neckline so exquisitely delicate when she'd first seen it, so feminine. Yet now it mocked her. What kind of a nightgown was Colette wearing to entice Adam?

Moving to her dressing table, she jerked the pins from her hair. Couldn't that man see what kind of woman Colette was? Jewel fumed as she picked up the ivory brush and jerked it through her hair, tossing the ebony mane over her shoulder to hang loose.

When she was finished, she moved to the door that connected her room with Adam's. She saw what she needed and headed straight for his liquor cabinet to pour herself a liberal portion of brandy. Tonight she didn't intend to feel anything.

Looking at the masculine bed, she wondered if he would even bother to come home. She held the glass up in mock salute. "Merry Christmas, Adam." A single tear rolled down her cheek, and quickly she wiped it away. Damned if she would cry over him when he wanted another.

Back in her room, she flung open the French doors. Cool wind smoothed the alcohol flush from her skin. Partially shielded from the full force of the winds, she stood on the balcony watching for anything and seeing nothing. The restless power of the coming storm seemed to ease the tension she felt. This would be a bad storm if the winds were any indication. The few trees she could see were being blown backwards by the force of the wind. The cold and biting gusts chafed her skin, but Jewel was indifferent as she stood lost in her misery.

Was he holding that woman, kissing her with the same lips that had touched hers? She hoped the storm would blow them both away. What hurt the most were Colette's stinging words coming back to her. "We will just see who Adam spends the night with." Evidently, Colette had won.

Jewel's eyes burned with unshed tears. Tipping the glass,

she gulped down another swig of brandy. Funny, it didn't even burn anymore. "This really is god-awful stuff."

Adam had looked so handsome tonight. His bronze skin accented by the snow-white shirt would set any woman's heart aflutter. And the darkness in his eyes had hidden a message she could not read. He was everything a woman could want, but Colette had made it clear Adam had been with her in London. Jewel felt stupid having thought otherwise. So, just where did *she* fit in?

Her jumbled thoughts were dulled by the brandy as she tried to remember once again what Adam had said earlier. Hadn't he told her that Colette meant nothing to him? Hadn't he been attentive to her tonight instead of Colette? And his Christmas present had left her breathless. Jewel reached up to touch the choker. She rubbed her fingers across it, feeling each opal burn into her skin. It was the one thing she hadn't taken off tonight. At least his present was a part of Adam she could keep for herself. Each little opal would remind her of his furious personality. He possessed a virile strength that couldn't be captured. He was a lot like this storm.

"Damn man," Jewel swore again for the dozenth time. Why did she keep thinking about him?

He was probably arranging for that Captain Lee to take her away, but she had a surprise for him. She would be leaving, but on her own terms.

Jewel was sure she'd seen Lee before. A flash of lightning streaked across the sky, and for a moment her back ached as if it had been struck. Draining the remaining brandy, Jewel felt the warmth in the pit of her stomach. A light drizzle began to fall. Soon the clouds would let loose the raindrops they had been holding all day.

She should go in, but she couldn't pry her fingers away from the railing as the drizzle mixed with her tears.

"Where are you Adam?" she said into the cold, wet night.

Seventeen

Adam's breath caught in his throat. Through the double doors of the bedroom, he glimpsed how the wind molded Jewel's thin white gown to her body, accenting every lush little curve. She appeared as an alluring apparition cloaked beneath a mane of long black hair that whipped about her face. Letting his breath out slowly, he tossed his greatcoat onto the chair beside the door. His jaw tightened, but his desire flamed. The little fool stood in the cold wind, staring out into the darkness.

In no time, he'd crossed the room. "This is a damn good way to catch your death!" he snapped, grabbing her by the arm. "I don't want you sick and near death like the first time I laid eyes on you."

Stunned at first, she didn't speak. Was he *really* here, or had she just conjured him up by merely thinking of him? It must be the damn rum—no brandy—she thought, her brain as murky as the darkness surrounding them. His fingers tightened when she didn't speak. Now she knew Adam was really here . . . in front of her . . . holding her . . . confusing her with his closeness.

"Did you hear me? Are you trying to cause your early demise?" Adam's eyes were as stormy as the night, and still she had no idea how he truly felt.

"Would you care?" She jerked her arm from his hand, stumbling backwards. "I—I think I've definitely had too much to drink."

Adam steadied her. A bolt of lightning flashed overhead. He placed his hands on her face and tilted it up until he could look into her eyes. Those rose-red lips were definitely made for kissing. His gaze caressed her pink cheeks as her eyes spat fire at him. Such a temptress!

Suddenly another bolt of lightning streaked across the sky, and Adam drank in Jewel's beauty. Thunder rumbled all around them, but neither of them moved. Adam didn't bat an eye because a more urgent storm brewed within him.

"You've been in my brandy again."

"And what if I have?" Her eyes had grown as black as his, a smoldering fire burning deep in their depths. "I'd have saved you some, but I expected Colette to warm you tonight."

He chuckled. "You're jealous."

"I am not!" she insisted, turning her head away.

But he knew better. Purposefully he reached to turn her around. An exasperated sigh left his lips. "I'm only going to say this one more time. The lady means nothing to me. Do you hear me, Jewel?" Finally, she nodded, and he could see tears glistening on her eyelashes before one escaped down her cheek. He reached up to wipe away the glistening drop. He saw the hurt in her eyes. The knowledge stirred him more than he cared to admit.

He slipped his arms with infinite care around her, then brushed her face with his lips. "Are those tears for me?" he whispered, placing a light kiss on her brow, the tip of her nose, and finally her moistened lips, where the taste of brandy still lingered. "I want you, Jewel. I have tried to stay away from you . . . God knows I've tried, but I can't."

Adam felt her tremble. He tightened his grip, pulling her body close to his chest. She melted against him, her thigh resting against his manhood. Sensual chills ran up his back.

Jewel's heart beat wildly within her breast. Dazed with pleasure, she kept hearing his words. He wanted her. Pleasure and anticipation coursed through her, yet a part of her still hesitated. What exactly did he want? Did he want to marry her? Did he want to stay with her for always? Her mind whirled giddily. She told herself to be careful, but her body seemed to know what it wanted. She clung to him. She grew hot—no, cold—no, both. And then time stood still.

His hot, wet mouth caressed her earlobes, then pressed tender kisses down her neck. She shuddered beneath his subtle seduction. His lips produced a warm, tantalizing blush that covered her body with fever and produced the most unusual yearning for something more. Should she stop him? Did she want to? Her heart yearned for his touch. She wanted to be held and protected in Adam's arms. Hadn't she always wanted this?

"I need you, Jewel. Don't send me away tonight." Adam's raspy voice choked with emotion as he buried his face in her hair and held her tight against him. Almost as if he were afraid of losing her.

Jewel pulled back and looked into his passion-filled eyes. If only she could read his thoughts. If only she knew how he felt about her. But he *did* want her. Burning desire made her weak. She didn't trust her voice as she nodded her head in response to his request.

"Are you sure?" Adam asked. Again she nodded her head, though she really wasn't sure at all. But she knew Adam would never hurt her.

Casting caution to the wind, Adam crushed Jewel hard against his body, cursing himself for wanting her with his very soul. He lifted her up into his arms and started across the room. He didn't stop at her bed, but headed straight for the master bedroom. This night might be the only night they'd have—one night that would have to last a lifetime.

She stood beside his bed with a vague uncertainty in her eyes of what she should do next.

But he knew.

He reached out and untied the pink ribbons that fastened her gown at the shoulders, then watched as it slid to the floor, leaving her body exposed to his view. She gasped and tried to cover herself, but he caught her arms and whispered, "Don't."

He rubbed his hands down her arms. "Your skin's so smooth, sweetheart," he murmured as his gaze took a slow journey over every inch of her frame while he drank in her beauty, a sensual smile coming to his lips.

Shyly, Jewel started unbuttoning his shirt, surrendering to the stormy splendor of his wonderful kisses. "I believe you once said I was a goddess." She tugged at the last button before pulling open his shirt and pushing it from his shoulders. Her palms glided over his bronzed skin. She caught the faint smell of musk, and couldn't resist brushing her lips across his chest. His every muscle tightened, and he shuddered.

Adam growled passionately. "Yes, I did. A goddess from the sea."

Outside, the full fury of the squall raged—just like the storm that had brought Jewel to him. But tonight the violent winds were mild compared to the inferno that brewed within his body.

Somewhere a shutter thumped against a wall. The rain lashed Briercliff. And the roar of the angry waves drifted through the open doors, and became music to them as it pounded the coast, releasing all its pent-up energy.

A flash of lightning illuminated the glistening bodies of the two lovers as they came to know each other. They sank down in bed. Caressing, touching, sharing themselves as they never had with anyone else. Jewel and Adam were caught in their own whirlwind, seeking a release that only they could provide.

Tonight, Jewel belonged to him, and after this night she'd never remember another. His kisses grew bolder. Her lavender fragrance engulfed him—a scent he'd come to know well.

Adam stared down into her infatuated eyes as he tenderly brushed a strand of dark hair from her cheek. He wanted to memorize her high cheekbones, her cute nose, and most of all her parted, moist lips. He might be leaving soon, but a part of her would be his tonight.

The same thought ran through Jewel's mind. Tonight she would become one with Adam, hoping he wouldn't soon forget her. She spoke with her eyes, wanting him to understand the unspoken words she'd never get to say.

She slipped her hands around his neck, drowning in this new world of sensuality. Her breasts were crushed against Adam's chest. His dark, curling hairs rubbed the tips of her nipples into firm, taut peaks. Reaching over, she laced her fingers through Adam's dark hair and pulled his lips to within her reach. She gazed deep into Adam's mesmerizing eyes, finding a burning passion that she was going to quench.

The storm whipped at the drapes. Another bolt of lightning streaked across the sky, shedding its light on their flushed bodies.

"I've never desired someone as much as I do you." Adam's admission sounded more like a growl just before he captured her lips. This time his kiss was different . . . hungry . . . urgent. His tongue plunged into her mouth, mating with her tongue. Soon their kisses matched the fury of the storm, becoming hotter and bolder as the fire between them built to a boiling point.

Adam's hands glided along Jewel's silky thighs before moving back to her ripe breasts. Trailing kisses down her neck, he lowered his head until he found her rose-tipped nipples, where he licked circles around the tight nubs. Her skin held the luster of creamy satin, and it felt smooth against him. He captured one trembling peak in his mouth, teasing it to the hardness of stone. She gasped as his other hand continued its path with agonizing slowness, parting her legs and finding the tempting flesh she offered him. With a little coaxing, she parted her legs, and his fingers slid through the curls down to her moist warmth. God, she was tight. He groaned. He could wait no longer. His hunger consumed his self-control.

He had to have her—Now!

Spreading her legs further apart with his knee, he positioned himself above her and drove deep inside her warmth. Too late he felt the tearing membrane as Jewel stiffened in his arms and cried out in pain.

"Christ! Why didn't you tell me?" Adam groaned out, feeling stupid that he'd rushed. If he'd known, he could have made it so much easier on her. Now he felt the pain as much as she did. He lay very still, even though his body demanded more. He throbbed, wanting to take all of her.

Jewel had been a virgin. All his other doubts vanished. There had never been another man. And he'd kill any man who would dare try and take her from him.

"It hurts, Adam," she cried, bringing him back to the moment at hand. Tears trickled down her face.

"I'm sorry, sweetheart, I didn't think. But trust me, the pain will ease in a moment." He kissed her tears away, giving her time to adjust to his size. Nibbling on her lips, he whispered, "You're mine, sweetheart, now and for always."

Slowly, he started to move, feeling her tightness surrounding his manhood. He shivered. She was driving him crazy with desire. He moved with the rhythm of love, building, driving, and finally consuming them both with a white heat that demanded satisfaction.

Jewel cried out with fulfillment. Slowly, she floated back down to earth on a cloud of contentment. There had been too much brandy, and too many new emotions for her tonight. Drained, she felt sleep beckon to her. Wrapped in the warmth of Adam's arms, she felt a sense of peace and safety claimed her. "I love you, Adam," she murmured just before sleep claimed her. But sleep had already claimed Adam, and he didn't appear to have heard her softly spoken words.

* * *

The hinges rattled on the bedroom door. "Who the hell is doing that infernal pounding?" Adam growled, jerking awake from sleep. He felt Jewel snuggled next to him in the dark, and pulled the cover up over her.

The insistent knocking again brought his attention back to the intruder. Sitting up, he bellowed, "Who the bloody hell is it?" Jewel stirred beside him.

"Surely, you wouldn't shoot me on sight, ol' boy," Jonathan said, coming in with a candle. "I know it's early, but before you go barking at me, I have to talk to you about Jewel." He walked up to the corner of the bed.

Adam was sitting up, shielding Jewel with his body as he lit a candle by the bed. She was hidden well and Jonathan hadn't seen her. He started to pace back and forth.

"This better be damn good, Jonathan. What time is it?"

"Five in the morning, and I had one hell of a time getting here with this storm, but what I heard couldn't wait."

Adam glanced out the window, observing the rain pelting the windows. He also noticed Jonathan was still dressed in his evening attire.

"I overheard Captain Lee tell Colette he was planning to pay you a special visit today. It seems his ship is anchored at Land's End, and it would be most convenient to whisk Jewel away."

Jonathan had Adam's interest now. "Are you sure?"

Annie chose the moment to stick her head through the open door. "What's goin' on in here? I be hearin' such a ruckus that I hurried up the stairs and canna find Jewel anywhere. Have ye be seein' her?"

"Damn," Adam swore, rubbing his chin. Hell, why didn't they just invite the whole bloody household into his bedroom?

Jewel lay perfectly still, afraid of detection.

"I'm too late," Jonathan said. "Damn! I knew I should have gotten here earlier." He threw his hands up. "Now what are we going to do?"

The commotion in front of Adam was becoming quite comical. "Silence!" he roared, realizing he wasn't going to get rid of either of them. "If both of you will just calm down a minute, I happen to know Jewel's whereabouts." Adam moved aside so they could see her hiding behind him.

Annie gasped, and her eyes grew as round as saucers before she turned to give Adam a disapproving look.

Jonathan laughed. "Sorry, ol' boy. Didn't know. Good morning, Jewel."

Adam turned to Jewel. Her face was absolutely scarlet as she clutched the blanket up under her chin. She didn't bother answering Jonathan. She merely nodded.

"The fact still remains, Adam, we need to get her away from here. And fast," Jonathan reminded him.

Adam's mind had already been working on that particular problem. "Annie, pack Jewel's things and prepare a hot bath. We'll go to the *Wind Jammer*. Jewel will sail with me."

"Are ye goin' tae marry the lass?" Annie asked.

"No, there isn't time." Adam frowned.

"Well, 'tisn't proper for a youn', unchaperoned lady tae be a travelin' with ye alone . . . just not right." Annie shook her head.

"Jesus, Annie, the damage has been done!" Adam didn't want to argue the point. He wasn't too sure of anything, only that danger was lurking near.

Jewel moaned after that statement, pulling the covers over her head. How embarrassing!

"I'll marry her," Jonathan suddenly said.

"The hell you will!" Adam's powerful voice rang out, silencing everyone.

Jewel cleared her throat and managed to find her voice, sliding the blanket down to her chin. "I'm sorry to be putting you both out." She looked at the men accusingly. "But I wouldn't marry either of you if you were the last men on earth!"

Adam looked over his shoulder at Jewel, then back at the

other two. This conversation was fast heading in the wrong direction. He sought to end it. "Annie, pack your bags, you're coming with us. Now, does that satisfy everyone?"

All three nodded their heads.

"Good! Now that we've wasted precious time, I suggest everyone get moving. Jonathan, ride ahead and tell Derek what's happening. At the first break in the storm, we'll set sail."

When they were alone again, Adam turned his attention back to Jewel. Rolling over, he placed his arms on either side of her head. "I'm sorry, sweetheart, for the intrusion." He kissed the tip of her nose. "I've ordered you a hot bath to soak in."

"Why?"

"Because you'll be sore after last night, and the bath will help," he gently explained. "Did you mean what you said?"

She blushed again. "What do you mean?"

"You really wouldn't marry me?"

"Are you proposing?" Jewel's brows lifted.

"No."

A slight smile touched her lips. "Then I guess you'll never know."

Adam looked down into liquid brown eyes, trying to discover his answer, but this time she'd shut him out.

Leaning down, he kissed her. When he finally pulled his mouth from hers he said, "We have some unfinished business to be settled at a later date."

Eighteen

After hurriedly packing her things, they were on their way. The coach moved with haste down the well-trodden road. Jewel pushed back into the red velvet seat, thankful for its warmth on such a stormy day. The murmur of Adam's and Annie's voices became the only sounds she heard while she rubbed the top of Duke's head, which he had propped lazily in her lap. The puppy lay on the seat to her left, and Adam claimed the other side. Jewel smiled down at her pet, glad Adam had agreed to let him come on the trip.

Watching the raindrops run down the coach window, Jewel wondered about their decision to brave the storm instead of waiting until the weather cleared. Though the wind howled outside the carriage, it didn't seem to hinder their progress.

Jewel caught glimpses of the English countryside through the rain. What she had thought of as home these last few months slipped quickly past her, and she wasn't sure exactly how she felt. A part of her was sad, yet she knew she had to find the secret to her past—and she hoped the answers would be forthcoming.

The vehicle swayed, and Jewel reached instinctively out to clutch Adam's arm. He pulled her closer while never missing a word of his conversation with Annie, seemingly unaware of Jewel's presence.

The pressure of his arm around her brought back memories of last night. His warm breath as he whispered her name. The feel of his strong arms as he'd held her tenderly. She had tried to put everything from her mind, but somehow it kept sneaking back into her thoughts. Did last night mean Adam loved her and wanted to marry her? He was taking her with him. Yet he had been given little choice since Lee had interfered. Jewel wondered how Adam felt.

Perhaps she was no more than just another conquest for him. After all, he hadn't said he loved her, nor had he made any promises. One thing she did know, remembering the passion she'd elicited. She definitely had some effect on him, whether good or bad.

By the time they reached the dock, the rain had turned into a cold drizzle. After their luggage was unloaded, Derek took charge of seeing Annie and their bags onto the ship, leaving Adam free to check his charts and make final preparations.

Derek showed Annie to her cabin, putting her trunk just inside the door. Picking up Jewel's bags, he started for Adam's cabin, and ran straight into Annie.

"Ye can be puttin' Jewel's trunks with mine," Annie instructed.

Derek stopped and stared at her. A crooked smile etched across his face. "I don't think that's what Adam had in mind."

Placing both hands on her hips, Annie resembled a lioness guarding her cub. "Trust me, mon. I be raisin' that lad, and deep down he does have a decent streak. I think this will be remindin' him."

Derek shook his head, giving into her wishes. "He ain't going to like this . . . could prove to be a mighty long voyage," he muttered.

"Quit yer grumblin'," Annie retorted, then grinned. "After all, Adam will be havin' ye for a roommate." She walked over and ran a hand over Derek's muscular arm. "A big stron' mon such as yerself can control him, and show him a little reason."

Derek decided he liked this spirited woman, and hoped

he'd get to know her better on this trip. "Annie, dear, you'd best get inside because your cloak is soaked."

"I will. But first I need tae be findin' Jewel."

"Don't worry. I'll go and bring her to you. She's saying good-bye to Jonathan. Now get in there, woman, and change into some dry clothes!"

Tears mixed with rain slipped down Jewel's face. She was drenched, but didn't care. "I'll truly miss you, Jonathan. You've become a good friend." She hugged him in farewell, and wondered if she would ever see him again. He'd made her laugh so many times over the last few months and helped her understand Adam's moods. Still, she wasn't certain she really knew the aloof Adam.

"I'll miss you, too, but you can count on me coming to America, especially now that you'll be there." Jonathan winked at her.

Hugging her for the last time, he said, "Adam cares for you, Jewel. But if he ever mistreats you, let me know." He glanced over his shoulder. "I believe we have an audience. Shall we give Adam something to think about?"

Jewel wasn't sure what Jonathan was talking about, but she didn't get a chance to say anything before he took her in his arms and kissed her. Not just a mere kiss on the cheek, but a kiss on the mouth that was slow and drawn out.

Her eyes widened in surprise. "What was that for?"

"For our audience. A little jealousy never hurt anyone." He grinned wickedly.

"You're a devil, Jonathan Hird!" She tapped him playfully on the arm. "And I'll miss you more than words can say. Please take care." Jewel reached up, placing a quick peck on his cheek, then turned away before she started crying again.

As she walked up the plank, she noticed Adam scowling at her. "Where has Annie gone?" she asked.

"Are you in the habit of kissing every man you meet?" he replied. His eyes held a dangerous gleam.

"He's a friend, Adam. I was just saying good-bye."

"A curtsy would have sufficed, madam," he pointed out before turning his back to her. "See Derek. He'll show you to the cabin." She could tell by Adam's tone that he wasn't pleased. Could he be jealous, as Jonathan had suggested? She felt a little better as she left him in search of Derek.

She tried not to act surprised when she found Annie already in Derek's cabin securing their things. Jewel had thought after last night that she would be in Adam's cabin. Apparently, Adam had other ideas on the subject. He'd gotten what he wanted. She'd been so stupid to think that he loved her.

After Jewel changed into some dry clothes, she and Annie set out to straighten up the small room and stow away their things.

The cabin had two neatly made beds against the walls. Two portholes would provide plenty of daylight and fresh air, and a whale-oil lamp would brighten the nighttime. A table sat at one end of the room with several chairs, and a potbelly stove stood in the corner of the room for warmth on the winter voyage. A washbasin, a looking glass, and cupboards to store their belongings completed the room. As Jewel glanced around, she decided the room was small but efficient, and strangely enough she felt at home.

In no time, they had their new quarters looking feminine. But to prepare for the rough seas ahead, everything that was loose had to be fastened down.

The ship lunged as it pulled away from the dock. Annie stumbled. Jewel reached out to steady her, at the same time thinking the movement of the ship didn't seem to bother her as it did her friend. Once again the feeling she'd been on a ship before became overpowering.

"Annie, we're under way. You'll have to develop sea legs before you're able to walk around the ship."

"And that will be takin' long? Ye don't seem tae be havin' tae hard of a go of it, lass."

"I'm just lucky. But you'll be walking around this ship before long."

Jewel felt giddy and sad all at the same time. She was sad to be leaving Jonathan and Briercliff, but on the other hand, she was excited to see what lay ahead. Most of all, she found she enjoyed being on a ship again.

The wind howled with mad laughter as it whipped at the sails while the men scurried to make sure all the riggings were secure. A gust of wind caught the sails, and a sailor atop the main topyard had to grab for support.

A wave smashed at the hull, picking the ship up and flinging her high upon the crests of the waves. It was a day fit for neither man nor beast.

Yet Adam stood at the helm, completely in charge. The drizzle pelted his face and the wind whipped at his coat and once again the blood raced through his veins, bringing the excitement that sailing always provided him. The *Wind Jammer* was a sturdy ship. He had no doubt she could handle any storm she ran into.

The damnable wind was his main problem, he thought as he kept a watchful eye. The wrong movement, and the ship would be swept into Cornwall's rocky shore. This wasn't exactly how he'd planned to spend Christmas Day.

Hours dragged by as the wind beat cruelly at the canvas sails, and it was quite late when Adam turned the ship over to one of his helmsman. Normally, he would have turned it over to Derek, but he'd sent him to the cabin earlier.

Adam stood on the deck, stretching his tired muscles before going below. It had been a long day, and he felt bone-weary. He wondered if Jewel had fallen asleep while she waited for him. Perhaps the storm had frightened her. But as soon as he pulled her in his arms, she would forget her fears. At least on this trip, it would feel good having her lying beside him.

That thought kept Adam's feet moving as he descended the stairs to the cabin. He opened the door. The soft glow of an oil lamp lit up the room as he entered and shut the door behind him. When he turned back around, the first thing that met his eyes was a hammock strung across the room. Derek's loud snoring indicated he enjoyed his sleep, but what the hell was he doing in here? He should be in *his* cabin. And where was Jewel?

Giving him a none-too-gentle shove, Adam gruffly asked, "Would you like to tell me what's going on here?"

"Aye, Cap'n." Derek blinked, trying to wake up. "It's about time you came to bed, son."

"So it is." Adam nodded. "But I didn't expect to find *you* as my bed partner. I had a more shapely form in mind."

Derek chuckled. "I know. I told Annie you wouldn't take to this, but she said you, being a decent man, would see she'd done the right thing."

"No doubt. I can hear her exact words, 'It just ain't proper.' And to think it was my idea to bring the woman along."

"She's a mighty strong-willed woman." Derek threw his head back and roared with laughter. "She just might be right for me."

"Good!" Adam crossed the room to the bed. "How about winning her over so I can have Jewel?"

"Cheer up. Maybe we'll have a fast crossing. Until then, I can always lend you a pillow to hold."

"You old codger." Adam threw a feather pillow at Derek. "I should make you sleep elsewhere, because I'm sure I'll hear about this the whole trip." Adam turned back to the door. "I'm going to check on Jewel. Be back in a moment."

Adam knocked on the door. After several minutes, it opened slowly and Jewel stood before him dressed in her robe. "Are you both all right?" he asked.

"I'm fine. But the sea is so rough that Annie is suffering from a bout of seasickness. I hope she'll recover soon." Jewel stared at him with a quizzical look; then suddenly she reached up and touched the side of his face.

"Are *you* all right? You appear tired."

The mere brush of her hand aroused him, and he cursed himself because of his weakness to this slip of a girl. And every day her hold upon him grew stronger. Maybe that was the real reason he'd brought her with him.

"Yes, I'll be fine with some sleep," Adam said gruffly. "I trust my men, but to be on the safe side, latch the door when I leave." Adam gazed at her a moment longer as he drank in her beauty. "Good night, and Merry Christmas, luv."

"Merry Christmas, Adam." Jewel gazed after him. Why, he hadn't even kissed her. Had last night even happened? She told herself his aloofness was because he was tired, but the thought was cold comfort. With a sigh, she did as he'd instructed and locked the door behind him.

Annie's touch of sickness lingered into the night. She alternated between holding her head over a bucket and dozing off. Jewel was glad to be able to take care of Annie and repay some of the kindness the older woman had shown her. Sometime in the wee hours of the morning, Annie's discomfort finally eased and she slept soundly.

Jewel rubbed her aching back. The bed felt good as she eased her weary bones down onto the soft mattress.

The familiar creaking of the ship, the howling winds, and the roaring of the waves transported Jewel into a deep sleep. With deep slumber came recognition of her past. She remembered tropical islands and her carefree days on Grand Terre with her uncles Pierre and Jean Lafitte. She also remembered Captain Lee and the battle fought on her ship. . . .

Black, murky smoke filled the air, mixing with the fading sunlight and casting an eerie orange glow over the battle scene. All were dead . . . dead and gone because she'd been foolish. Jewel's stomach tightened at the sight of the lifeless bodies going down with the ship, and she fought the bile rising in her throat. Nothing had turned out the way she'd planned. She'd miss her bodyguard, Ben, her gentle giant. Hot tears slid softly down her cheeks . . . now what? But she shook her head back and forth against the pillow, knowing somehow that she didn't want to see what would happen next.

She squirmed at her confinements. The small leather bindings wrapped tightly around each wrist bit painfully into her skin and firmly held her secured to the main cross beam. The ominous crack of the whip snapped Jewel's head up.

"You have one more chance to tell me what I want to know," Lee offered.

"I hope you rot in Hell!"

"Have it your way." Lee shrugged. Again he slapped the cat-o'-nine-tails nervously against his boot. "The lash has a nasty way of making one talk."

The straps whistled through the air as Lee brought them down on her back, producing a raw heat that surged through her. She pulled violently against her restraints. "I've hit you very lightly this time, but it's just the beginning. I intend to make each little cut a torture until you tell me what I want to know."

Jewel gasped. She choked back the screams that hovered on her lips. He knew about the map! But how had the captain found out?

Pain . . . so red . . . so hot . . . so burning, slowly sucked the very life from her body. The leather thongs sliced her skin. Again she jerked forward, trying to escape the agony.

Time after time the lash came down on her back. Think of home, think of anything, she silently screamed, but it didn't work. Her whole body wanted to wail out at the abuse she was receiving. There was no escaping the tor-

ture. She couldn't catch her breath before Lee once again laid the whip exactly where he wanted it. She felt a trickle of blood seep from the long gashes in her back, but she wouldn't give the captain the satisfaction of crying out. And he was right—she wouldn't forget Captain Lee.

Her head hung low. With the agony of excruciating pain . . . death would be welcome. She smelled her sweat and tasted the tears that ran freely down her cheeks. When had she begun to cry?

Please God, help me!

The sharp crack of the whip sounded again, and Jewel's head dropped forward, giving the appearance she'd passed out.

Finally, she heard Bud, the first mate, murmur softly to the captain so the rest of the crew couldn't hear. "Cap'n, if you kill her, you'll never find the treasure."

Lee raised his arm, hesitated, then lowered the whip. "Cut her down!" the captain bellowed. Again he mopped the blood from his chin. "Damn bitch, I should have killed her!"

And then there were bloody bodies. Once again, Jewel saw the picture of her crew lying dead at her feet. She clutched her throat. She couldn't breathe. Everything was drenched in blood red. The vivid scene produced a strangling terror within her.

She had to escape before the captain came back. She'd never taken a crew out to sea before, and she wouldn't have disobeyed her uncles if she hadn't thought they'd needed her help. Caught in a panic, she bolted straight up in bed.

Everything was dark. Where was she? Glancing around the room, Jewel didn't remember this bed. It took several minutes before reality returned and she realized she was aboard Adam's ship. She was safe. Or was she?

With shaky fingers, she touched her forehead and found

it damp with perspiration. Her rapid breathing had finally slowed and was returning to normal. What a nightmare! Now she had what she sought . . . her memory. She knew why Captain Lee had fabricated such a story, and she would be careful of him in the future. Provided she ever saw him again.

She could explain to Adam she wasn't related to the man . . . no, wait . . . she couldn't tell Adam anything! Her memory hadn't solved her predicament. It only presented other unsolvable problems.

Jewel bit her lip, uncertainty setting in. She didn't want to destroy the fragile relationship they had just built. She couldn't handle the look of revulsion on his face if he found out her relatives were pirates. Of course, Jean and Pierre were not like most pirates, but Adam wouldn't know that. If she only knew that he loved her, maybe then he could accept her past. But if he didn't . . . he was also very capable of turning her over to the authorities for attacking a British ship.

Exhausted from thinking, and finding no answers, Jewel slumped back down on the mattress. She wouldn't let Adam know she'd regained her memory. She would just handle one day at a time. But she would have to get word to Jean she was safe. He must be worried.

Jean was worried.

He refused to believe Jewel was dead. Somehow he would feel it if she were, but his heart told him differently, he thought as he stared out at the sea. Jean and Ben had set out searching for some small clue—anything to explain Jewel's disappearance, only to find nothing, not a scrap, not a hint of her fate. In their frustration, they had pilfered every ship that crossed their path, bringing home a shipload of goods to put in their already overflowing warehouses.

He'd become a superb smuggler with his band of cutthroats and sea ruffians armed with cutlasses, guns, and cannons, whom he nicely called privateers. He had also cleverly organized the fishermen into groups of smugglers to carry the plunder up to New Orleans, where the goods would command a high price.

Lafitte had acquired holdings in New Orleans. One of his purchases had been a blacksmith shop on Bourbon Street and a goods store on Rue Royale. The establishments, even though regular trade went on, were fronts for his smuggled goods and a place to buy slaves.

Jean's love for excitement usually kept him in trouble. Being a ladies' man, he frequently attended parties when in New Orleans. But all that had ceased when Jewel had disappeared. His niece had meant the world to him, and he wouldn't stop searching until he found her.

And he would find her!

The next morning Annie had improved.

"Would you like a little breakfast?" Jewel asked.

"Seein' as I might live tae see another day, I believe I could eat a wee bite." She sat up on the side of the bed, still looking very peaked. "Praise the Lord, the queasiness be gone."

They quickly dressed and then went in search of food. As they approached the galley, the smell of ham and coffee filled the air with heavenly aromas. The sound of sputtering and hissing prickled their ears. Adam stood as the ladies entered, motioning for them to sit with him.

"Are you feeling well this morning, Annie?"

"I do feel better, but still have a wee bit of trouble walkin' on this rollin' tub," she confessed.

Adam laughed. "It's a ship, Annie, not a tub. Trust me, you'll get used to it." He turned his attention to Jewel. "Are you having any trouble?"

Jewel shook her head. "I'm quite comfortable, thank you. You have a fine ship."

Adam liked her praise, but wasn't sure about her cheerfulness this morning. Especially after he'd spent a miserable night tossing and turning, trying to get her off his mind. For a man used to controlling his own thoughts, he seemed smitten by this little lady, and he damned sure didn't like it.

He'd somehow forgotten along the way that he was trying to discover her past. He'd also not given a second thought to taking her to his American home. What would he do with her when they arrived? Make her his mistress? He'd thought that, after the night when they'd made love, she would be easier to put from his mind. That was what he'd planned to do. Leave her behind.

But he *hadn't* left her behind. He was behaving no better than an animal when she was near him. Just the touch of her made him perspire.

Damn woman.

After breakfast, Jewel and Annie walked around, investigating the ship. Adam had told them they had free access to the ship, but not to interfere with the men's duties. He assured the ladies his men wouldn't bother them.

Jewel and Annie stood at the rail, looking out onto a now-calm sea.

" 'Tis beautiful." Annie's eyes shone as she watched the sea.

The Atlantic spread to the horizon like a sheet of tempered steel. Occasionally a flash of silver could be seen. But the easterly winds bit into Jewel's thin dress, and they realized they hadn't prepared properly to stay on deck for long. Jewel was glad now she had slipped her breeches into her luggage. They would definitely be more practical than these flimsy dresses, and warmer, too. Annie went below to their cabin.

Jewel stayed a few more minutes before she decided to go in, too. When she started below, she spotted a young cabin boy coming out of Adam's room. Not watching where he was going, he ran head on into Jewel, knocking them both down.

"Excuse me, my lady." The young boy blushed as he helped her to her feet. "Please, don't tell Captain Trent."

Jewel spoke softly, smiling at the young lad. "You're in such a hurry; maybe you should slow down just a mite. What's your name?"

"Andrew, my lady. But my friends call me Andy, and I can't slow down. I've got to show the captain I'm worth keeping on board ship." He sighed and sounded a little discouraged and completely out of breath.

"Sometimes haste makes twice the work." She stared down at the youthful face, feeling very motherly. "My name is Jewel. I hope we'll become friends, Andrew."

"It's a pleasure to meet you, my lady."

"Jewel," she corrected. "Aren't you a little young to be sailing?"

"No!" Andrew looked offended. I'm twelve years old, and will be thirteen pretty soon."

"Don't you have any family?"

"No, I've no one." A sad look entered his brown eyes. "Derek . . . well, he kinda took me in and said he'd teach me to sail."

"We have much in common. I don't have a mother or father either. Perhaps we should be friends." She winked, giving him a reassuring smile.

"Thank you, Miz Jewel, but please don't tell Captain Trent I knocked you down. I heard him talking to Derek about me. Captain said I was too young and had no business on a ship. I'm trying to stay out of his way and do everything just right. I'll show him I'm no baby!"

"I can see you're very grown up, and I'm sure you'll make a fine sailor." Jewel refrained from patting him on the head. He looked so young, but she knew he wouldn't like her to remind him of the fact. "I promise not to tell Adam, and you shouldn't be afraid of him. He's a fair man." Yet she wondered how true her statement was. How was the Duke of St. Ives going to treat her now that he'd had her?

"Call me Andy." He smiled, a look of adoration flashing in his eyes. "I like you, Miz Jewel; you're a real nice lady. Are you related to Captain Trent?"

"No," she answered slowly. "We're just friends. Andy," she said. "Would you like to help me take care of my puppy?"

"You have a puppy on board?" His eyes widened with excitement.

Jewel giggled. "Yes, but I had to promise Captain Trent I'd watch him carefully. Do you think you can help me?"

"Yes, my lady."

"Good."

She looked at Andy for a moment, then thought of a wonderful idea. "We're about the same size. Do you have an extra winter coat I can borrow?"

"Sure. Come with me, Miz Jewel." Taking her hand, he led her to his room. "I'm sure glad you're sailing with us."

Nineteen

Days aboard the *Wind Jammer* passed quickly.

The crew scurried about tying off ropes and mending riggings, oiling guns and cleaning decks. Of course, Jewel and Annie were not expected to do any cleaning, but they couldn't stand sitting idle, so they helped wherever needed.

And so everyone settled into a routine. Everyone except Adam, who seemed to grow more distant with each passing day.

One morning, having grown bored of the cabin, Jewel dressed in a pair of old breeches and Andy's coat, thinking this would be a good day to venture up on deck. The cold sea breeze ruffled her hair, making her feel carefree and much like her old self. Memories of Barataria Bay flooded her memory, and she could see herself aboard the ships anchored in the bay as she laughed and talked with Jean's men. Jean and Pierre had given in to her tomboy ways during those days, but were adamant about her dressing for dinner. They always cautioned her that she must never forget her femininity because she would need it to catch a husband one day.

Jewel reached down and pulled up her socks, thinking this was more like it . . . freedom to move about without the wind wrapping a dress around her legs. Adam had barely noticed her, or what she wore, so she didn't think he'd be a problem.

The crew, having seen her often by now, smiled their greetings. Some took a second look at her strange attire, but were polite and didn't comment. Thank goodness.

"If you're looking for Duke, he's lying over in that coil of rope—sound asleep . . . as always." Charlie laughed, pointing Jewel in the right direction. She saw a black nose resting on top of the coil.

"Thank you." Jewel nodded to the helmsman, Charlie Welfonder. Earlier they had talked and she'd learned he came from Hamburg. He was a quiet man, not boisterous like the rest of the crew.

"Who's at the helm?" Jewel asked.

"The captain himself, miss."

"Really?" Jewel decided to see for herself by paying the captain a visit. It irritated her how easily Adam could push her aside.

When she drew near, she could clearly see Adam standing beside the big wheel as he studied a map, his feet planted firmly on the deck and his arm propped on a wooden table. It gave her time to watch him. He was an enigma to her, always keeping her off guard, and she wondered if he ever thought of her. She remembered the magic of his hands when he had held her. She loved the fiery way his insistent kisses could make her head spin. At Briercliff, he had been different, but since coming aboard Adam had changed.

Perhaps he didn't think of her at all. Lately, he'd been like a cold stranger, avoiding her, and she wondered if he regretted bringing her with him.

Adam handled the ship as if she were a thoroughbred horse, responding to his slightest touch. He turned to say something to Derek, presenting his finely chiseled profile to her. He made a commanding figure, and she found herself wanting his attention, wanting to feel his strong arms around her again.

Enough of that kind of thinking, Jewel chided herself.

As she moved forward, his head came up and his gaze

traveled over her entire length, taking in every detail of her appearance.

"Hello, Adam. It's a beautiful day."

"It is," he acknowledged. "Why are you dressed in those clothes? We've had this discussion before." Adam eyed her coolly. "I have a ship full of men who haven't been with a woman in two weeks, and there you stand, looking extremely fetching in tight-fitting breeches. Do you have no brains, woman?"

So startled by his attack on her, Jewel was speechless. Maybe she had pushed him too far, she mused for one brief moment. She really hadn't thought about the sailors.

"Jewel!" Adam grabbed her arm. "You try my patience! Explain yourself."

"It's cold out here, Adam. You try wearing a skirt and have the biting wind blow up your dress. Can you not see the logic?"

Derek, who had been quiet, laughed. "I can just picture the captain in a skirt."

Adam shot him a murderous look.

"I believe I've some other things that need to be done," Derek said. He picked up several maps, tucked them under his arm, and left.

After Derek had walked off, Adam turned his attention back to her. "Where did you get that jacket? I don't remember purchasing it for you."

Heat ran through Jewel's veins and her body grew rigid. "Does the sight of me bring out this foul mood of yours or are you nasty to everyone?" Jewel exploded. "I asked Andy if I could borrow one of his. He said he didn't mind because he had two. I would have asked you, but I haven't seen much of you lately."

Adam looked out toward the sea as if trying to think of a good reason why he'd been avoiding her. "I've had some things to do, and charts to study."

A variety of different emotions filled her with sudden pain, and she felt empty. "I see," she said. Reality set in as she began to understand that Adam acted this way because he didn't want to be around her at all. Maybe she had misunderstood the way he'd felt Christmas Eve. Perhaps it had all been one-sided. After all, she had fallen willingly into his arms, much to her chagrin. She wished she could dismiss him from her mind as easily as he had her, but she missed his friendship.

Jewel looked up at the main topgallant sail, and saw Andy working on a rigging. "I see you've given Andy some different tasks to do. You know, he doesn't think you like him." She waited, challenging Adam to answer. "Do you?"

"I've nothing against Andrew. I just think he's too young to be at sea."

"You call him Andrew?"

"That is his name—isn't it?"

"Yes." Jewel grinned at the private joke. "Did you know he didn't have a home until Derek found him?"

Adam's brow arched. "No, I didn't."

"That's probably why Derek brought him on board ship, but I think he's young, too."

"I might point out that you're not very old yourself." He cocked a brow at her, and for a moment she glimpsed the old Adam. "Maybe, after we get home, I can find someplace nice for him. Andrew needs an education and some type of family."

They both watched Andy as he walked across the beam of the topgallant sail. He looked down and waved—a foolish mistake. A gust of wind caught him off balance and he plunged headfirst toward the deck. Luckily his foot caught in the riggings.

Hanging upside down, Andy yelled at the top of his lungs, "Help! Somebody help me!"

"Hold her steady!" Adam ordered, turning the wheel over to the crew member beside him. He ran to the mast.

Several sailors gathered around, all mumbling about what should be done.

"Hold on, Andy!" Charlie hollered. "The cap'n will be up after you in a minute."

They paid little attention to Jewel, who knew what had to be done. Adam was too heavy to get to the exact spot where Andy hung helplessly. The lad was much lighter, which was the reason they had sent Andy in the first place.

Having done this many times before, she jerked off her shoes and socks so she could grip the riggings better with her toes. She grabbed a knife beside the wheel. Putting it between her teeth, she ran past everyone else and started to climb the riggings.

"Jewel! Damn it, get down before you break your bloody neck!" Adam had been in the process of taking off his boots, but stopped when Jewel darted past him. He started after her, but Derek laid a hand on his arm, stopping him.

"Look at her, Adam. She climbs like a monkey and seems to know what she's about. Maybe it's wise to let her try. After all, she is much lighter than yourself."

"But if she falls . . ." He faltered. "It'd kill her." Adam teetered between concern and the impulse to wring her neck.

"Trust me, son."

They stood watching as she made her way up the ropes to Andy.

"Where did you learn to climb like that?" Andy asked, the surprise evident in his voice.

"Oh, I had some very good teachers."

"Miz Jewel, you shouldn't have come up here," Andy choked out from his precarious position. His face had turned red and his eyes were tinged with fear.

"Apparently, you're the one who shouldn't be up here, but I can always leave if you'd like," she teased, wrapping her legs in the ropes for support.

"No, please don't leave!" A slight panic touched Andy's voice as his eyes widened in horror.

Laughing, she tried to ease his distress. "Listen to me. Put your hands in the riggings so that when I cut this rope you'll not fall."

Below, Derek said to Adam, "You've got quite a woman. And it's quite apparent she has a good knowledge of ships." Derek kept his voice low so only Adam could hear. "I wonder where she could have learned that."

Adam wondered the same thing. Apparently, she knew quite a bit about ships. He watched her small frame move around the riggings. He had missed her, and that fact really didn't please him when he'd no intention of making her a permanent part of his life—but the truth was he wanted Jewel. She was aggravating, mysterious, stubborn, beautiful, and soft. And seeing her, knowing he couldn't touch her, was eating at his insides. Hadn't Derek complained this morning that he was meaner than a bear? That hadn't improved his disposition at all. The least little thing sent his temper flying.

Without warning the vessel swayed. Adam and the others struggled to keep their balance. Jewel's gasp was the only one he heard.

"Damn!" Adam knew it was his fault for leaving the ship in inexperienced hands. "Derek, take the wheel!" Adam couldn't take his eyes off Jewel while he waited for his friend to seize control of the ship.

Long minutes ticked by before the ship steadied herself.

Then Jewel finished cutting the last shred of rope, and Andy's legs fell. He grabbed the lines and slipped his feet onto the ropes to straighten himself, just as Jewel had instructed.

"Thank you." Andy sighed in relief. "Let's get down."

"You go ahead below while I tie off this loose rope."

When she set foot on the deck again, the men cheered her. All but one. She looked around in surprise, smiling at their enthusiasm, but her smile died when her gaze met Adam's.

Adam hadn't realized he'd been holding his breath until

Jewel stepped onto the deck. Tension coiled tight in his body. The damn woman could have been killed. He hadn't noticed her skills as the others had, for his anger had blocked everything else out. He walked over and gripped her arm. "Come with me."

The bright pink hue of Jewel's cheeks told him that she knew he wasn't pleased. She tossed her head back and tried to jerk free from his hand.

"It will be the last time you ever do anything that imprudent again," he bit out through clenched teeth.

Jewel half-walked and Adam half-dragged her across the deck and down the short hallway to his cabin. He didn't seem conscious of the painful grip he had on her arm, but she was getting ready to tell him in no uncertain terms.

After they reached his quarters, he shoved her inside. She whirled around to face him. Even in the dimness, she could see his cheek vibrate with rage as she stood rubbing the aching arm. Her anger steadily grew.

"You little fool, you could have easily broken your neck!"

"I grow tired of your insults today. I knew exactly what I was doing," she snapped back. "And I'm damn good at it, too. But you probably didn't bother to notice that, either."

Adam took her by the shoulders. "I did notice. And now may I ask, where did you learn so much about ships, Jewel? Am I to think you're withholding something from me?"

Terror struck her. How could she tell him about her horrible encounter with Lee? That she'd attacked an English ship. After all, Adam was British. He'd have her imprisoned.

"Where, Jewel?" He shook her in frustration.

She jerked away from him. "Apparently I've been on a ship before!" she retorted. "I acted on instinct. Other than that, I don't remember. Maybe I could be no better than a pirate," she stormed to gauge his reaction.

"I doubt that. A mistress would be more like it."

A loud crack echoed around the small room as she removed her stinging hand from the side of his arrogant face.

Infuriated with his high-handed attitude, she wondered how she could have ever wanted him. She'd wanted his attention. And she most definitely had it for the moment. Yet she hadn't missed the revulsion on his face at the mention of pirates.

"If you'd let me finish . . ." He rubbed his cheek. "I know firsthand you were not a mistress. More likely your father is in the shipping industry. From now on you'll take no more chances. Do you hear me, Jewel? No more. I'll not have it!"

"How can I not hear you the way you're shouting! Half the damn ship can probably hear you! You don't own me, Adam. I'll do as I damn well please!"

Adam pushed her back against the wall and placed his hands on either side of her. For just a brief moment she thought he might strike her. Yet she knew deep down he'd never really hurt her. The struggle to control his rage vibrated through his body. Never had she seen him so angry, not since that day at the mine.

"Let's get one thing straight. I'm captain of this ship. Do you understand? Captain! I'm master and law on this vessel. Everything here is done by my order. Everything!" His mouth clenched tighter. "If you ever do anything that ridiculous again, I'll have you locked in your room!"

He moved away before he gave in to his urge to shake some sense into her head. He could shut his eyes and see her strangling in the ropes. Just like at the mines, she had given no thought to her own safety. Massaging the back of his neck, he turned and poured himself a drink.

Jewel didn't move. She bit her bottom lip to keep it from trembling. Tired and drained, she didn't want to argue anymore. Besides, Adam refused to listen. While he had his back turned, she slipped quietly out the door.

Hearing the door click, Adam spun around. "Jewel, come here!" he shouted. He set his drink down and started to go after her, but thought better of it, knowing it probably would be better if he calmed down first.

* * *

For the next three days Adam didn't see Jewel at all. His mood grew blacker. Everyone who crossed his path fell subject to his ill temper.

On the third night, Derek had had about all he could take from the moody captain. He watched the young buck sitting on his bunk, looking as if he could explode at any moment.

"Adam, you probably don't want to hear this, but I'm going to have my say. Do you know what your problem is?"

"I don't have a problem," Adam growled.

"The hell you don't! Son, you're in love, and you're very much in love, if you ask me. You've been acting like a stud locked up in one pen with his filly in another. Now, you can go on making all of us miserable, or you can admit the truth and ask Jewel to marry you." Derek figured he would hear all kinds of protests, but Adam just sat on his bunk in a state of shock. Hell, the poor man hadn't even realized he loved the girl, Derek thought with a chuckle.

Adam stared, not really seeing Derek. Jewel made his blood throb through his veins, and he found he couldn't think straight because every time he shut his eyes, he could picture her lovely face. She affected him in ways he hadn't thought possible. Once he learned about her past, he expected his obsession would end, but so far the only thing he knew about her was that she was alone. She seemed helpless, but she wasn't—not when she could climb those damn ropes so well.

"So, son, what are you going to do? When you return to Four Oaks, you just can't keep her. She's not a pet."

Adam knew Derek spoke the truth. How in the hell had he let himself get so involved? Adam wondered. He only wanted to help the girl. Marriage. The strange word tumbled around in his mind. Marriage changed a person. He'd seen it happen many times before.

"You're going to give her up?"

"No!" Adam said, a little louder than he intended. The

girl was his. "If I marry her at least I can get rid of you for a roommate."

"That's my boy. I'll perform the services if you'll marry Annie and myself, too."

"You're joking."

"Nope. I asked her a few days ago."

"Congratulations!" Adam stood and slapped Derek on the back. "Now it's my turn, but first I'll have to get the lady to speak to me. That might prove difficult."

Adam decided to take the watch that night so he could think and let Charlie get some sleep. He knew with his restlessness he probably wouldn't be able to sleep anyway. Pulling a stocking cap down over his head for extra warmth, he jerked his collar up around his neck as he headed for the bow.

The wind could be biting at night. Maybe it was just what he needed.

Jewel tossed and turned, but sleep eluded her. She had been miserable since her fight with Adam. The man was impossible, and damn arrogant, too. Perhaps a walk would help.

She liked this time of night. It was quiet and peaceful. A new moon rode a sky full of stars that twinkled like diamonds as she took a breath of fresh salt air.

Beneath a star-studded sky, she walked the deck boards, unable to name her mood. Spotting Charlie at the helm, Jewel decided to go and talk to him. A wistful sigh escaped her. "Good evening, Charlie."

Adam froze at the sound of Jewel's soft voice. At first he thought he'd imagined it; then a slow, lazy smile touched his lips. So she believed he was Charlie.

"Aye, the moon is full. A lover's moon," Adam said, disguising his voice.

He heard Jewel's feet scrape as she sat down and leaned

against some coiled ropes. "Charlie, have you ever been in love?"

"Aye."

"Is it always so painful?"

Adam detected the sadness in her voice, and he felt a pang, knowing he'd been the cause. She couldn't guess the torture she'd put him through. "Are you in love?" he asked softly.

"Yes. But I'm afraid he doesn't love me," she whispered.

"Come over here." Adam bent down and lashed the wheel so he could have his hands free. Pulling off his cap, he turned to face Jewel. Her eyes shone soft and bright. He reached out, took her hand, and drew her near to him before she had a chance to run because he'd already seen her fleeting frown at being deceived.

Cupping the sides of her face, he tilted her chin upwards while he looked deep into her eyes.

Jewel's eyes widened, and he hadn't mistaken the panic as she realized it wasn't Charlie she had confessed her love to. "Of all the contemptible tricks!" She started to jerk away, but he held her fast.

"Jewel, I care for you a great deal." He placed a light kiss on her forehead. "When I scolded you like I did before, it was because I was frightened. I'm not used to feeling that way. I was afraid something would happen to you, and that I could not bear. I want to marry you." He lowered his mouth to hers and kissed her tenderly.

"Are you sure?" Jewel's voice shook with emotion as tears trickled down her face.

Wrapping her in his strong arms, he laid his cheek on top of her hair. "It has taken me a long time to realize the truth, but yes, I'm sure. Will you marry me, Jewel?"

"Adam, you don't know anything about me. What if something in my past turns up that is bad? Are you sure you'll still want me?" Jewel murmured into his chest, afraid of all her secrets.

"Sweetheart, we'll deal with that when the time comes. Your past can't be all that bad. I want to marry you, Jewel. I want to keep you in my arms. I want to make love to you, and I don't want to wait one minute longer . . . but it seems I'm forced to." He kissed the top of her head.

"Sweetheart," he told her, "tomorrow will be your wedding day."

Twenty

Sunshine streamed in through the porthole, bathing the room in shimmering light and waking Jewel from a blissful sleep. Had last night been real or had she dreamed it?

She touched her lips and found them still tender, proof that last night hadn't been a dream. She trembled with excitement. She couldn't wait to tell Annie.

Slipping from her bunk, Jewel moved over to Annie's bed and shook her. "Wake up I've got something to tell you."

Annie stretched. "I feel every ounce of my fifty-plus years this morning. Yer up bright and early, lass." She glanced at Jewel through sleepy eyes. "Why, yer positively glowing this morning. Did Adam ask ye to marry him?"

"You know . . . how did you know?" Jewel asked, puzzled.

"Derek be tellin' me last night. He said the mon had finally come to his senses, and I can see by yer face that ye said yes."

Jewel nodded.

"Well, I guess we'll be havin' a double wedding today." Annie grinned.

"You're getting married, too?" Jewel squealed with delight. After Annie confirmed the news, Jewel hugged her. "That's wonderful! I'm so happy for you. Derek is a fine man."

Jewel stood and nervously moved to the porthole. "Would you think me silly if I told you I was nervous?" She tugged at the bottom of her lip with her teeth. "Everything has happened so fast. Do you suppose I'm doing the right thing?"

"Of course ye are, lass. 'Tis only natural tae be jittery. I must be confessin' I'm a wee bit high-strung, too." Annie slipped out of bed and stretched. "Let's put this nervous energy to work, and be findin' something tae wear."

"Let's look through the trunks," Jewel suggested.

They spent the morning searching for the right garments. Then the remainder of Jewel's things were packed and moved to Adam's cabin. They had not seen the men all morning, but word had been sent that the wedding would take place just before sunset.

Jewel pondered how Adam would dress. She hadn't seen him in anything but sailor's garb since they had been aboard ship. It would be nice if they could have a large, elaborate wedding, but she knew that wasn't possible.

Her stomach tightened at the mere thought of her husband-to-be. She wondered if this feeling was love or seasickness. Adam had said he loved her . . . hadn't he? All day, she had to pinch herself to make sure it wasn't a dream.

As the day wore on, Jewel fought down her panic. She wanted to marry Adam, but she wished she'd been brave enough to tell him her memory had returned. Perhaps in a little while she could, but not yet.

She stood in front of the mirror, pulling on her sea-green dress. She wanted to wear white, but couldn't find anything appropriate. The gown of heavy satin had a simple cut, and would have to do. It had long, fitted sleeves and a high neck trimmed with beige lace. Her cheeks and mouth were the softest pink. The fire-opals around her neck reflected the green of the material, lending a special glow to her complexion. She sat brushing her hair until it flowed loose and silky about her shoulders.

"Are ye ready, lass?" Annie asked. She ran a hand over her cream-colored gown, looking very much like a bride.

Jewel stared at her reflection in the mirror. A slight disappointment crossed her face. "A bride should wear white, not green. I don't look like a bride, do I?"

Annie touched her arm. "Lass, ye are beautiful. Adam would want ye even if ye were in rags."

"As I recall, that's the way he found me."

Both chuckled and drank a toast to their upcoming marriages. One glass led to another, and soon only a small portion of the wine was left in the bottle.

A knock at the door brought them back to reality. Charlie stood at the door when Annie opened it. He blushed as he looked at them, then nodded his greeting.

"Captain said it's time. I came to escort you both topside."

They followed Charlie to the top deck. Jewel smiled when she saw the crew, all of whom had taken special care with their appearance. Clean-shaven with hair slicked back, they glanced at her, then looked quickly away and shifted their feet nervously. They seemed ready to celebrate their captain's marriage.

The sun had just met the horizon, and filled the sky with a blaze of orange. Vibrant flame-colored rays shot out from an orange ball mingled with copper and gold, contrasting with the cobalt blue of the sea. Jewel couldn't believe such beauty existed. It might not be in a church, but she definitely would have a memorable wedding under God's sky.

Nervously, she glanced around for Adam, and found him standing at the helm staring out to sea with Derek. Broad shoulders filled the same evening coat he'd worn at the Christmas party. He turned to Derek, giving her a view of his profile. She had every right to be nervous. After all, she was marrying a man she barely knew. Perhaps she should back out before it was too late. She should tell him she'd regained her memory. She should tell him she wasn't of his ranking. But he turned. Their eyes met. And she was hopelessly lost. No matter who she really was, she loved him.

He walked toward her, his steps long and effortless. He

took Jewel's hand. Her cold, icy fingers trembled. He smiled at her, slipping his arm around her waist.

She felt strangely calm from his closeness, and hoped this was a good sign.

"You're beautiful, sweetheart," he murmured just before they joined Annie and Derek.

"Derek, are you ready?" Adam asked.

"Aye."

"Let's begin."

They took their places in front of Adam while Jewel observed from the side. Annie couldn't take her eyes off Derek as she repeated her vows, and he held her hands when he spoke. The service was beautiful, and the love in their eyes unmistakable. Jewel smiled as Derek kissed Annie. It was beautiful . . . love knew no age.

Derek looked at Adam. "Now, son, it's your turn."

Adam took Jewel's hand, leading her over to where Annie and Derek had stood. The crew cheered. Adam smiled at his boisterous crew just as one of his men yelled, "It's about time, Captain."

Jewel blushed all the way to her toes. She peeked shyly up at Adam, and her blush deepened. Seeing the warmth of his smile, she felt her heart melt. His dark eyes held emotions she couldn't read, but his smile warmed her.

The brief service went by in a flash, and then Derek asked, "Do you take Adam Trent, Duke of St. Ives, to be your lawful wedded husband?"

"Yes," she said in a nervous voice that sounded strange. Was that really her voice? Was this really happening?

She heard the ceremony end. Derek laid a hand on both their heads. "What God hath brought together, let no man tear apart."

Adam slid his arm around Jewel's waist, pulling her to him in a possessive embrace. In a soft voice he murmured for her ears only, "If any man dare come between us, he'll be a dead man." He smiled sweetly, but she knew he meant every word.

Jewel raised an eyebrow in response. "Likewise, any woman, sir."

Somewhere from within the group of men a cheer rang out. "You going to stand there all night, Cap'n, or are you going to kiss her?"

Adam chuckled. "Should we oblige them, my dear?" He cradled her in his arms, but instead of a chaste kiss as she'd expected, he kissed her with a searing kiss meant to brand her for life. Adam raised his head and whispered huskily, "We will continue this tonight, sweetheart."

The men shouted their approval. Evidently they were happy that their captain had finally taken a wife.

The cook had prepared a feast, and had even found a case of champagne. Drinks flowed freely, and a festive mood prevailed as everyone enjoyed the celebration.

Jewel walked among the men, enjoying their lighthearted mood. Many of them played games and boasted of past feats. She found herself staring across the deck at Adam as he played a game of cards. God, the man was sinfully handsome. No man should look that good. And to think she was now looking at her husband. It gave her gooseflesh. He glanced up. His intense gaze caused her heart to skip a beat.

Smiling, she turned and went over to where a group of sailors gathered. She just couldn't stand around and stare at the man.

As darkness approached, lanterns cast a soft glow over the deck. The weather had blessed them with a mild winter day, and an unusually warm breeze lifted her hair and teased her face.

Jewel made her way into the crowd so she could see what they were doing. They had fashioned a bull's-eye on a board about twenty feet away. Wagers were placed on a barrel and then collected by the man with the best score. A sailor named

Billy had been the big winner so far. Andy was next to play. He stepped up, placing his wager on the barrel.

Billy threw his knife first, hitting a mark of forty. Then it was Andy's turn. He threw his blade and it landed on number thirty. Both men continued back and forth for a total of five throws. Billy's score was three forties and two thirties. Andy's was two thirties, two twenties, and a ten.

Billy tossed back his head, laughing. "I'm the winner and still champion." He held up the fistful of dollars he had collected off the barrel and continued to boast, daring any man to take his best shot.

Jewel looked at Andy's dejected face and felt sorry for him.

"Come back, Andy, when you grow up a mite," Billy gloated. "This here's a man's game." Billy's grin grew broader at the sight of Andy's red face.

Jewel looked at Billy scornfully. The man needed to be taken down a notch. "Billy, can I play your game?"

His mouth dropped open. "You can't be serious, mum."

"Oh, but I am."

"This is a man's game, mum. Captain Trent would have my hide if I let you do anything so dangerous."

"There is no danger to it, Billy. You're only throwing the knives at a target. Surely I'll be able to hit that board." She smiled, baiting him. "Besides, Adam is playing cards. He's not paying any attention. However, if you are afraid to face a woman, I quite understand."

"Well, I don't know. . . ." Billy hedged. She could tell he didn't want Captain Trent mad at him.

"We could make it interesting, if you'd like. I tell you what. I'll double the money you have in your hand."

The lights flickered in Billy's eyes as greed took over.

"It'll be like taking candy from a baby. All right, mum, you have a bet. Would you like to take a couple of throws to warm up?" Billy thought for a moment. "You have thrown a knife before?"

"Yes, I've thrown a little, but if you don't mind, I would like to use a knife I have in my cabin."

"Don't mind a bit, mum." He grinned.

She went to the cabin, quickly found her knife, and returned topside.

Jewel rejoined the men, who were laughing and carrying on—especially Billy. She couldn't help but hear his remark that this was going to be the easiest money he'd ever made.

Billy bowed. "Ladies first."

Jewel glanced at the target for only a moment before she sent her knife sailing through the air, hitting the bull's-eye just to the left. Still, her score was fifty.

Billy looked at Jewel, surprised. "Just a lucky shot." The rest of the men grew quiet as he stepped up and threw his knife. His mark was forty.

Jewel threw again . . . her aim true and dead center.

Billy muttered to himself about her damned luck as he threw again. "Bull's-eye—now that's better."

Adam had noticed Jewel leaving, and he wondered what she was up to, but his mind was brought back to the card game when Charlie spoke to him. Adam would play a few more hands, and then call it quits for tonight. But after a while he couldn't concentrate on the game. He stood, stretching his long legs. After he took some gibes from his card partners, he decided to find Jewel. He had seen her disappear into the group of men throwing knives. "No." Adam shook his head at the crazy thought. She couldn't possibly be—

He walked up behind the group and watched. The men moved apart, providing him with a good view.

It was the last throw. Billy threw another forty. Then Adam's wife stepped up and threw, and just like the previous four times, she hit the bull's-eye, this time to the right of center.

Billy shook his head. "That's the damnedest throwing I've ever seen. Here's your money."

"Thank you, Billy. It appears this is not only a man's

game, but perhaps a woman's, too." The men laughed at her comment. "Now, if you will excuse me, I have to go find Adam."

"You don't have to look far, madam."

Jewel turned and found her husband standing in the crowd behind her. The sailors fell quiet. She couldn't tell if Adam was angry or not.

Billy spoke first. "Didn't mean no harm, Cap'n."

Adam's deep chuckle seemed to relax his men. "Looks like my wife got the best of you, Billy."

"Aye, Cap'n, she throws a wicked knife. Best not make her too angry. Why, I bet *you* couldn't even beat her."

"Yeah, Captain, go ahead and throw. See if you can beat Miss Jewel." The rest of the crew joined in with the taunt, egging Adam on.

Jewel wasn't sure she liked this, but at least Adam's smile hadn't diminished.

"All right," Adam drawled. "Would you men like to put your money where your mouth is?"

The men eagerly placed their wagers on the barrel. "We know you're good, Cap'n, but yer miss's blade is in the bull's-eye."

Adam picked up a knife from the barrel, holding it in his hand, testing the balance. "This will do." He stepped up to the throwing line. Without hesitation he threw at the target. For just a moment no one said a word. Then Adam spoke first.

"I believe, gentlemen, I have just beat my wife." He collected his money off the barrel and then reached for Jewel.

She smiled at him. "Must you always show me up by doing everything better than I do?" Adam's knife had landed beside hers . . . dead center.

"Always, sweetheart," Adam said, grinning at her. He turned to the sailors. "Now if you will excuse us, I think we shall call it a night."

"Good night," Jewel said as they left the men. She was

glad Adam wasn't angry. She liked him when he was in this playful mood.

"Sweetheart, you never cease to amaze me. What are you going to do with your winnings?" Adam asked while they walked toward his cabin.

"I'm going to give the money to Andy. That's the reason I started playing. I was tired of seeing Billy boast. When he started teasing Andy, I thought he could use a good lesson."

They were standing at the door of Adam's cabin. "That was good of you, but tell me, what other hidden talents am I going to discover?" A wicked smile touched his lips.

"Well, maybe one or two others," she teased.

"Allow me." Adam swung her up in his arms and carried her over the threshold. Gently, he let her down; then he drew her against his body. The intensity of her feelings momentarily stopped her breathing while she anticipated his kiss. His arms closed around her, and she melted against him. His lips crushed her mouth. She felt as if she were drowning in sensual pleasure. He demanded more, and she gave it to him with a parting of her lips.

Her body flushed with a warmth that spread from head to toe and filled her with a longing she didn't quite understand. When Adam turned her around and started unbuttoning the back of her dress, desire weakened her knees to jelly. Her dress slipped from her shoulders. She heard his shuddered breathing when she faced him again.

Adam watched the pupils of Jewel's eyes grow wide, making her eyes black with desire, and he smiled lazily. He liked the fact that he was the cause of the passion that filled her. "I hope you enjoyed your wedding day, Mrs. Trent."

"Mmm," she murmured. "It was beautiful. I did have a hard time answering yes to that obedient part, though."

"I imagined you would." He chuckled. "Perhaps we can discuss that matter later." Adam finished pulling off his shirt as desire poured through his veins. He was anxious to feel her nipples against his chest. "For now, I have other plans."

Scooping Jewel up in his arms, he carried her over to the bed, where he finished removing his clothing.

He braced himself up on his elbows, then bent his head to kiss her. This was almost like their first time all over again, and he didn't want to rush. He brushed a kiss along her jaw before he sought her mouth again. This time her tongue met his. As she skillfully kissed him back, he heard his heartbeat racing in his ears.

Lost in their turbulent feelings, they enjoyed touching and exploring each other's bodies. Time seemed to stand still as they found pleasure with each caressing touch.

Adam pulled her hips next to him, making her feel his urgency. He felt her hands move across his chest as his kisses grew longer. Many women had been his before, but none had stirred his senses as this one did. He rubbed his hands ever so slowly down her velvety skin.

"You're so soft," he murmured in her ear.

A sigh escaped her lips. "Adam, I've never felt like this before." She became dizzy as delicious sensations filled her body. She felt as if she were floating in a sea of emotions over which she lacked control. He rolled on top of her, covering her lips with his.

"So beautiful," he breathed against her throat.

Lowering his head, he left a trail of kisses all the way to her breast. Jewel gasped as he took one peak into his mouth, teasing, sucking, nipping, making her moan with desire. His hand moved lower, and in a slow, circular motion he caressed the area between her legs, bringing her a desire of white-hot passion. The pressure of his fingertips increased as he caressed her breasts, causing her to arch her hips.

Her fever reached a pitch. She wanted some kind of release to this pressure Adam invoked in her.

"Does this feel good, Jewel?"

"Oh, yes, Adam . . . please . . ." Her voice was thick. It didn't sound normal. Her body trembled with need. "I want you."

She pulled his head back to her waiting lips and thrust her tongue deep in his mouth, wanting to taste all of him. She knew she'd never get enough. Her hand drifted lower until her fingers wrapped around his firm shaft. Not knowing exactly what to do, but wanting to give Adam the same pleasure he gave her, she instinctively moved her hand up and down to stroke him.

"My God, Jewel," Adam rasped, grabbing her hand. "I can't wait any longer, sweetheart."

He mounted her, driving deep and possessing her in every sense of the word, body and soul. They soared like the waves in the sea. The swells grew bigger and bigger, and when they could swell no longer, they reached a peak and crested, crashing down until once again it was calm and peaceful, their energy spent.

They murmured words of love—no pretense, just raw emotions. They couldn't seem to get enough of each other, and twice more that night they made love, exploring each other's body until they knew every inch. Adam taught Jewel the fine art of making love, and she taught him an intensity he had never known. Sometime in the early hours of morning, they fell into an exhausted sleep in each other's arms.

The next weeks were so peaceful that Jewel knew true contentment.

It was almost too perfect, and that frightened her. She wanted nothing to shatter her happiness, so she would wait until later to tell Adam of her past. After all, what could it harm?

Their days were spent doing everyday tasks, and their nights were filled with passionate lovemaking. One night Adam informed Jewel that they would be in New Orleans in a few weeks. Many emotions filled her. She would be at home—well, almost. At least she would be closer to her uncles, but she wouldn't be able to see them unless she told Adam.

Just what would the future bring at Four Oaks?

Early one morning, when Jewel went up to take the dog for a walk, she was surprised to be met by a chilling fog. The menace penetrated her clothes with ice-cold fingers and almost suffocated everything in its midst. The drifting mist muted everything. Even the sea. She could barely distinguish Adam at the helm, and he could not possibly see where he was going in this thick blanket of white.

Without warning, the shrouded outline of a ship appeared out of nowhere, a phantom ship that seemed to have been conjured up by the fog. She strained her eyes, trying to see if her imagination played tricks on her. Then she saw it. The deadly skull and crossbones flapping in the wind.

"Oh, God, I hope they're not my relatives," Jewel whispered as a sick feeling crept into the pit of her stomach.

It began slowly. The fog had hidden the pirate ship until it was upon them, too late to avoid a confrontation.

"Come about!" Adam called in command. "Man your guns, men!"

The first shot sailed over the *Wind Jammer*'s bow, hitting harmlessly on the far side. More shots were fired.

Adam had his hands full as he fought the wheel. He looked up, and his gaze met hers. "Jewel, get below and don't return until I come after you!" he bellowed. "Take Duke! I don't want either of you hurt!"

For once she did as instructed.

The blast of the *Wind Jammer*'s eighteen-pounders vibrated the air before they struck the enemy ship. Unfortunately, the damage was minor. The battle raged. As the ships drew closer, the pirate's sloop tried to rake the *Wind Jammer* with her broadside, but Adam quickly outmaneuvered them.

"Come about!" Now he became the aggressor. His ship

pivoted on the pirate's fouled bowsprit, and they fell close alongside each other, starboard to starboard, bow to stern, gun muzzles touching.

The scrape of the grappling hooks as they caught the side of the ship made the hair stand on Adam's neck. His sharpshooters quickly picked off the bloodthirsty pirates as they tried to board. But their numbers grew, and hand-to-hand combat could no longer be avoided.

Sword fights immediately broke out with the pirates that did make it across. The pirates were a scrubby lot clad in striped jerseys and stocking caps. The results of previous battles could be seen from the black patches over their eyes, and the scars on their faces and bodies.

The pirates began to outnumber the *Wind Jammer*'s crew. Adam lashed the wheel. He drew his sword and prepared to do battle. Death drew near.

Two pirates, spotting the captain of the ship, approached Adam from behind. "I've got the son of a whore. Prepare to die, mate!"

Adam's sixth sense took over, and he turned, sidestepping just in time to miss the thrust of the pirate's sword. "Gentlemen, it takes two of you? You do not fight fair." He laughed, mocking them. They were no match for his skills.

Below deck Jewel paced frantically about the room, listening for any sound that could tell them about the battle raging up top. "Annie, I can't stand not knowing what's happening."

"Just pray, lass, that our men are successful. I'd die if anythin' be happenin' tae Derek or Adam." She wrung her hands with worry. And Jewel could see the creases in Annie's forehead.

"I've got to peek out and see. We can't just sit here!" Jewel stopped pacing and looked at Annie. "What if things aren't going well? I only have my knife for protection." She eased over to the door. "I'm just going to look out."

"Be careful!" Annie warned. "Adam gave strict orders for ye to stay below."

Slowly, Jewel opened the door. Just for a peek. However, that was the only invitation Duke needed. He bounced out the door in a flash.

"Duke!" Jewel called as she chased after her dog.

By the time she caught him it was too late. They were in the midst of the battle. Her gaze went to the quarterdeck. Smoke curled, mixing with the fog around several sprawled bodies. The clanging of swords sounded all around her. If only she had a sword. But armed with merely a knife, Jewel knew she had to get below. Grabbing Duke by his collar, she started to stand and go back to the cabin.

But she was stopped short by a crafty-eyed pirate. He grabbed her by the hair, jerking her up to face him.

She screamed from the pain that shot through her head, and soon found herself face-to-face with the scruffy enemy. And thank God, she didn't recognize him. Duke barked and squirmed in her arms, and she finally had to let him go.

"Well, well, my pretty. What a tasty morsel you'd make."

"I'd let go of me if I were you," she calmly replied. Though calm wasn't how she felt.

The bloke gave another hard yank of her hair. She smelled the gunpowder and fresh blood on his dirty body. "What say you to that, my pretty?" he asked.

She refused to answer. Instead, she eased out the dagger she had slipped in her sleeve. He gave another jerk of her hair, demanding an answer. She waited for his guard to let down. Finally, he loosened his grip. She twisted and stuck the knife deep in his gut. He immediately released her, falling to the deck, writhing in pain.

Picking up Duke, she held him firmly under her arm before glancing quickly about her. She spotted Adam fighting with two men about twenty feet from her. He looked her way for only a moment, but it was enough for the marauder to pierce Adam's sword arm.

Jewel gasped. Adam never faltered as he switched sword hands, cutting the first man low, tumbling him to the ground.

He continued fighting the other buccaneer. Out of the corner of her eye, Jewel noticed a third pirate approaching Adam from behind.

Adam couldn't see him.

She had to do something.

Jerking her knife out of her victim, she poised the bloody knife by its point, reared back, and threw. Her knife covered the distance, hitting the pirate in the chest.

Adam must have heard the thud as he quickly glanced behind him. But he didn't turn until he'd finished the bloke in front of him. She saw his eyes widen as he realized that it had been Jewel who'd felled the sailor.

"Jewel, get below! Now!"

Blood soaked Adam's sleeve, and she'd been the cause by breaking his concentration. She stood uncertain, her bloody hand covering her mouth. She longed to go to him. His harsh voice finally shook her out of her stupor. Hastily, she retrieved her knife. Then, picking up her skirt, she turned and fled to the cabin, uncertain which was more daunting, the thought of the pirates storming the cabin or the anger in Adam's eyes when he'd seen her.

If the pirates came below, she would need some type of protection.

But a small knife wasn't much.

Twenty-one

Jewel could hear pistols firing, sword blades clashing, men shouting, but every time she heard the agonizing screams of men in pain—maybe dying—she had to close her eyes. Yet she couldn't shut out the thoughts of Adam lying in a pool of blood. Then she remembered she'd just killed two men. She'd never taken a life before.

In the past, her fencing and knife-throwing had always been a game she played with Jean and his men. Even Jean's journeys at sea had sounded like adventure—now she knew different. When the *Lin Fa* had engaged the British ship, she'd realized a little too late that attacks meant life and death. Still, she'd fought—but even then she hadn't taken anyone's life.

Duke lay at her feet, as if sensing her distress. She bent down and stroked his floppy ears. Suddenly, she looked at Annie, who sat rubbing her hands together. The air froze in Jewel's lungs.

"Listen. It's quiet. The battle's over," Jewel said.

Both women grew silent, listening intently for any noise that might indicate who had won. An eerie silence met their ears, until Duke ran over to the door and started growling.

Someone was coming. Perhaps whoever it was would keep on going.

The decisive footsteps grew closer.

Too close.

"Shh, Duke! Be quiet," Jewel whispered in desperation.

The footsteps slowed, then stopped right outside their door. Jewel's breath caught sharply in her throat. The frantic beating of her heart sounded in her ears while she focused on the turning doorknob.

Once again, Duke started to bark. A cold, sickening dread twisted in her stomach. She wrapped her fingers tightly around the hilt of her knife.

The door slammed back.

And Jewel released her breath with a long sigh of relief.

"Duke, is that any way to greet your master and namesake?" Adam said, bending down to the frisky puppy, who jumped up on his leg, demanding attention. After scratching the dog's head, Adam straightened with some difficulty and looked across the room. "It's over, ladies."

It was over. Relief flooded Jewel, but her eyes filled, giving her a watery image of Adam as she stood. His shirt had numerous tears from near-misses, and black sooty powder spotted its front.

Somehow she covered the distance and threw herself into his arms. He squeezed her tightly. Thank God, he'd survived.

She felt something sticky on her hand. "Adam, let me look at your arm. It's bleeding badly."

"It'll have to wait, luv. There are others worse off than I am." He gently touched the side of her face, letting her see his appreciation for her concern.

Annie, who had been silent, found her voice, pleading, "Not Derek?"

Adam put an arm around Annie. "No, he's fine, and is at the helm. We've lost precious time today. And men. Why don't you join Derek," Adam suggested.

Annie let the breath out that she'd been holding. "What happened to the pirates?"

"We were too much for them. They finally ran. If it hadn't been for this bloody fog, they'd never have gotten so close."

While Annie went to check on Derek, Jewel made Adam sit on the bunk so she could wrap something around his arm to absorb the blood. She tore linen strips to make a wide bandage.

"I don't have time for this." He frowned, attempting to get up.

Jewel shoved him back down, giving him a stern look. "If we don't stop the bleeding, you'll be no good to anyone." While he sat impatiently, she quickly finished her task. "There. That will control the bleeding until I can clean it up later."

Adam stood, pulling her up with him. "I don't know what I ever did without you, sweetheart." He placed a kiss on her forehead.

They looked at each other for a moment, neither saying a word. They didn't have to. Adam reluctantly put her away from him. "I could use your help on deck with the wounded," he said, already turning to leave.

"I'm coming."

When they reached the deck, Jewel noticed the fog hadn't improved. The sight of the wounds reminded her of her mishap with Lee. The thought of all the men dying made her stomach queasy, but now she could do something, and wasted little time before she started helping bandage and clean up the wounded crew members. The damage to the ship had to be repaired and, thank goodness, the men were soon patched up and ready to work. That is, all but one. Adam could be a stubborn man.

There had been several casualties, but Jewel hadn't asked Adam who they were. The pirates' bodies had already been removed from the deck. She saw a white canvas draped across a body, and went over to see who the victim was.

"No, Jewel!"

Adam's warning came too late. Pulling the sheet back, she screamed. Hot tears burned her eyes, cascading down her cheeks. "No! Not Charlie!" He had always been so nice to her.

She felt someone touch her shoulder, and turned to find

Adam beside her. She buried her head against his chest. "Charlie was such a good man," she sobbed.

"I know, sweetheart." Adam rubbed his hand up and down her back, trying to soothe her. "Those bloodthirsty pirates never give a damn who they kill! All they're interested in is money."

She stiffened at the mention of pirates. What would he do if he knew he held one in his arms? Would his love turn to hate? She wanted to cry even harder, but didn't.

"What's the matter?" he asked. He hugged her closer, then tilted her head up so he could see her expression.

"Nothing. Adam . . ." She looked up at him. "Do you believe all pirates are the same?"

"Yes, damn it! Look around you. The bloodthirsty pirates have killed some of my men." His angry voice told her what she had wanted to know. "But do not worry, sweetheart. You're safe."

Jewel shut her eyes for an instant. He would never understand when she told him. She felt Adam stumble against her, and she glanced quickly at his face. His coloring was a pasty white from loss of blood.

"Adam, we *must* take care of your arm."

"Not yet. We have to bury Charlie and the rest first."

Jewel wanted to argue, but figured it would do no good.

The men wrapped the bodies in sailcloth and stood poised at the rail while Adam spoke compassionate words. Jewel thought of her bodyguard, Ben. He'd died trying to save her life, and yet she hadn't been able to give him a decent burial. Tears started to fall freely from her eyes.

The sailors lifted the planks. She watched the frothing sea swallow the white bundles. Her stomach knotted and her heart twisted painfully because she'd never forgive herself for endangering her crew.

She watched the men as they stood by the railing, each seeming lost in his own thoughts. Slowly, they moved away from the side, going back to the work that needed to be done.

Jewel walked over to where Adam stood. He was slightly slumped as if he, too, carried the burden of war. "Now I'm going to take care of you. No arguments!"

Supporting his weight with her body, she helped him to their cabin. Once he was seated on the bunk, she skillfully stripped off his shirt and started to work. First, she gently sponged off the dried blood and cleaned his wound with water. It was a clean cut through the fatty flesh of his arm, and she didn't think it would cause him any trouble. Perhaps a little discomfort for a few days, but he'd be fine. Thank God.

Once she'd finished, she felt Adam's feverish eyes on her. His intense stare made her uncomfortable.

"What's wrong?" she asked, wondering if she'd misjudged the severity of his injury. "Are you in pain?"

"Yes, but the pain is not in my arm." He smiled lazily.

"How can you possibly think of *that* when . . . when you're hurt?"

"Sweetheart, when you're near me that's *all* I think about." Adam reached out, brushing the curve of her throat with his fingertips. "Make me forget, Jewel. Just make me forget." With his good arm, he pulled her down onto the bed beside him. The lines of his mouth gentled as he looked at her. Pulling her close, he draped his arm across her and fell into an exhausted sleep.

Jewel curled up beside him. His breathing indicated he was sleeping peacefully, and his warm body invited her to snuggle closer. Closing her eyes, she was thankful the day was over.

The next few weeks were tranquil, with no sign of pirates. One morning Jewel awoke to find Adam had already left their bed. That itself was not unusual, but this morning something felt different. She sat up in bed, stretching. Getting out from under the covers, she moved over to the metal washbasin and splashed water on her face. Staring down at the water in the bowl, she noticed it wasn't swaying. The ship wasn't moving.

Running over to the porthole, she looked out onto a bustling dock.

They had landed!

Footsteps sounded in the hallway, and she turned. Adam stood in the open doorway. "I was wondering if you were going to sleep through our homecoming."

Jewel moved toward him. "I can't believe we're finally here."

"We're in New Orleans, madam. My coach will take us to Four Oaks, so pack your things. You'll be going to your new home." He gave her a morning kiss.

"Is Annie packing?"

"Yes. She'll stay at the main house for a while," Adam explained. "Derek has a small home on my plantation, but it's in need of repairs. They'll reside at Four Oaks until the renovations can be made."

"Oh." At least not everyone would be unfamiliar.

After he left, Jewel dressed, choosing a burgundy wool gown that fit snugly at the waist and flared at the hips. The long sleeves would keep her warm and the dress was extremely comfortable for traveling. She brushed her hair until it shone with raven highlights. Her cheeks had taken on the same color as the dress.

Bundled up in her silver cape and hat, she went topside to join Adam by the rail.

"Welcome to New Orleans," Adam said in greeting.

Jewel studied the levee and wharves, noticing the bustle of activity. Dockworkers, both white and black, worked at unloading the ships. She glanced to her left. As far as she could see, huge sailing vessels rested at anchor, displaying flags of many different countries.

"This place is vast. And there are so many ships." Jewel pointed to one of the piers. "Are those bales of cotton over there?" The sounds of men grunting and groaning as they carried heavy crates off the ship floated in the air.

Adam's eyes followed the direction in which she pointed. "That's right. I'd say there are twenty thousand bales at the very least. That's what we grow at Four Oaks. And look, there's a load of tobacco coming in." Adam pointed to a ship just rounding the bend of the river.

Jewel turned and watched the ship's sails. "Tell me something about the city. It appears low. When I look over at those buildings, they seem lower than the Mississippi." Jewel had never been to New Orleans. Her uncles used to come frequently, but she had never been allowed to leave the island.

"You're very observant. In fact, the city is ten feet below the Gulf of Mexico. The earthen levees protect it on all sides from flood. The biggest problems they have are drainage and sanitation. You might say this city sits on top of the water, and if you dig down six feet, you'll surely find water; they even have to bury their dead above ground in tombs."

"Really?" Jewel frowned at the thought of coffins floating in water.

"That's the bad side. But the good side is the beauty of the city, and the many cultures that are found here. Besides Americans, there are Spanish, French, and Cajun. I think you'll like it here."

Jewel knew she'd like New Orleans if it was anything like her uncles said. "Where is Four Oaks?"

"About an hour's ride from here, and I believe it's about time to head that way. Why don't you go and get Annie? Our baggage is already on the carriage."

"What about Derek?" she asked.

"He will look after unloading the ship; then he'll take the *Wind Jammer* upriver to my private landing. He should join us at Four Oaks in a few days."

Jewel found Annie, and after saying good-bye to the crew they headed down the plank. She saw Andy trying to keep up with Duke at the bottom. Laughing, she took the dog's rope, then gave the boy a hug. "I won't say farewell, because I expect to see you when you visit Four Oaks."

Andy smiled. "Yes, mum, just as soon as I can."

Carriages of various sizes awaited their passengers. Jewel and Adam walked over to a huge black traveling chaise where a set of steps had been lowered. Jewel had to smile. If they had been in England, the duke's crest would have been boldly displayed. Evidently, Adam really did leave that aristocratic life behind when he came to America.

Putting Duke in the vehicle, Jewel prepared to climb in herself as another carriage pulled up. Several people turned to look at the gilded coach. It must be carrying someone important, Jewel thought.

The door opened, and a tall, serious-looking gentleman stepped out. "Adam Trent." The man threw up his hand, gaining Adam's attention. "I heard you were coming home." The portly gentleman moved toward them. "You've stayed away much too long."

"Governor Claiborne, it's good to see you. I trust you've gotten New Orleans under control," Adam answered with a smile.

Claiborne shook his head. "It's been tough, old friend, but I'm still working on it."

Adam had made a point of making the acquaintance of the first American governor of Louisiana.

"After you're settled in, I'd like to talk to you," the governor stated.

"We are headed to Four Oaks now. Perhaps in a few days we can meet."

"Wonderful. And once again, welcome home. Good day, Adam. Ma'am." He tipped his hat to Jewel.

"Charles," Adam said, stopping the governor, realizing he had not introduced Jewel.

"Yes?" Governor Claiborne turned back.

"I'd like to introduce you to my wife."

Surprise showed on the governor's face before he broke

into a wide grin. "A pleasure to meet you, Mrs. Trent. I've always said Adam had excellent taste."

"Thank you." Jewel blushed. "It's a pleasure to meet you."

When they were settled, Jewel asked, "The governor has a strange accent. Where is he from?"

"He was a Virginian."

"Then why did he choose Louisiana?"

"I'm not sure. Perhaps he wanted a challenge. Early in his political career, Claiborne realized that his task as governor of Louisiana would be a difficult one. Slowly but surely, he assembled some sort of order out of the chaos he found when he first came to New Orleans."

Annie and Jewel peered out the carriage windows as they left the docks. Horse-drawn wagons carried crates of merchandise to several large warehouses lining the streets. The area around the warehouses was filled with bars, bordellos, and boardinghouses that catered to boatmen. Jewel noticed some rough-looking creatures outside one bar. People walking down the street seemed to be going out of their way to avoid them.

"Who are those people?" Jewel pointed.

Adam glanced out the window. "They're Kaintocks from Kentucky, and you would do well to stay clear of them. They're vermin, and can be dangerous when drunk—which is usually the case. But even sober, they are despicable. Never trust a Kaintock, and don't come in this area unless I'm with you. Understood?"

Jewel agreed, and continued to stare out the window. They drove past the Vieux Carré, which was formed by the river, the Esplanade, the ruined old wall on Rampart Street, and the Faubourg Ste. Marie. Once they were away from the docks, the scenery changed completely. The tree-lined streets and the houses were magnificent. All the houses had either wrought-iron balconies or porticoes and projected an air of grace and elegance.

Once out of the city, Jewel noticed the lovely countryside

and the barren trees covered in gray moss. Finally, after an hour or so, their carriage turned into a long drive.

A row of live oaks lined both sides of the road, and at the end of the drive Jewel caught her first glance of Four Oaks.

Breathtaking was the only word to describe the massive house. The white mansion stood surrounded by four huge oak trees covered in Spanish moss. The house was not as big as Briercliff, but the slight difference didn't take away from the grandeur of Four Oaks. "It's magnificent, Adam," Jewel remarked, her voice filled with astonishment.

Eight Corinthian pillars graced the front of the house. Wisteria vines draped the two end pillars. Of course, it being winter, the vines lacked foliage, but in the spring beautiful lilac grape-shaped flowers would add grace and fragrance to the beautiful house.

As soon as the carriage stopped, Jewel saw a lovely young woman, who she assumed was Elizabeth, come flying down the front steps, evidently anxious to see her brother. The woman reached the carriage just as the door swung open and Adam climbed out. Elizabeth practically knocked him down as she threw herself in his arms and placed a kiss on his cheek.

"Adam, I've missed you so much!" She hugged her brother. Duke bounced out of the carriage, impatient to be on the ground again. He ran around Elizabeth, barking and wagging his tail. She giggled and bent down to rub his head. "I see you have acquired a pet."

Adam laughed. "That's not all I've acquired."

Jewel sat in the shadows of the carriage, so Elizabeth hadn't seen her or Annie. She watched the woman in Adam's arms. When she saw them standing side by side, there was no mistaking they were brother and sister. Elizabeth had a delicate and fragile face with Adam's features. Her dainty feet peeked out from under voluminous skirts. She was almost the same height as Adam, maybe three inches shorter, but still she appeared much taller than Jewel. Her long, shiny brown hair was tied back with blue ribbons.

"What do you mean, Adam?" Elizabeth asked at her twin brother's strange remark.

"I've brought some people to see you." He opened the door of the carriage and winked at Jewel. Motioning for Annie, he helped her down.

Squeals of delight erupted from Elizabeth. "Annie! I thought never to see you again!" Elizabeth cried and hugged her old nanny. "What finally made you decide to come?"

" 'Tis the apple of me eye. Ye've not changed a bit." Annie held Elizabeth at arm's length, looking her over. "Perhaps a wee bit too thin, but I'll be takin' care of that. As tae the reason I be comin', 'tis to be a chaperone tae yer brother's wife."

"Wife!" Elizabeth's eyes widened before she whirled on Adam.

Twenty-two

"Wife?" Elizabeth said again, then added, "Oh, my God, it's not Colette?"

Laughter burst from Adam's lips. "Sis, you've never been one to mince words. What if I tell you you've probably hurt her feelings?" he teased.

"That lady's hide is as thick as leather," Elizabeth said in a lower voice.

Jewel watched the scene outside the coach door. Yes, she definitely was going to like her new sister-in-law.

Adam moved back to the carriage. "Come, sweetheart, and meet your shy sister-in-law."

Jewel stepped down and moved toward Elizabeth, then curtsied, "I hope you approve."

Elizabeth embraced her, hugging her tightly. "Of course I do. I knew Adam had better sense than to marry that witch." An arched eyebrow showed her humorous surprise. "You're so beautiful." She smiled impishly. "Whatever made you look at my brother?"

Jewel winked at Elizabeth. "I'm not sure." She injected a mock-serious note into her voice. "It must have been his sparkling personality."

Arm and arm, the two new friends walked up the front steps together. Jewel was ready to start her new life at Four Oaks.

* * *

Spring had finally arrived at Four Oaks. A warm, gentle breeze fluttered in through the open French doors on the west wing, carrying the fragrance of wisteria vines that covered the veranda leading from the sitting room. Jewel leaned her head against the chair back, closed her eyes, and breathed in the wonderful damp smells of Four Oaks. She could picture the walkway where Elizabeth had planted a rainbow of pansies.

She opened her eyes and looked around her. The Southern plantation itself had a charming elegance, especially the foyer, which was graced with a double winding staircase.

Jewel was enjoying her new residence, but being so close to her uncles made her homesick. She could remember when she used to beg her uncles to take her to New Orleans— anything to get off the island—but they had always refused, saying it would be much too dangerous.

They'd taken great care to hide her when visitors came to the island. She recalled asking them if they were ashamed of her. Jean had become upset that she would think such a thing. And then he'd explained that she was their Achilles heel. If someone kidnapped her, her uncles would give everything they owned to get her back.

She wondered what her uncles would say when they found out she'd married. She sighed at that thought. It would take a lot of explaining on both sides.

She took a deep breath, filling her lungs with the scent of gardenias. Soon the roses would be blooming, adding their heady mixture of scents. It was evident that Elizabeth liked to work in the garden, because she'd planted flowers in every nook and cranny. Old, cracked red clay pots burst with color. Her vivacious personality was like a ray of sunshine to Jewel. One couldn't help but love Elizabeth.

In her short time at Four Oaks, Jewel had enjoyed getting to know her sister-in-law. Annie said she felt as if she had two daughters now, and sometimes wasn't quite sure which one could get into the most trouble.

Jewel noticed her sister-in-law had her share of gentlemen callers, but Elizabeth never seemed to be interested in any of them. One day Jewel asked Elizabeth which of the men she liked best—only to receive a shrug of her shoulders. "They're all boring," she later confessed.

Elizabeth probably didn't have time to think about men, since the running of the house had been left in her capable hands. Jewel hadn't made any changes in that arrangement, because she didn't want her new sister-in-law to feel she had been pushed out. Besides, Jewel had never run a house before and didn't have the slightest idea what to do.

The chirping birds seemed to be enjoying the bright sunny day. What a perfect time for their outing to the city. They needed to start preparing Annie's house so she and Derek could move, and they were going to have a summer party to introduce Jewel as Adam's wife. Since it had been winter when they'd arrived, Jewel hadn't met anyone.

Adam had made several business trips to plan his spring cotton crops, saying reluctantly that planting season would keep him busy. Jewel wanted to see the plantation he so loved, but she hadn't yet had that privilege, even though Adam had promised her a tour.

She had wanted to get word to her uncles that she was alive, but she wasn't sure just how she could accomplish the task. She remembered Jean speaking of a blacksmith shop he and Pierre owned in New Orleans. Maybe she could find this place and leave word of her safety; that is, if she could locate it.

Elizabeth swept into the room, breaking into Jewel's thoughts. "Are you ready to go? It's time to really show you New Orleans."

Jewel got up from her overstuffed stair and faced her sister-in-law. "I'm looking forward to going," she replied.

"I can't wait for you to taste the French pastries. Of course, we'll have to be fitted for our dresses first. The pastries will probably make our middles thick," Elizabeth teased, her eyes sparkling.

"Oh, do stop, Elizabeth. I didn't have any breakfast." Jewel tugged on her arm. They grabbed their things and left the room.

Outside, they were still chatting about food when they found Annie waiting in the carriage.

" 'Tis about time ye tae showed up," Annie scolded. "I thought I might have tae go shoppin' by meself."

"When are we supposed tae be meetin' Adam?" Annie asked.

"He said to meet him at one o'clock in the Café du Monde," Jewel told her.

They had chosen an open carriage so they could enjoy the fresh air and sunshine.

Upon reaching New Orleans, they rode along Esplanade Avenue, which was beautifully lined with Creole mansions set back from groves of lush banana trees. The festive streets of New Orleans carried the flavor of their Spanish and Creole influence. Once the carriage reached the shopping area, Jewel noticed the many window boxes, each decorated with assorted flowers that reflected the personality of the city—gay and bright with color.

The ladies stopped first at the famous House of St. Jacqueline. They pored over lace, ribbons, and material of very rich hues. After narrowing her selection to three, Jewel picked out a beautiful blue organza material with hand-painted orchids scattered over rich, heavy satin of the same color. A thick satin sash of teal blue would be worn at the waist, and a flimsy ruffle at the bodice in teal with traces of lavender completed the outfit.

Elizabeth picked out an attractive dress of buttercup yellow batiste. The sleeveless top featured tiny silk roses of buttercup yellow and white. Annie's vivid spring green dress had a skirt that hung with a dark green satin sash. After picking out the appropriate undergarments and shoes, the ladies proceeded to the next shop, very pleased with themselves.

Now they needed to get down to serious business, ordering supplies for Annie's house. New curtains were in order, as well as bedding, food supplies, and other necessities.

Adam was busy on the other side of town, talking with Governor Claiborne. He had put off his meeting with the governor until now because he had truly enjoyed the time spent with Jewel, though he realized he hadn't spent nearly enough time with her. But today had been perfect. When the ladies suggested it was time for them to go to town, Adam decided not to put off the meeting any longer.

Governor Claiborne told Adam that General Jackson was in Mobile. That bit of information was quite useful to Adam, for he had yet to meet with the general. He talked with Claiborne about New Orleans and what had been happening over the past year. But Adam was careful not to divulge the information he had obtained in England. That would be saved for Hawk alone.

"How is Lafitte?" Adam asked.

"That thief is a thorn in my flesh!" Claiborne slapped the desk with his hand. "The bloodcurdling sagas of ships being wrecked at sea is all I hear, and Lafitte swears he's innocent of any wrongdoing. If that wasn't enough, now he's smuggling slaves into New Orleans. Those bands of pirates are a constant headache!"

Claiborne stood, clasped his hands behind his back, and started to pace the room. "I'm not sure exactly what I can do with the pirate, seeing as Lafitte does pretty much as he pleases."

"Don't judge too hastily. We might need his ships before this war with England is over," Adam pointed out.

"Do you really think there will be war in Louisiana? I

myself think we'll be left out." Claiborne raised a brow and looked at Adam.

"I'm not too sure that will be the case." Adam narrowed his eyes thoughtfully. "The greatest attraction of New Orleans is its position; she regulates the mouth of the Mississippi, which means she controls the whole vast rich expanse between the Alleghenies and the Rockies, as you well know. Lose the Mississippi, and our young republic will not be able to expand. So I tell you again, a day might come when we will need Lafitte and his pirates."

"You might be right, but what good will it do? He can't be trusted," the governor protested.

"I know Lafitte. If he gives his word, it's as good as gold." The governor stood. "You'll have to prove that to me."

Adam left Governor Claiborne's, his decision made. It was time to visit his friend Lafitte, and then he would go to Mobile to see General Jackson.

Adam found his wife sitting at the Café du Monde, eating beignets and drinking café au lait. She was laughing over some remark that Annie had made, and Elizabeth looked amused, too. Seeing Jewel across the room made him swell with pride. She had definitely become a part of his life. He would hate leaving her, but as soon as this war was over, they could get back to a normal life.

He started over to the table where the ladies were sitting. He'd only taken a few steps when a young woman ran up, threw her arms around his neck, and planted a kiss firmly on his lips.

"Adam Trent, I didn't know you were back." Catherine Paulsboro smiled up at him.

Adam looked in dismay at the woman he used to keep company with before he'd gone to England. In fact, he'd seen quite a bit of her then. He'd forgotten all about her in the intervening months. He felt the heat sting his cheeks as he undraped her arms from around his neck.

"Catherine," he finally said, glancing at the table where

he had been heading, and noticing that he now had his wife's complete attention. "What a surprise."

"If you've been back a long time and haven't called on me, Adam Trent, I'll never forgive you." She put on her practiced pout.

"I've been back for several months. I have someone you should probably meet." Adam took Catherine by the elbow, escorting her past the gawking patrons and toward his wife's table.

Jewel watched Elizabeth turn to see what had caught her attention. "So, it's my brother." She giggled, holding a hand over her mouth. "I'd give a bundle to have a painting of him now." She leaned over to Jewel. "I don't think I've ever seen him blush before."

"I don't think I have either . . . he must be guilty."

"Perhaps in the past," Elizabeth agreed. "That young lady is someone Adam used to see before he left for England."

"I see." Adam must be the only man who could have women clinging to him in two countries.

They stopped in front of the table, and Catherine's eyes widened as she recognized Elizabeth and gave her a hug.

"Elizabeth, I can't believe my luck today. First I see Adam, and now you. It has been much too long since we've gotten together." She held out a lace-gloved hand. "Let's have lunch one day."

"That would be nice, Catherine. You are coming to our summer party in July, aren't you?" Elizabeth asked.

"Why, of course. I wouldn't miss it. It'll be like old times." Catherine looked at Adam, smiling sweetly. "You are going to be my escort?"

"No," Adam said gruffly. The damned woman was chattering so fast he couldn't introduce her to his wife. He stole a glance at Jewel. She purposely looked away from him, so he missed seeing the expression in her eyes.

"Catherine, perhaps I should introduce you to my relatives," Elizabeth jumped in. "I'd like you to meet my governess, Annie Pritchard . . . I mean Winters; she has just recently married."

"It's nice to meet you, Mrs. Winters, and congratulations," Catherine said. Then she addressed Elizabeth again. "I wasn't aware you had a governess, Elizabeth."

"Annie raised Adam and me at our home in England," Elizabeth explained.

"I see. You must have come home with Adam." Catherine smiled at Annie.

"Indeed, I did. 'Twas my first sea voyage."

"You have a lovely daughter, Mrs. Winters."

"Oh, Jewel isn't my daughter, even though I kind of adopted her," Annie said, patting Jewel's hand.

"I'm sorry, I just assumed—" Catherine began.

"I was getting ready to introduce her," Elizabeth broke in. "This"—Elizabeth pointed to Jewel—"is my sister-in-law, Jewel Trent."

"I wasn't aware you had two brothers. . . ." Catherine's voice trailed off and her face reddened.

"It's good to make your acquaintance." Jewel smiled at the young woman. "I can understand your confusion. Adam and I arrived in the winter months, and haven't had a chance to announce our marriage." She decided to ease the girl's embarrassment. She could tell Elizabeth was enjoying herself and wasn't about to enlighten Catherine. The poor girl still stood there with her mouth open and a look of horror in her eyes.

Adam moved to stand behind Jewel. His hand rested on her shoulder, and she resisted the urge to cut her gaze up to him. "I hope you will wish us both well."

"Yes, of course, it was . . . was just a surprise." Then, remembering her manners, Catherine added, "It's nice to meet you, Mrs. Trent. I hope you'll like it here in New Orleans."

"Thank you. It's a beautiful city."

Catherine gave her a genuine smile. "If y'all will excuse me, I've some errands to run for Mother. She has been ill."

"I'm sorry to hear that," Elizabeth said. "I hope it's nothing serious."

"The doctor said she needed bed rest for a couple of weeks, but she should be fine after that."

"Give her our regards," Adam said.

"Yes, I will. Good day." Catherine walked away from the group.

Adam took the chair next to Jewel and picked up a beignet that had been ordered for him. He was ravenous, and had just taken a bite when his sister decided to address him.

"What have you been up to, brother dear, besides entertaining Miss Catherine?" she asked with a teasing glance at Jewel.

Adam choked on his pastry, knowing what his sister meant. Taking a swallow of water to clear his throat, he said, "I had a meeting with Governor Claiborne." He decided to ignore his sister's barb. "How did you ladies enjoy your day?"

" 'Twas wonderful," Annie commented. "We obtained a few things for the house, and with the girls' help, I'll be havin' the cottage fixed up in no time."

"I'm glad to hear that," Adam said. "Derek has been grumbling about a place of his own. When you start working, if there is any heavy lifting to be done, you're to get help from the main house."

"Yes, sir," Annie said.

"What else did you do today?"

"We picked out dresses for the party." Elizabeth's excitement came through in her voice. "They're beautiful. You should see Jewel's."

Adam turned to his wife, looking at her for the first time since sitting down. He'd really love to see her without a dress, he quickly thought. She didn't appear angry over the earlier scene; however, he'd noticed she had been very quiet. Of course, with Elizabeth around, it was hard to get a word in.

He reached over and took Jewel's hand. "Are you going to be the belle of the ball, sweetheart?"

"I doubt that, not with all the beautiful young ladies I've seen in New Orleans. But then I guess you've probably made the rounds."

Annie and Elizabeth cleared their throats. "We have a little more shopping to do. We'll meet both of you in about an hour."

After saying good-bye, Adam turned his attention back to his wife. "You wouldn't be jealous . . . now would you, sweetheart?" He couldn't stop the grin spreading across his face.

"Of course not." She tilted her chin up.

"Well, I thought you handled the situation very gracefully." He rubbed his thumb across the back of her hand. "You could have been rude to Catherine, but you chose not to."

"Someone had to be pleasant," she snapped, and jerked her hand away. "The girl was heartbroken. Were you engaged to her, too?"

"No! I have never been engaged to anyone. If you will remember, I didn't even take time to be engaged to you." He grinned at her.

"Tell me, Adam, how many young ladies' hearts have I broken by marrying you?" Jewel raised a brow, awaiting his reply.

"Well, maybe one or two. But," he added quickly, "that was before I met you."

Jewel felt her heartbeat quicken. What a rogue. His magnetic charm was ever present. She should be angry with him, but she wasn't, especially when he smiled at her that way. Could he help it if women insisted on clinging to him? Just as long as Adam remembered he had a wife now . . . and by the smoldering look in his eyes, he definitely remembered that point.

Adam reached over to brush her lips with his. The chaste kiss had ended before it began. "Forgiven?" A devastating smile swept across his features.

Jewel returned his smile, surprised at his display of affection in a public place, yet pleased. "Yes."

"Good. I've another place I need to go before we return home." He wiped his mouth with the linen napkin, placed it on the table, and stood. "Would you like to go with me?"

Jewel stood, too. "The day is so beautiful. Can we walk?"

"Of course."

They left the restaurant and started strolling to a different part of town, one she hadn't yet seen.

"Where are we going?"

"The blacksmith shop," Adam answered.

If her husband had turned at that very moment and looked at her, he wouldn't have found much color in her cheeks. She had wanted to find the blacksmith shop, and now it was being laid in her lap.

Jewel could hear the blacksmiths hammering rhythmically. When they drew close, she saw the hot metal of a horseshoe lying upon an anvil. There were three blacksmiths in all.

The intense heat from the furnace had forced the huge men out of their shirts. One man stopped his pounding and inserted the finished horseshoe in water to cool. A loud hiss sounded from the sizzling metal. Back home, she'd seen many sailors without shirts, so the men didn't offend her. The man who had stopped now watched as Adam approached.

"I need to see Jake," Adam called out to the men. "I have some horses to be shod at Four Oaks."

"Yeah," the soot-faced blacksmith barked, his muscles bulging as he lifted the heavy hammers. "If ya want to see Jake, ya can find him in the back." He grunted and jerked his head in that direction before picking up another piece of red-hot metal.

Adam went back over to where Jewel stood. "The heat

from the furnace can be unbearable, so stand back away from the shed. Stay right here. I'll only be a few moments."

"I'll be fine."

"Were you listening?" His eyes twinkled, but she knew what he alluded to. "I said don't move."

"I'm not deaf. I'll be right here."

She watched Adam disappear around the corner into what she assumed to be an office. She took the opportunity to look around, but she didn't recognize anyone. How in the world was she going to get word to her uncles that she was alive? This might be her only chance.

Jewel hadn't been paying any attention to the blacksmith's conversation until she heard one of them mention Pierre.

"Excuse me?"

All three men looked her way, their astonishment showing that she had spoken to them.

"Did you mention Pierre Lafitte?"

"Yeah, lady, ya know him?"

"Yes, I do. Is he here?" She couldn't give him any information.

"Nope, but he will be in two weeks."

"And Jean?"

"Not sure when Jean will be coming. Unpredictable, he is, if ya want to see Pierre, though, come back in a few weeks. He's planning to stay a couple of days here. Ya want us to tell him ya were looking for him?"

"No, but thank you for the information." She noticed Adam rounding the corner.

Adam was glad to see his wife had obeyed him this time. He took her by the arm and they left, walking back to the Café du Monde to meet their carriage. A blacksmith would be coming out to Four Oaks next week. Some of the horses definitely needed shoeing, but the part Jewel didn't hear was a message he had left with Jake to inform Jean that he'd be paying him a visit. That way Adam wouldn't be shot on sight when he sailed into the bay.

Twenty-three

Jewel entered their bedroom at Four Oaks to find Adam's bag open on the bed. "What are you doing?"

"Packing."

"I can see that, but why?" Surprised at the panic that attacked her, she added, "Where are you going?"

He studied her for a long moment, and her heart plummeted. He was leaving her. Somehow he'd found out she had regained her memory and had been deceiving him the whole time.

"Sit down. We need to talk."

She didn't like the sound of that statement. Yet he didn't appear angry. She moved on shaky legs toward the bed. What was she going to do? What would she say?

Adam cleared his throat. "I need to tell you something, but you must promise not to repeat what I say."

Her panic eased a little. "All right."

"Since I've moved to Four Oaks, I've come to love my mother's country. And because I believe in the United States, I've had a secret mission over the last two years. Helping to gather information for Andrew Jackson."

She experienced a gamut of perplexing emotions. "You're a spy. But you're English!" Then she remembered he wouldn't have been in England at all if it hadn't been for his grandfather's death. Adam had told her so himself. Hadn't he mentioned to Annie he couldn't wait to get back to America? "Do you really think there will be a war?" Jewel asked as she watched Adam place two shirts in his valise.

"I'm afraid so. And if there is a war, I will fight."

"But it's dangerous!" Jewel jumped up and put her arms around Adam, hugging him to her. "Must you?"

"Yes, sweetheart. But remember, I'm fighting for you, Four Oaks, and most important, freedom to sail the seas without England's interference." He watched her slowly look up at him. He would hate leaving her, Adam thought as he stared at her soft brown eyes. Funny, he'd never believed he'd have a wife when it came time to fight.

"Will it be soon?"

"I'm not sure. I think we have some time." He let her go, then turned back to the bag. "That is one of the reasons I'm going to talk with General Jackson." Adam buckled the straps of his bag.

"Promise me you'll be careful," she said.

He smiled, touched by her fear for him. She didn't want him to go. He knew she didn't understand what this war was really about, and they hadn't settled down as man and wife yet, but when this war ended things would be different. She wouldn't be able to get him away from her.

He lovingly tipped her chin up and placed a tender kiss on her forehead. "I promise," he whispered, then turned his back, stepping lightly across the room and out the door. Even though Adam had explained his trip to see General Jackson, he hadn't bothered to tell Jewel about his friend Lafitte. How could one explain being friends with a pirate?

Derek met Adam as he boarded the ship. "You ready to sail, son?"

"Set our course for Barataria Bay, and holler if you need any help navigating." Adam chuckled as he went below to stow his gear, hearing Derek swearing in the salty language he knew best.

Adam pulled out a map. Barataria Bay lay between Bayou La Fourche and the river. The ten-foot-deep channel extended for seventy miles directly north toward New Orleans. After that, it broke into a series of bayous and swamps. He smiled. His friend had known what he was doing when he'd set up his camp. It was an aquatic wilderness made up of quaking prairies, cypress swamps, and twisting waterways. Most people couldn't navigate the hazardous region; therefore, the pirates had a safe haven.

Derek wound the ship through the twisted bayous, being very careful not to run aground. At last, they sailed into Barataria Bay, commonly known as Jean Lafitte's Bay.

As they rounded the point into the crystal blue water, Adam saw Jean, arms folded, waiting on the end of the pier. Evidently, the lookouts had spotted their ship long before it had neared the hideout.

"Welcome!" Jean shouted from the shore. He watched as Adam launched the dingy from the larger ship and rowed to the pier. "My friend the duke," Jean said with a laugh, knowing how Adam hated to have his title used here in America.

"Jean the notorious pirate," Adam grunted back at him.

"Come." Jean motioned in the direction of his house. "Let's go and find someplace where we can relax, my friend."

Adam had always admired Lafitte. His home wasn't a shack, but a large plantation house sitting high on a hill where Jean could watch every ship that sailed into his bay. They entered a huge den made light and airy with white cushioned furniture and bright green tropical plants. It wasn't what you'd expect of a pirate; however, it was a place where one could throw up one's feet and lounge without being disturbed.

"Where is Pierre?"

"He sailed about a week ago. I expect him back next Friday."

"Somehow, Jean, you look older." Strain lines etched the

swarthy skin around Jean's eyes, and he looked very tired. This wasn't the happy-go-lucky pirate Adam was used to seeing. "Is something wrong?"

"It shows, does it?" Jean took a swig of rum before continuing. "Ah, this rum somehow takes away the pain and makes me forget, if only for a moment," he mused.

"Forget what?"

"My niece," Jean said. "I lost her."

After waiting for Jean to elaborate, which he didn't, Adam asked, "What niece?"

"Pierre and I raised my sister's girl."

"Where did your keep her—New Orleans?"

"No, my friend. We raised her here."

"Why have I never heard you speak of her before?"

"Except for my men who live on the island, no one knew of her existence."

"I see."

"No offense, my friend, but we felt she was safer this way."

"So, what happened? Did she die?"

"No, I don't think so . . . perhaps I should explain. As I said, I raised my niece from a small girl." Jean paused, and the tensing of his jaw betrayed his deep frustrations. "She is now a woman, but little did I know my gang of thieves were teaching her to sail." Jean finished the rest of his rum. "To make a long story short, she went out on a ship that was seized and never returned."

"That's too bad. Do you know who attacked her?"

"No, and yes. I know it was an Englishman—no offense to you, my friend." Jean lifted his glass in salute.

"None taken, but what makes you think she's alive?"

Jean put a hand over his heart, patting it gently. "I'd know in here if she were dead." He grew quiet for a few moments. "The thought of her coming to harm tears at my gut."

Jean's face twisted in pain, yet there was an unmasked question in his eyes. "I haven't heard of anything," Adam said. "But then, of course, I've been in England. I'll keep my ears and eyes open for you. It would help if you knew the captain's name."

"I've one of my men down at the docks. He happened to be on her ship. As a matter of fact, to my knowledge, he was the only survivor. He'll recognize the bloke should he dare set foot on American soil." Hatred blazed in Jean's eyes. "God help him if he does!" Then he seemed to struggle as he regained his composure. "Let us talk about something more pleasant." He changed the subject. "I hear you've gotten married."

"I did, and to a very vivacious young lady. Jean, you wouldn't believe her. She's a rare jewel." Adam's grin spread across his face. "She's spirited and can handle a sword better than most men."

"Strange. I taught my niece to fence. She was quite good, too."

"Maybe one day they can meet each other. That is, after you find your niece."

Jean laughed. "I see you have finally found someone to tame you. I never thought I'd see the sparkle of love in your eyes, my friend. Your lady sounds like a handful."

"Well, it's not that bad." Adam chuckled at Lafitte's absurd observation. "Perhaps you can meet her soon."

"Do you think she would approve of a privateer?" Jean grinned.

Adam contemplated that for a minute. He wasn't sure, but gave Jewel the benefit of the doubt. "Of course. She isn't uppity like most of society's ladies."

"Then I'd consider it an honor." Jean raised his glass again in a salute. "Now tell me the reason for this unexpected visit." Jean looked pointedly at Adam. "Not that I'm not glad to see you."

"I've come to warn you about an impending visit."

"Visit? Sounds interesting." Jean stood. "Can I get you another drink before we start?"

Adam nodded. "When I was in England, I had the privilege of hearing some pretty interesting information. It seems the British Army is going to try and recruit you."

"Surely you pull my leg, my friend. Do you think we're headed for war?" Jean asked with grave look.

Adam nodded. "Yes, I do. That is the reason the British need your services. It would really put a notch in our defense to lose you and your men!"

"Then I look forward to their visit." Jean shook his head in utter disbelief. "But rest assured that my loyalties lie with the Americans. Have no doubt." Jean frowned. "Perhaps when I offer my services this time, Clairborne won't turn up his nose."

"They are a biased lot, I admit. But have no fear. As the time draws closer, they'll see the error of their ways."

After a pleasant dinner with the finest wine, Adam returned to his ship, bidding Jean good-bye until the next time.

"How did it go?" Derek inquired once Adam boarded.

"Fine. Jean is a good man. He'll let us know when the British contact him," Adam informed him.

"Where to now, son?"

"Back to New Orleans."

"I thought you were going to see General Jackson." Derek looked puzzled.

"I am, but first I need to meet a friend who should be arriving tomorrow." Adam started unbuttoning his shirt as he moved about the cabin. "My friend has decided to help in our fight, and will be traveling with me to meet Jackson."

"Anyone I know?"

Adam chuckled. "You're not going to believe it."

"Who?"

"Jonathan."

Derek slapped Adam on the back. "How in the hell did you ever accomplish that?"

"I'm not sure." Adam smiled as he pictured his old friend. "Perhaps he's just bored doing nothing with his life. Jonathan was a big help in gathering information when I was in England."

"I look forward to seeing him myself." Derek stood, stretching. "I'm kind of tired. I think I'll call it a night. We'll sail at daybreak."

"Good night, Derek."

Adam saw Jonathan's head above the group preparing to disembark from the ship. Adam didn't know why he enjoyed his friend's company so much, especially when he could be such a pain in the neck. But he had missed him, and was glad Jonathan had written word that he was coming to America.

Jonathan walked casually toward him, his ever-present lopsided grin evident. He had almost reached Adam when he hollered, "Where is Jewel?"

Adam shook his hand. "Wait a minute! Did you come to see me or my wife?"

"Actually, I came to make sure you were taking good care of your wife." Jonathan chuckled, always the demon.

"I should be jealous," Adam said as they walked to where their horses were tied. "You wouldn't try to take her . . . would you?"

"Egads, ol chap! I'm truly insulted." Jonathan grinned. "Besides, you're my best friend . . . and also a better shot than I am. What about my bags?" Jonathan asked.

"Don't worry. I've instructed one of my men to pick up your luggage and store it on my ship until we return. I thought, if it was all right with you, we would start out now, so we can make some traveling time before nightfall."

"After you, old boy."

The country sprawled between rivers and swamps as they made their way to Mobile. Low marshlands sucked at the horse's hooves as they rode, making their progress slower than normal. The heat and humidity soon took their toll on Jonathan, forcing him to discard his coat.

"Is it always this bloody hot?" Jonathan complained, wiping his brow.

Adam smiled. "I'm afraid so, especially this time of the year. It can get rather sultry, but you'll get used to it, just as soon as that English blood thins out."

"Very funny." Jonathan frowned. "While we're riding, tell me something about this famous general of yours. What kind of man is Jackson?"

Adam rubbed his chin. "That's hard to say. Let me see, what words should I use to describe him? How about obstinate? Yes, that's a good word. Obstinate with a vindictiveness toward his enemy that you wouldn't believe."

"Sounds like a real nice fellow, but should I trust my life to him?" Jonathan asked.

"Wait. Let me finish. The general's character is complex. He is a man of honor, courage, and above all things, a man who does not give his word lightly. And Jackson is honest, a true man of his word. However, he has a hair-trigger temper, especially to those who would utter slurs against himself or anyone he loves. If you think I have fought many duels, it's nothing compared to Jackson."

"You mean his temper is worse than yours?" Jonathan shook his head. "No, impossible!"

"Let's just say his temper is equal to mine." Adam raised an eyebrow at Jonathan's smart remark. "I'll give you an example. Jackson was at a convivial gathering. A gentleman by the name of Dickinson made a snide remark about the unconventionality of Rachel Jackson's marriage. By the way, Rachel is Andrew's wife. He heard this remark and warned Dickinson's father-in-law to restrain his son-in-law. But the offense was repeated. After some newspaper exchanges, Dickinson sent a card to a Nashville paper, the last paragraph of which stated that 'the Major General Jackson . . . is a worthless scoundrel, a poltroon, and coward.' "

"The man must have been a fool," Jonathan said, "if what you just told me is true."

"He was, but at that time I'm sure he didn't think so. Jackson at once challenged him, and of course, Dickinson accepted."

"I understand why he challenged him to a duel. You would have done the same. But what was so unconventional about Jackson's marriage?"

"That's another story, but seeing as we have a long ride ahead of us, I've plenty of time to tell you," Adam said, then continued with his story. "Rachel was married to a man named Robards before she married Jackson. Robards obtained a divorce through an act of the Virginia General Assembly. That's when Jackson married her. But what they didn't know was Robards had asked for and received only an enabling act, whereby if he could show cause, the marriage would be dissolved. It had to be printed in the newspaper and run for eight weeks consecutively. But Robards failed to do this for two years. Therefore, Rachel had been living in adultery with Jackson."

"I guess that's what you would call an unconventional marriage. What did Jackson do?"

"Jackson later went through the marriage ceremony again, but the scandal hung over their heads—and still does, he told me." Adam pulled out his canteen and offered Jonathan a drink. "Damn, it's hot today."

After Jonathan took a drink he said, "Interesting story, my friend. What happened after the challenge was made? I hope he blew the bloke's head off."

"At dawn, I think it was the month of May, Jackson faced his antagonist with pistols at twelve paces. Dickinson was known to be an expert shot, and Jackson was of a lesser skill. Jackson told me he knew he would be hit, perhaps mortally, but Dickinson had slandered his wife, and Jackson wouldn't back down."

"Neither would you," Jonathan commented. "But then, I've never seen a man who could even hold a candle to your marksmanship."

Adam laughed. "Thank you for that small token of praise. Now back to the story. One of his aides told me what happened. He said at the signal there was an instantaneous puff of smoke from Dickinson's pistol and Jackson felt a heavy shock in his side. He swayed momentarily, then straightened. The aide said there was a look of horror on Dickinson's face as he cried, 'Great God, have I missed him?' Dickinson recoiled a step, but resumed the mark upon the referee's order. Jackson raised his pistol and pulled the trigger. The hammer stopped at half-cock. Jackson remorselessly drew back the hammer and this time the gun fired, and Dickinson died that night."

"Was Jackson hurt?"

"He told me himself that he could feel the blood running from his wound down into his boot, but he mounted his horse and rode forty miles back to Nashville."

"I must say he doesn't sound like your ordinary man." Jonathan shook his head. "I can see why you like him."

The campground was dotted with white canvas tents like mushrooms on a forest floor. They rode between the rows of canvas, heading for Jackson's command post. A total of five regiments were camped here, just a little over two thousand men. It was midday, and most of the men hung around their tents, eating lunch or cleaning their rifles.

Adam and Jonathan stopped in front of Jackson's headquarters. Dismounting, they handed the reins to one of the general's aides and entered the tent.

General Jackson sat behind his desk, shoulders bent, looking at a map. Jonathan thought he didn't look as impressive as he had imagined from Adam's fabulous stories. Jackson's homely face tilted up, and Jonathan could see a scar running the length of one cheek. Probably another good story went with that scar. Jackson's voice, as he spoke to Adam, was not deep and bellowed, but high-pitched. Then the general turned, and Jonathan felt his eyes scrutinizing him. Jackson's eyes were a brilliant steel-blue, his look piercing as he searched Jonathan's face, trying to sum up what kind of man he was.

"Mr. Hird, it's a pleasure to have you join us. Adam has spoken often about you." Jackson extended his hand.

"Please call me Jonathan, and the pleasure is all mine, General." Jonathan felt the firm grip of his handshake.

"Sit down," Jackson commanded, pointing to some stools. "Let us talk."

"What are you looking at, General?" Adam asked.

"A map of the Gulf States." He pointed to a spot on the drawing. "I firmly believe the British will strike at Mobile."

"Why do you say that?" Adam asked.

"It seems perfectly obvious that the British will disembark at Mobile, and march overland to some river point above the Crescent City—maybe Baton Rouge—thus avoiding the treacherous delta country," he answered irritably.

"Maybe you are right," Adam acknowledged, "but I believe they will sail into New Orleans. I have information they'll offer Lafitte a deal to join forces with them, and who better than Lafitte knows those treacherous waterways?"

Jonathan's gaze rested on one of the aides standing near the door, who nearly choked when he heard Adam disagree with the general. Jonathan smiled. Evidently, nobody disagreed with Jackson.

The general stood, stretching his back and muscles. "I've not heard this bit of information. As you know, Adam, I'm not a man who readily changes his mind, but I do appreciate your input and would like to hear more. Let's just say we will see who is right in the end." Jackson grinned.

The meeting lasted a little over four hours. Both men shared the things they knew had been happening, and they both filled Jonathan in on everything he didn't know.

"I need your help, Adam," Jackson suddenly admitted.

"How can I assist you?"

"I need someone I can trust to go to Pensacola. There seems to be a bit of trouble down there."

"I hadn't expected to be away from home that long," Adam confessed. "However, if you'll send word to my wife, Jonathan and I will go on your mission."

"Agreed." Jackson shook Adam's hand. "I'll send one of my Choctaw scouts to Four Oaks."

Adam sat down and wrote a note to Jewel, telling her he would be away longer than he'd first thought. But he would try everything possible to be home in time for the party.

Jewel and Elizabeth had kept busy fixing up Annie's house, which now glistened from beeswax, and their hard work showed. Yellow curtains gave a light, airy look to the kitchen. The rooms seemed to glow as the sun trickled in through the windows.

Annie wiped a tear from her eye. "I never thought I'd be havin' anythin' so beautiful in all me born days. 'Tis truly a miracle."

Jewel hugged Annie. "You deserve every bit of it. Look how long you have taken care of everybody else."

"And look what a good job you did on Adam and me." Elizabeth giggled. "Why, we're simply perfect."

Elizabeth and Jewel walked back to the main house. It was a good distance, but they had decided the walk would do them good. As soon as they entered the main hall of Four Oaks, a butler appeared and handed a letter to Jewel. She was a bit worried when she first recognized Adam's writing, and quickly tore into the note.

"Is anything wrong?" Elizabeth asked.

"No, thank goodness. It just says they're going to be longer than expected."

"They?"

"He probably means General Jackson and himself."

"Well, why is he detained?" Elizabeth asked, peering over Jewel's shoulder.

"It seems General Jackson wants Adam to do something for him, but Adam doesn't explain anything."

"What about the party?" Elizabeth was getting excited. "The party is for both of you! Adam just *has* to be there!" Elizabeth declared, exasperated.

"Calm down. Adam said he *would* be here for the party." Jewel smiled at her sister-in-law, feeling she had her very own sister.

The next morning guaranteed a glorious day. Warm air caressed the morning glories, promising more heat by midday. The day wasn't hot, just pleasant and comfortable, nothing like the cold, clammy weather in England.

After a nice breakfast with Elizabeth, Jewel told her she was going for a ride in the country, which was almost the truth.

Jewel hurried to the stable. She moved past several stalls before picking out a mount that looked gentle and understanding.

Now, if she could just overpower this horse and let him know who was boss, she'd have a pleasurable ride into New Orleans. Surprisingly enough, what she'd learned in England came back to her once she mounted. She felt comfortable and somewhat in control.

The ride into New Orleans was enjoyable. Jewel smiled to herself at the thought of what everybody would have said if she had told them where she was going.

She couldn't wait to see her Uncle Pierre. How long had it been now? Over a year. He must be worried.

Jewel ignored the strange stares she received as she rode up to the blacksmith's shop. She had purposely worn a big hat and veil to hide her identity. She couldn't take the chance of word getting back to Adam.

Once she arrived, she lifted the veil so she could talk to the blacksmith. "I'd like to see Pierre, please."

"He isn't here," the blacksmith snapped without looking up.

"You said he would be here in two weeks." She dismounted and stood in front of him. She wasn't about to be put off. It had been a long ride to be dismissed so casually.

The big hulk of a man finally turned around. At first he seemed hesitant to answer her question. "We're expecting him, ma'am, but he hasn't come."

Another blacksmith spoke up, smiling at her. "You sure there ain't something I can do for you?"

"I'm positive." Jewel scowled at the man. She didn't like the way he looked at her. As she turned to head for the office she'd seen Adam go into the last time they'd been there, Jewel's hand came up slowly to the waistband of her skirt where she had hidden a knife.

As she suspected, the blacksmith who had spoken made a grab for her. She whirled just about the time he touched her, slicing his midsection.

"The bitch cut me!" he roared, grabbing his stomach and looking down at the blood staining his hands. "You little witch," he muttered. His eyes widened and he started toward her.

Jewel had been through too much to be afraid. All her training quickly returned as she took a stance, knife in hand. "I was playing with you the first time; however, if you lay another hand on me, I'll slit your throat."

That statement stopped him from advancing further as he contemplated whether she was bluffing.

From behind Jewel, men came flying out of the office

where she had been headed. "What's going on here?" they demanded.

Jewel glanced over her shoulder to see who approached her. The blacksmith lunged, but she was faster, and sidestepped him, leaving him face-down in the dirt.

"Jewel?" one of the men called from behind her.

A squeal of delight slipped from her lips as she ran and threw herself into his arms. "Dominique, is it really you?"

"Of course it is. We thought you were dead," he told Jewel, holding her back to get a better glance. "But look at you. You are fine, *petite?*"

"Yes, I am. And it's a long story how I happen to be here. I thought Pierre would be here today, and I wanted him to tell Jean I'm fine and would see him soon."

The blacksmith found his footing as he got up slowly. "You know her?"

"She's Jean's and Pierre's niece."

"Blimey!" The man swore as his face lost color.

"What happened to you?" Dominique asked, pointing at the blacksmith's middle.

"She cut me," he complained.

"Ah, it's but a mere scratch. If she had wanted to hurt you, mate, she'd have cut you to ribbons. After all, I taught her to handle a knife." Dominique chuckled. "And if Jean had been here, he'd slit your throat for touching his niece."

Jewel looked lovingly at the man she'd grown up with, Dominique You, Jean's first lieutenant. They moved into Jake's office, where they talked in private. Dominique promised he would notify Jean and Pierre that she was fine. Jewel told Dominique she had married, but wouldn't tell him to whom. She explained she had to inform her husband about her family first.

He walked with Jewel to her horse, fussing that she shouldn't have come alone. "You can't ride a horse," he said, surprised when he saw her mount.

"Shh, don't tell the animal," Jewel teased, bending over to kiss Dominique on the cheek.

Jewel felt content that at least one part of her problem was now solved.

What she didn't see when she left the blacksmith's shop was another pair of eyes that watched her from the alley.

Captain Lee grinned. He knew sooner or later Jewel would arrive. This was her uncle's shop, and he had been smart to bide his time and wait for her to make an appearance. He had dressed as a common sailor and made sure to disguise his accent. English sea captains were not welcome here now. His ship lay hidden safely in a cove where he had rowed to shore in a small boat. He was supposedly scouting for England; however, he had other plans, which included the young lady now riding off. He would be patient a while longer. There was a battle brewing and when it broke, everyone would be too busy to pay him much attention. That was when he would strike. He and the young lady would take a short sea voyage. And this time things would be different. He rubbed his finger slowly down his scarred cheek. There would be no escape—no mistakes. The little lady would lead him to a treasure—a treasure fit for a king. Or she'd die, just that simple.

Laughing in a sinister tone, Lee said out loud, "Yes, that is what I'll do. She hasn't seen the last of me yet!"

Twenty-four

Jewel sat before the large mirror at her dressing table, brushing her hair. Now that her hair had grown longer, falling below her shoulders, it took a long time to dry when washed, but today she had plenty to think about as she combed out the tangles.

Everything had been readied for the gala to announce her marriage to Adam. However, there seemed to be one problem . . . no husband. He hadn't come home. And she hadn't heard from him. She had swayed between anger and worrying that something awful had happened.

"I guess I'll just stand up and say, 'Ladies and Gentlemen, I'd like to introduce myself.' " Jewel waved her brush in the air. " 'I'm Adam's wife and, no, I haven't any idea as to the location of my husband.' " Jewel propped her chin on her hand and stared into the mirror, feeling sorry for herself.

The door opened behind her and Annie swept in, followed by a maid carrying Jewel's party dress. "I think ye might be needin' this tonight." Annie had the girl place the dress on the bed and went to stand behind Jewel.

"I don't feel much like a party."

"Now, we'll be havin' none of that, lass." Annie took the brush out of Jewel's hand and began arranging her hair. "If Adam said he would be here, then he will. But if the mon doesn't make it, ye can't let yer guests down." Annie frowned. "Where's yer spunk, lass?"

Jewel's gaze met her friend's in the mirror. Annie was

right, of course, and she *would* carry on tonight, whether Adam came or not. Sitting a little straighter, she squared her shoulders, preparing herself to handle whatever came about tonight.

"That's my girl." Annie finished adorning her hair with spring flowers, placing them in the curls on top of Jewel's head. She stood patiently while Annie began to fasten the tiny hooks at the back of her gown. Finally Jewel was ready, and with a bright smile from Annie, went downstairs.

She found Elizabeth at the bottom of the stairs, giving final instructions to the servants.

"You look like a queen. On second thought, a duchess," Elizabeth said as Jewel approached. "If you approve, I think we'll greet the guests over here." She pointed to the staircase.

"Whatever you think's best." Jewel tapped her fan against her hand. "I really dread meeting all these people I don't know. I feel so out of place here. As if I don't belong."

"Nonsense!" Elizabeth shook her hand. "I want you to stand beside me so I can introduce you." She reached out and grabbed Jewel's arm, pulling her right beside her. "I'll not forgive Adam for not being here."

"I'm sure he would have been here if he could have," Jewel declared, remembering that just a few moments ago she would have agreed with Elizabeth. "We'll just have to make do without him." She squeezed her sister-in-law's hand.

An endless line of strange faces greeted Jewel. I'll never remember these people, she thought. Everyone was nice and welcomed her, though they all seemed to want to know everything about her, such as where she came from and who she was related to. All inquired as to Adam's whereabouts, which managed to bring a blush to her cheeks.

"Who is that?" Jewel whispered to Elizabeth, nodding toward a very stunning lady entering the foyer.

"She's a cold-blooded snake, and that's the only nice thing

I can say about her," Elizabeth stated. "She is another who had designs on your husband."

Before Jewel could comment, the lady in question stood in front of her, and Elizabeth made the introduction.

"Bonnie Newman, may I present my sister-in-law, Jewel Trent."

"Why, I say, you're a pretty young thing," she gushed with Southern charm. "But then Adam always did have good taste in *his* women. It's downright shameful he hasn't bothered to make an appearance tonight. You must really feel the ninny."

Stunned, Jewel felt as if she'd been slapped. She hadn't expected this viciousness from a perfect stranger. How many of Adam's so-called lady friends lay in wait for her? The silence lingered while no one said a word. Jewel wanted to strike back and say something, but what the lady had said was true. She did feel the fool, and worse, she couldn't seem to utter a single word.

"Sorry, I'm late, sweetheart."

Jewel jerked around at the sound of her husband's vibrant voice. Adam had come home. He wore the latest in fashion as he strolled across the hallway in a fawn-colored coat with a white stock. His black knee-high boots glistened in the light from the candles. He slipped an arm around her shoulders, placing a quick kiss on her lips, before turning his attention to the guest.

Adam had heard Bonnie's crude remark and would personally like to strangle the bitch, but he had to rescue his wife first.

"Hello, Bonnie. I see you've not found a husband yet." Adam knew his remark would hit home. "Maybe you should go in and join the rest of our guests. You could test your luck tonight."

"I'd forgotten how mean you can be, Adam Trent." Bonnie's face glowed a vibrant red before she turned on her heels and stomped off toward the ballroom.

Bonnie had been the last of the arriving guests, Adam

noted. He turned Jewel to him. He had missed her, more than he cared to admit. "What . . . no hug . . . no kiss? Am I to assume you didn't miss me?"

His wife still stared at him, and he didn't think she was going to say anything, but finally she whispered, "I didn't think you were coming."

He drank in her beauty. Her cheeks and lips were the softest pink, the color of baby roses. Her eyes were liquid pools of brown, but in the very center gleamed specks of lavender picked up from her dress. He wasted little time taking her into his arms and savoring the sweetness of her mouth. He had a good mind to be rude and go upstairs. Let Elizabeth handle the party.

"All right, you two, stop that. Remember, you've a ballroom full of guests," Elizabeth reminded them.

Adam had forgotten his sister existed. "Elizabeth, you're a bore," he complained.

"Well, someone has to be. It's plain to see you have your wife deceived." Elizabeth cocked her head to the side and smiled.

"Come on, both of you," Adam said, taking their hands in his and pulling them behind him to the library.

"What is it?" Jewel asked, feeling slightly apprehensive.

Adam threw open the door, and Jewel saw a man standing with his back to them. At the sound of the door opening, he turned. "Jonathan!" She squealed, her hand flying over her mouth, before running over to give Jonathan a hug. "When did you get here? As a matter of fact, when did you and Adam both get here? It seems we know nothing that goes on in this house."

"If it is possible, my lady, you have grown lovelier since the last time I saw you." Jonathan bowed and kissed her hand. "And to answer your question, I went with your husband to meet General Jackson."

"Jonathan?" Elizabeth asked hesitantly.

Jonathan looked past Jewel to the lady standing in the doorway. "Elizabeth, you're no longer the child I remember."

"Of course not. I've grown up." Elizabeth turned completely around so he could see her. "What do you think?"

"I approve and demand the first dance with you, madam." Jonathan crossed the room and offered her his arm.

"Shall we, sweetheart?" Adam asked Jewel.

Jewel nodded when he placed his hand on her elbow. "Yes, I believe we are supposed to have the first dance."

They walked through the double doors of the ballroom to the gardens behind it where a dance floor had been constructed. Upon seeing Adam enter, the band started playing a waltz. He didn't stop, but led her out on the dance floor.

Jewel looked up at the body of heavenly stars twinkling down at them as he took her into his arms. "What a beautiful night." She sighed.

"Perhaps a night made for lovers." Adam smiled down at her. Their bodies touched as they glided across the dance floor with an easy grace that surprised her, since they had never actually danced before. The enchanting music captured their souls with its lyrical sound as they swirled around the garden. Jewel glanced up at Adam's handsome face. How could she be so lucky?

"I've missed you," she said, watching him as his gaze seemed to caress her face. The passion in Adam's eyes smoldered, and she knew he was keeping a tight control on his emotions.

Conscious of her softness, Adam felt the heat of her body searing through his clothes. But her softly spoken words became his undoing. His hold tightened on her. "Sweetheart, you don't know how much I've missed you."

After they finished the waltz, she didn't see much of Adam. Every time one dance ended someone was there asking her for the next dance, and she noticed Governor Claiborne spent a great deal of time talking to Adam.

Jewel had finished the last bit of her white wine when Jonathan claimed his dance.

"Are you enjoying yourself, Jonathan?"

"I am now." He grinned.

"I see you haven't lost that silver tongue of yours." Jewel lifted her brow slightly.

"You always could see through me." His eyes darkened as he turned serious. "Are you happy, Jewel?"

"Yes, I am." She felt her eyes mist slightly. "You've always had my best interest at heart, and I'll always love you dearly for being so sweet and being there when I needed you."

Jonathan smiled. "I'm glad Adam finally did the right thing and married you. I've seen him shy away from marriage so many times in the past."

"We had some rough times at sea, but finally solved some of our differences, or I think we have."

"Yes, you both are a little stubborn," he commented, as if the answers were obvious.

"Who, *me?*" Jewel pointed to herself and decided to change the subject before he asked about her memory. "I've seen you dancing with Elizabeth a few times. She's very sweet and has become a good friend."

"Sweet . . . Elizabeth? Remember, I grew up with the hellion, but I have to admit she has developed into quite a beauty."

Jewel saw a gleam in his eyes. Just maybe there could be something there. She would test him and find out. "Elizabeth has had a few marriage proposals since we've been home, but she keeps turning them down."

"Really? I can't picture Elizabeth married to just any man. She's too much like Adam." The dance ended and they moved to the side. "Will you excuse me, Jewel? I think I promised Elizabeth another dance."

"Yes, of course." Jewel tried to hide her smile as she opened a small fan to cool herself.

"Are you through dancing?" said the voice beside her.

"Not if you'd like to dance with me," Jewel said, smiling up at her husband and noticing he looked somewhat irritated.

"Well, you've danced with everybody here. I thought maybe I could have a turn," Adam snapped in a low voice.

"Isn't that what a hostess should do?" She didn't particularly like his tone. Especially since she'd endured boring small talk all night with strangers.

Adam didn't bother to reply, but escorted, or rather pulled, her to the dance floor just before the band called for the last dance. Neither said a word as they whirled around the floor. Both were definitely conscious of the energy radiating from their bodies. Adam guided her over to the side of the garden where the crowd had thinned.

"Let's take a walk," he growled.

She started not to go, but decided it might be better to be out of hearing range of their guests.

They stopped at the edge of a pool on the other side of the rose garden. Walking around the pool, they entered the gazebo, where they could have some privacy.

Before Adam could say a word, she whirled about to face him. Her eyes flashed with anger. "Don't you say a word, you pompous ass!"

"I beg your pardon," Adam bellowed.

"I said shut up!" She didn't care how angry he was. Her anger now matched his. "For weeks, I've worried that something had happened to you. You never bothered to write, not once. Then tonight I had to greet our guests by myself, and now when I try to be a good hostess and have to put up with men stepping all over my feet, you start accusing me of flirting!" Tears glistened on the edges of her eyelashes. "I'm trying to be a good wife, but where you're concerned it's almost impossible!"

He reached out and snatched her to him. His iron grip tightened, just a small reminder he could crush her if he so desired. His face was mere inches from hers as he said, "I'm sorry." He let his breath out slowly. "But the sight of men holding you close, when it has been so long since I've had the privilege, has driven me beyond reason. Once again my demon temper overruled my judgment."

Adam felt Jewel's body relax, and it warmed his heart. Just holding her seemed to ease his restless spirit. Something about her still scared him. He rarely thought about her lack of memory anymore. If she hadn't regained it by now, she probably wouldn't. But something nagged at him. Even though she had married him, he felt as if he didn't truly possess her. There was something she held away from him, and he couldn't figure out what it was.

His mouth eagerly took hers while his exploring hands caressed her body as he held her close. His warm breath brushed against her ear. Adam placed soft kisses on her neck, and soon felt her body tremble in his arms. It was all he needed to send him over the edge.

He stood back from her only a moment while he loosened his stock.

Jewel felt limp watching Adam disrobe. Her body already yearned for his kisses and touch. She, too, quickly pulled off her dress, frustrated by the knot she had just put in her corset.

Adam pulled her down on his lap. His knife quickly disposed of the ribbon and the corset fell away.

"Adam, you've ruined it!"

"I'll buy you another," he murmured huskily, turning her to face him. He took one of her breasts in his mouth, pulling her down on top of him as he lay back on the cushions. His tongue teased each nipple into hard buds. Then his teeth closed on one peak, causing Jewel to groan with longing. Adam's mouth traveled back to her pink lips, and he took her mouth with a blistering kiss. "I want you now, Jewel."

"Like this," she whispered, indicating she was on top.

"Yes, just like this." Adam held her hips, lifting her up before lowering her down on his throbbing manhood. God, she felt good! He moved her hips, feeling all of her velvety softness around him. Pulling her head down, Adam captured her lips again. He lost control and took her with a wild abandonment. They both climaxed as their bodies shuddered from pent-up emotion. Adam rolled her to the side, kissing her tender lips. "I've missed you, sweetheart."

"Will you be staying for a while?" Jewel murmured sleepily.

"Yes, for a while . . ."

Twenty-five

September 3, 1814

Thanks to his many friends and spies, Jean Lafitte knew what the British Army and Navy were thinking even before he was told.

So on this lovely morning in September as he watched the brig *Sophie, R.N.* come a-calling, Jean smiled and leaned back against a white column that supported his veranda while he wondered just what the British offer would be.

Unfortunately, he and his brother were now considered outlaws with a price on their heads. And poor Pierre had the unfortunate circumstance of now being a prisoner in the jail in New Orleans.

"That damn Claiborne!" Jean pushed away from the pillar, feeling the anger of his brother's imprisonment. At least he had confidence that his attorney would get Pierre out.

All these things weighed heavily on Jean's mind as he left the shade of the veranda to meet the crew of the *Sophie.*

He wasn't in a good mood.

"Good day, gentlemen," he said in his heavy French accent.

"Monsieur Lafitte, thank you for allowing us to come and make our proposal to you." Captain Lockyer shuffled his feet when Jean didn't bother to comment. "Let me introduce myself and my assistant. I am Captain Robert Lockyer, and this is Lieutenant Mark Williams."

Jean nodded at the introductions, but refused to shake their hands. "Come, let me escort you to my home. We'll dine there. Then we can discuss business."

Jean smiled secretly, noticing that his men jostled the Englishmen along the way as they walked to the main house. But what could these proper Englishmen expect from these ferocious Baratarians?

The British officers exchanged looks and started to hesitate, evidently thinking their coming here might not have been a good idea.

Looking over at the much-too-proper officers, Jean decided to rescue them. "These gentlemen are my guests," he said sternly, "and you would do well to remember that, men. Now, come." He swept his hand toward the veranda, ignoring the amused glances that passed between his men.

When they entered the sprawling house, Captain Lockyer looked surprised at the exquisite interior and how well Jean lived. Jean smiled. Just because he was an outlaw didn't mean he didn't have taste.

As dinner was served, a dinner that was probably far superior to the captain's everyday meals, Jean couldn't help thinking of Jewel. Had the British captured his niece? By heaven or hell, he would find out.

Jean plied the officers with his best rum and exquisite wine—stolen from a French ship, of course. After dinner they adjourned to a sitting area and the captain produced the letter.

Jean took the dispatch and an accompanying proclamation, reading both without comment. The letter stated that he would be in the British Navy with a rank of captain. He could have his lands as soon as they had peace, and a bonus of forty thousand dollars cash.

How absurd, Jean thought. Make him a captain . . . when he was already commander of his group of thieves. Give him land . . . that he already owned. And last but not least, an offer of forty thousand dollars when he had millions. *Bas-*

tards! These men had to be very stupid. They didn't deserve to win the war.

Since he considered himself a true diplomat and also very cunning, Jean smiled slowly. "Gentlemen, this offer leaves me . . . how would you say . . . perhaps, speechless? I would like to review it and get my affairs in order. I'll get back to you in a fortnight."

The men smiled and bade their farewells. Jean could see from their faces they were already congratulating themselves, thinking that the meeting had gone extremely well. Such fools.

As soon as the visitors had gone, Lafitte sat down and wrote to Adam and Governor Claiborne. Yes, he would fight with America, but first he had to get Pierre out of jail. Jean could not look for his niece with Pierre in danger.

To the governor, Jean suggested a pardon. He could handle the state people through his connections; it was the federal people that worried him.

But would he get his deal? Jean wondered.

The December morning dawned cold and wet. It wasn't a day fit for a parade, and all of New Orleans did so love a parade, but Adam knew the general wouldn't like the fuss.

Adam sat on the horse at the outskirts of town and waited for the general. He'd sent a carriage to fetch him, but doubted Jackson would take it.

Riding into the city, the commanding officer of the Seventh United States Military District cut a drab figure. He should have been covered with medals and gleaming with gold lace, but Jackson wore a leather cap on his head. A short, faded blue Spanish cloak was draped across his shoulders, and had been frogged over his chest against the chill, hiding his insignia and decorations.

He appeared damn tired, and it showed in his "damn-you" eyes. Adam knew how the man felt, for he felt much the same. He wanted to get on with his life, but unfortunately it would have to wait. Staring straight ahead, Adam and Jackson rode to the previously prepared quarters on Royal Street. They didn't bother to acknowledge the cheers from the crowd.

Once settled in, General Jackson met the engineers with whom he would have to work. He listened attentively to what they had to say.

When everyone had left, Adam tried to talk to the general about Jean and Pierre Lafitte.

"They are Hellish Banditti," Jackson stormed, coming to his feet.

"You've known me a long time," Adam stated, trying not to lose his temper. "I ask that you not make up your mind too quickly about the Lafittes. Sometimes things are not what they seem, and after you have had time to look around, you'll see I am correct."

Jackson sat back down. "Because I've known you a long time, I will think on this matter."

"Thank you, General. You'll not be sorry."

Unexpectedly, the office door swung open. "General Jackson, welcome to our city," Edward Livingston, a highly acclaimed lawyer, said in his deep voice.

"Edward, my old friend, how good it is to see you." Jackson beamed.

"Adam, as always, it's a pleasure." Edward shook his hand. "It looks like our mutual friend is in trouble."

"I just mentioned that very fact to the general."

Adam was glad that Edward Livingston worked for the Lafittes as their lawyer. Edward was a personal friend of Jackson's. Definitely more than any other man, he had the ear of the general. With Adam on one side and Edward on the other, they had the general convinced in no time to pardon their friends.

"I'm having a reception at my home tonight. I'd be honored if you both would attend," Edward said.

"I will see you both tonight, then." Adam took his leave, anxious to return home, if only for a night. Again, he found himself anxious to get this impending battle over with. He didn't want to go through life as he'd been doing. He wanted a meaningful life. He wanted a loving wife. But above all he wanted her trust. There had been few women in his life he could trust. He would bring Jewel, so she could meet the general.

Everybody had turned out, it seemed, for Livingston's party. There were six carriages waiting in front of them, Jewel observed as she peeked out the window, watching the ladies disembarking from the carriages. There were more than a sprinkling of aristocratic belles, which reminded her of Jonathan's party. From what Jewel had read, she decided she must be the most inexperienced party goer ever. But then most young ladies hadn't grown up the way she had. Then she thought of her uncles. She wouldn't change one minute of her childhood. Their love meant more than any fancy gatherings—their love and Adam's.

"Adam, are you sure I look proper? I had to get ready in such a hurry." Jewel fidgeted, smoothing out her gown. She wanted to make a good impression as his wife. She was sure he'd known much more sophisticated women in his past. "I should have put my hair up, shouldn't I?" She reached up, patting her hair.

Adam took her hand and held it firmly in his. "You're beautiful just the way you are, and I like your hair down. Just relax." He pulled out a flask of brandy. "Here, take one swallow and I'm sure you'll feel much better. I believe it's your favorite."

"You're never going to let me live that down," she said, laughing up at him. "Are you?"

Adam didn't get a chance to answer because the carriage

door opened and a footman waited to assist them from the vehicle.

"I wish Elizabeth and Jonathan could have joined us," Jewel commented to her husband's back as he stepped down and then turned to aid her.

"If I know Jonathan, he wanted to be alone with my sister. Remember, he's been gone, too."

"I suppose you're right. I think they make a lovely couple."

Adam arched a brow at her, and then placed her in front of him as they went through the receiving line.

"Jewel, may I introduce General Andrew Jackson," Adam said.

"It's a pleasure, General." Jewel extended her hand. She noted that he wore his dress uniform and his boots had been polished to a high luster.

"The pleasure is all mine," Jackson commented.

They entered a large ballroom, alight with candles and glistening chandeliers, which held a good number of people. Evidently Jewel and Adam had been among the last to arrive. Strolling among the guests, Adam finally settled in a small cluster of people that he seemed to know very well. Jewel half-listened, but she'd had the oddest feeling since entering the room.

For some strange reason she thought again of Jonathan's party and Captain Lee. After all these months, why would she think of that despicable man? Quickly glancing around the room to make sure he wasn't there, she breathed a sigh of relief. What a stupid feeling, she told herself. An Englishman wouldn't dare come to America unless it was to fight. She frowned again. Did that mean Lee would be coming?

It didn't matter, she finally convinced herself. He'd never be able to find her.

"I'll be right back." Adam squeezed her arm, then moved over to a cluster of men on the other side of the room, leaving her in the midst of a group of ladies talking about their latest quilting bee. Unfortunately, she'd never sewn a day in her life. Instead of sewing, she'd practiced with swords. Jewel smiled, wondering if she should change the subject.

"I'm glad you could come to my party," a male voice sounded beside her. She turned to find the general smiling at her as he extended his arm.

"Thank you for rescuing me," she murmured when they had moved away from the group.

"My pleasure." Jackson chuckled.

They began talking, and she found the man very interesting. She especially liked hearing the stories of some of the battles he had fought. He even told her a little bit about his wife, who was back home waiting for him. The time sped by quickly, until she overheard a conversation that a small group just behind them was having.

"You suppose they will hang that scoundrel Pierre Lafitte?" one man said.

"They have him locked in the jail, but there's not a jail built that can hold him," the other said with a laugh. "Especially while Jean is still loose. He's the dangerous one."

"Excuse me, General." Jewel went and got herself a glass of champagne. She found her throat suddenly very dry. That glass was soon followed by another. Her uncle was in jail. But why? He was so close. She had to see him. Glancing around for Adam, she noticed he was still in the group of men talking. It was perfect. She would take the carriage, see Pierre, and be back before Adam even noticed she was missing.

Slipping through the crowd, she hurried from the building to their waiting carriage. The driver, who was asleep, jumped when she grabbed his leg. "Please take me to the jail. It's urgent."

The short carriage ride took her directly to the middle of town. Jewel instructed the driver to wait, informing him she would be right back.

When she entered the jail, the sergeant in charge seemed reluctant to let her see Pierre. However, when Jewel informed him she had just come from Governor Claiborne's, and she'd be most happy to go back and get the governor, he changed his mind and let her in.

"You only have five minutes. Make it quick," the sergeant grumbled as he turned the key, allowing her entrance. She was thankful that he was leaving them alone.

Pierre didn't move at the sound of the jingling keys. He had a visitor, but her shadowed face meant nothing to him, so he waited for the jailor to let her into the cell. He wondered what tricks that nasty Claiborne had up his sleeve.

"You wish to see me, *mademoiselle?*" he said, his French accent thick.

She hesitantly moved into the light where he could see her, then said, "Uncle Pierre."

He came to his feet. "Are my eyes playing tricks on me, my love?" His soft-spoken words held a note of disbelief.

"I'm really here," she choked out before she embraced Pierre, laying her head on his shoulder.

"Jean was right." Pierre held her away from him, looking at her once again. "You're alive! But where have you been, and why haven't you contacted us?"

Blushing bright red, she proceeded to tell him about her memory loss, and all about Adam. She held nothing back this time.

Pierre smiled. "I would like to meet this husband of yours."

Jewel had been careful not to tell her uncle her last name, fearing that Uncle Jean might come after her. She didn't want to see Adam hurt—or her uncles. "You will meet him, but first I have to tell him about you and Jean."

"Ah, you're ashamed of us, *petite?*"

"No, Uncle Pierre! How can you say that?" She frowned. "It's just that—that you both are unusual. Even you have to admit, you're not like the local people around here."

Pierre chuckled. *"Oui,* I suppose our trade is a little different. Yet we are very prosperous."

"It's just that . . . well . . . I was thrust upon Adam with-out his having any say-so in the matter. He did marry me, and I believe he cares, but I must be sure of his love." She searched her uncle's face for understanding. "Every time we're together for a little while, I start to build my courage to tell him. Then he is called off to do something with the general, and we have to start all over again." Jewel sighed. "Please understand. I'm not sure I've explained it very well."

"Oui, petite, I do. And I think you worry too much. If he loves you, he'll not turn you away. He is the one who should worry. If Jean doesn't like him, he'll simply run him through." Pierre threw up his hand in a simple swordsman's gesture as his musical laughter rang out in the small area.

"I guess you've always been the calm one," Jewel admit-ted. "Listen." She reached out and grabbed his arm. "The guard is coming. Is there something I can do for you?" The footsteps kept advancing. "How will you get out?"

"My love." Pierre hugged her, then whispered in her ear so no one else could hear. "Do you really think Jean would leave me in here for long?"

Jewel looked at him. His smile told all. She kissed him on the cheek and ran to the coach, wasting little time in getting back to the party.

In the shadows, Adam stood outside the jail and waited for his carriage and wife to leave before crossing the street. Why would she be down here?

Well, he'd soon find out!

When he entered the building, the desk sergeant had his back to him, pouring a cup of coffee.

"Who did that lady come to see?" Adam said in a harsh voice.

"And what business is that of yours?" the sergeant replied without turning to face him.

"I'll not repeat myself," Adam growled.

The sergeant spun and choked on the hot liquid once his gaze locked with the black eyes that were now piercing his. It took several moments before he could speak.

"Mr. Trent! My apologies, sir. I didn't know it was you. The lady came to see Pierre Lafitte." He chuckled, raising his brow. "Probably one of his wenches."

That statement didn't please Adam worth a damn. And it was all he could do not to smash in the man's face. But then, the guard was just doing his duty. It was his friend in the next room Adam really wanted to hit. "Take me to him."

Why would she want to see Pierre? And how could Jewel possibly know him? All these questions tumbled through Adam's mind when he stepped into the cell, reminding him once again that he knew nothing about his wife.

"What? More company?" Pierre looked up and smiled when he saw Adam. "It's been a long time, old friend. I'm sorry you had to see me in here." Pierre gestured for Adam to sit down.

"I'm not so sure if . . ." Adam paused as he realized he was thinking out loud. He'd get the facts first. "Pierre, it's good to see old friends anytime, and I guess anyplace, but in my opinion you should not be in here," Adam said truthfully. "But the reason I came has nothing to do with you being held prisoner. Would you like to tell me why my *wife* came to see you?"

"Your wife hasn't been to see me, my friend." Pierre looked shocked when he placed his hand on his chest. "I didn't even know you were married."

"You didn't just have a visit from a young lady?" Adam questioned.

"*Oui,* my niece was here." Pierre's eyes snapped up. "My God, Adam! You're the *Adam* she spoke of!" Waves of laughter followed Pierre's statement as he held his middle.

Adam found nothing amusing about this situation, and he was getting ready to say so when it dawned on him what Pierre had said. "Niece. *Your niece?*"

Why hadn't he put everything together a long time ago? The accent, the fencing, her extensive knowledge about ships. And he'd wanted to know what boarding school she'd attended. "It's good to know Jewel sees fit to tell you about me. However, she hasn't bothered to tell me anything about you."

"A moment, please." Pierre stiffened. "Don't get your feathers ruffled, my friend." He grew serious. "Jewel is afraid to tell you that she's been raised in a very unconventional environment. Or by pirates, if you prefer. For some strange reason, she thinks you'll hate her." Pierre laughed again at his dumbfounded new nephew. "Wait until Jean finds out."

"Jean!" Adam laughed, too. "That is the *uncle* Jewel always referred to." He shook his head. "I can't believe I didn't put this all together when the truth has been all around me. Why, Jean and I even talked about her in an indirect way. He was talking about his niece, and I was talking about my wife. What a fool I've been."

"Are you going to say anything to her?" Pierre asked.

"No. Though I'll admit I'm angry that Jewel hasn't trusted me enough to tell me the truth. I'll wait until she divulges her secret."

"Be patient, my friend. Jewel has never been around men such as yourself. She is very naive when it comes to such things. Jean and I probably sheltered her way too much. Just give her time."

"My God, man. I am her husband! She should trust me!" Adam said, letting his irritation show.

Pierre got to his feet. "Promise me you'll have some patience."

"I'll try. But I will not make a promise I might not keep." It was the only concession Adam could make.

"At least you're an honest man. Just remember, she is our niece." Pierre chuckled. "You and Jean, kin . . . what a pair!"

Later that night Pierre had more visitors, ones he was especially glad to see. Jean's men broke Pierre out of prison, and Pierre was forced into hiding until things calmed down. Unfortunately, Pierre would have to wait to tell Jean about finding Jewel.

Jewel hurried up the steps and peeked into the ballroom. Looking quickly around the room for Adam and not finding him, she went off to freshen up and calm her flushed face.

When she entered the main drawing room, she noticed Adam talking with Jackson, and she headed over to them.

"If I've not told you, Adam," the general said, "I will do so now. Your wife is stunning, and she has completely captivated me."

Jewel blushed.

"It seems she has that effect on people. Thank you, Andrew," Adam said, acknowledging the compliment. "Not many men can *trust* their wives. I'm so glad mine is honest."

What a strange comment, Jewel thought, but said nothing, thinking her husband sounded a bit irritated.

"You're right about that, Adam." Jackson turned his attention back to Jewel. "I hope you will not think harsh of me for taking your husband once again, Mrs. Trent. I'm going to be needing him more now, so I'm afraid you'll not be seeing Adam very much."

"So soon?" Jewel asked, feeling the disappointment as it flooded her body. She watched the men shake their heads yes before she said, "No, General, I'll not hold it against you. The job has to be done." But she wanted to say, "How will I ever get to really know my husband?"

"Good, spoken like a real soldier's wife."

On the way home, Adam's irritation burned like a hot coal. "Sweetheart, have you ever noticed your accent is so much like the people of New Orleans? Do you suppose it's possible you came from here?" Adam watched her closely, waiting for her reply. Many emotions filtered across her face. He only wanted the truth.

Jewel blinked. Now was the time to tell him. She opened her mouth to speak . . . she hesitated . . . then lost the struggle. What if she lost him? Couldn't he just say he loved her no matter who she was? "Yes, it's possible. However, I could be French, the accent is so similar." Coward, she chided herself. Would she ever tell him?

Damn, Adam thought. He wanted to shake her. He had given her a chance, and again she'd avoided the truth. Damn it all, he didn't like Jewel lying to him. He loved her. Couldn't she see that and trust him?

A cold silence settled around them as neither said a word the rest of the way home. When they reached Four Oaks, Adam packed his bag.

"I'm leaving tonight." He turned to look at Jewel as she stood behind him, watching.

"But I thought it wouldn't be until tomorrow."

"My plans have changed," he answered gruffly. He started to pick up his bag and leave, but the expression on her face stopped him. He swore to himself, put the bag down, then pulled her into his arms.

Adam struggled with his emotions. But in the end he did leave, not giving in to the temptation to stay. This was better than losing his temper with her, and he had many things to sort through his mind. Maybe when this battle was over, they could sit down and talk, but right now he'd have to stay focused on what lay ahead. All of New Orleans could be in danger.

After Adam left, Jewel cried herself to sleep. His hug had been strange. It had felt so final, as if he'd never return. She should have told him. Why didn't she tell him the truth? Jewel scolded herself.

She hadn't even told him she loved him.

Twenty-six

Now was Jean's chance.

His attorney arranged a meeting with Jackson. Jean had heard that the general was having a hard time doing his job with what he'd been given. "So, why not sweeten the deal to my advantage?" he said out loud, then laughed as he dismounted from his white stallion, tied the reins, then climbed the steps of a secluded cabin.

He knocked on the door and upon hearing "Enter," moved into the room. Jackson stood and frowned.

"General. I'm Jean Lafitte." He nodded, not offering to shake the general's hand.

"Be seated," Jackson said gruffly as he took his seat behind the desk. "What can I do for you, Lafitte?"

"Jean, if you please." Lafitte grinned. He liked keeping the general off balance. "It's not what you can do for me, but what *I* can do for you, General."

"Really?"

"Oui. I believe you're in need of flints."

"I am." Jackson stood abruptly and went over to look out the window. "A good general is one who wins battles, but with what I've been given to work with, the task seems all but impossible."

"That's why I'm here. I have seventy-five hundred flints and a crew of men who'd fight anyone at the drop of a hat."

Jackson turned back from the window. "Interesting. But why be so generous when you've been treated so badly?"

"I have no love for the British." Jean shrugged. "And I'll not buffalo you. In exchange for the flints, I want a full pardon for my brother and my men. Upon your signed agreement, we'll be ready to take up arms and fight with you."

Jackson moved over to stand in front of Lafitte. "You have your agreement, Jean. Perhaps I've misjudged you. Adam Trent told me I'd seek your help before this battle was over. Needless to say, I should have listened to him sooner."

It was still early morning when Jackson left to inspect his defenses. Most of the area, he discovered, was either swamp or open water. There were only two possible avenues of approach to the city. Adam had advised Jackson that the British would more than likely take Chef Menteur Road. Adam's reason was valid. It was one of the few roads that were solid and would support the weight of cannons. Now that Jackson saw the road, he agreed with Adam. Chef Menteur Road ran from just north of the city, northeast to a strip of land known as the Plain of Gentilly. It reached to Lake Borgne, which connected with the sound between the Chandeleur Islands.

Adam arrived just as the general finished his inspection. "I see you decided to study the road yourself?" Adam raised a brow, questioning the general.

"Of course. You know I investigate everything."

Adam had begun explaining the region to General Jackson when a distant rider appeared. Upon reaching them, the courier jerked back on the reins. "I've a dispatch for the general."

Adam watched as Jackson read the note, then shook his head. "It's bad news. Lieutenant Catesby Jones says the British have attacked five of his gunboats." The general looked over at Adam. "It seems Jones had to retreat into the shallow waters of Lake Borgne. Jones said they were enormously outnumbered, but they fought well."

"Did any of his crews survive?" Adam asked.

"His crews are either dead or now prisoners." The general wadded up the letter.

"Damn," Adam swore. "That means the gate is wide open for the British. This isn't a good sign. I hope you have a trick or two up your sleeve, General. We're going to need it."

Their moods were somber as they hurried back to New Orleans. Adam had done well keeping his mind on the upcoming battle, but now his thoughts were on Jewel and his sister. He prayed they didn't venture from the plantation. They would be safe there. He'd left a few men to watch over them, but if the British started moving inland, he would find Jonathan and together they would protect his family.

"I think you should send for your nephew, Brigadier Coffee," Adam suggested, trying to put his mind back to the main objective. "He's at Baton Rouge, and I think we could use his twenty-five hundred Tennessee militiamen," Adam said. "The quicker the better."

It was three o'clock in the afternoon when Major Villeré and his friend Dussau de la Croix, both breathless, entered the command post at Royal Street. "We would like to see General Jackson urgently!"

The desk sergeant, seeing no need to hurry, spat out the tobacco he was chewing. Wiping his mouth with the back of his hand, he stated casually, "The general is busy. Have a seat and I'll tell him you're here."

"Are you deaf? I said it was urgent, man!" Major Velleré protested.

"No, I ain't deaf!" The sergeant slammed his hand down on the desk. "You're not a military man, even though you're referred to as 'Major.' It's a courtesy title, and you've no right to demand anything."

Adam was in his office. The commotion outside the door

drew his attention. He went to investigate. "What's the trouble here?"

"Adam." A look of relief flooded the major's face upon seeing someone he knew. "I must see the general. The British have taken over my plantation. We just came from there, barely escaping with our lives!" Overly excited, he lapsed into French, and it was hard to understand what he was saying. Dussau de la Croix, after catching his breath, began to babble about the number of soldiers.

Adam understood Major Villeré enough to take him and his friend in to see Jackson himself, leaving the sputtering sergeant behind him.

They entered the general's office unannounced. "Andrew, I think these men have some information for you. It sounds important."

Jackson listened carefully, nodding as Villeré recounted what had happened at his plantation.

"I was asleep on the veranda, and when I awoke, I was surrounded by Redcoats. I couldn't believe it! They came in just as if they owned the place. I knew you had to be told, General, so I jerked free from the man holding me and vaulted the railing. I ran like hell and headed for the swamp. They were shooting at me the whole time. They followed, but stopped dead in their tracks when I entered the swamp. I lost them, met my friend, and we came straight here, General."

Adam watched Jackson as he realized the full meaning of what the major had said. Jackson's face had grown pale, but other than that he showed no outward emotion.

"How many men do you think they have?"

"It looked to be a brigade, maybe two thousand men."

"I see," Jackson said. Turning his back to the men, he walked over to his window—a habit that Adam had learned meant the general was deep in thought. Jackson remained quiet for several moments. Slowly, he turned back to the men who waited for him to speak.

"Major, this day you've performed a brave deed, and I thank you." He cleared his throat. "Tom," he yelled for the desk sergeant.

"Yes, sir, General."

"Get my horse and my sword."

"What are you going to do?" Adam asked.

"If they want a fight, then by God, gentlemen, we'll give them a fight!" Jackson cried. "We will fight them tonight! Right now!"

The sun hung low in the sky when Adam and his men set out. He had been given what seemed like an impossible task to perform, but by God, perform it he would. They traveled at a steady pace, not stopping until they saw the first glow of the enemy's campfires.

Adam nudged his horse into a trot over to Jackson's side. "Look, General. The Redcoats are in a bare sugarcane field, with no trees for protection. Perhaps they will be easy pickings after all."

"It's perfect." Jackson grinned.

He waited until dark before giving the command to attack. A white mist had settled in, making the flashes from the muskets' fire seem eerie. The gun smoke hung in the air, mixing with the mist and causing poor visibility. At times they couldn't even see where they were firing.

The fighting grew fierce and bloody. However, the superior discipline of the British soldiers was apparent, and at last that discipline began to tell. Andrew Jackson did something he usually didn't do; he ordered a retreat.

"Where to?" Adam hollered over his shoulder.

"Rodriguez Canal. We will regroup there."

The British didn't pursue. They'd had enough for one night.

"We'll regroup and attack in the morning," Jackson said.

"I don't think that's such a good idea."

"Why, Adam?"

"I just talked to Jonathan. He went with the Choctaw scouts to check on the enemy. He heard them say they thought any man like this American general crazy enough to attack at night must have fifty thousand troops. Jonathan said the British were being heavily reinforced."

"I see your point. That does make a difference. But we won't retreat again! It's not in my nature." Jackson rubbed his chin in thought. "Have you an account of our dead and wounded?"

"Yes, we had twenty-four killed and at least a hundred wounded."

I'm disappointed we didn't get a victory," Jackson confessed. "But at least we showed the British that Americans can fight."

And so the wait began. This time they would wait for the British to attack.

The Rodriguez Canal, a man-made irrigation ditch about ten feet wide and three quarters of a mile long, extended from the river. Because of the lowness of the Mississippi, there wasn't any water in the canal now, and the Americans found it the perfect place to dig in. They placed bales of cotton up on the banks for extra protection from bullets, being careful to cover the bales with dirt for fear of fire.

The men worked hard, forgoing sleep. The general and Adam hadn't slept either. They were there to drive their men on, knowing time was of the essence.

But when morning dawned, there was no attack, so everyone dug in and waited. Jackson was not idle, but feverishly busy having supplies brought out from the city. They searched for every available firearm that could be found while reinforcing their positions.

The weather turned miserable and it rained much of the time. The nights were cold and damp. Some men didn't even have tents where they could sleep and escape the weather. The cold ground was their only bed, and threadbare blankets their only comfort. They huddled near the campfires to receive what little warmth they could provide. Adam worried about the men being cold and wet. He prayed none of the men developed consumption. They couldn't afford to lose good men.

Adam was also concerned about their commander. Jackson seldom got more than an hour of sleep, and he had developed dysentery. The general wouldn't let it stop him, even though he was a walking, wincing skeleton. He constantly checked on his troops, scolding or encouraging them.

On the morning of December twenty-seventh, a loud explosion rocked the area. Adam and the general wondered what it could be. Later they found out it was their ship, the *Carolina*.

The *Carolina* had been pounding the British with gunfire. The English had issued orders to mount four twenty-four-pound howitzers on the levee. They had a lucky hit, sending a red-hot ball into the magazine of the *Carolina*. She exploded with a roar that rattled windows clear up in New Orleans, and then she sank.

It was the day after Christmas, and a more miserable Christmas Jewel couldn't remember. She and Elizabeth tried to make the best of things, but they missed Adam and Jonathan. Since they hadn't received any word on what was happening, they were forced to sit and wait . . . and wonder . . . and most of all worry. One night they did hear volleys of gunfire, and assumed a battle of some sort had occurred.

"I'll just die if something happens to Jonathan," Elizabeth confided to Jewel.

"You know how experienced they are, Elizabeth. I'm sure they will be just fine. Wait and see." Jewel tried to sound optimistic. She had worried many times something might happen to Adam, and she'd give anything to see him. And this time she would tell Adam just how much she loved him. And she'd fight to make him love her.

The next day Elizabeth said she was going for a ride. Jewel didn't think it was a good idea with the British troops about.

"Don't be silly, Jewel. I'm English, remember? Besides, we haven't seen any soldiers, and I just have to get out of this house. I promise I'll stay on Four Oaks land." Elizabeth rode off, vowing she wouldn't go far.

When the sky grew dark and Elizabeth hadn't returned, Jewel began pacing the floor, reprimanding herself for not accompanying her sister-in-law.

A noise in the distance stopped Jewel's pacing. She listened. The sound of a horse galloping out front got her attention. "Thank goodness, Elizabeth is home!"

Relieved, Jewel ran to the front door. She pulled it open, and her smile faded instantly. It wasn't Elizabeth, but a boy with a package in his hand.

"I have a package for Mrs. Jewel Trent."

"I am Jewel Trent." something was wrong. She could feel it. Her hands shook as she took the note. Looking up, she found the boy was still waiting. "Is there something else?" she asked before reading the note.

"I was instructed to wait for a reply, ma'am."

"A reply?" Jewel gave him a blank look. "A reply?" she questioned again. Who in the world was the message from? She wasted little time reading the note. Then she opened the package. "No!" She shook her head. This just couldn't be possible. It was a nightmare. She felt the color drain from her face, and she was having a difficult time breathing.

The boy reached out and touched her arm. "You all right, miss?"

"Yes," she stammered, trying to gather her thoughts. "If you'll come in and wait I will pen my reply."

Captain Lee had Elizabeth in his possession. So Jewel

would not think he was making idle threats, he had sent a small token . . . Elizabeth's chemise.

Lee had come back to haunt her.

Jewel prayed Lee wouldn't harm Elizabeth, even though he had threatened to in the letter. Then it dawned on Jewel . . . Lee wouldn't hurt Elizabeth . . . *she* was the one Lee wanted because only she could take him to the treasure.

Jewel moved numbly, void of all emotion. It was time. She'd known that one day it would happen, and now was the time to pay the price. She wrote the response that Captain Lee expected, and handed it back to the boy.

"Take this as quickly as possible!" she instructed.

She watched as the boy rode in the direction of New Orleans. Turning, she went in the house and climbed the stairs to her room. Walking over to her closet, she rummaged around in the bottom and found what she was looking for— her men's clothing.

Packing only a few things, she left all the beautiful gowns Adam had given her. She would have little need of them now and she would leave with what she'd come with—nothing.

Now for the last task, a note to Adam. Jewel's eyes moistened at the thought of her husband. She would always remember the picnic when Adam had first kissed her, and the snowy day when they had gotten the Christmas greenery. But most of all she would remember their first Christmas Eve when Adam had given her two special gifts: a beautiful necklace and the gift of love.

With shaky fingers, she picked up a pen and wrote Adam a note explaining everything. The thought that she would never see him again brought a sadness to her heart that was almost too painful to bear.

But bear it she must. However, she couldn't bear to say good-bye to Annie. Besides, Annie might try to stop her.

* * *

The early morning sun had just etched its way up in the darkened sky. The note to Adam was finished and lay on his desk where he would be able to find it. How many times had she wished that she had told Adam the truth?

Her identity had endangered Elizabeth's life, but no more would she lie. The truth was in the note. She could imagine the look of disgust when Adam found out she was a pirate's niece. He would hate her, not only for what she was, but for not telling him sooner.

"I'm sorry, Adam," Jewel whispered. Perhaps, all things considered, it would be for the best. This way he wouldn't come after her, because he wouldn't know where to look.

Dressed in the pants and jacket, Jewel slipped a knife in her waistband. She had some unfinished business to take care of, and the knife might prove useful.

She reached out her hand and touched the necklace. She didn't feel much like a lady now. She was not worthy of his present. It was given to someone Adam had thought he knew. But he would discover he hadn't known her at all. Raising her hand to her cheek, she wiped the tears that trickled down. "Good-bye, my love."

Jewel stayed low in the saddle. She could hear the fighting in the distance as she rode toward New Orleans. Her thoughts were jumbled in her, and she was too numb with fear to worry about the war.

She rode to the specified wharf, and noticed it was away from the main docks. Dismounting, she waited for what seemed like a lifetime—her lifetime, slowly slipping away. Then she heard the splashing of oars as they hit the water, stroking slowly and steadily. She watched a small boat glide over to the pier. Two men flanked Elizabeth in the middle of the boat. She appeared fine. Jewel breathed a sigh of relief.

When the boat was tied, Captain Lee stepped up on the pier. He turned and pulled Elizabeth up to stand beside him.

She started toward Jewel, but Lee seized her, wrapping his hand in Elizabeth's hair and yanking her back to his side. She screamed, but wisely said nothing.

"Are you ready, Jewel?" Captain Lee asked.

"I'm ready. You did promise to let Elizabeth go." Her voice sounded calm, smooth.

"I'll let her go, providing you don't give me any trouble. I'll have your word on it now!"

"You have it. But first I'd like to say good-bye to my sister-in-law in private."

"No tricks," Lee threatened, signaling his men to raise their guns and keep them aimed on Jewel. "Or you both die."

"No tricks," Jewel promised.

Elizabeth ran all the way to Jewel, throwing her arms around her. "You can't go with this man, Jewel. He'll kill you," she whispered.

"Are you all right?" Jewel checked her sister-in-law over to make sure she was unharmed.

"Yes . . . yes." Elizabeth hesitated. "I'm fine, but why does this man want you? He's cruel. Tears streamed down her face.

"Please don't cry, Elizabeth. I'll be fine. I've left a note for Adam explaining everything." She hugged Elizabeth tightly, knowing she wouldn't see her again. "Take care of Adam for me. Now, leave immediately. I won't set foot in that boat until you've gone."

"You sound as if you're not coming back." Elizabeth's eyes grew wide, but she left, and Jewel watched until Elizabeth was safely away.

Reluctantly, Jewel walked to the pier and climbed down in the boat. Her life with Adam was over. Surviving would be her only goal now, and she wasn't sure at this moment if she wanted to survive. She sat quietly as the small boat headed toward the larger ship.

Once they were on board, Captain Lee grabbed Jewel by

the arm, jerking her in front of him. "I'll personally search you this time. The last encounter is still fresh in my mind. I only have to look in the mirror to be reminded of how dangerous you can be."

He found the knife she had tucked in her waistband, and smiled. "We don't want to have another incident. Perhaps you'd like a scar to match mine?" His sinister laugh sounded all around her as he ran the cold steel blade across her face. But it was only to frighten her this time. He searched her once more, his hands lingering intimately over the curves of her body.

Jewel squirmed and slapped his hands away. Lee snarled, drawing back his hand. The blow came quickly, knocking Jewel to her knees. Blood trickled from the side of her mouth as she raised her head and glanced at Lee. She knew hatred burned deep in her eyes.

"Now, my lovely, where is the map?"

"I don't have it."

"What!" Lee yanked her to him. Twisting his hands in her long, raven tresses, he jerked her head back.

"I gave it to my husband."

"Then he shall die!" Lee roared.

"No! Leave Adam out of this." Jewel began to feel a new panic. She didn't want Adam to be in danger because of her. "I don't need the map. I can take you there."

"How do I know you are to be trusted?"

"You don't," Jewel declared.

"Damn you!" Lee twisted her hair tighter, causing Jewel to wince in pain. "I should shoot you now!"

"Then you'll never be rich." Jewel smiled, knowing that for a while at least, she had the upper hand.

Disgusted, Captain Lee threw her away from him. "Which way do we sail, Duchess?"

At first she didn't answer, but decided it would be easier to get away from Captain Lee once they were on the island.

"Set your course for the Bay of Pirates."

"You heard the duchess, Bud. Set your course and throw our lovely lady in the hold until we reach clear water."

Twenty-seven

If patience was a virtue, then Jewel's bodyguard, Ben, would surely be rewarded. He had faithfully watched the docks and everybody around them for months. Dominique had told him about seeing Jewel, and Ben had a hunch the English captain hadn't given up his search for the treasure.

Ben had grown suspicious of an isolated wharf that had been abandoned for many years. His vigil grew into long days as he watched the activities there. He was just about to give up when he saw *him*—the captain.

Ben had scrutinized the captain's coming and goings. He had not been absolutely sure he had the right man, until today when he saw Jewel with him. Now Ben knew he'd been correct.

At this very moment, he wanted to choke the life out of the Englishman. But Ben knew if he interfered now, they would kill Jewel without hesitation. He was sure that she'd be safe until Captain Lee got what he wanted. Ben knew all too well how brutal Lee could be from by the last time they'd met. . . .

Ben could still picture the petite young lady who had stood at the helm of the ship, firmly gripping the wheel. Long, black hair swirled about her shoulders, and the excitement of the upcoming battle glowed in her dark eyes.

"Your uncles will have my hide," Ben said, shaking his head. A storm brewed not only on the high seas, but within the woman who commanded *The Morning Star*. She liked adventure too much. "We've wandered too far from home, Jewel. Perhaps we should quit while we're ahead. These English waters are not to my likin'."

Jewel looked affectionately at her sworn protector. "Haven't we been successful thus far? Besides, Uncle Jean and Uncle Pierre won't be half so angry when we show them our bounty." She pointed to the ship on the horizon. "Just look at that English brig. She sits heavy in the water, a sure indication her hold is full of valuables." She smiled devilishly. "Won't my uncles be disappointed more if we pass up this opportunity?"

"You know good and well they don't want this kind of life for you. I should have never let you twist me around your little finger. Ben sighed. This beautiful young woman had but to bat her eyes and any man would die to do her bidding.

He turned to look at the approaching brig. "Something ain't right . . . I've got a bad feelin'." He pointed at the brig. "Don't you think it strange they're not makin' much of an effort to escape?"

"Ben, you worry too much." Jewel motioned for the first mate to take the wheel. "Come about!" she shouted before picking up the spyglass.

The glass never made it to her eye as a heavy barrage of cannon fire slammed into *The Morning Star*. Just as the mast snapped, Ben threw Jewel to the deck and covered her body with his.

It had been a deadly trap.

Now, as Ben stood staring at his sworn enemy, it seemed strange to be able to put a name to the face that had haunted him these past two years. What was he going to do? He didn't want to leave Jewel, but as one man he could do little.

Jean was the answer.

Jean would know what to do, and where the captain was headed. However, Ben would first obtain a promise from

Jean that he'd have the pleasure of killing Captain Lee himself.

The once-dry trench was now muddy from rain. A dismal morning dawned, and with it a fog-drenched day began, obscuring all vision beyond fifty feet. Voices, muted by the heavy mist, could be heard up and down the trench.

Jackson stood half-shivering in the crispness of the morning. Adam knew how the man felt. The cold seemed to penetrate even his own bones. Adam watched Jackson. He stared into the chilling fog as if he could pierce it with his eyes by sheer willpower. "What I wouldn't give for a cup of hot coffee," the general said. "That commodity has been scarce since the British set up their blockade. Wait . . ." Jackson lifted his nose to sniff the air. "Do you smell the wonderful aroma? It's exactly what I seek."

Adam turned toward the scent and saw the red shirts of Lafitte's men. Adam and Jackson moved over to where Dominique You sat drinking a cup of the dark brew. Jackson asked, "Do you mind if I have a cup of coffee with you?"

"Of course not, General. Help yourself."

Jackson smacked his lips, savoring the hot liquid. "This is the best coffee I've ever tasted," he complimented the man. "Where did you get it?" He laughed before answering his own question. "Smuggled it, I suppose?"

The Baratarian only grinned, and the general moved on, inspecting his troops. Adam walked beside him, nodding and answering questions.

The very core of their defense would be the frontier hunters. Despite homespun shirts and coonskin caps, they were deadly with the long rifles they carried.

A light breeze began to strip the fog away, and without warning, the defenders stared at a rank of scarlet coats. Quickly, Adam took his position behind several bales of hay.

The British began advancing, and compared to Jackson's

ragamuffins, they were splendidly dressed. Their discipline was evident in the perfectly straight lines they maintained. Stern, brave soldiers in red coats and white cross belts would be a good target for the frontier hunters.

The drummers could be heard in the background, pounding a rhythmic beat for the men to march to. The British soldiers moved forward, bayonets fixed, each step perfect.

The Americans waited, and listened, fingers poised on the triggers, waiting for just the right moment. They looked forward to bagging a few.

The first shot rang out. It was the only invitation the Americans needed as they began firing rifle volleys at a long range that could not be believed. The British rifles had only a hundred-yard range, but the American rifles could shoot a distance of three hundred yards.

Instead of the Americans firing a volley, then stopping to reload, they fired in waves. As soon as one man fired, another was there to take his place while the first man reloaded. Clouds of smoke, streaked by flashes of fire, shrouded the American ramparts. Every shot counted, for the frontier hunters were deadly accurate.

"Unbelievable!" Pakenham, the British commander, gaped at the continuous, concentrated fire of the Americans. "It's fatal. Never have my troops faced gunfire at such a range."

After watching the carnage of the first attack, Pakenham wasn't sure what to do. As if his prayers were answered, he received renewed hope. The Ninety-Third Foot Regiment marched across the field from the river. Those Scotland Highlanders had never known defeat.

"Let's see how the Americans handle these men!" Pakenham laughed, thinking he had the perfect answer.

The Highlanders swung onto the battle front, their bagpipes skirling the blood-stirring music of Scotland.

"What's that god-awful sound?" some of Jean's men shouted.

Adam, who had been fighting by their side, readily supplied the answer. "Those, gentlemen, are bagpipes. I suspect we are getting ready to taste some gunfire from Scotland."

"Look!" Dominique chuckled as he pointed toward the field. "Just how tough can they be?" Dominique laughed. "Look at them . . . they're wearing skirts!"

"Bring them on!" the pirates shouted. "We'll send them running back to their mothers." A cheer swept through the soldiers as they positioned their rifles and took aim. Adam would have laughed if the situation hadn't been so serious.

There was something majestic about the Highlanders' advance. Time and again they closed ranks as their men fell, but always they marched forward.

Adam noticed a horse and rider cut across the field. Just what fool could that be? Before Adam could blink, the rider was shot and fell from his horse.

"Hand me a spyglass," Adam shouted. He looked at the downed rider. "My God, it's Jonathan!" What in the world could he have been thinking of, to try such a dangerous stunt? "Cover me, men," Adam shouted over the gunfire. "I'm going after him."

"Are you crazy?" Jean protested. "You'll be shot, too!"

"Not if your aim is accurate, my friend."

Adam zigzagged across the field, staying close to the ground, until he reached Jonathan, who hadn't move since he'd fallen. Blood plastered his shirt and he had a nasty chest wound. For a moment, Adam thought the worst. With two fingers, he checked his friend's throat for a pulse and found it strong. Thank goodness. Now he could personally kill him for trying such a stupid stunt, Adam swore to himself.

He needed to get Jonathan back to the rampart. In order to do that, he would have to stand, making a perfect target for the British, but he had little choice. They would both be killed if they stayed there.

Adam swung Jonathan over his shoulder and started running. It was much farther than he'd first thought. The back of his legs started to burn. His labored breathing grew louder in his ears with each step until it had blocked out the guns altogether. A bullet whizzed by, much too close for comfort. *Only a few more steps. I can make it. Just keep running. We're almost there.* Three feet in front of the rampart a searing pain hit his side and he yelled as grabbed for the wound. The impact sent them both tumbling into the ditch.

"Adam's been shot!" Jean jumped to his feet. "Run and fetch the doc."

After Jean was sure neither man was in danger, he again took his position. Jean looked around him. *Something was wrong. He could feel it in his bones.* Someone called his name. He swung in the direction of the sound.

Ben ran toward him as if the demons of Hell were on his heels. Jean didn't know the man could move that fast. Something must definitely be wrong.

"What's the trouble, Ben?"

"They have Jewel . . . I've found Jewel . . . they have her!"

"Wait! You've found Jewel?" Jean was shocked. How could Ben have found his niece *here?* "Is she all right?" He clasped his hands on Ben's meaty arms. "Where is she?"

"She's here, I found her . . . *They* have her!" Ben kept repeating himself. "Where's Pierre?"

"Pierre's in hiding. Some of the men took him to a hideout when they broke him out of jail. But he should be back at the compound when this battle is finished. Why do you ask?"

"I was with them when they freed Pierre, and he said he'd seen Jewel."

"I don't understand any of this . . . who has Jewel?" Jean shouted as he shook the big bear of a man.

"That English captain. I heard his men call him Captain Lee."

After a long pause, during which Jean fought for self-control, he gathered enough men to handle a ship, leaving the rest behind. He knew where Lee would be headed, and Jean intended to meet him there. Unfortunately, the captain had a head start.

Having left the fighting behind, Jean stopped when he heard the Americans wildly cheering in the background. The battle must be over. He grinned, feeling a deep satisfaction for his small part in it.

The Battle of New Orleans had ended. It was a crushing defeat for the British Army. Adam stood staring out over the field strewn with bodies forgetting his own pain. The British had lost more than two thousand men killed, wounded, or taken prisoner. The Americans' loss was seventy-one, with only thirteen of those killed.

The battle had been fierce, Adam thought, but thank God victory was theirs. He still wore the bloodstained shirt as he tried to help others worse off than himself. Jonathan had been moved to a hospital where Adam knew he'd receive excellent care. Now it was *his* turn. After the doctor extracted the bullet, he wrapped Adam's side with long strips to contain the bleeding, and told him to stay off his feet for the next forty-eight hours. But Adam's only thought was to get home to his wife.

By the time Adam returned to the field, Jean seemed to have disappeared and no one knew where he'd gone. Adam bade the general farewell. He was going home.

Four Oaks was a welcome sight indeed as Adam slid from his horse and stumbled to the front doors.

"Jewel!" Adam shouted when he entered the house. It was much too quiet; an eerie feeling prevailed. "Jewel, where are you?" Adam repeated his bellowed cry, and it echoed around the house.

He heard footsteps upstairs, and moved to the staircase. Elizabeth came flying down the steps, throwing her arms around his neck. "Thank God, you're home!" She stepped back and saw the bloodstain on his shirt. "Oh, my God, you've been hurt!"

"A small flesh wound." Adam tried to smile. "I'll be fine, but where is Jewel?"

"Adam, it was awful!" An odd look entered Elizabeth's eyes, and she hung her head.

Adam's muscles tightened. The hair stood up on the back of his neck as his apprehension grew. He took Elizabeth by the arm and escorted her to the library. Still holding her with his good hand, he winced as he sloshed liquor into a glass. Christ, he needed some brandy, bad.

"For once in your life, dear sister, don't be rattled. Where is Jewel?"

"Gone."

Adam took a deep breath, forcing himself to remain calm until he got the full story. Elizabeth looked as if she could become hysterical at any moment, and he didn't need that. He needed his wife.

Adam's voice softened. "Tell me what happened."

Elizabeth twisted the white lace handkerchief she clutched in her trembling fingers. "I went riding the day after Christmas." She held up her hand. "I know I wasn't supposed to, but I had to get away from the house. If only I had listened to Jewel, none of this would have occurred."

"What wouldn't have happened?"

"Two men approached as I sat in a small coffeehouse. They told me they had been sent by Jewel and I was to accompany them. I thought something had happened to you or Jonathan." Elizabeth gave him a pleading look before continuing. "The men took me to a dock, but Jewel was nowhere to be found. By the time I realized something was wrong, a cape had been thrown over my head. The next thing I knew, I was on a ship. It was awful, Adam." She started to cry.

"Keep on, Elizabeth. Tell me everything." Adam's voice

held a dull edge. He dreaded what was to come. A muscle throbbed in his jaw as he fought to control his temper.

"They threw me in a small dark room. I don't know how long I stayed there. It seemed like a day. Then *he* came. He brought an oil lamp, so I could see his face."

"Who, Elizabeth?"

"I never heard his name, but someone addressed him as 'Captain.' He was a hard-looking man. I'd never seen him before. The whole time he talked to me he ran his hand over a long, nasty scar that ran across his face, and there was hatred in his eyes. I didn't understand why." Elizabeth frowned. "He was calm at first, but when he began talking about Jewel, he changed. He started pacing the room and became wild with agitation. Then he . . . ," Elizabeth choked. "He . . . oh, Adam, it was so awful." She sobbed.

"What, Elizabeth?" Every muscle strained in Adam's body as the rage brewed within him. "Tell me!"

"I can't tell you—" She became hysterical and cried just that much harder, shaking her head.

Adam tried to calm her down. They were losing precious time. "I want to know if he hurt you, Elizabeth. Remember, Jewel's life could be in danger. You must tell me!"

"He made me take off all my clothes," Elizabeth whispered in a small voice.

Adam felt as if someone had slammed a fist into his midsection. He took Elizabeth in his arms, rocking her back and forth, not trusting his voice at this very moment.

"When he was finished with me . . . ," Elizabeth said, choking on her tears, "he said that was a small payment you owed him." Adam tensed. "He told me to put on my clothes, all but my chemise. That he kept and sent to Jewel with a note. He said I'd better pray she complied with his demands, or he would let every man on the ship have a turn with me. Oh, God, Adam! I was so afraid," she sobbed. Sniffing, she asked, "Do you know who he is?"

Adam continued rocking Elizabeth, stroking her hair while

she cried. "Yes, I know who he is," he said tersely. "Finish your story. What happened to Jewel?"

"She did as the note requested, and traded places with me."

"Traded places?" Adam wasn't sure he could take much more.

"I begged her not to go, but she didn't have any choice. They had guns pointed at her." Elizabeth pulled back and looked at him. "Jewel was so brave. She made sure I was safe before she left with them."

"Did Jewel say anything?"

"No. She didn't even look back as she stepped into their boat—wait a minute, Jewel did say something. She said she left a note in your room." Elizabeth leaned back away from Adam. "You have to find her, Adam! She gave herself up for me."

Adam kissed his sister on the forehead before hurrying to the door. "I'll have Annie come and stay with you. I'm going after Jewel."

"Adam do you know who the man was?" Elizabeth asked again.

"Yes, Elizabeth." His gaze drifted to the stairs. "He's a dead man."

As soon as Adam entered his chambers, he saw the necklace and the note on which it laid. His face turned grim. Damn, he was tired. He poured himself another brandy and sat down with the note. Slowly, Adam opened the note and read.

Dear Adam,

Where do I start? I remember my identity. My name is Jewel Bona. Why haven't I told you until now? I have asked myself that question a thousand times.

I realize now that I could never fit into your life. You were born of royal blood. I'm but a mere commoner.

I suppose I was afraid of the revulsion I would see in

your eyes. You see, my uncles are Jean and Pierre Lafitte. They are pirates, but they are kind and gentle to me. They raised me from a small child. I cannot let your family, or you, suffer for my past; therefore, I am leaving. Take care, Adam.

Love,
Jewel

Damn! Why hadn't he been here? She'd had so little faith in him. Perhaps she had never loved him at all, and she definitely hadn't trusted him. He read the note again. She loved him. He knew it, but there were no pleas to come after her. He let the note slip from his fingers. Did she think he cared what her background was? He ran his hand through his hair as his eyes misted. The pain he felt at reading the note was ten times worse than his wound. Jewel should have confided in him; then she would have known Lafitte was his friend.

"Wait," he mumbled. Did Jean know anything about this? No, he couldn't have. They had fought together. Pierre had evidently never had a chance to tell his brother about Jewel before he'd gone into hiding.

Adam jumped to his feet. He needed to find Jean Lafitte, but he would have to move fast. Adam knew Captain Lee would kill Jewel just as soon as he got his hands on the treasure. Adam stopped by his desk, picking up the other half of the map. Jean would know where this mysterious hidden treasure lay buried. He must be the one with the other half of the map.

Adam went by Elizabeth's room to tell her he was leaving. She looked up as he entered the room. "Adam, where is Jonathan?"

"I'm sorry." Adam placed his hand on Elizabeth's shoulder. He'd been so wrapped up in his own thoughts, he hadn't even thought of Jonathan. "He's been shot, Elizabeth, and is being treated at St. John's Hospital. The doctors assured me he would be fine. Perhaps you and Annie should go and bring him home. I'll be back in a few days." Adam gave his sister a hug, then turned to leave, but stopped and turned back. "You will be all right?"

"Yes, Adam. Bring Jewel home safely."

"I will," Adam said, but he wondered if he would bring Jewel home at all. By the time he reached Jewel, she could be dead. And if she wasn't, there was still the note. The note had sounded final. Somehow he had to convince Jewel that her past meant nothing to him.

Twenty-eight

It was dark and damp in the hold where Jewel had been thrown. A faint scratching noise came from an obscure corner, and she could swear a pair of red eyes glared at her, leaving Jewel to wonder what animal lurked there. She pulled her knees up tight to her body and wrapped her arms around them. She had always hated the dark.

The ship swayed, and Jewel grabbed the side of the vessel as a deafening explosion boomed very close to the ship. The stench of gunpowder filled the air. Another detonation sent her tossing about with the rest of the cargo. More gunfire ensued, and the faint sound of people yelling surrounded her. She strained, trying to hear more, but the noise soon faded into the background.

Jewel assumed they must have survived the battle. She shut her eyes and prayed Adam was safe.

For now she had to concentrate on her own situation. She had to remember anything she could about the Bay of Pirates. A long time had passed since she and Jean had been there. Being a child at the time, she hadn't known the importance of the treasure. A few bits and pieces began to form in her mind, but nothing that would help her escape. She knew Jean probably had some kind of safeguard for intruders. Perhaps when they arrived on the island, she'd remember something that might save her life. One thing she was sure of. She'd go down fighting.

Her thoughts again turned to Adam. What would he think

when he read the note? Would he be angry or glad to be rid of her? She lacked answers for her questions. As the agonizing reality settled upon her, she sighed. No matter how badly she might want to, she would never fit into Adam's world. Her eyes moistened, and she wiped her nose on her sleeve. If only things could have been different. He'd been raised by a stern father and grandfather who believed a man had to be hard to survive. She knew underneath Adam's hard exterior lay a heart of gold.

She would give anything to be in Adam's arms just once more, and feel his lips on her face, and hear him murmur soft-spoken love words . . . but that was not to be . . . fate had dealt her a different hand.

The hatch opened and bright sunlight poured in through the small opening. A stabbing pain shot through Jewel's head as she covered her eyes against the brilliant light. The rats scurried for cover and she jerked her foot back. Reluctantly, she removed her hands and blinked, trying to adjust to the glare. She wasn't sure how long she'd been cramped up in this squalid, dark hole, but her stomach told her she'd been days without food.

"The captain said you're to come up top," the sailor who opened the hatch shouted down at her.

Her tight muscles protested and cramped as she slowly inched her way to her feet. She moved over toward the stairs, where she had to wait a minute for the circulation to return to her feet before she climbed the ladder. Upon reaching the top, she stretched and shook her arms, trying to limber up her muscles.

"Where's this bloody island, Your Highness?" Captain Lee shouted at her. "Or have you lied to me yet again?"

"I spoke the truth. It's not an island any normal sailor can find. If it were, there would be no treasure." Jewel's voice was filled with all the contempt she felt for this savage who called himself a man. "Let me see your charts, and I'll check to see how far off course we are."

Grudgingly, Lee stepped aside. She pointed the way across the map, her fingers tracing the route they should take.

"Bloody hell, you can read a chart. You might be worth keeping . . . with a little taming, that is," Lee sneered. "There's little chance you'll escape now, so you can remain on deck. Adrian, bring her some food. She'll be of little use to me dead."

The sea breeze felt good blowing in her hair, and even in her present situation Jewel found a little peace, but at least her stomach was soon full. Not having to worry about the rats as she had in the hole, she curled up on a tarp and slept soundly for the first time in days.

The next morning the sun rose early in the clear blue sky. Not a cloud could be seen. Jewel peeked over the railing and smiled.

She saw the first signs of the dark shore of Jean's private island. The Bay of Pirates was a strange island. Instead of sand, millions of tiny shells coated the beach that stretched around the island for ten miles. Surrounded by coral reefs, the coast was flat with an elevated interior and steep cliffs.

Jewel, Captain Lee, and two of his men rowed to shore. Upon stepping out on the beach, they pulled the boat up on dry land. Tiny shells crunched and snapped as they walked inland away from the shore. Their feet would have been cut to ribbons if they hadn't been wearing shoes.

"It's going to be a long walk," Jewel informed Lee.

"Lead the way, and remember, no tricks," he warned. "I'll be watching you."

They moved along the rocky shore in a northeasterly direction, until they came to a slope where they began their slow climb, following a trail to a point where it dropped over the side of a cliff and appeared to be a dead end.

A path that led nowhere.

"What bloody trick are you trying to pull?" Lee grabbed her arm.

Jewel closed her eyes and thought back. She could remember twigs and branches—yes, the path was hidden. "Give me a minute. I was but a child the last time I came here."

Moving over to the thicket, she began removing the brush that revealed the descending path. She heard Lee take a deep breath, but he didn't say anything as he started down the footpath behind her.

The steep slope was difficult to maneuver, and Jewel had to be careful not to lose her footing. It turned out to be a precipitous expedition when Lee tripped and slid ten feet down the slope. He got up and glared at Jewel when she passed him with a smile on her lips. Finally, they emerged at the base of the cliff.

Jewel stood looking around as the others finished their descent. Pleasant, girlish memories swirled in her head. She could almost hear a child's carefree laughter echoing among the cliffs. Memories of her childhood came flowing back, and she was thankful, hoping those memories would soon bring the answer she sought—the way to escape.

As they walked down the beach, the shoreline once again changed. Rugged, sharp cliffs gave way to a flat beach littered with boulders the size of heads. A variety of green seaweed grew atop the smooth boulders. She and Jean had called this area the graveyard, because it appeared that sailors been buried straight up in the sand, leaving only their heads above the ground. It was still a scary sight.

"My God, what is that?" Captain Lee exclaimed.

"It's a graveyard."

"Who's buried there?" Lee demanded.

"All the unsuccessful men who have tried to take the treasure chest." Jewel's laughter held an eerie sound, and she saw the uncertainty on the captain's face.

"You witch! You've led me into a trap." Lee took her by the shoulders and shook her. "Stop laughing this instant!"

"Wait. Wait a minute," she protested. "It's just a myth. A story Jean made up for me when I was little. Unless you're afraid of rocks, I suggest we go on."

"I don't care for your jokes." Lee shoved her none too gently. "Just remember you've made a fool of me for the last time."

Several caverns lay ahead scattered in different directions. She looked at each one while trying to remember. Finally, she spotted the one she sought. To get to the cavern, they would have to wade through a small cove, which lay just under a cliff.

Jewel stopped and stared at the water before entering the cove. A dull picture flooded her memory. Suddenly, Jean's warning came back to her. She was careful not to smile or give anything away. She just might have a surprise for Lee after all.

"There is a small cave over there." Jewel pointed to the end of a narrow gully. "That's where the treasure is hidden."

Everyone crossed the cove, but only Captain Lee followed Jewel into the cavern. A torch had been conveniently placed at the entrance, which Lee lit as he followed her. It took a few moments for Jewel's eyes to adjust to the darkness of the damp hole. Being careful not to trip over the stones on the cavern floor, she inched her way to the back of the cave, noticing the faint smell of seawater. A shelf built into the stone wall lay just ahead. She couldn't see anything at first, so she began pushing the loose rocks away, until she saw the wooden chest. She tried tugging on the box, but it wouldn't budge.

"This is what you seek." Jewel pointed to the strongbox.

Lee shoved her aside and went to the treasure. Excitement seemed to fill him as he grunted and groaned, pulling on the wooden chest. It took several tries before he worked it loose. The brown chest came complete with a large black lock. But it was quickly disposed of when Lee shot it off with his pistol. However, the rusty hinges on the lid wouldn't budge. Picking up a rock, he struck the lid over and over again. Time seemed to stand still as he focused on the chest. The noise of his struggles echoed on the walls as his face broke out in a fine sweat.

Finally, Lee was rewarded for his efforts as the lid moved. Lifting it carefully, he gasped at the array of dazzling rubies, diamonds, and emeralds that lay before him. He held the torch closer for a better look, and watched the jewels sparkle beneath the light. He raked back the gems. Under them lay gold coins worth a king's ransom.

Jewel knew her life would now be in danger. Captain Lee had what he wanted: a treasure chest that would make him as rich as a king. Now it was time to set her plan in motion. She prayed it would work. Jewel stared at Lee, but didn't really see him as she remembered her uncle's warning about the small cove they had come through. The tide there was dangerous—nature's own trap and a watery coffin to those who didn't heed the warnings.

She had glanced at the tide briefly when they'd come across the cove. The tide had been out, but would soon start coming in. It came in at the incredible speed of an inch a minute. The water from the cove would back into the caverns where they now stood, and would keep rising to a height of forty to fifty feet. The tide would be a death trap. She just had to make sure it wasn't *her* death trap.

"How will you carry the chest?" she asked Lee.

"Why do you think I brought along two big men?" He laughed. "Go get them."

It took all three men struggling with the chest to get it up the narrow gully to the edge of the cove. They had to stop often because of the chest's weight, grumbling about the treasure each time, and at the moment were paying little attention to Jewel.

She glanced at the small cove. Already the tide had shifted

and had started to come in. It looked to be knee deep. Taking a deep breath, she remembered the warning. She would have to hurry.

Patiently, she waited for the two men to pick up the chest again. Captain Lee followed behind, holding the back of the strongbox while Jewel led the way. They all started forward, and she knew this was her chance. She darted ahead and ran, heading straight for the water.

"Look, Captain, she's getting away!"

They dropped their load, and Lee pulled out his pistol. Taking careful aim, he cocked the trigger. "I might as well kill her now because I don't need her anymore. I have what I want." A devious smile touched his lips as he squeezed the trigger. The bullet hit its target. Captain Lee laughed as he watched Jewel fall face-first to the ground. "That, my dear girl, was for this ugly scar." His hand went to his cheek. "I said I would get even!"

A searing pain shot through Jewel as the bullet slammed into her shoulder, knocking her to the ground. Gasping, she tried to catch her breath. Slowly she lifted her head to look at the rising water. "Be calm," she cautioned herself. *You must get up. . . . You must hurry. . . .*

Pulling herself up to her knees, she heard Lee reloading his gun. She found her footing and half staggered into the cove. Struggling against the water to get her stability, she waded through the rough tide. Twice she lost her balance and slid under the water, feeling the sharp sting of salt. The last time, she felt the tug of the undertow as it began to suck her out with the tide. Knowing she was fighting for her life gave Jewel a final burst of energy. She regained her balance and thrust her head out of the water, taking deep breaths of air. She fought the waist-high current and crawled to the other side before collapsing in the dry sand.

Lee's men had entered the edge of the water in pursuit of Jewel. But Captain Lee made them come back and get the chest. The three of them entered the cove with their treasure. Lee fired again, but missed Jewel this time.

"We'll never make it, Captain. Let's leave the chest."

"I'll not leave without it! And I will shoot you if you try. Now I strongly suggest you carry that box. It's only a little water and will not kill you."

Lee realized his folly in the middle of the inlet. It was much deeper than it looked. The sand acted like quicksand, trapping their feet and pulling them under. The incoming water swirled around their necks. Their gurgled cries filled the air as the sea slowly rose . . . inch by inch . . . minute by minute . . .

Jewel heard the frantic screams of the men fading as the sea swept them to their watery graves. Then there was silence. Only the call of the seagulls floated in the breeze. She smiled, knowing justice had been done. Greed knew no mercy, she thought before lapsing into unconsciousness.

Jean and his men had already secured Captain Lee's ship. Jean and Dominique were preparing to go ashore when Ben stopped them.

"You aren't going without me," he shouted. "I want to kill that bastard!"

"Come on, Ben." Jean smiled grimly, knowing Ben was so angry he wouldn't need a gun.

They made the long climb up the cliff and then down the other side. Jean noticed the brush had been moved, and he knew they were on the right trail. Many things ran through his mind. He just hoped he would be in time. Without a weapon, Jewel could suffer at Lee's hand.

They had just passed the graveyard when Jean looked up ahead and spotted a body lying in the sand. Icy fingers of fear crept up his back. He stood where he was, paralyzed. He had waited all this time to see Jewel again, and now he might be deprived.

"Damn," he swore, before breaking into a run. "Please don't let me be too late."

In no time, Jean covered the distance and was beside Jewel. He rolled her over and brushed the hair and sand from her face. Blood stained the sand beneath her, and her face was pale. He bent down, putting his ear to her mouth. Thank goodness! She was breathing.

"Jewel." Jean shook her. "Speak to me, *cherie*. Where are the others?" he asked.

Her eyes fluttered open, "Adam?" she mumbled.

"No, *cherie*. It's Jean."

"Uncle Jean." Jewel tried to lift her hand. She wanted to touch him to make sure he was real, but the pain stopped her. "Jean, they took the treasure," she sobbed. "I'm sorry. I've let you down."

He laughed that smooth laugh she always remembered. *"Cherie,* you are my treasure. I can always replace mere trinkets and gold, but I can never replace you."

"But our blood pact." Jewel knew she sounded like a child. He rocked her back and forth. *"Petite,* the blood pact was made with a child and was part of a child's game. You're a woman now, and sometimes things change."

"Yes, you're right," she agreed. "I've changed, Jean. I'm married now."

"So I've heard." Jean motioned to Ben. "Help me carry her back to the ship."

"I want to kill that captain!" Ben had looked everywhere for Lee, but couldn't find him. "Where is he, Jean?" Ben muttered.

"It's too late. The sea took care of him for you, my friend," Jean explained.

"Damn, I've been cheated," Ben grumbled, swearing up a blue streak.

"Ben, is that you?" Jewel's weak voice sounded faint even to her. "I thought you were dead."

"Who, me?" Ben grinned. "You know they can't kill an old bear like me." He bent down and picked her up.

She moaned the minute Ben touched her. Excruciating pain shot through her body just before she passed out.

"I've hurt, her, Jean." Ben's voice was filled with concern.

Jean looked at his niece. "She's just passed out, my friend. It probably will be better in the long run, especially when we start climbing that cliff to return to the ship."

"I'll take care of her, Jean! Nobody will ever touch her again!" Ben cradled the burden in his arms.

"I'm sure they won't, Ben. However, I am a little concerned. She has lost way too much blood. Let's not waste any time in getting her home."

Twenty-nine

Crazed with fever by the time he reached Grand Terre, Adam was only standing up straight because of sheer determination and an iron will.

Pierre was sitting in the study when Adam stormed in, dragging three of Pierre's best men with him.

"Where is Jean?" Adam shouted. Beads of perspiration dotted his brow.

"He's gone, left on his ship two days ago," Pierre explained. "What's wrong, my friend?"

"Jewel! They have Jewel!" Adam's fever had reached such a pitch, his speech had become slurred.

"I know." Pierre smiled at the man staggering in front of him.

"Then why in hell are you still here? You're her uncle!" Adam shook his head. "I've got to go and find her." He now saw two Pierres and would slug the man if he could figure out which one to hit.

"The only place you're going is to bed." Pierre laughed at Adam's swaying body. "Rest easy. Jean has gone after Jewel."

It took four men and Pierre hitting Adam over the head with a bottle of his best rum before Adam was persuaded to go to bed.

"Ah, love!" Pierre smiled. "It must be wonderful."

* * *

It was not a quiet time at Grand Terre. Jewel was in one room and Adam in another. Jean attended Jewel, and Pierre, who had lost the flip of the coin, tried to take care of Adam.

Jewel and Adam spent the next week in and out of fevered sleeps, having absolutely no idea where they were.

Jewel called for Adam in her crazed state. Jean was beside himself with worry that she wouldn't recover. He couldn't lose her, he just couldn't, now that he had found her again. He diligently bathed Jewel's forehead and arms, trying to cool the raging fever.

Of course, Jewel now belonged to Adam, but that was fine with Jean. He couldn't have chosen better himself. One thing was sure. Adam was definitely man enough to handle her. "Hell, Adam is almost as good as I am," Jean said out loud, then smiled over his humor.

He stood up, stretching. Damn, he was getting old. Every muscle and joint ached from being bent over the sick bed. Jewel slept peacefully now, so he left to check on the other patient.

"How's it going, Pierre?" Jean started laughing at the sight before him. His brother was sprawled across Adam's body as Adam thrashed wildly about. Pierre had a damp cloth, trying to wipe Adam's face with very little success.

"I'm glad the bloke is sick, or I probably couldn't handle him." Pierre laughed at himself. "You want to exchange patients?"

"And deprive you of all this exercise? I think not."

"And Jewel?" Pierre asked, giving up his struggles with Adam.

"Finally, she is sleeping peacefully. I think the fever has broken. She keeps calling for Adam, though."

"He keeps mumbling Jewel's name, too."

"Let's relax and have some rum," Jean suggested.

After half a bottle of rum, the two brothers sat laughing over Jean's brilliant idea.

"You probably shouldn't have done it, Jean." Pierre chortled.

"Yeah, you're probably right. But hell, she wanted him and he wanted her, and we were running ourselves ragged. It made perfect sense to me. Now, they are both in the same bed. Our lives should be easier."

"I hope you're right." Pierre laughed again.

"Of course, I'm right. Let Mother Nature take her turn in the healing process." Jean smiled as he sipped his rum. He was quite pleased with himself. Yes, sir, he was sure Mother Nature would solve all their problems.

Contentment filled Jewel. The warmth of Adam's body made her relax, and she had calmed down. She felt someone nibbling on her ear, and she moaned from the pleasure she experienced. "At least, my love, I can still have you in my dreams," Jewel murmured as she turned to welcome Adam's kisses. This dream felt so real. "I'm sorry I never told you the truth, but I thought you'd send me away. Oh, please don't leave me, Adam," Jewel whispered against his lips.

Her dream lover captured her mouth with hungry violence as his arms enfolded her. She never wanted to wake up from this delicious dream.

"I love you, Jewel Bona," Adam whispered tenderly.

Jewel's eyes flew open. It was real! She was here in bed with Adam! "I—I don't understand. Where? How?" Jewel couldn't seem to get a complete sentence out. The last thing she remembered she'd been on the beach. She'd been shot and Jean was there . . . not Adam . . . but how?

Adam smiled. "Even with one-word sentences, you still manage to ask all your questions at once." He brushed her lips softly with his. "Don't ever change. I love you just the way you are."

"But the note. Didn't you find it?" Jewel's confusion grew. Adam should be disgusted with her now that he had found out she was related to pirates, but he was smiling. She looked wildly around at her surroundings. This was not Adam's house . . . it was Jean's. But how did Adam get here? Something strange had happened. She'd told Pierre about her marriage, but she hadn't mentioned Adam's name.

"Yes, I did get the note." Adam propped up on his good elbow so he could see her better. "I must say you have little faith in me, sweetheart."

"I do, Adam. I really do. But you're a duke. And I'm nothing."

"You are *my* wife."

"Then you don't mind?" Jewel's eyes widened as she waited for his reply.

"Jean and Pierre are friends of mine, and when it boils down to it, we're all pirates at heart. I was born into my title, which is something I cannot help, the same as you can't help where you were raised."

"I'm sorry I didn't trust you." Jewel's heart hammered with love. With her good arm, she pulled Adam to her for a long-awaited kiss. This time she held nothing back, for she knew Adam loved her for who she was. There would be no more lies between them. She heard his quick intake of breath when she bumped his side.

"What's wrong?" Her gaze scanned his body. "You've a bandage?"

"This is my war wound, sweetheart. I got it saving my fool friend Jonathan."

"Is Jonathan all right?" She watched Adam nod. "Your wound isn't serious?" He shook his head.

"You mean we both have wounds?"

"That appears to be the case. Didn't you know women are supposed to be soft and gentle and never play with guns and swords?" Adam teased.

"I guess I never learned that in finishing school." Jewel giggled. "And you're sure Jonathan is going to be all right?"

Adam's brow raised slightly. "I sent Elizabeth to tend to

him. And if she doesn't kill Jonathan with her nursing, I'm sure he'll be just fine. But I don't want to talk about Jonathan. . . ." She saw a fire burning deep in Adam's eyes.

Adam stared at her beautiful face. The thought of almost losing her ripped agonizingly through his chest. Life had been dull before she'd stormed in. He'd been but a mere shadow of a man without her. This slip of a woman had taught him patience and she had eased his cynical outlook on life. And he knew he'd move Heaven and Hell to keep her close.

"I love you, Adam."

The silkily spoken words stirred him with a flaming desire that only Jewel could quench.

"I love you, too, sweetheart. You want to compare wounds?" Adam teased as he gazed down tenderly at the beauty beneath him.

"I'd rather make love . . . that is, if you're able," Jewel purred.

With a wolfish grin, Adam pulled her into his arms before answering. "Sweetheart, I'm always able where you're concerned!"

AUTHOR'S NOTE

I hoped you enjoyed *The Duke's Lady* as much as I enjoyed writing it. I would love to hear your comments. You can write to me at the address below. Please send an SASE if you'd like a reply. The first fan letter I receive will get a special gift from me.

Thank You,

Brenda K. Jernigan
Rt. 4, Box 281-B
Lillington, N.C. 27546

ROMANCE FROM JANELLE TAYLOR

YOU WON'T WANT TO READ
JUST ONE—KATHERINE STONE

ROOMMATES   (0-8217-5206-5, $6.99/$7.99)
No one could have prepared Carrie for the monumental
changes she would face when she met her new circle of friends
at Stanford University. Once their lives intertwined and became
woven into the tapestry of the times, they would never be the
same.

TWINS   (0-8217-5207-3, $6.99/$7.99)
Brook and Melanie Chandler were so different, it was hard to
believe they were sisters. One was a dark, serious, ambitious
New York attorney; the other, a golden, glamourous, sophisticated supermodel. But they were more than sisters—they were
twins and more alike than even they knew . . .

THE CARLTON CLUB   (0-8217-5204-9, $6.99/$7.99)
It was the place to see and be seen, the only place to be. And
for those who frequented the playground of the very rich, it
was a way of life. Mark, Kathleen, Leslie and Janet—they
worked together, played together, and loved together, all behind
exclusive gates of the *Carlton Club*.